The Other World

D. D. Riessen

The Other World - Fantasy

This book is a work of fiction. Names, characters, places and incidents are either products of the author's imagination or are used fictitiously. Any resemblance to actual events, locales or persons is entirely coincidental.

Library of Congress Control Number: 2015930476
ISBN 10 - 0991663063
ISBN:13- 978-0-9916630-6-4

ddr
books

San Diego, CA 92119

To Phelan, who planted the idea of Capn Dog many years ago.

Cheers!

Once in a blue moon. Maybe such a thing is not a time, a place or a color..., certainly not an event that can be predicted.

Perhaps a blue moon is born at the first hint of something not following the natural order of things, not behaving.

It challenges the reality of what *is* and a chain reaction begins...,

Ben let out the Genoa sheet and watched the sail fill with the cool breeze coming in from the stern, waiting until he felt it tug before tying off to the cleat. He walked the boom across the deck to the opposite side and adjusted the sheet so that the main sail could fill as well.

This was a gentle ride, stern of the boat rising gracefully with the incoming swells, pushing the boat along, sails collapsing slightly as they glided with the wave, glowing with the orange tinted, waning light of the day.

Ben glanced over at the dog sitting on top of the cabin, his nose raised into the air.

"Wing and wing. That's what they call it, Capn. Easy ride into a pretty town. Lot's a pretty girls here, too. And I'm gonna find me one."

Capn didn't know about any of that. He jumped down to the deck and made his way up to the bow where he found a good place to sit and watch.

"Gonna be some free anchorage comin' up," said Ben. "Let me know when you see some boats at anchor. It'll be on yur left."

Capn didn't know about any of that either. What he did know is that he smelled land and that it was a good smell compared to the month of damp, salty air out on the open ocean.

Sitting there, gliding with the boat across the glistening water, still a half mile from their destination, he had already detected wafts of grilled meats, fried tortillas, hamburgers and fries, a thousand other scents mixing together with the distant sounds of the freeways, horns, the steady buzz of a vibrant city.

"Heads up!" Ben untied the halyard from the cleat and began to let the front sail drop. Clanking against the mast, they formed a loose pile across the deck, still wanting to balloon out with the breeze.

Ben came forward, folded the sail and pulled it back toward the cabin where he tied everything down. He

1

brushed his hands off on his pants.

"That'll cut our speed in half. No sense hurryin' to get anywhere. Just have to do more work sooner. Mmm, Capn. You smell that? Tacos. Carne asada. I'll get you some, too. I see your nose is wet. You're as excited as me, aren't you, boy?"

Ben knelt down, opened the hatch and retrieved the rusty anchor that he stored inside. He made sure the chain was secured to the ring and pulled out several more feet, until he came to the rope attachment. Seeing that the connection was good, he set the rope out so that it wouldn't tangle, felt it hit bottom and played out another fifty feet for good measure. He tied that off and then wandered back to the stern.

"Yep. Gonna be a good night, Capn. We'll get somethin' to eat and lay low until morning. You're gonna have to stay onboard until I take care of some business."

He was taking too long. Capn climbed the steps leading up to the deck for the hundredth time, spotted Ben's dinghy tied up at the dock and searched the shoreline for Ben. Nothing.

Two days, waiting, food dish empty, water dish stale and running low.

Capn considered jumping overboard, swimming to shore and searching for Ben. But if he couldn't find him, then what? He knew he couldn't get back on board without Ben's help.

No. He said to stay and guard the boat. That's what he said.

Capn circled the deck, checking for new scents and, finding none, went below, jumped up on Ben's bed and waited. There was nothing more to do.

It was late afternoon when he heard human voices. Coming up on deck, he spotted the harbor patrol boat approaching and began to bark.

That did not stop them. They pulled up to the boat, tied off to one of the cleats and boarded, all the while talking calmly to Capn, who retreated back down into the cabin.

When they followed, Capn curled his lips, showed his teeth and snarled. The humans retreated, and when they did return, shot him with a tranquilizer dart...,

Wincing at the smell of some kind of potent antibacterial wash, Capn opened his eyes and found himself lying on a hard concrete floor.

This was a small enclosure, three windowless concrete walls and a steel screen in front, with enough room to get up and turn but not enough to walk around a bit. Attempting to stand, his legs got wobbly and he fell into a metal dish full of water.

"You're in the bad cage."

The voice had come from across the aisle, from another dog, one with a freshly brushed long, silky coat and

3

freshly clipped nails.

"What?"

"You're in the bad cage. Dogs that stay in that cage don't make it."

"I'm not staying."

"There's no way out, except when they come get you."

"They?"

"The humans, in the morning." She pointed with her nose. "They'll take you to that room over there."

"And this is bad..., how?"

"It's a death room."

"How do you know?"

"Dogs and humans go in. Just the humans come out."

"Maybe they let them go. Maybe...,"

"I don't think so."

"How come they don't take you?"

"I've got a collar."

"A what?"

"Around my neck. It lets them know that my master will come get me."

"But I have a master, I...,"

"You don't have a collar," said Magic, "You're as good as dead."

Capn turned away. If true, how could this be? Surely his master would come get him and they'd go back to the boat and sail off to the next place like they always do.

He sniffed the corners of his cage pushing here and there with his nose.

If you can get in there's gotta be a way out. It only makes sense.

But the screen, steel hard, did not budge and refused to be chewed and the ground was as hard as cement.

Kathryn kicked off her shoes, leaned back in the chair and put her feet up on the coffee table. She turned on the light at the side of her chair, took a sip of wine and retrieved the book from the table.

"Two hundred pages. Are you ready?"

Paul plopped down on the couch and pulled a pillow in behind his head. "It's gonna go all night?"

"Until we're done, whenever that is."

"OK. It's your birthday. I can think of a million other things I'd rather do for mine."

"This is your punishment for forgetting. And for getting a D in Science."

"Mr. Cobb. I hate that teacher. He just puts me to sleep."

"First class after lunch. Maybe that's it."

"No. It's him. His voice is monotone. He doesn't show any enthusiasm. And if he doesn't have it, how can I?" Paul turned so that he was on his side, facing his mother. "OK. What's the title?"

"The Other World."

"What's it about?"

"Says here, beware if we read this story on the night of a blue moon."

"What's a blue moon?"

"The third full moon in a quarter that has four."

"What?"

"Twelve months in a year, right?"

"OK. So?"

"How many months in a quarter?"

"Three."

"How often do we have a full moon?"

"Every month."

"Actually, it's every twenty-nine days. So, if we have four full moons in a quarter, the third one is called a blue moon."

"I thought 'blue moon' meant the moon looked blue."

"Could be. What would cause that?"

"I don't know. Dirty air?"

"You know what blue moon means, don't you? A rare event, once in a blue moon. You've heard that?"

"I'll go with dirty air. What should we be aware of?"

"It says that this accounting took place on the night of a blue moon. He warns that if this story is read on the night of a blue moon, these events might somehow transcend time."

"Riiight. Where'd you find this book?"

"Higgins Bookstore, downtown."

"That place is creepy."

"You're the teenager. You're supposed to like creepy."

"You're the Mom. You're supposed to not like it."

"Gotta keep my mind young. Here goes...,"

"Does it say what that event is?"

"It says, read on...,"

"In 1883, I was a cabin boy on the sailing ship, Nerissa. On this, my first voyage, two days out, I learned that we were carrying, besides passengers, a shipment of wild animals bound for private zoos.

There were rumors that someone on board possessed a stone, a firestone with great magical powers. No one knew if that was true, or if it was, who had it. The manifest stated "common jewelry" but a brother-in-law of the second mate said he saw the container that held it, itself with magical properties to keep the power of the stone inside. Of course, all of us were curious.

Being forced to help in the galley, not one of my primary duties but where I spent most of my time, I was unable to investigate the whereabouts of the stone, but I always kept my ears open to the scuttlebutt when the crews came down to eat.

On that second day, we encountered a terrible storm and, while weathering that, ran into an uncharted island.

While the crew was attempting to make repairs, I was told to accompany Bardolf onto the island. I missed the rising of the moon, but talking to Flabby Max later on, I heard that it came out of the clouds as large as a pumpkin, glowing blue.

Everyone on board knew something big was going to happen but no one had any idea what. This is my story."

Oskar – 1883

My father died when I was twelve. My mother needed help in the fields so I was forced to quit school. I didn't like it but there was no way that she could work the fields, handle all of the chores and still take care of my baby sister.

One night, sometime after supper, my Uncle Fernando showed up on our doorstep. He and my mother got into a big argument.

"The boy needs an education," he said.

"So does my daughter. I need him for the harvest."

"One year. Just give me one year."

They argued past my bedtime. Next morning, I was surprised to learn that I would be leaving with my uncle. Two days later we arrived at Mogadishu.

I had never been in a city before and was amazed by all of the commotion, people haggling over prices, sitting in the shade sipping tea, all the colors and noises and smells. I was in awe of everything.

But on our first night in town, Fernando got drunk and lost me, that's right..., me, in a card game to the Captain of a ship.

I thought I'd never see my family again and was greatly saddened. But when I saw Nerissa, such a beautiful ship, I couldn't believe my luck. She had three masts and I couldn't even count how many sails.

For one year my training would be as a cabin boy, starting the next morning when we headed out with the tide. When I asked where we were going, I was told that our destination would be revealed once we were at sea.

I wanted to talk to the crew and find out where they had been and what kinds of work they did. It was a whole new world and I couldn't get my questions answered fast enough.

I was given a damp, sweaty-smelling bunk next to the galley where I shared a tiny room with Sulley, the ship's cook, who smelled bad. Sulley was not a happy man...,

"Clear them dishes, boy. Get 'em washed and put away! Hurry up! They're gonna wanna eat and you're slowr'n molasses."

"I have to help up on deck."

"You wanna go up there?" He handed me a bucket full of garbage. "Here. Empty this. Ya got one minute. If ya ain't back, I'm comin' to get ya."

I hauled the pot up the steps thinking that this might be a good thing. But the wind caught the door when I opened it and it pulled me right out onto the deck.

I wasn't used to the rolling of the ship, lost my balance and fell over to the rail where an errant wave came out of nowhere, filled the pot and ripped it out of my hands...,

"Where's the pot?"

"Got away."

"Got away...., where?"

"A wave caught it."

"What?"

"I was goin' overboard."

"Better you than the pot!"

"It happened so fast that...,"

"Can't do nothin' right, ya worthless pile a dung!"

You would think that working with Sulley would be the worst part of this voyage. That's true. But for the first two days, I was so seasick that I couldn't eat. It did not help that I was forced to stay below and clean dirty pots and pans while the walls swayed with the rolling of the ship.

I took every opportunity to get away. The rest of the ship was magical, to me anyway. In the forward hold I discovered where the animals were kept. I would've gone inside but the door was locked. I waited for some sounds, hoping to discover what kinds of animals, but heard nothing more than the occasional snort or quiet growl.

I was instructed to stay away from the 'special passengers' onboard. Two of the women from that group always came to the galley to take food back to their cabin, accompanied by one of the men.

One of my duties was to pick up the dirty dishes. They never opened their door more than a few inches, just enough to pass the dishes out and they always stood in the doorway so that I could not see inside.

Once, standing at the rail, mid-ship, just outside the crew's quarters and looking aft, I saw the entire party, a sickly old man, white hair and beard, leaning on a cane, looking out over the rail, two younger men, one with a closely trimmed black beard and short hair, the other with longer hair, almost shoulder length, and a goatee. Neither of them looked friendly.

I counted three middle aged women. I know there were three because they all wore different colored scarves, and a younger girl about my age. Our eyes met once. Hers were dark and curious. We both quickly looked away...,

Flabby Max was shading his eyes with his hand and looking up at the sky when I joined him at the wheel.

"Got some weather comin'," he said, pointing at the eastern horizon.

"I don't see anything."

"Keep lookin'. In 'bout an hour you'll see some clouds."

"How can you tell?"

With a big grin, Flabby Max touched his nose. "I can smell it."

"What happens to all of those sails? If they get wet, do they get too heavy? We won't tip over, will we?"

He laughed. "No. Uppers will come down, maybe more if the winds pick up. I'm thinkin' it's gonna blow pretty good since the storm's that far away and already I can smell it."

"Who's taking care of the animals?"

"Bardolf. Don't think he likes to sail. Saw him at the rail last night spilling his guts."

"When does he check on the animals?"

"Don't know he has. I think he's gotta get over being sick first and that ain't gonna happen until after this storm."

"Do you know where we're going?"

Flabby Max shook his head. "No. Captain gives me new coordinates every so often, mostly east. I guessin' Singapore, maybe some place in Sumatra or Indonesia. If we was headed to Perth, we'd be headin' south more. Captain keeps calling it the other world. Don't know what he means by that."

"Do you know anything about a magical stone?"

Flabby Max made a face that went from a smile to a grimace. "That's the other thing. We got them strange folks onboard, don't want to talk to nobody, Lord knows what kind of animals. Their cages were covered when they brought them onboard. The Captain with all of his secrets and some kind of magical stone. What kind of magic, I'm wonderin'."

"So, you don't know anything either?"

"Make you a deal, Oskar. You keep your ears open down in the galley and I'll keep mine open up here. You hear anything you let me know and I'll do the same."

"It's a deal."

Sails sounding like thundering drums, the rain hit in several short, sudden bursts before it really came down.

"I told the Captain we was headin' into weather," said Flabby Max, yelling over the wind. "But this is a green crew. Most of 'em never been in a storm at sea before. If they had, they'd a worked a little faster gettin' them sails down."

I was getting nervous about Nerissa's bow. It seemed to be dipping deeper and deeper into the swells. "Are we going to sink?"

Flabby Max shook his head. "No. We're in open ocean. As long as we don't run into nothin' we'll be all right, soon as we get them sails down. It's gettin' dark, gonna be harder to see."

"Something I can do to help?"

He laughed. "Don't ask them kinda questions, Oskar. They'll put you up there on the spars and that'll get you killed for sure. Look at 'em. Wet canvas is heavy canvas, wind blowin' like the devil. No, Oskar. Get below. I know you don't like Sulley, but he's better than a wave washin' you overboard. You know we can't turn around."

Flabby Max was right. But once I got down inside the crew's quarters, instead of going toward the galley, I went the other way, toward the cargo hold. I spotted Bardolf before he saw me and hid behind a row of crates as he passed by, looking green. When he was gone, I continued on to the door where the animals were kept and discovered that it was unlocked.

As I was opening the door, the bow of the ship pitched upward and, had I not been holding onto the handle, would've fallen down. I felt light on my feet, almost like floating and it was eerily quiet until we smashed into the next wave. I heard a loud crash come from inside the room and, hanging onto the handle to steady myself, pushed the door open. But before I could go in, Sulley appeared out of nowhere.

"Going somewhere?"

"I was just gonna check on the animals."

"Since when's that yer job?"

"Bardolf's sick. I was gonna help."

He grabbed me by the ear and started dragging me back to the galley.

"We got work to do!"

"But....,"

I never even saw it coming. He spun me around and kicked me in the butt so hard it hurt for the next two days.

"Ever I catch ya sneakin' off like that again, I'll flog ya myself! And if ya lose another pot I'll throw ya in after it! Maybe a shark'll getcha and take yer legs off. You'll bleed to death while fish are eatin' ya. How'd ya like that?"

"But....,"

"Move!"

When Sulley's neck got as red as his face, there was no arguing. Back at work in the galley, I had time to wonder about what was going to happen next. I wouldn't have long to wait.

They could barely see where the water was coming from, pouring in through the air vent above, but they could all tell that it was getting deeper. Hitting that wave, the force of the collision broke the tie holding the chimpanzee's cage to the bulkhead. Sliding across the floor, following the rolling motion of the ship, the cage crossed the room and crashed into the opposite wall. Bars slightly ajar, Baby squeezed out through the opening and stood on top of the cage.

"Baby! Come here! Come to Mama."

Baby was not paying attention. Everything's going crazy! It's so loud! She turned and ran to a stack of crates, climbed up to the top and folded her arms over her head.

"Ama!"

Amber tried squeezing through the bars, tried pulling them apart, but no matter what, she could not get through. "Baby! Come here!"

Shivering and afraid, waiting for her mother, Baby noticed another sound, clank – clink..., clink.

Always the curious one, she found a ring, a large brass ring hanging from a hook, banging against a wooden beam. She touched it lightly and then, wanting to be sure, poked a little harder. Finally, she plucked it from the wall.

All of the animals had seen how this thing was somehow linked to the opening and closing of their cages. And all of them knew it held some sort of magical power over their freedom.

An older chimp, Far, watched from a dark corner of the room. "Baby," he said, gently. "Come here. Show me your new toy."

Baby knew that voice. They had played together not long ago, out in the forest, swinging through the trees. Yes. That voice reminded her of good times, sitting in the shadows of a sunny day eating fruit..., happy. They

14

had played tag together. She found her way to Far and showed him the keys.

"Bro," said Bander, pleading at the bars after Far had figured out how to work the lock. "We gotta stick together."

"Later, maybe."

"You'll need protection," said Kintar, a cheetah. "I'm the one for that."

"Right," said Far. "Just what I need."

He fiddled with the lock on Amber's cage until it clicked. Coming out, she gathered up Baby from Far's shoulders and headed for a drier spot.

"I can help," said Kintar, pacing.

Far shook his head. "What am I? Bananas?"

"Over here," said a voice from the corner. I'm the one you need.

"I don't think so," said Far.

"You won't have a chance later. They'll just shoot you. We're in this together."

"Riiiight," said Kintar. "The one thing we agree on."

"Makes no sense, none of this," said Far. "And it makes less sense to have you two running loose in the same place as me."

"You're gonna have to fight your way out."

"True," said Far. "But I'll know my enemy is in front of me." He glanced over at Amber on his way to the door. "Stay here. I'll be back."

A single lantern turned down low, creaking with the rolling of the ship as it swung from the steel eye screwed into the beam above, was all that lit the room. Bunks, stacked high on either side, stinking with the smell of humans, wet clothes and damp wood, provided lots of places for someone to hide. Far cautiously crossed the room and discovered two sets of stairs leading up, one on his left and one on the right. Both had doors at the top. Going straight, a dark hallway with another door at the other end, closed.

Sitting, Far studied his options. The scents coming from the tops of the stairs, from beneath the drafty doors, were those of the ocean, not like home, but at least it was fresh air. Going into the hallway? Possibly a dead end.

Suddenly, the door on his right swung open. In came the rain, the wind and humans, soaked and dripping.

"Thought I was gonna die! Rope wrapped itself 'round my leg!"

"Shoulda seen him dancin'!"

"Got hit by that wave," someone mumbled. "Coulda been fish bait, hadn't a been for...,"

Far hid behind the stairs, crouching beneath the steps. The humans turned up the lantern. Their shadows danced thickly across the walls.

Holding onto the bunk for balance as he doffed his oilskins, one of the men spotted Far behind the stairs. His mind whirled with the impossibility of what his eyes were seeing and, for a few seconds, was speechless. But then...,

"Monkey! We got a monkey in here! Behind the stairs!"

Far turned and ran into the hallway but did not have time to think about how to open the door. Humans closing in, he turned, raised his arms, showed his teeth and charged straight at them, shrieking. Everybody stepped aside and let him pass.

A few stragglers were coming in through the door at the

top of the stairs. Before they even noticed his presence, Far scampered up the steps, nudged his way through their legs, ran out onto the deck and discovered the storm as the door slammed shut behind him.

Shielding his eyes against the salty spray, he made his way to the railing and looked out over the dark sea. Nothing but angry water, big waves and whistling wind.

Using the side of the cabin for shelter, Far made his way back toward the stern, where Flabby Max spotted him and started yelling.

"Over there! A chimpanzee!"

Seeing the humans advance, Far found refuge up in the rigging and hid in the sails between the men above and those on the deck below. And there he waited, looking out between the spars and staring at the endless watery horizon.

Shielding his eyes from the rain, he wondered what had happened to the lazy days where he could find a quiet branch with a little food and spend the afternoon. What had happened to the times when he could close his eyes, listen to the chatter of the forest and not feel afraid?

The crews were working two hours on, two hours off. They rotated through the galley around the clock. I had no time to do anything but clean up the constant mess. I had to work two hours before I was allowed one hour of sleep and that's how it was all night long.

Sometime around midnight, there was great commotion about an animal loose on the ship. Some said it was like something they'd never seen before, with four legs, long hairy arms and able to leap through the spars, looking for blood. Others said it was a gorilla that was going to gnaw at the rigging and destroy the ship.

I heard that the Captain was going to shoot it but between the waves sweeping across the deck, the ship tossing about like a toy in the storm, face-stinging salty spray and the gunpowder getting wet, the chance of a ricochet back down to the deck, he decided to wait until later.

After that, I heard that Bardolf came out of his room long enough to spot the animal, saw that it was a chimpanzee, said it was harmless and that he would take care of it in the morning. When everyone kept bothering him by banging on his door, he claimed that he would shoot the next one that did so. That's the last that I heard about Bardolf.

Sometime around five, I began to notice that the storm was waning, not that I could go up on deck and see for myself, but that Nerissa was rolling more steadily with the swells.

I was curious to see what the weather was like and certainly needed a breath of fresh air. Down in the galley, air is already stale before anyone does anything. Add to that, the smell of Sulley, his terrible cooking and the constant mess and you'll know why I was always wanting to get away.

I also wanted to see the animal trapped up in the rigging. What must it be thinking? How were they going to get it down? I was pretty sure the captain would not put up with it for very long.

While cleaning pots and pans I had lots of time to think about things...,

Understanding quite quickly that Far's ability to maneuver through the rigging was superior to theirs, the humans stopped chasing him. In the end, Far had the best view.

But looking in every direction, he saw only mountains of water, rolling, angry, windswept and endless. Not a tree to be found.

A huge disappointment. Confined in the cage, in the dark, rolling belly of Nerissa, Far imagined that, given the chance, they could make their escape back into the forest. But out here, there was nothing. Why escape if there's no place else to go?

Looking ahead, into the direction that they were going, Far noticed, standing out against all of the other moving shades of gray, one darker shadow, a vague outline stretching up from the sea on his right, disappearing into the clouds and then reappearing on his left, continuing back down to meet the water. Far wasn't sure what to think of it. Whatever it was, it was not bothered by wind or sea.

Fascinated by this unmoving thing in front him, Far climbed even higher in the rigging to get a better view. Whatever it was, it appeared to be getting closer.

Long blurred, black vertical streaks within it began to look like rock slides. Other dark patches began to look like stands of trees up near the ridge.

I think I know what it is. Still..., too dark to tell.

I was standing at the cabin door waiting for them to give me the dirty dishes when I heard someone shouting. I couldn't hear what, but from the excitement in their voices, I knew it was important. I ran over to the rail hoping to hear what they were saying, a dangerous move in this weather. Several of the crew were pointing and yelling, shouting. "Land! Land! Dead ahead!"

Flabby Max had said there was nothing around for hundreds of miles! Were we blown off course? Was this an uncharted island? My mind raced for some kind of answer. I heard the Captain yelling.

"Hard to port! Turn the bloody wheel!"

The ship's bottom scraped against something. I thought it was sand because it sounded like a very long, but loud, "Shhhhh."

That slowed Nerissa a bit. Suddenly the deck was very unsteady, leaning downward to the starboard side, the one I was on.

The woman appeared at the door at about that same time, holding the dirty dishes with both hands, steadying them, when Nerissa hit bottom.

A sickening sound, rock, wood and waves. Nerissa pitched violently to starboard as it slowly creaked to a halt, swells hitting us from the opposite side.

The woman fell to her left, dishes crashing. She managed to stay in her room, but the girl standing behind her stumbled out of the door, wide-eyed and screaming, as she fell toward me. Her feet were already beneath the rail, sea licking her shoes, when I finally managed to catch her hand.

Nerissa was rocking in the swells. It felt like we were stopped on top of a shoal with the sea coming in from the opposite side. There were moments when it was possible to pull her up, others when it was all I could do to keep us both from falling into the frenzied, frothy water.

Finally, and with great difficulty, we were both standing

at the rail for what seemed like an eternity. We attempted to make our way back to the cabin but our timing had to be just right. The deck was too wet and steep for us to make a mistake.

The two bearded men appeared at the doorway shouting something in a language that I could not understand. They formed a human link, one hanging onto the doorway and holding hands with the other, who extended his hand to me. I waited until I knew Nerissa would roll the other way and then made the commitment, the girl and I each hanging onto the other for dear life.

Far found Amber back near the cages, holding Baby, wide-eyed and crying. He grabbed her hand and pulled her toward the stairs. "This way."

They hurried out from the cargo area, through the deserted crew's quarters and up onto deck. Using the cabin as a shield from the waves, Far headed for the railing on the low side and pointed to the island.

"There," he said. "That's where we want to go."

Amber started to tell him, but before she could say anything, he pointed to a barrel bobbing in the water, in and out of view, nearly fifty feet away.

"And there's our chance."

Amber looked at the water doubtfully. "I'm not a good swimmer."

"I'll hold Baby. Stay close and jump as far away from this thing as you can."

Looking down, Amber tightened her grip on the railing. Timing was the thing. Sometimes the waves were as high as the deck, yet a twenty-foot drop before hitting the sea was just as possible. At no time could she see bottom.

"When?"

He touched her hand. "When you're ready. I'll jump with you."

She had started to tell Far that she could not swim. But he had risked his life to rescue them and certainly if they stayed with the ship they would be put back in the cages and either die trying to get out, or die in them, prisoners of this creature and the humans.

No. Their only chance was with the sea. Knowing how to swim had nothing to do with it. She leaned over, kissed Baby on her cheek and squeezed Far's hand. Together, they climbed to the top of the rail and leaped into the churning water.

Coughing and gagging, fighting the waves the same way she'd fight a swarm of angry bees, Amber flailed her arms and tried to run, going down in the process. Far pulled her back up.

"Relax," he said. "Don't fight it."

"Baby!" Amber coughed. "Where's Baby?"

"I got her," Far gasped. "Don't let go. Kick your legs. Move your arms like this."

Not finding the barrel, they headed for the island. But after several minutes, Far realized that they were not making any progress. "Something's wrong," he gasped. "We're not getting closer."

With her keel stuck in the sand and the swells hitting her other side, Nerissa's rolling motion was acting like a giant pump in the waves, each successive roll of the ship sucking water in beneath her hull and, rolling back, spitting it out all at once.

"Harder! We're going backward!"

"I'm kicking!"

Theirs was a gallant attempt and then a frantic attempt. They struggled until they could almost reach out and touch Nerissa's side.

Amber feeling more tired than ever before, spit out the salty water, coughing. "Baby! I love you. Thank you, Far. We tried."

Nerissa groaned as she rolled with the receding wave, sails momentarily defying wind. When the ship was nearly standing on her keel, belly exposed, Amber and Far exchanged glances, knowing they were caught.

"Don't give up," said Far solemnly. "Take a deep breath."

Capn couldn't actually see the lights, but he could see the glow coming from them on either end of the corridor. Located somewhere in the middle, his cage was in the darkest area, which was just fine.

And even though he couldn't see most of them, Capn was thinking that there must be at least another twenty or thirty dogs in the place, yelping, whining, barking or howling.

What's the point? Help is not arriving. So, shut up. You don't like how you're being treated? Get over it.

That's how Capn had always felt. He never knew his father and his mother had been killed shortly after he was born, hit by a truck when she tried to cross a street.

Capn, barely a month old at the time, saw it with his own eyes, saw her spilled out all over the road and he learned right then and there that life was going to be tough.

Not knowing what to eat or where to go, Capn begged for food, scrounged through the human's garbage, doing whatever it took to get the next bite, until Benjamin Bartman III came along, picked him up and took him back to his boat. They were partners.

So it didn't make sense that he would not show up now. What was it about a collar? If a collar keeps you from being killed and if his master loved him as much as Capn thought he did, surely he would have given him a collar.

Across the aisle, up near the ceiling behind Magic's cage, fresh night air drifted into the room through a vent along with a narrow view of the night sky, moonlight showing through.

Capn watched with interest. On the boat he would have howled. He would have stood up on the cabin and, with Ben laughing and singing out of tune, they would have howled at the moon together from somewhere out in the middle of the sea.

He checked his cage again for a way out, hoping that

he might discover something he'd missed all of the previous times, but every search provided no clues. He was trapped, at the mercy of whoever was holding him.

If they come to take me away in the morning, would that be early or late? Master sleeps in a bit. He might not even be awake. He might not even know that I'm missing. How can he come get me if he's still sleeping? How can I explain?

A bit of a draft, a slight breeze coming in through the opening above Magic's cage brought with it the fresh scent of rain. Capn settled down in the middle of his space, closed his eyes and listened to the first few drops hitting the roof. Minutes later, the lingering light of the moon was snuffed out.

Nothing to do but wait. Closing his eyes, Capn drifted into an odd, fitful dream...,

Nighttime, standing on the bank of some kind of pond or lake, impossible to know until he got beyond the cattails and reeds growing along the shore. To his right, sloping upward, what started out with grass and low shrubs soon was pocked with larger rocks, boulders, a much steeper incline all the way up to the top, faint against the night sky. The ground was wet, the air thick with the smell of a fresh rain, decaying leaves and damp earth.

Exploring along the bank, a small opening in the vegetation revealed a fallen tree, roots uprooted on the shore, trunk extending out into the water. Capn jumped on top and ventured out as far as he could, until the branches began to sink.

The lake was about a half mile across, the far side being contained by what looked like the highest peak. The left side of the mountain sloped down into some kind of high, grass covered terrain while the drop on the right was sharp and abrupt and, judging from the lack of visible land beyond the horizon of the water, all downhill. Between that area and where he was standing, a forest, beyond which he could not see. If it was possible to circumvent the lake, Capn figured that he could do it in a day.

The mountain was glowing dimly with the light of the

approaching morning, a faint reflection across the calm waters of the lake. With the branch sinking ever lower into cool water, Capn turned and headed back to shore. Wanting to mark this spot for future reference, Capn raised his leg.

"STOP!"

Instinctively, he jumped away, tripped over a rock and stumbled into the mud. The voice had come from beneath the log. Inching closer, Capn peered into the shadow and spotted a small set of eyes peering back.

"Somebody there?"

"What are you doing?"

"What?"

"On my house!"

"Sorry, I...,"

"How would you like it if I did that where you lived?"

"Sorry," said Capn, inching closer. "I'm lost, and...,"

"Stay back! I'm poisonous."

"Oh. Sorry, I...,"

"Get back!"

"I'm lost. Where am I?"

"What?"

"Where am I?"

"Here." *A sound of shuffling from beneath the log.* "Obvious."

"What's the name of this place?"

"I just said, here. Now, go."

"I'm trying. But I'm lost."

"I can't help you! I'm here, but I'm not lost. You have the problem."

"But...,"

"Scram!"

"I don't know which way to go."

"Figure it out."

"I'm trying."

"Not here. Figure it out over there."

"Where?"

"I don't care! Get out of here!"

"This is the first place I can remember being. I...,"

"I can't help you with that either. Obviously you have some problems. I wish you the best of luck in solving them..., over there."

"How big is this place?"

"How would I know? I never leave this spot."

"Never?"

"Not your business."

"I cannot imagine going nowhere. Do you have legs?"

"Of course, I have legs!"

"What are you? All I see is eyes."

"It doesn't matter what I am! I'm here. I'm not lost. I'm happy. Don't mess with it."

Capn turned and studied the ridge behind them. "You're right. Not your problem. Maybe I'll go up there, see what I can see."

"Good plan."

"I'll come back and let you know what I've found."

"Please, don't."

Capn followed the shoreline south, until he came across a grassy field that sloped upward and became the gully between two ridges leading up to the top. The ridge on the right, closer, appeared to be an easier hike.

Nearing the highest point, a steady breeze, bringing with it bits of sand, smells of the ocean and the distant boom of waves crashing into rock far below. The top of the ridge was worn smooth.

Standing at the edge, looking out over the endless sea, Capn was greatly disappointed. The ocean was familiar, but not where he was standing.

Looking right, windswept trees populated small nooks and crannies along the cliffs, sparse growth on steep, rocky terrain for another mile before the cliffs curved out of view. Looking left, a steep and tenuous descent down to the water, to the waves that washed over a rocky peninsula, half hidden in the sea.

Turning, Capn headed back toward the lake. He stopped at the top of the ridge and looked out over the island, estimated the size of the lake and searched for the best way to get to the other side.

North of Nerissa, Far stumbled up through the waves and onto the rocks. When he was finally able to stand without the water knocking him over, he untangled himself from the kelp.

Once in kelp always in kelp, unless you're a fish or can walk on water. Wrapped up in the stuff, Far learned that the waves wash over, around and through kelp rather than move it along. And it's only when the big set comes in that everything happens at once in that driving tumble onto shore.

Once on the rocks, Far climbed up until he was out of the splash and most of the spray. There, he found a flat rock, sprawled out and closed his eyes.

He was trying to remember if he had ever actually been happy and was wondering at the same time if living was worth all of the trouble. How much, he wondered, did it take just to get by in this world?

Shari, with her big hazel eyes and ready smile, was always full of fun and laughter and ready to play a joke on anyone. Far had loved her since the very first time he had seen her. Shari and Far, he dreamed of the day. But Shari was not as enamored with Far. She chose another more fun-loving mate.

Rather than watch them and their playful antics, Far moved away from the center of the group and chose instead the more quiet life on the fringes of the clan. Soon that became his preferred way of life.

That was also where Far came to know Luone. It was her quiet beauty that Far found fascinating, along with her dark, mysterious eyes and subtle smile. They became friends and Far dreamed of the day that they might be together.

But it turned out that Luone's interest in Far was to get to know his best friend, Shan. When those two got together, Far felt twice betrayed. No longer trusting anyone, he chose instead to live alone. He kept track of the

29

others and they, he. But the distance between them was always at a maximum.

Being alone, Far had time to think of things. He wondered about clouds, why they move, why they're white and gray and orange and black and purple and why sometimes they rain and most times they don't. He wondered why the other chimps made so much noise and why water only went downhill and wondered why things don't fall up. Far thought of things the other chimps couldn't even imagine.

Over time, he became a legend. He knew where to find food while others failed and often saw danger before the others. Many came to like his quiet power. Some even thought he should be their leader. Far would have none of that.

He stayed away, always on the fringes. He had no desire to be hurt again and shunned the invitations to join them. No, thank you. Joy in life comes from being alone.

The attack had come without warning. Thinking back about it, Far realized that it was the red bird that had given them away. He remembered seeing it the day before, how it flew through the trees and followed the clan from a distance.

Far, being at the fringes of the clan's movements and out of sight, had watched as it tracked the others and had wondered about that. The night before the attack, he had even stayed up late thinking about it. The macaw's actions were unnatural and it bothered him.

When he did get to sleep his dreams were troubled and it wasn't until early morning before he finally got some real rest. He was sleeping hard when it happened.

The attack was before sun-up. The humans had dart guns with tranquilizers, nets and rope and the whole thing was over in less than an hour. Prisoners were taken to the creature and placed down inside its' belly.

Caught in the gentle roll of the ship, sitting inside his cage in the dark and listening to the creaking sounds of the creature, Far knew that he was slipping again. He did everything he could to avoid it, to stop those old, forgotten feelings. But no matter how hard he tried, he discovered that his thoughts always returned to Amber.

Maybe it was because of the way she handled Baby, attentive, yet firm and always with love. Maybe it was the way she kept quiet when everyone else found a need to make noise. Maybe it was because her mate had been killed, and now, except for Baby, she was alone.

Far had wondered about all of these things while they were locked inside the cages. But he finally concluded, the reason didn't matter. He felt himself hopelessly attracted to her and no matter how many barriers he put up, no matter how much he tried to deny these feelings, he was unable to stop them.

For a moment, back when they were standing at the rail, studying the island, he thought they had a chance. He even let himself hope, something he hadn't done in a long time, for a chance to share his love, something he then realized that he desperately needed to do. Go with your heart. The rest will follow.

And then, together, they discovered how bad, how utterly destructive the sea can be. They had tried. They had fought for their lives and their freedom but they, as a team, had failed.

Lying on the rocks, Far felt the tears well up and drip away. He listened to the waves crashing onto shore, felt the heat of the morning sun, imagined clouds passing by when the light dimmed and the air cooled, smelled the salty air, heard the flies buzzing around his head, listened to the wind as it blew over one ear while hearing the sounds of waves gurgling up through the rocks with his other. Far cared about none of it.

Somehow, between the waves and creature and rocks and sand and kelp and more waves and bad luck and whatever else happened in those first few minutes, he had let go. He knew Amber went down. He felt her hand slip away and, just before she disappeared down into the murky water, had seen her looking back. Their eyes met and they both knew it was over.

Somehow Far had come back to the surface even though

he didn't know why. And somehow he still had hold of Baby. The wooden plank had appeared from nowhere. Far quickly grabbed hold and got Baby to do the same.

The dive back down to find Amber was when everything went wrong. Between the ship and the shoal and the temper of the sea, visibility was less than ten feet. Far had gone down, found nothing, then returned to the surface and discovered that Baby and the wood were gone.

It was then, in those next few moments frantically searching for Baby and Amber that something hit him from behind. Far felt the pain, felt his limbs refuse to respond, felt the sea pour down his throat and that was all he remembered until finding himself tangled up in the kelp just off shore.

Living did not matter. Even if the humans and their creature disappeared never to be seen again, even if this new world had all the food one could want, it still did not matter. With Amber's and Baby's death now on his shoulders, with no one to share this freedom with, Far was content to lay on the rocks until he died...., until a curious, hungry crab bit him on the toe.

Far swatted it away. "Hey! I'm not dead yet! Get out of here!"

Standing at the rail, mid-ship on Nerissa's port side, I could see how, miraculously, the sand bar had slowed the ship before we sailed into the rocks. South of us, the peninsula had broken up the waves before they hit us on the beam. They had actually helped keep us off of the rocks. Damage was minimal, repairs were needed, but the problem of getting the ship back into deeper water remained.

The crew dropped two longboats into the water, each carrying an anchor, coils of rope and a crew of three, who rowed to two different locations, one forward and one aft of Nerissa's starboard side and about a hundred yards away from the ship.

When they reached their locations, the men dropped the anchors. On deck, the crew started turning giant winches, reeling the anchors in, waiting for them to set.

Before long, I could hear the scraping sounds from Nerissa's hull being pulled over the sand, crunching and creaking, everyone waiting for something to break. Others, ready with tar and caulking, inspected the ship from bow to stern looking for leaks, ruptures, split boards, anything that might be a danger when we returned to the open sea.

When I saw Bardolf approaching the Captain, I moved close enough to hear their conversation...,

"Three of my chimps are missing. I want to go get them. Can you spare a couple of your crew?"

"Impossible. We're working around the clock already."

"Just one day."

"A luxury we don't have."

"It was not me that ran your ship aground. I want an opportunity to search for my animals. That's all I'm asking."

"And you'd want to borrow a longboat?"

"Yes."

"And you'd want help loading and unloading your equipment?"

"If you can spare it, yes."

"And, of course, you'd want food."

"I would hope so. Yes."

"See how many distractions you'll cause? That's what I'm talking about. My answer is no."

"I had the animals confined. The keys were not where I left them and the animals don't know how to unlock the cages. Someone on the ship let them out. That makes my problem your problem. You are liable."

"There is no proof that any of my crew released them."

"Sulley said it was Oskar. Caught him at the door. He's your responsibility."

"And he says he didn't do it."

At this point in the conversation, both of them turned and studied me. I pretended to be interested in something to the south, over on the peninsula, and shaded my eyes to confirm that lie.

"How about the boy goes with me?"

"Sulley says he's needed in the galley."

"One day. Just give me one day."

The Captain seemed irritated with the whole conversation. He tapped the old tobacco out of his pipe, reloaded from a bag stuffed inside a pocket on his vest and carefully packed it in. "You can leave tonight. Take the boy with you. Keep an eye on the ship. If I raise a red flag, you've got four hours to get back. If you can't make it I'll leave you both behind." And with that he stomped away.

Perched on Bardolf's shoulder, Ekko fanned her red wings. Watching Bardolf's intent gaze toward the island, she knew where she would be working. She screeched loudly and let him know that she was ready.

"Soon," said Bardolf, quietly. "Your time will come...., tonight."

Sulley was not at all happy about losing my help. He pleaded with the Captain but that got him nowhere. I could hardly keep from smiling as I packed my things and went topside.

I thought that it was going to be fun going ashore. What else might we find? People? What kinds of animals? Buried treasure? Looking back, I was so naïve. I should have been more concerned about Bardolf.

Loaded with supplies, the longboat floated heavily on the swells, reached the end of its tether, came about abruptly, drifted back toward the mother ship and hit the hull with a soft, wooden thud.

Climbing over Nerissa's rail, Bardolf descended the rope ladder down to the water and, stepping onboard, held the boat steady. He motioned for me to follow. I climbed down, jumped in, stepped over several crates and coils of rope and seated myself at the bow.

Bardolf whistled softly. Ekko glided down from the rail and landed on top of a box near the stern of the boat. After struggling to untie the wet, swollen rope, Bardolf finally pulled out his knife, cut free, and pushed away.

"We'll be landing next to that rock," he said, pointing toward the cove. "See it, boy?"

"My name is Oskar."

"Your name's whatever I call you."

"It's Oskar."

"Could be a lot worse."

"I did not open any cage. I didn't even go into the room."

"Don't lie to me, boy. I'll cut your tongue out."

"But I didn't!"

"Shut up."

I sat in silence, watching the shore approach. Going in with the surf, the longboat took on a bit of water over the stern. I knew that one of the next several swells was going to give us a fast ride in so I grabbed the rope that was attached to the boat's bow and held it in my lap. "I can't swim."

"Too bad."

"What if the boat tips over?"

"Save my gear."

"But....,"

"We're here to get my animals back." Bardolf said, coldly. "If we don't, you've got a big problem. I'll sell your hide if I have to." He pointed to a clearing near the top of the bluff. "We'll camp up there, if we can get to it. We've got to haul all of this stuff up before morning. Work hard and you might get some sleep. We'll head out before sun-up."

"How will you know where to find the animals?"

"Macaw does that."

Oskar turned and studied the bird. "How'd you train it to do that?"

"We take care of each other."

A swell started to break about twenty feet behind us. Bardolf buried the oars deep and pulled hard. We surged ahead. Looking down, I watched the bow cut through the water and felt the boat shudder. I clutched the sides and braced my feet against the frame. Ekko took to wing and followed overhead as the boat planed toward shore. When we hit bottom, I jumped out with the rope, ran up onto shore, turned and pulled.

"Harder! Put your back into it."

We pulled the boat up on shore, tied it to a large rock and then unloaded our supplies.

"Climb's steep," said Bardolf, looking up. "Carry as much as you can. Don't want to make too many trips."

Over the next two hours we made three trips up the cliffs and established camp in a small clearing within the trees. I was dead tired and tomorrow was going to be a long day. After some jerky, hard tack and a little water, I felt refreshed. I was desperately in need of sleep. We called it a night.

I wondered if one of us should stand watch. We did not know what else was on the island. I wanted to bring the subject up, but was afraid that he'd agree and tell me to take the first two hours. I knew that I could not do that.

Bardolf seemed unconcerned about the matter so I said nothing. Then I noticed that the macaw took a branch close by and that it had a good perspective of everything around us. I then realized that she was the alarm if danger presented itself.

I was so excited about having the chance to see how Bardolf trapped the animals, how he and Ekko communicated, and just having a chance to explore an unknown island, that it took me a long time to finally get to sleep.

Capn did not have to climb all the way up to the top of the mountain to confirm that he was on an island. Looking out at the miles and miles of blue water and endless skies, he felt a terrible sadness settling in. This island was going to be his home.

Not that it was a bad place. Just not what he was expecting. He was going to have to decide where to live, how to survive and what he was going to do next.

The lake appeared tiny from this height and shimmered with the afternoon sun when the clouds permitted, they themselves at the mercy of the trailing winds of the storm. Capn identified the ridge that he had climbed earlier in the morning and thought he spotted the fallen tree by the lake.

Looking south, the island trailed into the sea in bits and pieces, disappearing here, reappearing there. At the farthest end the land curved east sharply, like the crook of a finger, and formed a tiny cove.

Capn had to look twice to be sure. Leaning into the breeze, ears forward, wet nose and furrowed brow, he studied the tiny object.

Is that a rock? Animal? Or..., what?

Something...,

He immediately started back down, heading south.

No sense going back to the lake yet. I have to check the whole island anyway. Might as well go there next. What is that?

Capn followed the terrain down, always taking the easiest way and not taking too many chances. But when he reached a point where he had to make a choice, left, the most expedient way, the trail would be across rocky terrain that eventually dropped down to the sea or, going right, an easier time of it, more trees and rolling terrain but leading away from the cove. Straight ahead, a sharply dropping ravine that was not even a consideration for travel. Capn went left.

It was a ship, a much larger sailing vessel than he had ever seen and a chance to get off of the island. Searching for an easy way down, Capn spotted Far climbing up. "Hello!"

Far turned toward the sound but was staring up into the sun. He shielded his eyes. "Where are you?"

"Over here."

Capn pushed a small rock over the edge. It bounced and clacked down across the rocks and catapulted into the waves.

"I don't know you. Go away."

"I can help you....,"

"I don't need help."

"But it looks like you're trapped and....,"

"I said, go away."

"You don't want help?"

"No. You're bothering me!" Far dismissed the dog with a wave of his hand. "Go!"

"I'm new here," said Capn. "But I don't know how I got here."

"Better than how I got here," said Far, thinking of the kelp experience.

"I think there are humans and a boat over there."

"Probably," said Far, thinking of Amber and Baby.

"Are they friendly?"

Far sighed. "No. It is a ship of death. Don't go near it."

"Do you know where they're going?"

"To their deaths. Now, go away."

"I don't know whether you're going up or down," said Capn. "But if you're trying to get up here, you can't do it from there. Go back down to the ridge below and then go left. That will get you up here."

"You're sure of this?"

"I can see it from here."

"How come you want to help me?"

"I'd like some help myself."

Far climbed back down to the ridge backwards, studied the two different possibilities and then headed left. He had contemplated going that way earlier but the other path looked like it would be faster. Capn watched from above, following the ridge to his right, keeping in pace with Far's ascent.

"I don't know anything about this place," said Far, meeting him at the top. "I just arrived."

"How did you get here?"

Far pointed at Nerissa. "On that. Stay away from it. They will take you away."

"To where? I don't want to be trapped here."

"What do you mean..., trapped?"

"This is an island. We're surrounded by water. I just saw it." Capn pointed with his nose. "From up there."

"How did you get here?"

"I don't know."

"You were born here?"

"No. This is my first day."

Far scratched his head, not knowing how to reply.

They started the descent down toward the cove, Capn wanting to get a closer look at Nerissa and Far wanting stay as far away it from it as possible, except for his compelling need to find out what happened to Amber and Baby.

We spent the night up on a bluff that overlooked the cove, about one hundred feet above the water. Nerissa was anchored about a half mile out, almost directly east of us. The beach on the north side of the cove was sandy and, being shielded from the swells, Bardolf figured that would be a good place to search for footprints.

Breakfast, stale bread, beef jerky and strong, black coffee, eaten quickly and in silence. Even before Bardolf had finished chewing, he was picking up gear and strapping it on. He gulped the last of his coffee and, as if breakfast was over for both of us, pointed to a net for me to carry.

I stuffed the rest of my breakfast into my pockets and picked up the net. But it seemed to have a mind of its' own, mostly wanting to do everything except stay folded. When I put it on my shoulder, it slid off of the other side. While picking it up, another fold got loose and went the other way. Trying to get that under control, another section became tangled in my feet.

Soon, I was tangled up in the whole mess. If ever a more obstinate thing was ever made, I could not imagine what it might be. Bardolf, baffled by my incompetence, finally came over, pulled me away from the mess and coiled a rope around the net.

"Quit foolin' around, boy. We got a lot of work to do."

Between us and that beach, we discovered a fast running stream feeding the waterfall down to the cove. We had two choices. We could either lug some equipment back down to the boat and row over to the beach, or follow the water inland and look for a place to cross. We headed inland. That was my vote as well, not that it was counted.

We kept the river within sight as we worked our way upstream. We discovered one spot where it might be possible to cross, but I think Bardolf was as anxious as me to see where all of the water was coming from.

What an odd sensation, walking though a rain soaked

41

pine forest after spending days rolling in the sea. We hadn't gone very far when we came to a more opportune place to cross, where the riverbed flattened out and, if one were careful jumping rock to rock, it could be a way across, also an easy way to get washed downstream.

Ekko joined us, landing on Bardolf's outstretched arm. She does not give a hoot about me. I'm starting to think that she perceives me as a competitor for his attention, the way she looks at me sometimes, leaning forward with a cold, hard stare. Just a thought in the back of my mind.

"There," said Bardolf, almost in a whisper. He pointed to a footprint in the mud and motioned for me to stop. Kneeling down beside the track, he studied the print for a minute or so and then allowed me to approach.

"Dog," he said quietly. "Going that way."

"But we're looking for chimps, right?"

"We'll take whatever we can sell." He readjusted his gear and headed north. "Stay sharp, boy. And be quiet."

I did not like that Bardolf was going to try to capture the dog. It was not fair that it should be a victim of the crew's inability to steer the ship and Bardolf's inability to keep his animals locked up.

If this island was unexplored, the dog may not even have a fear of humans. It would be an easy catch. I found a piece of jerky in my pocket, ripped off a quick bite and, chewing, hurried to follow.

Knowing that Bardolf was interested in the tracks, Ekko took to the air, heading north, searching for whatever made them.

As soon as he saw the bird, Far tapped Capn's shoulder and pointed. "Up there! Follow me! Don't let her see you."

They ducked beneath a small scrub pine and hid near the base. Following Far's gaze, Capn spotted the bird, a red macaw circling high above.

"That bird," said Far, peering out through the branches, "is a spy."

"What?"

"She tells the humans where we are."

"Why?"

"Don't know, but she does. When the humans know where we are, they come get us."

"Why?"

"They'll put you on that ship and take you away."

"To where?" Capn glanced over at Far. "Better than being trapped here."

"That's your opinion."

"All she has to do is see me?"

"Do *not* do that while you are with me. We should travel alone. I can see that now."

"I don't know that I want to go on the ship. But I have to go look."

"We will travel alone. I have other plans."

"What is your plan?"

Far was silent for a minute. "I was lucky. I'm hoping that two others made it as well."

"I see." Capn watched Ekko circle one last time and then veer south, flying close to the rocks as she glided down toward the cove. "These other two, they are like you?"

"Yes, Baby and her mother, Amber."

"If I find them, how will I let you know?"

"We need a meeting place."

"You remember the lake I pointed out on our way down?"

"Of course."

"On the other side of the lake is a fallen tree. It's not that far and it's easy to recognize. If I find them, that's where I'll take them. Tonight, after sunset?"

"I'll be there," said Far as he stepped out from beneath the branches.

Far slowly made his way back down to the water. Guilt was overwhelming. It wasn't fair, asking them to jump. But the barrel was right in front of them, ready to give a helping hand and it wasn't going to be there for very long.

If they stayed with the ship, then what? Back into the cages, trusting your fate to the humans? Was that better? Alive, but imprisoned? Or, trapped on an island, as the dog had said.

Far stood just out of reach of the water and watched the wave roll into the cove, splash against the cliffs and then retreat back into the next incoming swell, causing unknown things to happen in the middle.

He knew that he could go back up and around, but he also wanted to see what had washed up into the rocks, hoping at the same time that he didn't find a body.

This would have to be a fast crossing. Whatever he discovered on his way to the other side could be no more than just remembering about it, because there was not enough time to stop.

Timing was the thing. Far noticed a lull in the waves every so often and began to judge, by watching the waves further out, when that was going to happen.

When he thought conditions were right, Far leaped down into the receding wave and held onto the rock until the water was down to his knees. He splashed his way forward across the steep, sandy floor and had an urge to run closer to the back of the cove, hoping to get a better view of what was stuffed into the rocks.

But the sound of the next wave breaking, sooner than expected, got him sprinting for the other side. The wave roared in, shoulder high, as he jumped up onto the rocks.

Far sat on the other side and watched the next few waves roll through, fascinated by the gurgling, whoosh sounds of the wave breaking onto shore, and studied the cove from this side, until he was satisfied that no bodies had been washed in.

The next cove was farther across and the beach sloped down just as sharply. Several areas of the cove were just plain rock, One was tall enough to stay above the water and it was to there that Far headed.

Standing on top, safe from the surf, Far looked back into the cove and spotted a wooden plank, much like the one he'd gotten Baby to hang onto.

Several more waves passed through, each causing seaweed and kelp and parts and pieces to gurgle up with the water, but Baby was not part of it.

Finally, Far hurried across to the other side, scampered over the rocks, anxious to see what was in the main cove.

Bardolf wanted to explore the area leading back down to the cove. We crossed at the same place as the dog, jumping from rock to rock over the swift moving waterfall.

He took the net from me before I attempted to cross, not because he was concerned about me, more like he didn't want to lose the net. As soon as I reached the other side, it was mine to carry again.

The dog's tracks did not lead down toward the cove. Rather, at a point where we had to make a choice, Bardolf guessed that the dog headed north, toward the mountain, while our destination was east, down to the cove.

Ekko met us when we stepped out onto the sand. I could not understand her cackling, but Bardolf must've gotten something out of it because he was quick to follow the bird over to an island of rocks. I say island because that's what it would be if the tide was high. At this point, they were just rocks jutting up out of the sand, full of kelp and seaweed and some kind of flying bugs that liked to bite.

In the midst of the rocks we found the female chimp. It looked like she had drowned, but when Bardolf touched her, she moved. It was not an arm or leg moving or even so much as rolling to one side. Rather, she moved a finger and we saw her eyes flutter.

We untangled her from the kelp and took her to the west end of the cove where she could be treated in the shade. Before long, we had her sitting up. That's when Bardolf put her arms through the openings of a harness, secured it, and attached the other end to me.

"Lose the chimp, boy, and you'd better just keep going."

"What if she tries to bite?"

"Don't hurt her."

"I have to be able to defend myself."

Bardolf has a gaze that could freeze a fire. His look told me that I'd be better off taking it from the chimp than from him. I had little doubt that he would not hesitate to hurt me if he were so inclined.

I began to realize the depths of trouble that I was in. There were no witnesses. I was at his mercy. Actually, I was at the mercy of the chimp as well.

He spent another hour searching the cove but found nothing more. I was lucky in that I was told to give the chimp fresh water and bits of food. She took little water and refused all food.

That hour with her in the shade was a welcome respite and for that I was grateful. Cove searched, we headed back up toward the lake, me with the chimp in tow.

Far spotted Ekko and the humans before they saw him. He ducked behind some rocks and watched as they extracted Amber from the kelp.

His urge to join her was overwhelming, but he knew what the result would be, another tranquilizer dart and then he would be back on the ship.

He watched as they carried her into the shade and, feeling great relief at the sight of it, finally saw Amber move on her own.

And he watched with great interest as Bardolf strapped the harness onto Amber and tied the other end of the rope to the boy. They picked up their things and left, going back the way they'd arrived, Amber in tow.

They would be easy to follow. But how to break the link between Amber and the boy? Even if that was possible, how could it be done without alerting everyone?

Where was Baby? Had he somehow missed her back in the cove where he saw that plank of wood? Was the climb up those cliffs possible for a baby chimp? Far returned to the previous cove and looked. It would be a difficult climb for the little one.

Returning to the main cove, he checked the sky for birds and, not seeing Ekko, hurried to follow the humans.

If Baby did make that climb, where would she go? Higher up the mountain? No. She would head for the trees, right into the arms of her mother and the humans.

Coming up from the cove, Bardolf was getting impatient. He gave me the knapsack containing our supplies, extra rope and water and told me to wait at the crossing.

I did not care for this situation because the chimpanzee was acting more aggressive as she regained strength. I tried to convince Bardolf that we could keep up but he would have none of it, saying that we were both too noisy and too slow. He went ahead with only a coil of rope, his tranquilizer gun and some water. I was left with the task of moving everything else up to the crossing.

The chimp seemed to sense my struggling and began to pull back, acting like an anchor. At one point she stopped altogether, hanging onto a sapling and planting her feet. We had a tug of war for a minute or two, until I finally set all of the gear down and took the game seriously.

When she realized that I was stronger and that I could win, she let go of the tree and charged, teeth bared. It was all that I could do to defend myself. She jumped square into my chest, knocked me down, and it was only my quick reaction, rolling onto my stomach, curling into a ball and covering my neck with my arms, that saved me.

When she had taught me who was boss, she backed off and waited to see what I would do next. I was very careful to move slowly. I offered her some food, which she took, watching me suspiciously as she ate, and some water, which she drank.

During that time, I finished my breakfast, relishing even the stale bread, and waited until she too was done.

Finally, I gathered up the gear and headed upstream. She trailed behind, setting the pace. It took us about an hour to reach the crossing.

There was no way that I was going to attempt to cross either with the gear or with a chimpanzee in tow. We settled in along the bank in the shade of a small pine and waited for Bardolf.

Baby was hiding beneath a fern when Capn first spotted her. She was staring blankly at the ground, arms hugging herself. Capn approached slowly.

"Hello," he said, gently.

She let out a short shriek and darted further back into the brush.

"I won't hurt you," said Capn, making no attempt to follow. "I didn't mean to scare you."

Baby inched deeper into the damp shadows. She waited quietly, eyes wide, hardly daring to breathe.

"Someone is looking for you," said Capn. "I can take you to him."

None of that made any sense. And for Baby, it didn't matter. Until she heard the word Ama, or saw her mother, she was not going to move.

Capn sat in front of the fern and waited. She was right to not come out. She had to learn that he wasn't dangerous. He made himself a little more comfortable, positioning so that he could keep an eye on her, and waited.

A noise, a twig snapping. Capn turned his head toward the sound, listening. Then he whispered to Baby. "There's something coming. Don't move. Don't make a sound. I'll be back."

Baby wasn't sure what to do. Follow the advice of some dog she did not know? Hardly. Go back out to the opening and see what's coming? Hardly. Instead she did the one thing that she thought was the best, wait and be quiet, see what happens next.

Minutes later, Bardolf stepped into her view, his boots taking up most of what she could see.

The urge to turn and run was overwhelming but somehow the dog's warning rang true. This was a bad human, Even Ama said so. Don't go near this man. She held her breath and waited.

Bardolf ran his hand through the brush, pulling it back here and there, searching. Then he turned and headed in the other direction, into the area where the dog had disappeared.

"Ama?" Baby whispered quietly. "Ama?"

Minutes later, the dog reappeared, stuck his nose into the opening.

"Baby. Come with me. I can take you to your papa."

Baby did not know, "Papa." And she did not know this dog. She did know that the human was bad and that this dog was running from it. Does that make the dog a friend? No. She backed away.

"Hurry!" Capn glanced over his shoulder. "He's coming back. If you're not going to follow, hide!"

Capn paused at the crossing. There, in the shade of the tree, one of the humans and the baby's mother. Under normal circumstances, he would approach them, might even join them.

But his first commitment was to meet Far over by the fallen tree. If the human caught the baby and it was reunited with its mother, that would be fine. If he did not capture the baby, then Far would want to know where it was.

In any case, he had information that needed to deliver, his first priority. Whatever happens after that is a different issue.

Capn crossed over the falls and headed up the bank. The west side of the island was already in shadows by the time he reached the tree with most of the light being reflected across the lake from the mountain on the eastern side.

Croaker spotted the dog before it saw him and quickly headed for cover under the trunk. Capn caught a glimpse of him going in and found a comfortable place to sit near the frog's hiding spot.

"Guess what?"

"Why are you back?"

"I said that I'd tell you what I found."

"And I said, no need. Yet, here you are."

"This is an island."

"I don't know, island."

"We're surrounded by the sea."

"I have no use for this information."

"It means that we're trapped here and...,"

"No. I am here but not trapped. You are here, lost and trapped. The problems are all yours. Now, go away."

"I'm supposed to meet someone here."

"Don't bring others around. It is dangerous for me."

"I thought you were poisonous."

"I am. But who knows before they take a bite? A lot of

good it does me then."

"At least you won't get eaten."

"How many pieces will I be in? Get out of here!"

"There is a ship on the other...,"

"I don't know, ship."

"It floats on water."

"I can float on water."

"It carries humans across the sea."

"I don't want to know about humans. Go away. Others are going to wonder why you're standing here."

"One question. And then I'll go."

"Do it and be gone."

"I passed whole colonies of frogs on the way over. Why are you living over here, alone?"

"That's it? That's the best question you've got? All of this knowledge and you ask that?"

"Yes."

"Listen to them! They're a bunch of babbling morons. Night and day, on and on and on. Noise, noise, noise. And you ask why I don't want to be a part of that?"

"Well, all of the others are...,"

"I don't care what all of the others are! You've had your question, move along."

"Do you want to know about...,"

"No. None of this concerns me. Why won't you go away?"

Both of us must've dozed off. Bardolf was towering over us when I first became aware of his presence. He nudged me with his boot and motioned for me to stand. When I was slow getting up, he grabbed me by the shoulders, stood me up and slapped me.

I could feel the heat pouring into my cheek, that stinging sensation, burning. I was determined not to cry even though my eyes were watering. He led me back to the crossing, the chimpanzee in tow, and pointed out several tracks, those of a dog.

"You were sleeping, boy. You coulda' had it! Get your stuff."

"Where are we going?"

"To catch the dog."

"What about the other chimps?"

"Don't know that they lived."

Darkness comes quickly on this island. As soon as the sun passes over the western ridge, shadows move like demons across the land. Not like out on the sea where there is nothing to stop the sun from horizon to horizon. For a while I could see the reflection of the mountain, still caught in the fading light, reflecting back in the lake. Everything took on an orange glow. When that was gone, it was night.

Ekko led us to an old, decaying, fallen tree on the west side of the lake. We had been tracking the animal, traveling through the brush away from the shoreline. From time to time Bardolf would venture down to the water and inspect the tracks, hurry back and then we'd move on.

We were still about fifty feet away from the trunk when Bardolf motioned for me to stop and be quiet. I was not going to argue with that. I could not remember ever being so tired. The chimp did not protest either.

For the last hour she had been taking every opportunity to sit down. Whenever I paused over the next step, how to get around a bush or from one rock to another, she sat.

Until then, I had no idea how much trouble dead weight could be. I quickly learned to coax her up before taking that next step.

We spotted the dog sitting next to the roots of the tree. Its coat appeared gray in the dim light, not shaggy and not short. Its ears looked like they could stand up but were both cocked. And, the oddest thing, the dog's mouth appeared to smile, like that of a hyena. When it stood, I thought it would move on but instead it meandered up into the brush.

Bardolf quietly set his gear down, motioned for me to stay put and loaded a dart into his tranquilizer gun. A few minutes later, the dog reappeared, looked in both directions along the shoreline, as if expecting something. When it turned and headed back up into the brush, Bardolf, silent as a cat, made his way to the trunk of the tree.

It became a waiting game. Hardly daring to breathe, I was transfixed by the empty space between Bardolf and the brush.

Frogs, croaking from somewhere in the distance, filled the silence of the night. On occasion, when for some strange reason, all of them would stop, I could hear water lapping up onto shore.

I became aware of the light of a rising moon. I did not understand at first what I was seeing because the moon was still behind the mountain.

The reflection of the moon's light was not the bright yellow that I was accustomed to. I had seen darker yellows, golden, and I'd seen gray moons through the clouds. I even saw an orange moon once. On this night the edges of the mountain, were glowing blue, reflecting across the lake.

The dog stepped out into the clearing and was looking north along the shoreline when Bardolf cautiously stood, raised his gun and took aim. It would be an easy hit, only twenty feet.

I remember the silence of the night being shredded by the shrieking sound of some kind of growling thing. It came out of the darkness from my right at a full run and headed straight for Bardolf who, being hit from behind, fell over the trunk of the tree as the gun went off.

And then the female chimp was all over me. She was on my back, at my throat, biting my hands. I managed to throw her off and for a second or two thought that maybe I could put a net over her. But she took off in the direction of that thing, whatever it was, dragging me along and getting very angry when I didn't keep up. It was easy for her to scramble around a bush or through some thick brush to keep her forward progress at high speed.

I was not so adept. My hands were already bleeding from her bites and running through thorny vines in the dark did not help.

Everything was a blur to me until we stopped somewhere in the trees. My clothes were torn and I had so many wounds I didn't know where to start looking to see how I was.

A second, larger chimpanzee joined us. After a quick exchange of hellos with her, he attempted to figure out how to get her out of the harness, and then turned and stared at me.

I did not know what to think when the dog joined us in the clearing. The male chimp and the dog seemed to have some kind of knowledge of each other and it appeared that they were friends!

After a minute or two, when the three of them decided to go somewhere and when the female chimp was slow to follow, I suddenly found myself on the wrong end of the rope.

They tried to separate the rope from the harness. When that failed the female tried chewing the rope but soon gave up, I think when she realized that it was going to take a long time. The male chimp tried pulling it apart, jumping up and down it and finally got all the way over to me. He examined the knot and then looked up with a pleading expression.

I didn't know what to do. If I untied the chimp Bardolf would kill me. I was pretty sure of that. If I didn't die, I'd probably wish that I had.

These chimps didn't seem to want to hurt me. I think that they reasoned that, dead, I would be more trouble than alive, where they could at least coax me along.

This actually fit both of our needs. I was not releasing the chimp, merely trying to control her, making sure she didn't get away. Even Bardolf would have to see my reasoning with that.

The dog seemed to have some sense of where he was going and the chimps trusted him enough to follow. Soon, all of us were trekking away from the evil man Bardolf and I felt some sense of pride in my ability to work with the animals.

Adeptly jumping from rock to rock across the stream, the dog went first. The male chimp was next, splashing a bit here and there but making it across quickly. The female chimp turned, studied me, and I had the oddest sensation of déjà vu, except that his time she was leading the way, it was night and the river was sparkling blue.

About halfway across, she made a jump that I knew I could not make. Suddenly the rope was tight between us. We were only about three feet above the water at this point and, had I been able to see bottom, I might have tried to walk it. As it was, the current was too strong to take the chance.

The female chimp seemed to recognize my dilemma. She jumped back to the rock that I was on and headed in the easier, longer path to get us across. Anyone who thinks a chimpanzee cannot problem solve is wrong.

At some point in our journey the dog slowed and began sniffing through the foliage. The chimps started making a lot of noise and I started worrying that Bardolf was going to catch up.

Isn't that funny? I was more worried about him than them. Before long, I heard a squeaky noise from somewhere deep in the brush and a baby chimp came out and jumped into her mama's arms.

I was touched by this and found myself wondering how my mother was doing back home. So many things had happened in the last several days that I hadn't had time to think about it.

How simple my life had been! What happened to Uncle Ferdinand? Would he go back and say that he lost me in a card game? No. He was not an honest man. If anything, he would say that I was a fast learner and very busy with my studies. He would be right about that.

There were now five of us standing together and none of us had any idea of what we were going to do. I felt this impending doom following me. No, not following. Surrounding me. It was coming down like a cloud becoming dense fog and its name was Bardolf.

The chimps wanted to be together and I was the one keeping them apart. Who was I to doom their future because I would not untie a simple knot? Certainly they wanted to be rid of me.

If I untied the knot, I could tell Bardolf that it came loose during the struggle. Certainly I looked like I'd been in one. I didn't think that he would believe it, but the story was better than anything else I could come up with.

And it would be dangerous, probably deadly, for the chimp to be loose with a harness and eight feet of rope still attached.

If I removed the harness, and this is what I wanted to do so she wouldn't get hung up on a branch somewhere high up in a tree, that would be deadly for me. I could not adequately explain to Bardolf how that happened.

The only other alternative was to somehow sever the rope linking us, closest to her end so that all she really had was the harness. That would also be hard to explain as the rope was new and of high quality.

Put more simply, it was either the chimp's freedom in exchange for my life, or their captivity and my unhappiness for being responsible for it.

If I did remove the harness and I still wanted to live, obvious, I had two choices, get back out to the ship before Bardolf and plead my case to the Captain, or go hide somewhere on the island until Bardolf returned to Nerissa and they sailed away. None of these choices were appealing.

The dog's ears perked up and there was no question that something was approaching. The chimps were becoming increasingly irritated with my indecision.

Heart pounding in my ears, knowing what I was going to do, I reached down and unbuckled the harness from the female chimp. As soon as she realized that she was free, she grabbed her baby, turned and raced off to catch up to the male. She did look back one last time. I would like to think it was a look of thanks. It felt like one.

I did not have time to untie the knot linking me to the harness. Something was approaching from the rear and I was not about to hang around and see what it was. I quickly wrapped the rope around the harness and followed the dog through the trees until we came out into a field of tall grass.

I knew that running through tall grass was not good. Our trail would be easy to follow even at night. Looking up, I noticed that the moon was now clearing the mountain, as big as a pumpkin and glowing bluer than ever, plenty of light.

I did not know why I was following the dog. I suppose because all of us were of one mind about escaping from Bardolf.

Whatever reasons the dog had for running away now belonged to it. I had my own. By following the dog, I was putting it at risk. So, one of the times when it ran right, I ran left.

As much as he liked mud, slept in it, ate in it, lived his whole life in it, Croaker loved even more to come out of the lake clean. His favorite rock, a flat one that sloped down into the water, served that purpose exactly.

During the day it was excellent for heating up and, when it got too warm, slipping into the cool water or, if it got too cold, back out, perfect temperature control without mud.

Tonight, sitting on the rock just up from the water, the moon seemed like it was just a hop away. Bugs were plentiful with all this light and except for all of the noisemakers, Croaker glanced disdainfully toward the hundreds of frogs further south along the shoreline, peaceful.

The talon surrounded him before he even had a chance to jump. The bird had come in from behind, its moon shadow trailing. Croaker twisted part way around, enough to see the red feathers of a macaw.

"I'm poisonous! Let go!"

"I don't want to eat you," said Ekko, in her raspy voice. "But I have a question."

"Put me down!"

Ekko opened her wings and headed out over the lake. "You were talking to the dog."

"We didn't talk. I was telling it to go away."

"I was watching. More was said than that."

"He's slow. I had to explain over and over."

"Are there more dogs than one?"

"I don't know. This was the first time I saw that one."

"Where does it live?"

"How would I know?"

"This is an island. There have to be more."

"I don't know what you're talking about."

Gaining altitude, Croaker was noticing how small his home was compared to the vastness of the lake. He'd always thought that the entire world was what he could see. Yet, here was something that was not only bigger than what he imagined, but bigger than anything he could ever imagine.

"Since it's an island...," Ekko was saying.

"I don't know island," Croaker replied, now wishing that he had let the dog explain.

Ekko veered east, flew over the forest and followed the runoff down toward the cove and out along the southern peninsula. "An island is land surrounded by water. It goes on forever."

Waves, a million times larger than anything Croaker had ever seen, crashed into the rocky shoreline with a thunderous roar. He twisted around so that he could study Ekko's wings. "How did you get here? Fly?"

"I am with the humans."

She flew above Nerissa, circled it once and turned back. "On that. It floats on water."

"I can float on water."

"That water is salty and it's full of big fish. You would be eaten before you could die."

"Oh. Where did you come from?"

"From another world far away."

"Where are we going?"

"To find the dog. Then we'll see how valuable you are."

Sameer carefully set his tea down and studied his granddaughter, so young, beautiful, and so, restless. "Mahin, what is wrong? If we were on land I would say that you have ants in your pants. But I don't think this ship has ants. Rats, yes."

Normally Mahin would smile at her grandfather's jokes. But there were more pressing concerns on her mind. "Three meals," she said. "He has not picked up our dishes for three meals."

Musheer threw up his hands. "It's the boy again! She cannot take her mind off of the boy."

"Father, because of him, I am here. How empty would this room feel if I had drowned? Please, tell me."

"My child. That is not a fair argument. Of course, his actions were heroic. But you must remember, he was trying to save his own life as well. It is us who saved him."

"You did not answer my question. Imagine me gone, my limp body sinking down to the bottom of the sea."

Sameer, who had the habit of stroking his long white beard as he listened to their conversation, held up his hand. "Enough of this. Mahin is right. We owe the boy some kind of reward. Perhaps some gold at the end of our journey?"

Mahin put her hands on her hips, tilted her head and gave a hard stare at her grandfather. She was the only one that could get away with such behavior. "Grandfather, it is not gold that will help him. Where is he? I think he's in danger."

"It is not our duty to protect him," said Musheer, reaching for his tea.

"And it was not his to save me. Can't we find out where he is?"

Kashif, who was sitting beneath a lantern on the other side of the room, put down his book. "I already have. He is on the island with the trapper, looking for some animals that escaped. They will be back in the morning."

"Why didn't you tell me? You knew that I was concerned."

"It takes away from your studies."

"Studies, studies, studies. I'm sick of studies! This is a voyage of a lifetime and we're confined to this cabin."

"This is not a trustworthy crew," said Musheer. "We paid good money to have...,"

"That will be settled later," said Sameer. "Mahin, the boy is on the island. We are here on the ship. What can we do?"

"I want to empower the stone. I want to see."

"Impossible," said both Kashif and Musheer at the same time from opposite ends of the room.

"My child," Sameer stroked his beard slowly. "Where are we going to find a place on this ship where we can reveal the stone? There will be a mutiny and we will be the ones to perish."

"All I want to do is see," said Mahin. "I am not going to interfere."

"That's what you always say," Musheer replied. "And yet we always seem to have complications. You're too young. Your training is not complete."

"You've always said experience is the best teacher. What better time than now?"

"Never when the stone is at risk. When we get to our destination...,"

"It will be too late. I owe him my life. It is my duty to repay that."

Kashif leaned into the light and asked, "Why do you think he is in danger?"

"I have seen that trapper, an evil man. The boy is in trouble."

"Such strong feelings for someone you don't even know," said Musheer. "He's not one of us, just a poor slave boy for the cook. Why should we jeopardize the stone for such a child?"

"He did save your daughter," Kashif reminded him. "Is that not worth something to you?"

"Of course! But..., the stone?"

"Enough of this," said Sameer. "Kashif, bring me the stone. You women, cover the windows with the thickest blankets. Musheer, step outside and keep watch. No one comes inside."

"But father...,"

"Do it!"

Flying just above most of the treetops and veering sharply around the others, Ekko followed the stream back up toward the lake. She went north at the crossing and circled above her last known encounter with Bardolf.

"You're making me dizzy," said Croaker.

"We have to go up. I'm looking for someone."

Flying north over another grove of trees, zipping along at unimaginable speeds, Croaker wondered why he wasn't born with wings. Flying was a truly wonderful thing! In just these last several minutes he had learned more than he had in his entire life.

Why..., with wings I could...,

"Over there," said Ekko.

Bardolf was walking through a patch of high grass heading toward the lake. Ekko glided overhead. "I'm with him. Let's see what he's chasing."

"That's a..., what?"

"Human."

"They always walk on their back legs?"

"Yes."

"Looks like they should fall over."

"Sometimes they do."

They spotted the boy coming out of the grass and heading for the shoreline.

"You can put me down here," said Croaker. "I'll find my way home."

"Where is the mother?"

"What mother?"

"She was tied to the boy."

"Apparently you know more about this than me. I'm pretty much useless. If you just let me get to the water, I'll find my way home."

"You're with me until we find the dog."

"What if we don't?"

"Then, you're useless."

"Then..., what?"

"I haven't thought about it. Your home's way on the other side of the lake."

"That sounds like you're not taking me back."

"We shall see."

"If this is an island," Croaker wondered. "How did that dog get here?"

"Don't know."

"He must have wings."

"Dog's," Ekko snorted, "don't have wings."

"How else did he get here?"

"Even I could not fly that far."

"He arrived this morning. When did you get here?"

"This morning."

"He must have come with you."

"He was not on the ship."

They spotted the dog lying beneath a scrub oak near the base of the mountain. Hearing the fluttering of wings, looking up, Capn had to blink twice to confirm what he was seeing.

"I will set you down," said Ekko, landing. "Don't even think about getting away."

Feeling the earth beneath him, Croaker readjusted all of his body parts and turned to the dog. "All because of you. How many things were out there trampling around my house last night?"

"I was trying to get a baby back to its mother."

"Oh."

"It was supposed to be a secret meeting," said Capn, glancing over at Ekko. "We were followed."

"My master wants his property back," said Ekko.

"But he was...,"

"Wait," said Croaker. "Did that happen?"

"Did what happen?"

"Did the baby whatever get back together with the mother whatever?"

"Yes. Last I saw, they were heading...," Capn trailed off, watching Ekko.

"Are you still looking for a way off of the island?"

"I thought you didn't know what an island was."

"I do now. And I can see now why you want to go. You're trapped!"

"That's what I've been saying."

"So, why are you running from the ones that can take you away?"

"I don't know. I haven't had time to think about it."

"The humans are over at the lake," said Croaker, thinking that maybe this was a truly wonderful plan, getting the bird to take him back to the water. "It's not far. Let's see if they're friendly. I'll go with you."

"Why are you with this bird? I've been told that it's an enemy."

"For those who want to stay," Croaker replied. "But that's not you. You want to go!"

Sameer, eyes closed, held his arms out, palms facing the quiet glow of the stone. "It is an island of dreams, a harbor for refugees fleeing a storm, a ship's worst nightmare, an escape for those imprisoned. This island of dreams poses a danger for two of our party that have gone ashore, a man and a boy."

"Not the man," Mahin corrected, her face glowing softly in the light. "The boy."

"Patience, Mahin. First we must coax the stone to let us see."

"This island is a mystery," Sameer continued. "It exists on none of our charts. Nor is it mentioned in all of our books. I, Sameer, keeper of the stone, humbly request to see what transpires on this island."

Not a sound in the dim room except for the creaking of the ship, occasional footsteps outside the walls, whispers of muffled words poking through the moon's light. Gathered around the stone's soft glow, they sat in silence.

"My child," said Sameer, at last. "I believe that there are too many distractions. Perhaps we can try again later."

"Please hear my case," said Mahin, embracing the stone's light. "Was it not for this boy's action, I would be lying at the bottom of the sea. He is a kind boy. I have seen his face and I believe this to be true. He is brave. He risked his life to save mine. Why, I ask, am I to be deprived the vision of his fate when I feel that his life is in danger? I just want to see. I am Mahin, proud granddaughter of Sameer, keeper of the stone."

Flowing outward like golden plumes of smoke, turning to black when they reached the walls, shadows filled the corners of the room, bleeding together like a liquid until they covered the dim, blank walls and, except for the stone, engulfed the room into total darkness.

Above the stone, the vision of an endless sea, golden with the lingering light of the day. And on the horizon, an island, a black dot against the sun's bright light, with a shadow across the water a thousand times longer than it was tall.

With the rising moon, running through a forest, thick with the moon's blue light, a boy looking over his shoulder, searching for something he could not see. They were running together, the boy and a dog.

Had I thought about it at the time, I would have realized that going left would take me back toward the lake. The dog was correct going right, heading up onto high ground. Plenty of places to hide up there, lots of big boulders, rock slides, pockets of trees and steep slopes.

Bardolf may be good at tracking and he was bigger, stronger and older than me, but he was also heavier. I probably could have out-climbed him.

When I realized that I was at the lake's edge and standing in mud, I knew that Bardolf could follow my tracks almost as fast as I could make them. I ran along the shoreline until I came to a marshy area, made sure my tracks led into the water, and then waded back the other way, hoping to pass by my original spot before Bardolf approached the lake.

I continued wading along the shoreline, staying in shallow water and trying not to splash. I came upon a large growth of reeds stretching out into the lake.

I thought it was my good fortune to have such a wonderful hiding place. But as I was working my way in, the rope and harness got caught up in the stalks of the plants.

I was only waist deep in water and still exposed, standing at the edge of plants trying to untangle the mess when Bardolf caught up to me...,

"Travelin' a little light, aren't you, boy?"

"She got away."

"I can see that. Question is, how'd she unbuckle that harness? Pretty smart for a chimp, wouldn't you say?"

"Don't know how she managed, especially while she was running."

"Looks like a whole army was travelin' together. You didn't put up a fight?"

I held out my arms for proof, sleeves torn and bloody. "They were going to kill me."

He seemed to contemplate that for a minute. "Had they,

I'd still have me a chimp, wouldn't I? Cause you'd a been dead weight. Probably the others woulda hung around mama. I coulda had them too."

"It all happened so fast."

Standing at the shoreline, Bardolf slowly unfolded the leather bag that held his tranquilizer darts. "Well, it's gonna slow down for you now, so you won't need to worry about keeping up."

"What are you going to do?"

"Way I see it, you've had all the chances you're gonna get. You let them loose on the ship...,"

"I did not do that. Why would I do that?"

"Been askin' myself the same question. Can't find a good reason. Not for the first time and not for this one. You're just a bleedin' heart. You think those chimps will be better off here than where I'm takin' them?"

I had to admit that I did not know where he was taking them and whether or not the place would be better.

"So," he loaded a dart into the gun. "You're going to meet with a little condition. Accidentally drowned in the lake. In about a minute, you're going to go to sleep. Problem is, you're going to fall down into water. I'm being good to you, boy. You won't feel a thing. Not like what I was gonna to do."

Kathryn placed a bookmark in between the pages and closed the book. "Let's take a break. My wine glass is empty and I need to use the rest room. Shall we get some snacks?"

"I don't believe you," Paul groaned, getting up. "You pick the very moment that something big is going to happen and you close the book?"

"Whatever it is, I would like to appreciate it with an empty bladder and a full glass of wine."

"Popcorn?"

"Can't. I'll get the pages greasy."

Paul opened the cupboard, retrieved a packet of popcorn, ripped off the cellophane and tossed it into the microwave. "You know the kid won't die. He's the one who wrote the story."

"Don't ruin it."

"Ice cream?"

"Sure. I'll be right back."

Kathryn returned to the smell of popcorn. Paul settled back into the couch with a bowl of the stuff and a root beer float. Sitting on the coffee table in front of her chair was a bowl of ice cream, complete with chopped strawberries, chocolate syrup drizzle and a full glass of wine.

"You're being awfully nice. It's not like you."

"I didn't get you a present either so that's it."

"Just bring your grades up in science."

"I could get into science," said Paul, scooping a bit of ice cream out of his float. "What I need is stimulus, total submersion in the subject. That's how I learn, hands on. Like what's his name, Oskar? That kid is using everything he's got to stay alive, if the story is true. Too bad, it's fiction."

"It doesn't say, fiction."

"It doesn't say autobiography either."

"No. It says, beware. You've already heard that part."

"Point is, that's how you learn. They can preach all they

want in school, but unless you back it up with hands on, you've got nothing, unless it's Math or Physics."

"You still got a D. You can do better."

"Oh, forgot to ask. How did your interview go today?"

"It's after midnight. Yesterday?"

"Right."

"I didn't get the job."

"Oh, sorry."

"Me too. Now you won't get that raise in your allowance."

"I'm even more sorry."

"Did your dad send you any money?"

"No. Let's get back to the story."

I thought Bardolf would hurt me. I was pretty sure of that. There was no way that the chimp could unbuckle the harness by herself and I wasn't going to convince him otherwise, even if she had.

I thought he would hurt me but I did not think that he would try to kill me. What a perfect alibi! I drowned helping him trap his animals.

That's what it would look like. Everybody knew I couldn't swim. With all of the bites, scrapes and scratches, who would think to look for a little pinhole? The rope connecting me to the harness was soaked. I could not untie the knot.

Eight feet. That's what I had to move around in. I yanked the harness several times, trying to break it loose, but it had hooked itself onto something solid deeper down. Glancing over at Bardolf, I saw that he was casually taking aim. A quick deep breath and I went underwater.

That's the worst part, not knowing what's happening up there. I knew he was out there. But was he waiting for me to come up for air? Or was he casually wading out into the water to get a closer shot? My being underwater wasn't going to help if he was only a few feet away.

Under normal circumstances, I would never open my eyes underwater. I discovered that it wasn't so bad and that, with the moon's bright light, I could see the why the harness was stuck. One of the leather straps had wrapped itself around an old sunken log. I did not have enough air to do anything about it. I crawled as far into the reeds as I could go and surfaced, gasping for air.

What an odd feeling, waiting for the bang, waiting to get hit and knowing I will never wake up. My heart was pounding in my chest and I could hear it banging in my ears.

Gulping in air and trying to be quiet about it, I quietly wiped the water from my eyes, turned and looked for Bardolf. He was not where I thought he would be and not anywhere else that I could see.

Another deep breath and I untangled the harness from the log. I was now free to move around, but I didn't know if that was a good or a bad thing.

Was I better off staying quiet and keeping still? Probably not. If the situation was turned around and I had the gun, this would be the first place I'd look. Was I better off going deeper into the reeds? Compared to Bardolf, yes.

Something slid past my ankle. I felt it go by, long and smooth, not afraid of my presence. I did not like that feeling at all and was hesitant to continue further into the reeds. My imagination was telling me that it could wrap itself around my leg and not let go or, worse, pull me under.

The lake bottom dipped sharply and it was not long before the water was up to my shoulders. I didn't dare go any farther. Bardolf wouldn't even have to shoot. I would drown myself trying to get away from drowning by Bardolf.

It is very difficult to turn around when standing on the edge of a lake bottom sloping down. The effort put me into deeper water. I was now facing the way I came but my balance was backwards.

Holding onto the rope and harness was not making anything any easier. Another step deeper into the water helped me regain my balance, but the water was up to my neck. Desperate, I threw the harness into the reeds, felt it grab hold of something, and began to pull myself back into shallower water.

It was when the rope began pulling me that I realized that Bardolf was on the other end. I tried resisting but he was heavier and in shallower water. He had a snarl on his face, jaw set hard behind his beard, teeth glowing blue with the moon's light. I knew I was doomed.

I believe that it was the astonishment on my face that caused Bardolf to turn and look back toward shore. His red macaw landed along the shoreline, making clicking noises as the dog stepped out of the brush.

Bardolf was as struck by this strange scene as I. He

quietly started back toward shore, pulling me along. It was then that I realized that he did not have his gun with him. When the rope tightened between us, he looked back with a look that would kill, but I already figured I was as good as dead anyway, so I resisted.

He had to make a choice. My guess was that dawn was about two hours away and I knew that it would take at least an hour, more like two, to get back to our camp. It would take another hour to load supplies back into the boat. The way I figured it, Bardolf had to choose between me and the dog.

He made a quick attempt to tangle the harness into the reeds and then quietly waded toward shore. The dog did not seem to be afraid of humans.

As Bardolf neared the shoreline, the dog actually came over to greet him. It did not take more than a minute for Bardolf to put a rope around the dog's neck. During that time I was untangling the harness from the reeds and planning my escape.

I didn't know how I was going to get back to the ship. I knew my ride would not be with him and was wondering if I could drag a log out into the water and make my way with that. I also was thinking I could find a place away from Bardolf, but in view of the ship, and build a fire to get the Captain's attention. The recent storm dampened that idea.

I knew that I could not go back into the reeds in the same direction. The water was over my head. While deciding which way to go, Bardolf casually picked up his gun, turned off the safety and aimed it at me.

"He's going to kill the boy!" Mahin gasped.

"Not kill," Kashif corrected. "That's a tranquilizer gun. He's going to put the boy to sleep."

"Same thing as murder," said Sameer. "The boy will drown."

"What happened to his clothes?" Mahin wondered. "He's bleeding. What has happened?"

"I don't understand about the dog," Kashif replied. "Where did it come from? Is this place populated? Is this just a small island or part of something bigger? Perhaps we should ask the Captain for a one day delay."

"Don't be foolish," Sameer warned. "We already don't trust this crew. The sooner we leave, the better."

"What about the boy?" Mahin replied coldly. "He's going to die and you're talking about exploring the island? I can't believe it!"

"My child," Sameer began in his calm voice.

"Please stop calling me a child. Grandfather, my name is Mahin."

Sameer smiled, loving his granddaughter's spunk. "Mahin, there is nothing we can do. They are on the island. We are here on the ship. If he shoots that gun, the boy will drown. We will know the truth if the boy does not return to the ship and, no matter what that man tells the Captain, we will say nothing because that will jeopardize the stone. I am sorry that you had to see this."

"I ask the stone," said Mahin, holding her arms out to embrace the stone's glow, "to help me save the boy. Justice is not being served!"

"Mahin, stop!" Sameer's voice hardened. "Do not ask such things from the stone. It is not your place or authority."

"He-saved-my-life. I implore the stone to help me. Sitting here on the ship, I am powerless! Perhaps the dog can help? What is its training? Will it allow one human to kill another while it just sits there and does *nothing*?"

Freedom to roam about the island unfettered was wonderful, but having no place else to go after the island had been explored was the same thing as being trapped.

With the rope now looped around his neck, even roaming the island was impossible. Capn had this feeling that his world had just gotten smaller. He glanced over at Ekko. "Why do you stay with this human?"

"We go everywhere. I've seen jungles, deserts, mountains and cities. And now we're traveling across an ocean. Why would I not stay with him?"

"He treats you well?"

"He has never hurt me. If not for him, I would be just one bird in a million flying through the trees fighting over food."

"Where are you going next?"

"What does it matter? It won't be here."

Bardolf, taking his time and enjoying the moment, aimed the gun at Oskar.

"The boy looks scared."

"He should be. He let the mother go."

"I saw them get back together. It was a good thing. They are happy."

"They already were, on the ship."

"They jumped off to get away."

"They belong to this human."

"Nobody owns anybody else."

And that, Capn realized, was what this rope was all about. Willingly, he had joined the human. And what was the first thing he did? Grab a rope.

It was all about possessions. The boy let the chimps be together, something they obviously wanted, and now he was going to be punished for that?

Down in the mud, Croaker quietly inched toward the water. He was only a hop away, probably more like two, a short one to get closer to the water and then a long one to get some depth and he was wondering if this bird would follow. Take the chance? Yes!

One hop, two hops. Croaker was airborne and ready to land in the lake, free from both of them! In an explosion of red feathers, Ekko was there with him. She nabbed Croaker's back leg just as his nose touched the water. "No you don't!"

"Fly poop!" Croaker yelled. Twisting around, he yelled at the dog. "Run! It's a trap! Don't stand there! Run!"

Capn turned and headed for the high grass, pulling Bardolf off balance. When the rope tightened around his neck, and when he knew he was going to lose the battle, he turned and attacked. They went down together, struggling, rolling in and out of the water..., BANG!

Capn yelped when he felt the needle go in. Where did that come from? Didn't the human drop the gun when they began to fight? Looking toward the pain, he saw the dart dangling from his right flank.

Spinning, around and around, the island was moving in directions that his feet could not follow. Tilting his head, Capn wondered why the lake appeared sideways, why the moon, glowing brightly in the water, did not slide down to the ground.

Look! Over there, the boy! How did he do that?

Disappear beneath the water upside down?

What is this thing that's strangling me?

Moon..., so bright! Feels like it's going right on through...,

When the dog turned and ran, I went underwater. I had untangled the harness and wrapped the rope around it. Holding it close so it couldn't get loose, I made my way back into the reeds. I knew which way not to go and there were many more places to hide closer to the shore.

I was hoping that Bardolf was going to be busy with the dog and that I was no longer worth the effort. Certainly the money for the dog was better for him than killing me for revenge. I didn't think he'd have enough time for both.

He was already going to have a hard time carrying the dog and all of his gear back to camp and crossing the river wasn't going to be easy if the dog was not steady enough to walk by the time they reached it.

Staying underwater, I was amazed at how well I could see. The water was clear and pure as long as I hadn't disturbed the muddy bottom. Moonbeams, glowing, blue shafts of light slanted down through the water lighting my way. I felt like I was wandering through some kind of enchanted forest. So amazed was I with this view that I forgot that I was holding my breath. In a sudden, noisy surfacing, I gasped for air.

I took in a large gulp, something that I could let out slowly, quietly, while I held onto the reeds for support. I was dizzy to the point of fainting and even had to laugh at the thought that in the end I drowned myself.

My head cleared quickly enough and before long my breathing was back to normal. I wanted to see what happened with Bardolf and the dog. I had to know what happened. How long should I wait before looking? Five minutes? Ten? An hour? How much time was I ready to spend before doing so?

Staying low, my nose just above the water, I started venturing toward shore. The moonbeams were so bright that the reeds cast thick black shadows across glowing stalks, diagonals across verticals. I felt like I was wading through a thousand piece mosaic.

Bardolf was busy tying a muzzle around the dog's snout when I began to notice a change in the moon's light. A thin cloud was passing overhead. The feeling was like turning down a lantern in a dark room.

Within a minute or two, quite suddenly, we were standing in a night so dark that it was impossible to see more than a few feet. A breeze accompanied this change and I found myself standing in a chorus of rustling leaves.

I could no longer see what Bardolf was doing. Surely the lack of light affected him the same as me. How would he find his way back? Would I be able to follow? Did I want to follow?

The reality of my predicament hit me. I was going to be stranded in this place forever if I did not find a way back to the ship. He would not be my ride.

I heard some rustling of equipment from Bardolf's area, something clanking, a metal sound. I saw a couple of brilliant flashes, his face intent as he hunched over this thing sitting on the ground. I could not tell what it was and was wondering how it would affect me.

Within a minute or so, he held up a lantern. From the way that the light came out of the front, I determined that three of the sides were metal, the fourth glass, and that there was some kind of mirror behind the flame that focused the light out front, a handy little thing to have when the lights go out.

He shined the beam out toward the reeds and I was not slow going underwater. Looking up toward the surface, I waited until I saw the light flicker away before I came up for air. He did not concern himself with me any more, choosing instead to gather his gear. Dog on his shoulders, he headed back toward camp.

Coming out of the water, I tried to follow but he had the advantage of light. How odd that the darkness that I wanted while running and hiding was here with me now when I needed light. I stumbled my way forward following Bardolf as best I could, but it was not long before he was way ahead of me.

What a desolate feeling! I began to imagine my life alone, stumbling around in this place trying to survive. How long might it be before another ship came along?

And my mother, what would she think happened to me? Wandering after Bardolf, I felt my eyes tearing up. I could not believe that barely more than a week had passed since I woke up in my own bed. I yearned to be home, working in the fields. At least I knew I'd be alive at the end of the day and that there would be a hot meal waiting for me when I came through the door.

As I followed Bardolf, I began to wonder what was I going to do. How would I live here? What was there to eat? How severe was the weather? What kinds of dangers would I encounter? I did not like any of these questions.

Looking up, there were two layers of clouds, an upper tier that moved with a wind that I could not feel down on the ground, and a thinner veil that lingered over the valley through which a blue glow was permeating, giving everything a ghostly look.

Hiding back in the rocks, I saw that Bardolf had tied the dog to a tree and was busy hauling his gear across the river. By now I knew the path, having crossed it three times.

While watching Bardolf, hoping that he would fall, I debated about sneaking over to the dog and untying the knot. I owed it one even if it did not realize that it had saved my life.

It was a short debate. Releasing the dog would bring the same result as putting a gun to my head and pulling the trigger. Bardolf would hunt me down.

The dog did not look that stable anyway. It was standing, yes. But it was wobbly and it kept shaking its head, ears flapping in its attempts to clear out the fog. In that condition, it probably could not escape. The dog still looked like it was smiling and if it were not for the circumstances, I would have laughed.

While watching Bardolf's return for the dog, when he was about half way across, I noticed a brighter light forming to the west of our location, from the high ridge on the opposite side of the lake.

A break in both the upper and lower layers of clouds allowed a shaft of moonlight to pour down like water, no, more like a mist of light tumbling down through the nooks and crannies of the ridge, over the ravines and through the trees.

Bardolf was as taken with this scene as I. Both of us were below the level of the lake so we could not see what actually happened when this light crossed over the water, but a glowing reflection from it lit the underside of the lower layer of clouds, giving me the feeling that I was flying high above them, looking down. I kept thinking that, sooner or later, this condition would break apart, but that did not happen.

When we could see the full moon clearly, the dog began to howl in two or three different pitches, starting low, going up an octave and coming back to some vague note in the middle, more or less.

Bardolf untied the dog from the tree and began to lead it across the rapids. There was some disagreement between them as to which route that they were going to take, and more than once the rope between them grew taunt. I knew this feeling, having experienced it with the chimpanzee.

When they were about half way across, the moonlight was so bright and the shadows so thick that it seemed like there were two worlds, one of light and one of dark, each holding its own against the other.

I had never seen such a phenomena and was surprised at how easily I could focus on one or the other. At a moment when the shadows prevailed, the dog disappeared.

All that was left was a freely dangling noose in the water. Bardolf pulled it in, examined it, and then turned his gaze downstream. I knew he would find nothing. The dog did not go over the falls. It disappeared.

At some point I must have forgotten my situation and stood up to better witness the event. Suddenly Ekko was flying over my head, chattering noisily.

When I realized that Bardolf was staring at me, I turned and headed back into the trees.

Ekko kept me in her sights and chattered away, following me through the trees. If I thought I had enough time, I would've stopped and thrown rocks at her. That would be a costly mistake.

I also knew that the last thing I wanted to do was go back to the lake. I began to follow the terrain up, wanting to get to some big rocks, places that would be hard for Bardolf to follow, hopefully with lots of places to hide.

I couldn't figure out why he was still coming after me. Yes, I took the harness off of the chimp, but he lost the dog all on his own. I had nothing to do with that. It was the rope that he put around the dog's neck that made it want to run. Not quite true. The dog did not run until his bird chased that frog. That must've spooked the dog.

Heading up, I crossed over a patch of low grass and many smaller clusters of boulders, stuff that appeared to have been formed by rock slides, boulders that kept going after the main slide came to a halt.

Darting from one to another, I headed for the way that would give me the advantage, up steep slopes when possible and into areas that would give me a lot of cover from both Bardolf and Ekko. I figured that Bardolf was at least eighty pounds heavier than me, and if he decided to pursue me with his gear, add another fifty pounds. I did not think that he could keep up.

Ekko continued to fly back and forth between Bardolf and me, cackling like an old witch. But it soon became apparent that Bardolf was running out of determination to do me in. He still had to carry his gear back to camp and load it into the boat. Dawn was on the horizon, less than an hour away, when I heard his call to Ekko, a long, shrill whistle. I knew that I had won the battle. I was going to live.

Obviously, this put me back to the problem of getting back to the ship. What next? I started heading east in the hope that I could catch a glimpse of Nerissa. My climb took me up into another stand of trees along the upper ridge, and it was while passing through there that the male chimpanzee and I crossed paths.

We studied each other for a while. I should say that he studied me while I just watched him, hoping that he wasn't going to be aggressive. Eventually, he came down from the tree and headed east, the direction that I was already going.

We traveled together for a while, not that we were actually traveling together, just both going in the same direction at the same time, me choosing the same path, him in the lead because he was much better at choosing which path, and he was faster.

When we got to the top of the ridge Nerissa came into view. How beautiful she was, standing tall in the water, floating gracefully in the cove, tops of her masts glowing with the first rays of the day.

Both the chimp and I stood there for a while, looking down at the ship. I wanted so much to be back on board, wouldn't mind the dirty dishes, smelly Sulley, trading stories with Flabby Max, sailing off into the horizon, seeing the girl again.

What was her name? I didn't even know. I wanted to tell her that I was thinking about her all the time when I wasn't busy trying to save my life. We would both laugh at that.

I also knew that I was doomed. Nerissa was poised for departing the cove, her bow now facing east, and I was almost a mile away. To get to her I had two choices, try and follow the ridge south across extremely rocky terrain, or head down to the water and try to make my way south across the beach.

I say beach because that is what I thought would be down there. I couldn't see from where I stood. Somehow, my mind had already determined that the passage would be flat and that I could run along the shoreline waving my arms and shouting when I got close. Surely the Captain would be watching for our return. Would he have his telescope out? Would he be checking the shoreline looking for clues?

The chimp began heading down the ridge. When I didn't follow, he stopped, turned and looked back at me, and waited. I still had not made up my mind what to do.

Either way, even if I made it to the cove, I still had to get out to the ship. If they didn't see me, how was that going to be possible? I was on the north side of the cove while Nerissa was anchored in the south.

I took a few steps, heading in the same direction as the chimp. When he thought that I was following, he turned and led our way down the ridge. I figured that I had I might as well go since I did not have a better plan.

Sameer leaned back against the pillows stacked between him and the wall. "Mahin, the boy will not be killed by the trapper. We have seen. It is time to put the stone away."

"He is not yet on the ship."

"I am sorry. We have already taken too many chances."

Kashif cleared his throat. "Some things must be left to fate. You cannot control everything."

"I haven't controlled anything. All I've done is see."

"Not true. You have intercepted a dream. There will be a resettling of accounts."

As much as Mahin hated her studies, and even more so how she was still treated as a child, she did have great respect for Kashif's ability to understand the workings of the stone. "How so?"

"The dog's action saved the life of the boy. You implored the stone to communicate with the dog. The dog had to question its own motives."

Mahin smiled. "Is that such a bad thing? The dog was being led away with a rope around its neck. It was trapped. I helped set it free."

"You have intercepted a dream that will no longer reach its normal conclusion. You have changed the outcome."

"For the better, I believe."

"You have little understanding of such things. You might be sending the dog back to its death."

"But the boy lives."

"Once again, is that a good thing? If he cannot return to the ship, what will his life be like? It might have been better that he died in the lake. Or, perhaps the trapper would need help carrying the animals and supplies back, and a truce could be made. We won't know."

"If the trapper returns without the boy, we must notify the Captain that he is still alive."

"Impossible," said Sameer. "That will reveal the stone."

"Grandfather...,"

"Stop! There is no arguing on this point. The boy's fate is in his own hands."

"We can't just leave him there!"

"Yes, we can. The Captain is the one that will decide the boy's fate and that will depend on whether, or not, he believes the trapper."

Heart pounding, Capn awoke with a start. Turning his head slowly, taking it all in, he rediscovered the three cement walls, the concrete floor, the steel screen across the front of his cage.

I was crossing a river. There was..., a man and a boy. I was on an island. I remember...,

"You were howling," said Magic, from across the aisle. "How primitive."

Capn squinted into the light. The voice was vaguely familiar, but he couldn't put a face to the sound. Moonlight, filtering in through an opening up on the wall was blinding. He got up and moved out of the light. "I must have been dreaming," he said, still thinking of crossing the rapids. "I think I was seeing a moon."

"You got them started," said Magic. "Everybody's howling. Now, how am I going to get back to sleep?"

A dream? Was that all it was? Running all over the island, searching for an escape, fighting with the human, being shot? It was all a dream?

Reality, sinking in.

No collar. I have no collar. I'm going to die in the morning. Is that what she said? And she's worried about sleeping?

Capn glanced over at Magic. "That's your problem."

"Rude," said Magic, turning away.

Once again, Capn sniffed the perimeter of his cage, checking for an escape, testing here and there. Nothing had changed. The food was stale, floor sanitized and deodorized, and the cage was not big enough, not after sailing across the sea.

The chimp led me down to the water. We stayed above the waves, but were still low enough that we caught the spray. Any ideas that I had about running along the beach waving my arms were destroyed. Trying to get to the ship from here would be a far more difficult task than working my way along the ridge.

I figured that it was time for us to part ways, but for one thing. The chimp appeared to be looking for something. We were still traveling toward the ship, so I stayed with him.

We made pretty good progress crossing over the numerous inlets that covered the eastern shoreline. We encountered a cove that was too wide to cross without getting hit by a second wave.

The chimpanzee ran to an outcropping of rocks in the middle where he could wait for the water to wash through. But to my surprise, he turned and waited for me.

I was curious about that and began to wonder if I was following some hunger starved, crazed chimpanzee, well on my way to becoming one of them.

I joined him on top of the rocks and, while we waited for our chance to continue on, was wondering why he was down here. Was he looking for food? Maybe hoping that I could help him get back onto the ship? Where were mama and baby? My questions had no answers. He saw his chance to go and I was quick to follow.

At the following cove the chimp began to chatter excitedly. I was thinking that the ship must be around the next inlet or two and was anxious to move on, but the chimp protested when I started to leave.

He was bringing my attention to a wooden plank that was stuffed beneath mounds of kelp, locked in between the rocks, moving side to side a bit when waves washed through, obviously, my passage if I could get it free.

The question was, how far away was the ship? Actually, there were many questions. Would the board hold me up? Which way was the current going? What if something tried to eat me on the way out? Could I get to the ship on time?

That last question depended on how soon Bardolf returned to the ship. Had his progress been any faster than mine? He had a heavier load and still had to carry his equipment down to the boat and row out to the ship.

And then there was the final question. What would the Captain do? Would he believe Bardolf? Send a search party?

I went over to the plank and began to remove kelp from the top of the pile, wondering how much had been gambled when I was won in a game of cards.

And at this thought, I had to laugh. Sulley would certainly want me back on the ship and would argue for my return.

The chimp sat on the rocks above and watched.

To make it out past the swells I had to go with determination. There was no water calm enough where I could hang onto the board to see if it would hold me up. The swells were breaking close to shore and the drop-off was steep. Back at the lake, had I had more time, I could have taught myself how to swim. But this was not calm lake water. I didn't know what to do. As a result, my first timid approach into the waves actually took me backward into the rocks. I was terrified to push that board out into the unknown.

Getting out past the breakers was the hardest part. I was greatly relieved to see that the board held me up. At first I felt like I was trying to walk on water and getting nothing for my efforts except winded.

Hanging onto the board, and laying myself out flat behind it, worked. Kicking gave me forward momentum. But I discovered that if I got on top and held the plank in place with my legs, I could paddle and make better progress. I headed out, wanting to get past where a big set of waves could take me back in.

Glancing back at the shoreline, I could see the chimpanzee standing on the rock shielding his eyes from the glare of the sun. When he saw that I had gotten past the swells and that the board would keep me afloat, he turned and headed back up the cliffs.

It was a debt repaid, that's what I was thinking. He was with his family. I don't know if he had thought all of that through, but I'd like to think so.

Nerissa came into view when I was about a hundred yards away from the shoreline. How magnificent she looked from the water! How wonderful it would be to get back on board, get some food, change of clothes, get some rest, heal my wounds.

It was then that I realized that I was in pain all over. I just hadn't had time to think about it. The salt water was working its way into all of my scratches and bites. Then it occurred to me that I was bleeding into the water.

Oh, what is down there? What kinds of things can smell blood in the water? Sulley talked about sharks, over and over, how they come in and take big hunks of flesh, grabbing the meat and shaking it until something breaks free, and about barracuda, how they come streaking in with their razor teeth, ten or twenty taking you apart quickly, piece by piece.

I was paddling harder than ever but not making the kind of progress that I expected. It did not take long, a minute or two of not paddling, to see that the current was driving me backward.

Of course. That was the same sea that kept Nerissa off of the rocks, coming in from the south-west. I would have to paddle twice as hard to get close enough that they might spot me.

That was another thing. Knowing that I could not swim, who would bother to look out into the swells to see if I was here?

Kashif volunteered for the task of accompanying Mahin while she stepped outside for a breath of fresh air. She was supposed to go only as far as the rail nearest their cabin door, but as soon as she heard it close behind them, she turned left and headed toward the bow of the ship.

Kashif hurried to catch up to her. "Mahin! What are you doing?"

"I want to know something."

"Please stop. We can discuss it at the rail. It is forbidden for you to do this."

Mahin stopped abruptly, turned and met Kashif's worried look with a hard stare. "I am going to look through that man's spyglass. I want to see for myself."

"Impossible. You are not allowed to speak with any of these...,"

"Stupid rules. Rules, rules, rules! What good do they do? I ask you, Kashif. Tell me. What have I learned with all of these rules?"

"We will both get into trouble. Please, let's go over to the rail and discuss what we can do."

Mahin turned on her heel and continued on. "The ship is being prepared to leave. There is no more time for discussion."

Kashif threw up his hands in disbelief. "Mahin! Stop!"

Flabby Max watched their approach with a slightly crooked smile. Ah, yes, women. Can't live with them, can't live without them. Just need one when we get to port, someone to drink with, have a little fun. Can't imagine traveling with one, and they've got four. They must be going crazy in there.

To his surprise, Mahin walked straight up to him pointed at the spyglass hanging by a leather strap around his chest. Flabby Max was going to say no because he didn't want her accidentally dropping it overboard, forever lost, especially this glass with its excellent optics.

But when she smiled, his heart melted. He handed it to her with a smile while Kashif looked on suspiciously.

"Put the strap around your neck," said Flabby Max. "So you don't drop it."

She looked at him quizzically. He pointed to the strap and then to her neck. Understanding, she followed his advice with another smile, turned and went straight to the rail.

It took her a few minutes to understand how to adjust the magnification. Kashif showed her how to adjust the focus. As soon as she understood the mechanics, she scanned the cove for clues.

"The trapper has loaded his things into the boat. The boy is not with him. He is stranded."

"We will have to wait and see what the trapper tells the Captain," Kashif replied. "Let's go back."

"No. Not until I know what happened to the boy. I will be stuck in the cabin and not allowed out."

"There is nothing to do until we know this man's story."

"Then we will stand here and wait to hear it."

"Mahin, don't be foolish. You cannot understand their language. Even if you hear every word, you will still not know what he says."

"And that is what my studies should be teaching me. I need to know these things that will help me when my family is gone."

"But your family is not gone. We are here with you."

"And you are allowing a murder to take place. What kind of lesson is that?"

"This ship, this crew, these are things that will not be with you in the future. What do you care about them? They are not like us."

"Kashif, the boy saved my life. How many times must I state this? I will help him, even if I have to sink this ship to do so."

"Mahin...,"

"Kashif, if anyone understands this, it is you. I need your help. Will you stand with me?"

Kashif rolled his eyes and raised his hands in a helpless gesture to the sky. "How difficult she can be!"

"Kashif?"

"Yes, Mahin," he said with a sigh. "You already know that I will help."

Mahin smiled. "You speak a bit of their language. Perhaps we can stand near the Captain when the trapper comes aboard."

Flabby Max was getting worried. The girl had yet to give back his spyglass. Surely, in their culture, borrow meant the same thing. You don't borrow something and then assume that it is yours because it's never returned. He hadn't said anything yet, but there was going to be a culture clash pretty soon.

She hadn't removed the strap from around her neck, immediate grounds for return. He could not understand anything that she and her escort were saying, even though he knew some Spanish, a little French, Italian and he could curse in several languages. But the sounds coming out of their mouths was like nothing he had ever heard, words formed at the back of the throat.

The girl kept looking from Bardolf's boat and back to the island, checking from the harbor all the way up to the top of the mountain. Clearly she was interested in Oskar's fate, so at least they were on the same side of that issue anyway.

When Bardolf came alongside, waving and shouting, they followed the Captain over to where a rope ladder was dropped over the side.

"He is saying," said Kashif, "something about an accident."

"He is lying," Mahin replied.

"You must understand that the existence of the stone is not to be revealed at all costs, Mahin. That is the one stipulation that I must insist upon."

Mahin frowned. "A stone is more valuable than a human life? What else is he saying?"

"He is saying that there is a lake and that fresh water is available."

"Fluff," said Mahin. "He is changing the subject. We don't need fresh water."

"He says that the boy was attacked by the chimpanzees."

"Whose fault is that? He was tied to the chimpanzee!

How can this man lie so easily? Has he no scruples?"

"I cannot answer that question. I am only repeating what I hear. Here comes your father."

"Crap."

I thought I saw a fin, dark gray, further out. I tried to raise myself off of the plank to get a better look, but the plank would have none of that. Me going higher pushed the board further down into the water and then it became a battle to see who would stay on top. I lost that battle twice and did not like it. No. I had to stay prone and paddle as hard as I could.

My worries about bleeding really did not matter anymore. If I didn't make it back to the ship I was probably going to die soon anyway. Might as well make the stand here.

I yelled on occasion but no one heard. I had made progress and had cut the distance between us in half. But when I considered how small the ship was still and then thought about how small I must be to them, I was not optimistic.

The ship popped into and out of view, depending on whether I was in the trough or on the apex of the swells. I figured that I must be just a dot to them, if anything.

The fin reappeared, closer this time, and I found new energy to paddle. I had gotten better at keeping the board beneath me by lying down on the back two thirds of the plank so that the front of the board stayed out of the water.

My forward progress pushed the board against my body so that I could hold it in place longer and kick as well as paddle.

I didn't think I could feel any new pain but I started becoming aware of the slivers that my arms and legs were suffering due to rubbing against the edges of the board.

I was filled with a feeling of doom. Sulley said that the sharks come up from below, out of the deep and will take a bite even before you know that they are there.

There was nothing for me to do but paddle for my life. My only other option was to head toward land and surf the waves into the rocks. That didn't sound too good either.

If I was feeling doom before, I cannot describe the depths of my sorrow when I saw Nerissa's main sail being raised.

Obvious. Bardolf beat me back, told a convincing story, convincing enough that they were not going to send a search party and that the ship was going to raise anchor and head out to sea.

"Mahin! Go back to the cabin immediately! I command it!"

"Father, the boy...,"

"Enough of the boy! You have disobeyed me for the last time. Kashif? How can you allow this to happen?"

"Musheer, this girl is so headstrong that she is hard to refuse...,"

"Even you. I cannot believe it!"

Musheer grabbed Mahin by the arm and started to lead her back to the cabin. Flabby Max stepped in front of the three of them.

"Begging your pardon," said Flabby Max. "Not until I get my glass back."

Musheer had no idea what he was talking about. He began to lead Mahin around the man, but Flabby Max blocked their way. He pointed to the strap around Mahin's neck. "Don't mind you borrowin' it, but I do need it back."

Musheer began to yell. Flabby Max had no idea what he was saying but one thing for sure, the glass was not going to leave his sight. He held his ground. The Captain came over to see what the commotion was all about.

While they were hashing it all out, Mahin held the scope up to her eye and scanned the shoreline one more time, sure that she would see something. Disappointed, she turned the glass to the surf. It was then that she spotted a shark fin popping in and out of view.

She kept waiting for it to reappear, wave after wave, frustrating seconds of doubt. And then, just for a second, she spotted Oskar hanging onto the board, paddling. "There! He's out there!"

She handed the glass back to Flabby Max, stomped on her father's foot, tore away from his grasp and ran toward the rope ladder. In a flash she was over the side, climbing down to the longboat, unsure of what to do next.

Row? She had heard the term and knew what it meant

103

but had never done such a thing.

The boat was not like the ship at all. It rocked easily from side to side, having a round bottom. Stumbling over Bardolf's equipment, she made her way to the oars, hoping to get away before her father could stop her, and then realized that she was still tied to the ship.

Kashif joined her. Jumping into the boat from three steps up, he unsheathed his knife, cut them loose and pushed away from the mother ship.

"We might as well keep going, Mahin. We will never get out of trouble now."

"The boy is out there. I saw him."

"I don't see anything."

"Keep looking. How do I get this thing to move?"

"I will row. You come to the bow and tell me which way to go."

"I will call for him. Do you know his name, Kashif?"

"Yes," he replied, pulling on the oars and feeling the boat surge ahead. "His name is Oskar."

I could not understand what was happening. Nerissa's sails were being fastened back onto the spars! I found this sight very encouraging and it gave me renewed strength to paddle on.

I did not think I had any left. I had not eaten since breakfast the morning before and I had not stopped running, one way or the other, since then. The only thing that kept me going at this point was the fear of dying.

The shark fin appeared between me and the surf for the first time, disconcerting because now I realized that it was still interested and that it was familiar with my location. I think if I was a bleeding fish it would have already attacked.

Maybe, I was hoping, it didn't like the smell of my blood and was just keeping me in mind in case it couldn't find something better.

Dropping the sails is a major event. I sure wanted to be a whole lot closer to see what caused it. As I neared the ship, I saw that several people were standing along the rail, the side closest to me. My hopes soared. Did someone see me? Flabby Max had that spyglass that he always carried. Maybe he was looking.

Did Bardolf confess? Change his story? I doubted that. One thing for sure, if I survived this part I would have to be extra vigilant on the ship. I did not want to run into Bardolf up on the deck at night. I had no doubts that he would throw me overboard.

On the other hand, I was a witness, the only witness to the disappearance of the dog. He would want answers and only I could provide them. Would he call a truce so that we could discuss things? There was a lot to talk about.

To my horror, I spotted a second fin in the water. At first I thought it was the same shark. But then, as I was watching the one in front of me, the second one appeared off to my right, between me and the shore.

Nothing gets your attention like a shark. I paddled as

hard as I could and stopped all the worrying and wondering about what would happen on the ship. First things first. I had to live long enough to get there.

I had never heard her voice before so I thought I was going, or had already gone mad. No food, fight or flight for a whole day, hiking miles of rough terrain, swimming the seas with a wooden plank and circling sharks, and I kept hearing this voice calling my name. I was thinking my time had come.

The boat came out of nowhere. The ocean is deceiving like that. Several times I spotted objects in the water, when I was riding the peak of a swell and it was doing the same, and when that moment had passed never saw the object again. Things can be right there with you and you might never know. Such was the case with the boat, coming toward me, only fifty feet away.

I tried to yell, but I think not much sound came out. I got up on the board as best I could and waved. As the boat closed the distance between us, to my horror, I realized that it was the same boat that Bardolf and I had taken to shore. A moment of panic. I tried to turn around and get away, thinking Bardolf would just shoot me out here. I had no place else to go.

The boat came alongside and I was astounded to see the girl sitting at the bow of the boat, reaching out and calling my name. We held each other's hands. Not quite. She held one of my hands with both of hers. I was not about to let go of the board until I knew I was going to actually be able to get into the boat.

I later learned that his name was Kashif and I will be eternally grateful for his effort to pull me out of the water. I knew that the boat had a round bottom and was concerned that it would tip if all three of us were on the same side. He instructed the girl to get on the opposite side, kept his weight in the center of the boat and pulled me out.

I could not believe that I was safe. I felt like this was a false dream, something to make me feel OK about dying. The boat did not seem real even though I was sprawled out across Bardolf's gear.

The man rowing us back toward Nerissa smiled at me. I did not know how to respond to that. It had been so long since I'd seen a smile.

The girl, sitting above me, began pulling my hair away from my eyes and dabbing me with a handkerchief to dry me off.

How hopeless is that? I started laughing at the absurdity of it, me, bleeding from countless wounds, soaking wet, and she has a little piece of cloth? I was laughing so hard and then I was crying. I don't know when it changed from one to the other.

We were crying together, the two of us..., and hugging. I do not remember any more after that.

Back at sea. I could feel the steady rolling of the ship, sheets straining against the cleats, creaking down through the wood, the foul smell of Sulley's bed.

My bunk, above his, was too short for me to stretch out completely because it had been filled with supplies before Sulley discovered that I was going to be sleeping there. He had to move a lot of stuff out of the cubicle and was not too happy about it. Not everything got moved. That's how short my bed was.

It all felt good, that part anyway. I was back on the ship. The rest of me felt terrible, covered with bandages and gauzes and ointments and whatever. All of my fingers worked and I could wiggle my toes and move my legs and feet. Overall, I was in pretty good shape. I just hurt everywhere.

The smells of Sulley's lousy cooking drifted into my space and suddenly I was famished. How long since I had eaten? What had happened to Bardolf? What things had transpired? I was dying to do two things, eat and go talk to Flabby Max.

Of course, seeing the girl was at the top of my list but I did not know if that was ever going to be possible. At least I should be allowed to thank both her and that man for saving my life.

Thinking back about my experience, I probably would have died, if not from the sharks, then from crashing back into the rocks, and if not from that, then from something else on the island later on.

I was turned on my bunk so that I was facing the bulkhead. I did not hear Flabby Max come in behind me...,

"Hey, Oskar. You still kicking?"

What a wonderful sound that was! I rolled over in my bunk, not an easy task. I had to turn my hips first, get my knees across and then follow them around with my shoulders. If I tried to do it all at once I wouldn't fit. I'd be glad when we used up these supplies. Flabby Max was holding a cupful of Sulley's terrible broth.

"Max!"

He handed me the soup with a big grin. "This probably won't help either, but it's better than the poop deck."

I laughed. It hurt. The soup was not as bad as I remembered. "What day is it?"

"What does it matter? How are you feeling?"

I smiled. Even that hurt. "Glad to be alive."

"Lucky to be alive. If it weren't for that girl…,"

"What's her name?"

"Mahin."

"Mahin." I rolled the name around in my mind. What a wonderful sound. I liked how it lingered on the tip of my tongue. "Mahin."

"Took my glass and wouldn't give it back until she found you. Got some spunk, that one."

"Who was the man rowing the boat?"

"His name is Kashif, her uncle.

I took another sip of soup. It tasted a lot worse, so bad that it helped my pain go away. Maybe there was something to Sulley's cooking. "What happened to Bardolf?"

"That's something we got to talk about, one of the reasons I'm here, actually. He claims that you let the chimps go. Wants the Captain to pay damages."

"He tried to kill me."

"Don't doubt that. I'm pretty sure he don't want you talking to the Captain."

Flabby Max handed me a thin leather strap and a sheath. The knife, with a carved whale bone handle, was sleek and sharp with a four inch blade.

"It's not much. Thought you might need this. I'd strap it on if I were you, keep it out of sight, but handy."

"That bad?"

"You never know."

"Who doctored me up?"

"Musheer, Mahin's father. He's a doctor."

"I have to thank them."

Flabby Max laughed. "First you gotta get past Sulley's cooking and then Bardolf. Gotta go. They're expectin' me

109

topside."

"Thanks, Max."

I got my answer. It did not sound like Bardolf wanted to negotiate. Then again, maybe Flabby Max was just being cautious.

A ship is a very small thing, days at sea. Sooner or later you run into everyone.

I did not have permission to go to their cabin, but I had to thank Mahin and her family for saving my life. After dinner's mess had been cleaned, I climbed the steps leading up out of the galley, stepped out onto the deck and, not seeing Bardolf, went to their cabin and knocked on their door.

I was still a mess, black and blue all over and the inflamed areas, mostly where the chimp had bitten me, were slowly looking less angry. I couldn't do dishes because of the bandages on my hands.

Sulley checked my wounds every day and, rest assured, as soon as I was up to that task, my hands would be back into the water.

One of the women answered the door and, as usual, blocked my view. She had no dirty dishes for me and the timing of my arrival was wrong. I wanted very much to ask for Mahin but was afraid that if they thought I was going to use this episode as an excuse to see her, my opportunity would be blocked. She looked at me questioningly.

"Kashif."

I don't think that that was what she was expecting. A surprised looked passed over her face. Just as quickly, she recovered.

"Kashif?"

Smiling, I nodded. "Yes, please."

Kashif came to the door and took the place of the woman. The opening between the door and the bulkhead stayed the same. "Oskar," he smiled. "How are you?"

Once again I was surprised by this man. How he could look so mean one moment and so kind the next? His eyes were narrow and dark, hard to read, but they sparkled when he smiled. His beard, which I've mentioned before, was a goatee, and that gave him a mean look. Perhaps this was a front, something to keep undesirables at a distance. That must have been it because, inside, I felt that he was a gentle man. This time I could return his smile. I held out my hand. "Thank you for saving my life."

He took my hand and shook it, not squeezing too hard. I think he was being careful of the bandages. "Oskar, you brave, very brave. You..., you are welcome."

I wanted very much to ask for Mahin. I wanted to say her name. I hoped that she was standing behind Kashif. "Please thank, Musheer. He is a good doctor. I feel good."

Kashif seemed surprised that I knew Musheer's name and profession. "Yes. Good doctor. He says, hello."

I couldn't stand it any longer. I had to say her name and what I felt. "And please tell Mahin that she is a very brave girl and I thank her from here." I put my hand on my heart.

Kashif translated that back into the room. It was met with silence. Had I overstepped my bounds? "And please tell her, next time to bring a larger handkerchief."

Kashif started laughing. He translated that back into the room, to much laughter. The door swung open, much to Kashif's surprise and Mahin pulled me into the room.

I don't think that this was what anyone was expecting. She gave me a big hug while the room grew quiet. Suddenly, I was very nervous.

Mahin said something to Kashif. "She says, thank you for saving her life. Now..., even."

Musheer came over and examined my wounds. Then he instructed me to sit while he crossed the room and retrieved his bag. He removed several of the old bandages, treated the wounds and placed clean bandages over them.

When he was done, I stood and smiled. "Thank you, Doctor Musheer. I thank all of you. You are so kind." I wanted to stay but knew that I could not, so I headed for the door while Kashif translated this. Even the women smiled.

The one person that did not smile was the old man. I hardly noticed him sitting over in the corner. But when I became aware of his presence, the way he studied me, my every move, listening intently to Kashif's translations, I felt as if I was in the presence of a great power. I don't know why I felt that.

I turned back to Kashif. "Please tell everyone that I can bring extra food if they would like. I will do this anytime for them, night or day."

Kashif translated this and it was met with much laughter. "They say," said Kashif, stifling a laugh as he opened the door, "No, thank you. Anything but that."

I started laughing. Good. We had something in common. We all hated Sulley's cooking. I exchanged as many glances as I could with Mahin before I went out the door.

I felt good about what had transpired, so good that I let my guard down. Bardolf's hand was over my mouth before I even knew that he was there. He dragged me back into the shadows and pinned me up against the bulkhead.

"Been a long time coming, boy."

"My name is Oskar."

"What happened to the dog?"

My heart started pounding. "I had no part in that. "You did that all by yourself."

"What did you see?"

At last, something to bargain with. "You call me Oskar. And you stop harassing me."

He tightened his grip on my collar. Looking into his eyes, I could see the anguish building. This was a disturbed and driven man.

"The dog. What - did – you - see?"

"Deal?"

"I don't make deals."

"Then, I won't talk. You'll never know."

This was my only chance. His forearm leaned heavily against my chest. I couldn't move my arms enough to get to the knife. Even if I could, I'm not sure that I'd use it.

At what point would I draw a knife? Surely, if I could draw it now, even if I stuck him with it, was that going to save my life? I didn't think so. This man would just get madder.

So, answering my own question, I'll use it like a wild man if I think I'm going overboard and not before.

Bardolf suddenly loosened his grip and backed away. I was so surprised by this move that I ducked, thinking that he was going to hit me. Then I noticed that he was standing straight up, too straight. Kashif was standing behind Bardolf, holding his head back by his hair and a knife at Bardolf's throat.

He smiled. "No, no."

Bardolf had no choice. His arms hung limp at his sides. Kashif waited a few seconds longer than necessary and then let Bardolf go, cautiously, gently. Still keeping his knife ready, he smiled at Bardolf. "So sorry."

I think Bardolf actually thought he could win in this situation. I could see him calculating, his eyes steady, weighing the odds. But Kashif did not appear to be any kind of pushover. I do not think that he was afraid. I was amazed how gracefully he got out of a very tense situation, apologizing to Bardolf, allowing him to save face at the same time. I hoped that Bardolf would take the hint. Instead, he turned to go.

"Bardolf."

He stopped, turned back and tilted his head in a mocking way, waiting for me to say something.

"The dog disappeared. It did not go down the rapids."

"Then..., where?"

"Do you remember how there was light and then shadows, on and off?"

"I do."

"It happened during a shadow. You were half way across. It was only dark for a few seconds. It was there..., and then it was gone. It did not go downstream. I had a good view."

He studied me for a minute, weighing my words. "Then..., where?"

"Into the shadow. That's all I know."

A long, quiet minute passed between the three of us, Kashif with knife, Bardolf exchanging glances with the two of us, me just hoping that this moment would pass with no one getting hurt.

I did not know how long this journey was going to take or what I would do when it was over, probably try to work my way back home. I fully understood that I needed allies, people that I could trust, and I was very appreciative of Kashif's help. Between Flabby Max and Kashif, I felt that I had a pretty good start.

I think Bardolf was recalculating as well. Maybe he was thinking that I might be of some use after all, better alive than dead. I could certainly help take care of the animals if he wasn't up to it.

Standing there in the lee of the wind, in the shadows of the bulkhead on a moonlit night, I believe that some kind of truce was quietly being formed. After a long pause, Bardolf looked at me and nodded. "Thanks for sayin'."

He still wouldn't call me by name but he did say thanks. I felt like a million pounds had been lifted off of my shoulders. I still did not know if he was going to try and kill me, and that weighed heavily on my mind. There might still be an 'accident' waiting for me, just needing a time and place.

But he did say thanks. Hoping to prolong this tenuous moment of good will, I was looking for some kind of opportunity to show that I was worthy of something more than being a target. I did not have long to wait. Swells were up to twenty feet, winds to thirty knots. Nerissa was weathering the conditions just fine, pitching and rolling with the sea and wet everywhere on deck.

Flabby Max reported that Bardolf was too seasick to tend to his animals. He was surprised when I knocked on his door and, standing there in the weather, offered my help. He looked at me suspiciously.

"Why do you want to help me?"

"I'm just offering. I'll have an excuse to get out of the galley, something different for me to do."

"I tried to kill you."

"I noticed."

"So..., why you want to help me?"

"The animals probably need attention."

"You want to let some more loose?"

"I've never been in that room. I let the mama go in the forest. Yes. Maybe, by helping you I can pay off some of the loss."

Bardolf had this mocking mannerism that he used with me most of the time, folding his arms, cocking his head and waiting for some profound words that I was going to utter. He assumed that now, leaning against the doorway. "A cage broke loose during the storm. I saw how the baby could get out, not the mama. But mama's cage was unlocked, same as with the male. Found the keys on the floor. Now..., how did those keys do that by them-

116

selves?"

"Ask Sulley. He never saw me in the room. He dragged me back to the galley. I never even got a chance to look in. That's the truth."

I could tell Bardolf was not weathering the storm very well. There were moments where he looked like he needed to heave. At least he didn't tell me to go die somewhere and slam the door.

"What happened on the island?" he asked, at last.

"What do you mean?"

"When that moonlight broke through."

I shrugged. "There were two layers of clouds...,"

"Saw that. Something else was happening."

"Right."

"What do you know about a magic stone?"

I shrugged again. "I heard that there was one. That's all I know."

"It was a blue moon."

Shivering, I nodded.

"You sure that dog didn't go downstream?"

"I would've seen. The dog was there, rope around its' neck while you led it across the stream. During the time that it was dark, he disappeared, only about five seconds. It wouldn't have had time to go down the rapids out of my view."

Bardolf shook his head doubtfully, looking green again. "Gotta go."

He abruptly closed the door. I smiled. Good. Two meetings and I'm not dead yet. And now I knew that Bardolf did not have the stone. That was something Flabby Max and I had discussed.

The story of the dog's disappearance became a topic of conversation around the ship. Bardolf's reputation as a skilled trapper was wider than I had suspected.

Yes. I was very impressed with his ability to track the animals and even more impressed with his ability to hunt me down so quickly. When word got out that he had lost an animal, not escaped, but disappeared while tethered, that was reason for speculation.

But we did not have time to consider the possibilities. The island was behind us and Teluk Betung was our destination. After departing from the island, two days out, we began to see ash floating in the swells, falling out of the sky and, with a nightly heavy dew, sticking onto the deck. It wasn't long before we spotted a human body drifting in the water.

We hove to while the Captain dispatched a boat to retrieve the body. It was of a young man who looked like he had been badly burned, at least the parts that the fish hadn't eaten. This was the first of many distressing signs that something major had occurred. Flabby Max had a theory.

"I was at the helm during the storm. One wave was bigger than all the others, twice, maybe three times, you remember that? Just before, I heard thunder when I didn't see lightning and was wondering about that. Had to hang onto the wheel to keep from falling, thinking maybe something fell outta the sky and landed in the ocean or maybe something came up from below. I'm telling you, Oskar. Too many things aren't right."

I had to agree. The time on the island seemed like it was just a dream and I had to keep looking at my wounds to make sure that it really happened. Being led through a blue moon forest by a chimpanzee is not something that you can relate to another human being without them laughing, so I kept quiet about that.

Walking underwater with my eyes open while being

stalked by a crazed man with a tranquilizer gun did not seem real either, or swimming with the sharks, or being hugged by Mahin.

I began to think that maybe I was still at home, sleeping in my bed, dreaming, having to wake up in the morning and get to work in the fields. It was time to harvest corn.

It was after we had retrieved pumice out of the water that we realized a volcano had erupted somewhere in the direction of our destination. That would explain the blue moon, maybe, certainly the orange sun.

Many in the crew did not want to head into a death trap, at least that's what they were calling it, and wanted to turn around. The Captain said that Teluk Betung was our destination and that we were going to reach it. Tension mounted on the ship.

Bardolf especially was wanting to continue on. I learned that he was low on supplies for the animals and was anxious for Nerissa to get to port. There was also a geologist on board, Geoffrey Bard from London, who was going to study Krakatoa, a volcano that had been active for some time. It was Mr. Bard who suggested that we might be too late for his studies, but lucky enough to miss the actual event.

That night, when I went to pick up the dirty dishes, Kashif invited me inside. I was offered a cup of tea, which I accepted, and was seated across a table from Kashif and Musheer. I tried very hard to keep my eyes off of Mahin, who was seated among the three other women at the far end of the room. I did not see the old man, whose name I later learned was Sameer, but suspected that he was resting (or listening) behind a screen positioned behind Kashif and Musheer.

"Oskar," said Kashif. "Are you..., free man?"

I did not know how to answer that. Paid for my services? No. Free as in not a slave? Not really. I answered quite simply. "No. I am not free." I figured that this pretty much answered both questions.

"You are..., slave for cook?"

I smiled. "No. For Captain."

This was translated to the others. There followed much discussion between them in the next several minutes, time that my eyes wandered the room, landing on Mahin more often than was polite. Each of us smiled at the other. I felt like I was in Heaven. Finally Kashif returned his gaze to me.

"How much..., money, for help Captain?"

"Nothing." I replied. "No money."

Again, much discussion.

"How you be..., slave?" Kashif asked.

"Card game," I explained. "My uncle lost me in a bet."

Kashif was certainly not understanding that. He shook his head doubtfully, not knowing how to translate. "Uncle bet..., you?"

"Yes," I smiled.

I thought that they would laugh at that. In a way it was funny even though it would take me many years to see the humor in it. But translated to the others, the room became very quiet. I think that they were astounded that a relative so close as an uncle would even think to put his nephew at risk. They exchanged glances quietly, each assessing the other's reaction to such news. Kashif looked back at me.

"For..., how long?"

"One year."

Musheer and Kashif discussed something at length. I was hoping it was something like, let's buy the boy and have him be with us. Wouldn't that be nice? No more Sulley. No more dishes. Maybe they wanted me to teach them English. Mahin would be my student!

"Three more days, Teluk Betung," said Kashif. "Yes?"

I nodded. "I think so." I reminded myself to be more informed. Time for me to quit dwelling on the past and make myself valuable. Next stop after the night's clean-up, Flabby Max.

When I returned to the galley, probably taking a good twenty minutes longer than I should have, I expected to get another twisted ear and a tongue lashing. By now, I should have cleared the tables and, since I wasn't washing, been finishing up and getting everything ready for the next meal. Not having this done cuts into Sulley's rest time, so you can understand what I was expecting.

Sulley was just finishing up clearing the dishes when I returned carrying Mahin's family's dishes. "Where ya been, boy?"

"My name's Oskar."

"Ya been with them, Oskar?"

"Them?"

"Them strange ones. Yur carryin' their dishes."

"The doctor wanted to check my bandages."

I didn't want to get into any lengthy conversation about Mahin and her family. They wanted their privacy and I intended to keep it that way, except for Flabby Max. I headed for the sink with their dishes. Sulley followed with what he'd cleared off of the tables.

"Ya didn't tell him ya got work to do?"

"I didn't think it would take so long."

"Yur getting' friendly with 'em, aren't ya?"

"They did save my life."

Sulley smiled. I found that, I hate to use the word, astounding, but that's what it was. I did not think that Sulley knew how to smile.

"Got to swim with the sharks, did ya? How'd it feel, Oskar?"

"I was too tired to care." And that was the truth. I don't think I could have made it to the ship by myself. The lifeboat and Mahin's outstretched arms will be embedded into my memory until the day I die.

"How long fore we get to port?"

"Three days, I think. I'm going to talk to Flabby Max after I'm done here. I'll let you know."

121

"What are ya hearin' about the ash?"

It suddenly occurred to me that Sulley spent almost all of his time below deck. His was about the most thankless job on the ship and he was probably working eighteen to twenty hours a day. He didn't get much chance to talk to anyone.

"The Englishman, Bard, thinks it was a volcano."

"What's the Captain say?"

"He doesn't know either."

"We're still headin' to Teluk Betung."

That was a statement, not a question. Yet, he was expecting an answer. "Far as I know. Like I said, I'm going to talk to Flabby Max after I'm done here. I'll let you know."

"There's some on the crew don't want to go."

"I heard. Sulley, why don't you take a break. I'll finish up."

I don't think he knew how to handle the offer. I wondered if anyone ever offered to help.

"Why would ya want to do that?"

"You deserve a break."

"Ya can't wash dishes with them bandages."

"I think I'm healed enough by now."

Sulley did not know what to think. He looked around the room, measuring how much longer it was going to take. I could see it in his eyes.

And then he looked at me, wondering if I was up to the task. Because if I wasn't, it's hard to explain to a hungry crew why the meal is not ready. I wondered if anyone ever showed him any kindness and was suddenly curious as to where he came from and how he wound up here. How was he raised? Did his father beat him? Maybe he was never around.

I can still see my father's face. And I remember his laughter. Even that will fade with time. Ours was a happy family until he died. I'd only been gone from home for ten days and already that life seemed like it was from a different life.

Sulley looked around the room one last time and then

122

headed for the steps leading topside. "Thanks, Oskar."

Flabby Max had a worried, far away look when I approached him at the wheel. He did not see me coming and for him to miss something was actually kind of a big thing.

"Hey, Max."

He jumped at the sound. "Oh, Oskar. Geez. You scared me."

"You were thinking about something. Where were you?"

"I'm just wonderin' what the next big thing's gonna be."

"I heard they found another body."

"Two. People are wonderin' what we're sailing into. I'm tellin' you, Oskar, I've never seen this kind of..., disturbance. That's what I'm feelin'. And I don't know which side is going to win, those wantin' to keep goin' or those wantin' to turn around."

"Win?"

"Somethin's up. I think we got trouble brewin'."

"How's that?"

"I'm seein' a lot of sideways glances, kind of a silent communication, if you know what I mean. There's somethin' going on. And if we keep finding bodies, it's gonna get worse."

"Who's behind it?"

"Don't think anybody's behind it, more like common opinion. But if there was a leader, my guess is Sanjay."

"Don't know him."

"Wears a black head band, gold earring, dark skin. He smiles a lot, but his eyes never do."

"I know who."

I almost couldn't believe what I was hearing. Yes, there are always disgruntled people no matter what. Living on the ship, the food is bad, living quarters cramped, too much work, not enough pay, but on a ship that is to be expected.

At least that was my thinking. To me, the biggest thing is to get back to land, hopefully to where you wanted to go. To sabotage that effort seemed unthinkable. "Mutiny, Max? Is that what you're saying?"

"I ain't sayin' it, just thinkin' it. You know how I can smell weather? I can smell trouble."

"Are we still heading for Teluk Betung?"

"Two and a half days by my calculations."

"What happens if there is a mutiny?"

Flabby Max smiled grimly. "Never seen one, so I don't know. I just hope whoever's got control knows they need me to steer the ship."

"Will they make the Captain walk the plank?"

I was also wondering if I would have to walk the plank since I was the Captain's property. Would someone else inherit me? Would they honor the one year limit or would it be for life?

"I think first they gotta catch him and tie him up. And that'll be no easy task. How many guns you think he carries?"

I shrugged. "Never thought about it. Just the one, I guess. On his hip."

"Take a closer look. Three, hip, shoulder and one strapped to his calf beneath his pants. Bardolf will want to make Teluk Betung cause that's when he'll get paid. So, if anything happens, I'd guess he's on the Captain's side. He won't care if the place is burnin' down as long as he gets his money."

"If it was a volcano, his customers might already be dead."

"That's the chance you take. If that volcano explosion caused the thunder that I heard during the storm, and then that big wave that followed, and with us that far away, that must been something to see. Our stop at that island might've saved our lives. If we'd a been a little closer, who knows?"

"What do you think we're going to find?"

"I'm thinkin'," Flabby Max, tightened his grip on the wheel, checked the compass and looked out at the sea.

"I'm thinkin' Teluk Betung might not even be there any-more. You know, Oskar. If the wind's blowin' the wrong way and that explosion's as big as I'm thinkin', then you got to wonder what happened close by. If fire didn't kill everyone, maybe the sea rose up and finished the job."

"What if Teluk Betung's gone?"

"We're gonna need supplies. Got to find another port. If the place is covered in ash or if it washed away, there's going to be nothing for us there."

Flabby Max was opening my eyes to a whole bunch of possibilities. I had to be up in four hours to help Sul-ley with breakfast. Instead of time slowing down, like I thought it would out at sea, it seemed to be speeding up.

On my way back to my bunk, I noticed Sanjay stand-ing just outside the crew's quarters, talking to two other men. They grew quiet as I passed by. Sanjay smiled and nodded.

I went straight through the galley to my bunk, decid-ing along the way that I was going to sleep facing the doorway with my knife ready. Climbing up to my bunk, I discovered that Sulley had cleared out the supplies. For the first time since the voyage began I was able to stretch out in my bunk.

Kathryn placed a bookmark into the pages and closed the book. "OK. Time for a refill. And it's your turn to read."

Paul yawned. "Me? It's your birthday. I give you the pleasure."

"You're not weaseling out of it. You owe."

"So, what happens if we read this on a blue moon?"

"He never said. I think we have to get to the end of the story."

"Let's just read it now and be done with it."

"No. I want to know how we get to the end. If you read the end first, you spoil everything."

"But at least you'll know if it was worth it."

"What part of this story has not fascinated you? I actually want to see what happens next. Don't you?"

"It's a fantasy novel."

"That has never been stated. It is Oskar's story."

"As told by Oskar. That doesn't make it true."

"He never asked us to believe his story. He told us to beware."

"Same thing, fiction."

"So, history lesson. What happened to Teluk Betung when Krakatoa erupted in eighteen-eighty-three?"

"No idea."

"If you were on the ship, would you turn around or keep going?"

Paul got up, headed for the kitchenette on the other side of the counter. "Tea?'

Kathryn set the book down and got up with a sigh. "Wine. You didn't answer my question."

Paul filled a cup with water, put it in the microwave and gave it a minute. "I don't know. They've got an orange sun, blue moon and bodies floating out in the ocean. That doesn't sound like a beach resort."

"You still didn't answer my question."

"No radios back then? No way to verify anything?"

Kathryn poured herself another glass of wine. "I don't think radios were invented until around the turn of the century."

"Nineteen hundred?"

"Can't believe that you even asked that. Of course. So, unless there is another ship going the other way, they have no way of knowing. Back to the question. Would you turn around or keep going?"

"Are they more than half way? Because if they've gone too far, they may not have enough supplies to turn around."

"I'm sure that's on the Captain's mind."

Paul retrieved his cup, dropped a tea bag into the steaming water and returned to the couch. "I'd keep going. I'd want to know what happened."

Kathryn sipped her wine, set the glass down, opened the book and handed it to Paul. "Me too. Your turn."

Kashif invited me back into their cabin the following morning. I explained that I had to help Sulley first, as that was my duty. When I returned, as before, Musheer and Kashif sat across the table from me, all of us sitting on pillows on the floor, and offered tea, which I accepted.

Kashif and Musheer lifted their cups for a toast. Hesitantly, I did the same. Kashif smiled.

"Oskar, you free man."

I didn't know what to think about that. Did he mean that the Captain no longer owned me? If that was the case, I was now a passenger on the ship without money. What would I do when we arrived at Teluk Betung? How would I get back home?

Being free suddenly had an awful lot of bad implications. If there was going to be a mutiny, I was a free man. I hoped they would believe that. Was there any paperwork involved in this deal? If so, who had it? If I'm free, shouldn't that paperwork be mine?

I smiled at Musheer and Kashif. "What?"

"We..., decide. We buy..., you."

"You *bought* me?"

"From Captain. You, no work for ship..., more."

"What will I do? I have no money."

"We..., help." Kashif clinked his cup to mine. "Now, you free."

I drank to that, as did Musheer. "Thank you. How may I help you?"

Glancing over at Mahin, I saw that she was beaming. I felt my heart just about leap out of my chest. Picking up a book, Musheer spoke to Kashif.

"He says, please help, go to English."

Translate? You bet. How odd that I was feeling sorry for myself two weeks ago because I had to work the fields rather than go to school. Overnight I became a slave. And now I'm a free man, back in school, teaching? Life is strange. "Who will help me? I don't know your words."

Kashif and Musheer discussed this at length. "All," said Kashif, with a wave of his hand to the others. "We learn English."

I smiled and raised my cup. "For teaching."

As we were toasting the new deal someone started pounding on the door. "Mutiny!" they were yelling. "Mutiny onboard!"

Kashif looked at me quizzically.

I pointed toward the bow. "Captain..., Teluk Betung. Others, go back to Mogadishu." I pointed toward the stern.

Kashif nodded and translated. As soon as Musheer understood mutiny, he was up strapping on a sword. He stood by the door while Kashif retrieved his sword and two knives. The old man, Sameer, went to the far part of the room, retrieved a crossbow, sat in the darkest area and did not take his eyes off of the door. The women joined him.

I had no idea what to do. I did not think it appropriate that I join the women in the corner, but who was I to attempt to fight with grown men? If I took no stand and did not fight, was I coward? Would I be looked at with disdain? I did not want to kill or be killed. Why can't people get along?

If people still thought that I was the property of the Captain, would I not be bound to help defend his cause? Would I be considered the enemy?

The door was kicked open. A burly man with an oar stepped in shouting for us to surrender. Musheer engaged him with his sword. I was hearing shouts and screams from all over the ship, someone running across the top of the cabin. Another man came through the door. Kashif cut him up before he even knew he was in trouble. Kashif kicked him out of the room and followed, now going to help Musheer who was defending himself from two attackers.

I started for the doorway wondering what I was going to do. I was no match for even the feeblest of these men.

Certainly, if I engaged anyone in battle, I would be hurt badly.

As I was stepping out onto the deck I heard someone yell, "No!" A man's voice coming from inside the cabin, Sameer's. He motioned for me to join them in the corner of the room and to stand in front of the women. He handed me a gun. I had never held a gun before.

Thomkins came through the door next, followed by Klicker. Both of these men were friends of Sanjay so I had a pretty good idea whose side they were on. When they approached us, Sameer shot Thomkins in the chest with the bolt from the crossbow. The force knocked him clean out of the room. Klicker turned to go but Sanjay appeared in the doorway, with a smile.

"Look at all them pretty girls."

He entered boldly, bloody knife in hand. I pointed the gun at the two of them.

Sanjay laughed. "You only got one shot. One of us is gonna get ya."

I could tell by the nervous look on Klicker's face that he was not as determined as Sanjay to follow through with the threat. He had already decided to leave before

"You won't pull that trigger," Sanjay said quietly, approaching. "You haven't got it in you."

He was within lunging range and still approaching slowly, quietly, calmly, and with a smile. I remembered what Flabby Max said, "He smiles, but his eyes never do."

Looking into them, I could see where that was true. When he was too close and when he made a sudden move, I pulled the trigger.

Sanjay flew backward onto the floor, flopping around like a fish out of the water, bleeding profusely. I had shot through his stomach. My ears were ringing with the explosion and somewhere behind me I heard screaming. I pulled out my knife and flashed it around like I knew how to use it. Suddenly, there were three women at my side, each of them holding knives. Klicker hurried out of the room.

The mutiny was put down quickly, three men dead,

several wounded. Musheer, who was not hurt, was busy tending the wounded for most of the rest of the day. Kashif had sustained a pretty bad bump on his head and had several bruises where he'd been attacked with a belaying pin.

Sulley was surprised when I walked into the galley, went over to the sink and began to clean up.

"Not yur job," he said. "Captain says yur a free man."

"Free, or not," I said, scrubbing out a pot. "You still have dirty dishes. We can be done in an hour if you stop talking and get back to work."

"I can't pay ya nothin'."

"I'm not asking for anything. Thanks for cleaning out my bunk."

"I owed ya," Sulley replied. He turned back to his work. "Heard ya shot Sanjay."

"He deserved it. He shouldn't have come into a private room."

"How'd ya get a gun?"

"The old man told me to stand in front of the women and handed me a gun. I was defending them."

"Some on the ship are thinkin' yur a traitor."

"They are wrong. It is them that are traitors."

"Just lettin' ya know. Keep an eye out."

"I will. Thanks, Sulley."

A new set of problems, figuring out who doesn't like me now. "What's going to happen to the prisoners?"

"Used to make em walk the plank. Captain's takin' em to Teluk Betung, for hangin' I guess."

"If Teluk Betung's still there."

"Captain says 'bout two days."

"If it's still there."

"I'm hopin'. Cause I need a lot of stiff drinks to make this go away."

"You do that in every port, Sulley?"

Sulley smiled. "Just the ones that have liquor."

That night after cleanup I went topside for a non-existent breath of fresh air. Nerissa was covered in ash. The moon, if it did show through at all, was a ghostly gray leaning toward midnight blue. My lungs were heavy with dirty air, everyone was complaining of the sulfur smell and by now we all agreed that the event had been a volcano. We had no expectations of what we were sailing into, but most all of us agreed it would be a scene of immeasurable destruction.

Kashif, who was standing guard outside their cabin door, motioned for me to join him. Inside their cabin, I was again seated across the table from Musheer and Kashif and served tea.

"Oskar, Teluk Betung, two days, yes?"

I nodded. "Yes."

Both Kashif and Musheer seemed worried. Looking around the room, I could see that everyone was in a melancholy mood. I guessed that they had discussed something concerning me and were now attempting to inform me of their decision.

"Teluk Betung, you go, us." Kashif motioned with his hands to include the rest of his family.

I nodded. "Yes, I will go with you."

"Teluk Betung, no more, you go..., home."

I had not even considered this. Yes. Of course, I'd love to go home. But that would mean that I leave these people behind. I glanced over at Mahin who was looking down at her feet. How could I turn away from her? If I went back home I would always wonder what happened to her and her family. I felt like this was my new family. We had, after all, saved each other's lives.

If I went home, I could see myself back in the fields, unable to go to school, digging holes in the ground, planting seeds and hoping they would grow. That was the future waiting for me. Would I someday be able to have a wife? How would she compare to Mahin? Thinking it through, I did not want to go home.

"Kashif. If Teluk Betung is gone, I will stay with your family and help."

Kashif shook his head. "If Teluk Betung no more, we..., home. English, no."

I did not like how this conversation was going. It did not seem right that in a time of crisis they were refusing my help. Did they think that I would be a burden? Knowing English was going to be essential in any case, by my thinking anyway.

Flabby Max had told me how Teluk Betung was only a few feet above the sea and how a big wave could destroy it in minutes. If that was the case, we'd need supplies. We would have to find another port, something out of the range of the volcano. Surely two languages were better than one going into a foreign port. Nerissa could not turn around now, not according to Sulley, who knew how much food was available.

"If Teluk Betung is gone, all of us need help," I said. "Together, we are stronger. I am a free man. I choose to stay."

Sameer twisted the long strands of gray hairs at the sides of his mouth and then patted them back into the rest of his beard. The candle, sitting on the table between the three of them, cast a flickering play of shadows back onto the walls of the room.

"You say that the boy saw the disappearance of the dog?"

Kashif nodded. "That is what he said."

"It is very unusual to witness such an event. You are positive?"

"He said that the dog disappeared into the shadow."

"This boy continues to travel in a path parallel to ours. Even when we attempt to discourage him from doing so. Why does he not want to go home? Did you offer to pay for his passage?"

"I did. Perhaps there is a reason that our lives are intertwined with his."

"There is not," said Musheer. "The boy is not one of us. He never will be. It is time for him to go."

"You do not like Mahin's attraction to him," Kashif replied. "Or, his to her."

Sameer waved off that comment with a gesture of patience, holding his hand up and then mimicking patting the last words down to the table. "He has been with us in dangerous situations two times and both times has proven his loyalty and his worth."

"And he has shown his courage to be that of a lion when faced with danger," Kashif added. "I would be proud to have him on our side."

Musheer set his cup down hard. "Absurd. He is not one of us. How will we keep the stone a secret from someone so close? Impossible."

"First," said Sameer, "we must know what happened at Teluk Betung. If my brother and his family are gone, there is nothing for us there. We will then have to arrange passage back. When will that happen? And with

136

whom? It is to our advantage to keep the boy with us."
He glanced over at Musheer. "But always at a distance."

"They will ask questions," Musheer replied. "They will
want to know why this boy is traveling with us. His presence will attract attention."

Kashif smiled. "A perfect alibi. He is teaching us English in exchange for passage back home. We are helping
him. He is helping us. We would be viewed in a more
friendly light."

"We will be viewed more," Musheer answered, dryly.

Mahin stood, walked across the room and joined them
at the table. "If I may say something...,"

"You may not," said Musheer. "This is the men's discussion. Go back with the others."

"You are discussing my future."

"We are discussing the boy."

"He is in my future."

"Mahin! Go sit!"

"Grandfather, please hear my case. I will not marry
anyone that I do not choose to marry."

"Mahin!"

"I will kill myself first. Oskar may not be the one, but I
will not reject him because of someone else's opinion."

Sameer motioned for her to sit at the table. "Mahin,
your father is right. The stone must remain a secret from
all outsiders."

"If I marry him, he will not be an outsider."

"You will not marry him," Musheer replied. "He is just
a poor boy from a poor family who lost him in a game of
cards. Pitiful."

"Father, you keep forgetting that, if not for him, I would
not be here."

"I have not forgotten. You and Kashif saved his life as
well. I have tended his wounds and we have bought his
freedom. We have even offered to pay for his passage back
home. Our debt is more than repaid."

"Why," Mahin said, coldly, "is everything measured so?
Does my heart have no say in such matters?"

"We give him his freedom and what does he do? He goes

back to the galley to help the cook! The boy will never rise above a trivial and meaningless life. Mahin, your future holds more for you than what this boy can provide."

Kashif quietly listened to the exchange between them. "There is one item that needs to be resolved. Mahin requested that the stone intervene, which it did. The dog may seem insignificant, but it played a crucial role in saving the boy. Like it, or not, we all owe a debt to the stone for doing so and it will be measured in our actions to help the dog. We changed its fate. We are responsible. Mahin, let this be a lesson to you. All things are connected. When you change one, you change them all."

"You said that Oskar saw the dog disappear into a shadow," Mahin replied. "This was the dog's dream. He was not really there. How does that matter?"

"It is still a debt. And unfortunately, two occupants on this ship have witnessed the power of this stone, one that is very close to us and one that hunts and captures things for his living. I have heard that this trapper is very interested in how the dog disappeared. I do not think that this matter is over."

We are at anchor offshore near what used to be Teluk Betung. The Captain has dispatched all boats to shore and I have been instructed to stay.

What I see is maybe a mile of mud and destruction before I see any resemblance of a town. Whatever came through washed through with a vengeance that is beyond my ability to explain. No one could survive this. I am surprised that we did not see a thousand dead bodies floating past the ship as we approached our destination.

Kashif and Musheer have gone ashore and instructed me to stay in their cabin and help with any of the women's or Sameer's needs. I am happy to do this, especially happy that now am trusted enough to be allowed inside the cabin while they are gone.

During their absence, Kashif has requested that I write down my experiences on the island, everything, beginning to end. I explained that, in my mind, the experience is over and that there is nothing more for me to do about it. Yet he insists that I especially write about the dog. I puzzled over that.

"How did you know about the dog?"

"You talk with trapper."

"Why do you want to know about the dog?"

"How..., go away?"

"It disappeared into the shadow."

"How?"

"I don't know."

"Dog help you?"

"Yes." To me, this was an odd question. How could Kashif even suspect that the dog and I had some kind of interaction? One would almost have to be there to even ask such a question. The only other way to have that information would be to talk with Bardolf and I didn't think that that had happened.

He handed me a book, hardbound, all blank pages, and a quill and ink. "For me, you write..., everything. I come back..., you read."

After they had gone, I sat at my normal place at the table and began to write. It was very hard for me to concentrate with Mahin in the room. But I was also under the sharp eye of Sameer, who sat close by.

I had wondered what the women do all day long, day after day on the ship, and was finally given a glimpse into their world. Lessons. It was all about lessons for the first two hours. I could not understand anything anyone was saying, but several times they pointed to a phrase in a book and began to discuss something about it.

Mahin and I exchanged glances several times, each time with a quiet smile, until the oldest of the women scolded her. At least that's what I think happened because she did not look up again. Actually, that was a good thing because it allowed me to get back to my writing.

After studies, everyone, including me, had tea and some kind of sweet rice for a snack. This time was very short, only about fifteen to twenty minutes. I had returned to my writing and was recounting my excursion through the trees with the chimpanzees, all of us following that dog and thinking that no one would ever believe this, when the eldest of the women stood and began to stretch.

I assumed, perhaps incorrectly, that she was Sameer's wife. Her intonation to the others seemed to be one of authority while theirs was of subservience. Mahin seemed to disregard much of that and was going along with the rest, more from boredom than desire or obedience.

They started by holding their hands out fully to their sides, fingers outstretched, and then joining them above their heads, palms upward. From there they began to twist side to side, then frontward and backward. I was surprised how limber each of them were and found myself watching more than writing, until Sameer tapped me on the shoulder and pointed to the paper.

It was hard to ignore their movements. Soon, they were moving as a group in some kind of synchronized motion that I suspected had something to do with defense, appearing as flowing motion from one stance to another, each with a wave of the arm or hand as if to deflect a blow. They moved like cats and I was more than envious of their abilities.

I finished my writing before Kashif and Musheer returned. I knew that Sulley would need help in the galley and excused myself from the room, leaving the book behind.

Kashif was correct in asking me to reconstruct the events on the island. It brought the dog into focus. I had been so intent on saving my life that the dog's disappearance was not so spectacular.

Under normal circumstances, witnessing that would be foremost in my mind. After dinner, I was summoned back to their cabin.

"Sameer brother," Kashif explained. "No more."

I looked over at Sameer. Losing his brother would be like me losing my little sister, only with many more years more of memories.

Suddenly I was lonely for her, for my home. How must it feel back there with me gone. Has it only been two weeks? "I am so sorry to hear this. Please accept my deepest sympathies."

Sameer was looking blankly straight ahead. Hearing Kashif's translation, he turned his head slowly and studied me. And then he nodded and returned his gaze to someplace that I could not see.

"We go..., Jakarta," said Kashif.

I had heard this from Flabby Max. The Captain had delivered what fresh water he could from Nerissa's stock and delivered most all of our medical supplies and food to what was left of the town. Several of the crew elected to stay and help while others, needing medical attention, were helped onboard for our next destination, Jakarta. "Yes. Next port, Jakarta."

He pointed to the book that I had been writing all day. "Please, you read."

As I read my story, he translated to the others. Several times I heard ooh's and ahh's. Many times there was much conversation before they allowed me to continue.

In the end, Kashif smiled and thanked me for my work. And then he took a more serious tone.

"Oskar, dog help you, yes?"

"Yes."

"Now..., dog where?"

"I don't know. In the shadow."

"Shadow of blue moon?"

"Yes. I guess that you could say that."

Kashif held his hand above the table, palm facing downward. "Oskar, you here. You help someone," he raised his hand a little higher, "you here. Better, yes?"

I nodded, trying to figure out what he was getting at. "Yes."

"You take from someone," he lowered his hand. "No good. Yes?"

"Yes." I thought that he was trying to explain that stealing or taking from someone was bad, and giving or helping was good. My parents had already taught me and why we were having this conversation was a complete mystery. Kashif was insistent on my understanding the idea that my own personal power depended on paying back what I owed to others, in this case the dog.

"I cannot help the dog," I explained. "It is gone."

He shook his head. "You cannot see, yes. Gone? No. You help dog."

"How?"

"We go, Jakarta." He pointed to the account of my experiences on the island. "This, you send..., London for become book."

"How does that help the dog?"

Kashif looked up toward the roof of the cabin, but I could see that his vision went far beyond the limitations of the structure. "Blue moon, yes?"

"Yes."

"Dog, blue moon, together. Someday, maybe come back. This story, somebody read and help dog."

"I never asked the dog for help. It did what it did for some other reason. Why do I owe it anything?"

It was Kashif's quick glance over at Musheer and then

to Mahin that got me to thinking that something else was going on. If there was a price to pay, I was the one being asked to do so.

Was it going to hurt me to send this story to London? No. I never planned on going there anyway, so that part did not matter. By sending this, I was helping the family that had already done so much to help me. I will always be grateful for that and I will always return the favor, not to mention more chances to be with Mahin. I just wanted to know why.

"Kashif, I will do as you say. Someday, on the night of a blue moon, someone will read my story and find a way to help the dog."

My raised cup was met with his and we shared a smile. "To the dog."

I felt like some kind of tension had just been released out of the room, a general sigh of relief. I sipped my tea, stole a glance at Mahin and set my cup down.

"Kashif, a very powerful magic was also on the island that night. I know this to be true. Perhaps you can help me to understand."

Leaving, Kashif followed me out the door. We stood at the rail and talked well past midnight. I told him that my father was a poor farmer and that he died very young. When he asked about my schooling, I explained that I had to work in the fields so that we, my mother, little sister and I, could make enough money to eat and that we were very poor, but honest and hard working. He nodded his head knowingly. I felt comfortable telling him these things.

When I asked about his family, he was hesitant to go into detail about the reasons for their journey other than to say that Sameer wanted to visit his brother. When I inquired about what the women were doing when they practiced those exotic exercises, he just smiled and said that it was a dance that they had invented.

Somewhere behind us, Krakatoa was still trying to stay alive, belching up plumes of steam, rumbling across the sea. Miles away, we could still feel her power. On the ship, the night was warm and the sea was calm.

"Everybody sleep," Kashif said, at last.

I thought he was referring to everyone aboard Nerissa. "Except you, me, Flabby Max and whoever's up there in the crow's nest."

It felt like the conversation was over. I had to get up in two hours and help Sulley and was about to say good night and head for my bunk when he spoke.

"Everybody dream."

Obvious. I did not know why Kashif said such a thing. "Right. Everybody dreams when they sleep."

"Some dreams good. Some bad, yes?"

"Right."

"Some weak, some..., very strong, yes?"

"Right."

Using his hands to mimic the shape of a large ball, Kashif opened his arms fully as if to embrace the sky. "Dreams..., over there, yes?"

Not quite sure where this is going. "Yes."

"Sometimes," Kashif took a serious tone, "strong dream come here."

"What do you mean?"

"Sometimes..., mix. Both..., together."

I thought he meant daydreams. Everyone does that, thinks about one thing while doing another. "It's called daydream, Kashif."

He shook his head. "Sometimes dream come here."

I shook my head. "No. Not together. Dreams cannot come here."

Kashif shrugged my comment off with a smile. "Tomorrow, very busy. Good night, Oskar." And with that he headed back to his cabin.

I was instantly asleep when I hit my bunk and it seemed like I had just closed my eyes when Sulley nudged me awake two hours later. My eyes were burning and I felt like I was sleepwalking for the first half hour.

But as I began to get into the routine of work, my mind kept wandering back to Kashif's words. The notion of dreams coming into our world was so absurd that I disregarded the idea without giving it any thought.

If Kashif was leading into an explanation of the events on the island, I had discouraged him from continuing. How could I have been so blundering? How else could the dog disappear so completely?

It was real. I saw it. Bardolf had a rope around it. We both would agree that the dog was as real as the island, as real as him trying to kill me. I checked my wounds again just to be sure.

We would arrive at Jakarta soon. I was more than anxious to speak with Kashif. Suddenly, so many questions, so little time. Was Nerissa going back to Teluk Betung? If so, would Bardolf go ashore at Jakarta with his animals? If Mahin and her family left the ship, was I going with them? If that did not happen, what would I do?

The idea of being an ocean away from home without any money is a lonely feeling, desolate.

Jakarta – September, 1883

These will be my last words into this journal. We have arrived at Jakarta and I have been instructed by Kashif to gather my things. I am to accompany his family back to Mogadishu. We don't know which ship, but my new job will be to teach his family English.

In the event that you have read this far and would like some sort of accounting, Bardolf has a buyer for his animals in exchange for a ship going back to the island. I don't know why, but this scares me.

Nerissa is now being loaded with emergency supplies and will sail back to Teluk Betung with Flabby Max at the helm.

We gave each other a hug when I said good-bye. He wouldn't take his knife back, said that I'd probably need it one time or another and if I didn't, so much the better. I will miss him.

Sulley, last seen, was heading for the bad parts of town. He shook my hand when he left and thanked me for being a friend. I couldn't help but think that he had an awful lot of strange tales to tell. Somebody should write a story about him.

If you've read this on a blue moon, and if my story has inspired in you a feeling that anything is possible, that a little magic is never far away, then you are of the same mind as I.

And if that is true, the dog may be out there and need a little help. Maybe this accounting of events will reach someone who is in a position to provide some. If so, go with my best wishes.

Safe journey.

P. S. I may never know why the dog decided to run at that very moment. I am beginning to believe that there is more to life than what meets the eye.

Kashif has already suggested such a thing and you may rest assured that on our return voyage I will be questioning him the entire way. If I have time, maybe I will start another journal.

Until then, thank you and good-bye,

Oskar
September 1883

The Morning After...,

Kathryn awoke with a start. It took her a while, looking around the room, surprised that she wasn't still out on the sea. She rolled over in bed and checked the clock, almost nine.

Too much wine, she was thinking. How many glasses did I have? Only three?

I remember giving Paul the book and I remember him starting to read. Did we finish?

That's right, Krakatoa, 1883. Jakarta. Nerissa was going back to Teluk Betung, Oskar staying with Mahin's family.

Why won't this room stop moving?

She did not remember going to bed or saying good-night to Paul. She did not remember turning out the lights or closing the windows or locking the doors. Kathryn felt like she was still living in some kind of dream. She pinched her forearm just to be sure. Yep, it hurt.

Paul stepped into the living room, yawning and rubbing his eyes, his hair wild with the night's adventure. Kathryn was standing in the doorway to her room, studying the scene of last night's reading, hoping to find some clue that would help her understand her present state of mind.

"Paul, how'd you sleep?"

He looked at her blankly. "Why is the room moving?"

"You feel it, too, huh?"

"I don't remember going to bed."

"Me either. I was thinking maybe I drank too much wine."

"I don't have school today, right?"

"Right."

"Good, cause I feel like crap."

"Too much sugar. You deserve it."

"Too much wine. You deserve it. So, are we done with the book? Your birthday celebration is over now, right? Can my life get back to normal?"

"One more thing," said Kathryn. "Go get cleaned up. Be

149

ready to go in fifteen."

"Where are we going?"

"I'll tell you on the way."

"To where?"

She hustled Paul out of the house, into the car and started the engine. "Fasten your seat belt."

Paul twisted around, grabbed the key and slid it into place with a click. "Where are we going?"

"To the animal shelter."

"You're kidding, right?"

"No."

"Mom, are you forgetting that they don't allow dogs in our apartment?"

"I haven't forgotten."

"So, why?"

"How many people on this planet?"

"What does that have to do with anything?"

"How many people?"

"I don't know, five billion?"

"How many do you think read that story last night?"

"We're the only ones crazy enough. Actually, that's just you. I wouldn't have done it."

"So, what are the dog's odds of being saved?"

"I get it, one in five billion."

"Now, isn't that worth the effort? What if we saved that dog?"

"We still can't keep it."

"What if there is more to life than what we can see?"

"Mom, you're letting the story go to your head."

"Maybe. Tell me, Paul, honestly, are you happy with what you're doing with your life right now?"

"I don't get it."

"You got a D in Science...,"

"That's Mr. Cobb."

"Not the point. I know you. You love science, you've always been more than curious about everything. You're moody now...,"

"I'm a teenager. What do you expect?"

"I don't like my job. I don't like those apartments. I feel

150

like we're being smothered."

"Now I get it. You're willing to drive across town on a one-in-five billion chance that your life will get better if you save the dog. Are you on something?"

"I'm on for a change."

"Do you miss Dad?"

"What kind of question is that?"

"You want change. Doesn't that mean that you're tired of the old? If you're thinking about the old, you must miss him sometimes."

"You're not supposed to think like that for at least another twenty years."

"Do you?"

"Sometimes. Most times, not."

"What do you miss?"

"I'm not going there. I don't miss him enough to want him back, if that's what you're getting at."

"Do you still love him?"

"Only historically. Actually, I'm enjoying being independent. We just need to make a little more money so that we can be really independent, like buy a house with a little land. Wouldn't that be nice?"

"Might as well make it lake front property since we're dreaming, with our own pier."

"You know what I like? I like that I can choose my own friends and be my own person. That's one of the problems with being attached. You have to put up with your spouse's friends."

"School's not much different. Got to put up with everybody. Mr. Cobb, Mr. Cobb, Mr. Cobb. I should teach that class, put a little oomph into it."

"You'd be a good teacher."

"They don't make enough. Are we going to stop for breakfast?"

"So many dogs. I don't know. None of them stand out."

"Nice try, Mom. One in five billion, right?"

"What does the dog look like, in your mind?"

"All I remember is that it looked like it was smiling, like a hyena."

"None of these dogs are smiling."

"I wouldn't be smiling either if I was stuck in here. Now can we go have breakfast?"

Kathryn turned and headed back to the door. "Well, I had high hopes. Let's go."

"Bacon and eggs and a stack of pancakes on the side."

"You're having oatmeal."

"Think of it, all that syrup soaking into those delicious hot cakes, crispy bacon and two eggs over easy. It's calling me."

"You're going to die of a heart attack before forty. Don't you dare die before me. Oatmeal it is for you."

Kelly looked up from her monitor when they came through the door. Still holding the phone to her ear, she smiled and motioned for them to wait.

"This will just take a second."

Paul found a seat, Kathryn waited at the counter. Kelly was repeating while typing.

"He was..., what? Shot? Oh, my. And he died..., I see. Yes, we have the dog. This morning, yes. Ok. Thank you."

Kelly hung up and finished typing the end of the sentence, hitting the period with finality and a smile. "Sorry. Didn't find what you were looking for?"

"No. What was that about a dog?"

"An old one, in the back. Sickly, undernourished, owner was shot in some kind of drug deal. The dog was stranded out on a boat in the harbor."

"Can we see this dog?"

Kelly pushed a red button on her console. "He might

152

not be with us anymore."

"Hey, Kelly. What's up?"

"Have you started yet?"

"Did three, two more to go."

"Stop. We've got some folks here that want to take a look."

"You're kidding me, right?"

"Nope. They want to see."

"Hey Joe, hold off. Ok. Give us a few minutes and then send 'em back."

Kelly smiled. "Well, you're in luck. Don't know if that's a good or bad thing, the condition these dogs are in."

"You say the dog's owner was shot?"

"Drug deal gone bad. Poor dog was out there for three days without food or water. After seventy-two hours, you've got to move your boat. That's when they linked the victim to the boat."

Paul got up from his chair and joined them at the counter. "What does the dog look like?"

"Oddest thing," said Kelly. "It looked like it was smiling."

"Great," said Paul, opening the menu and turning to the breakfast section. "Now we've got an old dog that we can't keep, cost us a hundred dollars that we don't have and...,"

"Quit whining. We're on to something. What are the odds that they were going to put down a smiling dog this morning?"

"Smelly dog, you mean. What are we going to do with it? We can't take it home."

"We'll move. I'm going to have the Number One Special, one egg, hash browns, two strips of bacon and toast. How about you?"

"Number Three with extra bacon and a stack of pancakes."

"No wonder we're always broke."

"I'm a growing boy. I need my nourishment."

"That's not nourishment."

"Right. When are they going to be done grooming the dog?"

"About another hour. Hey, check this out. Here's the article about that guy being shot."

"What's it say?"

"Says his boat is being auctioned off today at the Coast Guard Station downtown."

"Mom, don't go there. We're already...,"

"Says the boat's name is, Spittin' Image. I like that. It's a sailboat."

"You don't know the first thing about boats and nothing about sailing."

"Paul, where is your spirit of adventure? You never used to be such a downer. What's your dad doing to you?"

"I'm just trying to be realistic."

"It's a forty-two foot sailboat, sleeps six, has a galley, chart room, shower, self contained, solar panels...,"

"Is that an advertisement or a report on the crime?"

"His name was Ben, died of gunshot wounds, no known

relatives. We're going there, Paul. I want to see the dog's reaction when it sees the boat."

"Are you going to bid on it?"

"Depends. If we can get it for a song, why not?"

"Why not? You're kidding, right? Where will we keep it? Even if we had a place, how will we get it there? Do you know anything about how to start and stop a boat? And then there's the sail problem. How do you hoist them? Take them down? How do you keep from killing yourself?"

"They have books that teach you that sort of thing. You may not be familiar with that concept."

"Funny. What if they give you twenty-fours hours to get the boat out of there? After we get the engine started, if it even has an engine, where are we going to take it?"

"They did mention that seventy-two hour free anchorage."

"We don't know how to drop an anchor."

"How hard can that be? Throw it overboard and wait for it to hit bottom."

"And then tie it off?"

"Right."

"What happens if you drop anchor at low tide and then the tide comes in and you're five feet higher?"

"Hmm. You've got a point. OK. Just give it some slack."

"How much slack? If you don't put out as much slack as everyone else, it seems like you might be running into each other when the tide runs the other way."

"In any case, we would have three days to figure things out."

"If we can get to shore. Does this thing come with a dingy? Geez, Mom."

"What do you think the dog's reaction is going to be?"

"If it doesn't die of old age first? Don't know. If that was his home, he'll recognize it."

"Aren't all of these coincidences exiting?"

"You know what's exciting? Here comes the waitress."

Kathryn and Paul, made late waiting for the dog that still wasn't done being groomed, said they'd be back later and then hurried off to the Coast Guard Station. A crowd had gathered in the auction area outside, about thirty to forty people plus a couple of reporters. Spittin' Image was tied up to the first finger off of the main dock.

"Mom, the boat's a wreck. Look at it."

"Beautiful lines. I'll bet she was awesome when she was new."

"She? It's a she?"

"All boats are she's."

"It's old. Forget it, Mom. We don't have the money. What do marinas charge to dock a boat that big? It might be more than our rent."

"Our rent? I'm the one that pays it."

"Someone said that the two happiest days of a boat owner's life is the day he buys it and the day he sells it?"

"Where did you hear that?"

Paul shrugged. "Probably from an ex-boat owner."

Kathryn pointed to a table located to the side of the crowd. "Over there. We have to register if we're going to bid."

A short squeal blared out of the speaker as the man turned on the mike. "May I have your attention, please? If everybody is ready, we will begin bidding for Spittin' Image. The boat is not registered with the state so whoever purchases it will have to pay taxes and registration. We will also require that the boat is insured prior to leaving the dock. The new owner will be allowed to keep the boat here for up to seventy-two hours...,"

"Let's see," said Paul. "Taxes, registration, insurance, docking fees, repairs. I think we're looking at ten thousand, Mom, just for starters."

"Shh."

"All proceeds will be used to provide for more classes on water safety, rules of the road...,"

"What's your number, Mom?"

"Twelve."

"We're only bidding against eleven others? That shouldn't be too bad."

"It only takes one."

"There will be three bidding opportunities. Please note that there are three stubs with your paperwork, each with a place to write your bid and each identifying you as the bidder. We will accept bids for Bid Number One for the next fifteen minutes.

After we tally the results, we will announce the highest two bids and the average of those two will be the starting point for Bid Number Two. That process will repeat through Bid Number Three. Spittin' Image will go to the highest bidder. Best of luck to all of you. Thank you for coming out today to support this cause."

Paul nudged Kathryn toward the boat. "Let's go look. We've got fifteen minutes."

Stepping onboard, Spitting Image rocked gently. Paul headed for the cockpit, checked out the wheel, all of the cleats within reach, each with a rope going to one place or another. He found the depth gauge, knot meter, wind speed indicator, fuel, all the stuff needed to help keep control of the boat.

"Deck wood is old," said Kathryn. "Look how gray it is."

"That's teak, Mom. It'll clean up."

"How do you know?"

"I helped Terry clean her Dad's boat. They have stuff for that. You just rub it on and hose it off. The wood looks brand new."

"What have you discovered here? Looks complicated."

"Actually, I'm starting to like the idea. I'm too young to drive, but wow, look at this!"

"You know what all those gauges are for?"

"Most of 'em."

"Let's take a quick look below."

Coming down the steps, Kathryn held her nose. "Oh my God. What died down here?"

"Yea, stinks pretty bad."

"Nice room though. Look at that. All of the cupboards

and drawers have latches on them. Never really thought about it. Everything moves out on the ocean."

"Check this out. Here's where the dog sleeps." Paul pointed to the magic marker scribbling on the fiberglass. "His name's Capn."

Kathryn hurried through the galley, checked out the chart room, head, shower and forward cabin long enough to get a feel for what life might be like living in much smaller quarters. "We'd better hurry up or we won't get a chance to bid."

Paul checked out the main cabin at the stern. "Pretty cool. That's my room back there."

Kathryn hurried up the steps. "Don't count on it. What do you think? Can we live on it?"

"Are you kidding me? This would be awesome! How much are you going to bid?"

"I don't know, a thousand?"

"They'll probably laugh at it, but you'll have two more bids after that."

"Ladies and gentlemen, the two highest bids were three thousand five hundred dollars and five thousand dollars. The next round of bidding will start at four thousand two hundred and fifty dollars. I repeat, the next round of bidding will start at four thousand two hundred and fifty dollars. We will accept bids for Round Two for the next thirty minutes. Thank you."

Kathryn let out a sigh. "My credit card's good up to ten thousand. What do you think?"

"Live in those dumpy apartments or live on a forty-two foot yacht? Do I get the berth in the back?"

"No. I haven't even seen it yet. You're right. I'm crazy for doing this. I can't afford it. You'll have to change schools or I'll have to drive you. My job is farther away."

"Mom. Let's go look again." Paul put his arm around her shoulder and led her back to the dock. "Check out the Captain's cabin. It's pretty cool. I want to look at the engine and the rigging and see what kind of condition it's in. If it's a dump, forget it. But I think it would be pretty cool living out here."

"You're all right, Paul."

Walking down the dock, Paul pointed out the hull. "Fiberglass. That'll buff out. It'll take me a few of days...,"

"There's a dinghy. See it? Tied up to the back."

"It's called the stern. You'd better learn the lingo."

"Am I crazy? What am I doing?"

"Captain's quarters, Mom. Go look."

Kathryn headed for the Captain's quarters while Paul explored the engine compartment. He stared into the dark abyss long enough to know that it was a diesel engine and that maybe it might be leaking somewhere and that he needed a flashlight to really know what was going on, but he didn't see any water, a good sign.

"I like the Captain's quarters, Paul. You lose. I'm going to put a sign over the door, Captain Kathryn."

"We'd better get back. What's your new bid going to

be?"

"I'm thinking seven thousand."

"That sounds about right, seven for the boat, one for taxes, insurance and registration, and then we'll live on beans and rice for the next month or two. It's still worth it."

"I'm going to have to get a second job."

"Maybe I can work part time somewhere."

"No, you won't. If I buy this boat, I'd better see your grades go up to straight A's"

"School is so boring. I learn faster than they teach. I have to keep waiting for everyone else to catch up."

"Mr. Cobb would disagree with that, apparently."

"Mom...,"

"No ifs, ands or buts. If he's slow, it's your job to pick it up. Push him harder. Make him earn his money. I don't buy your excuses, Paul."

"Ladies and gentlemen, the two highest bids for Spittin' Image were ten thousand and eleven thousand dollars. We will be accepting bids for the third and final round of bidding for the next thirty minutes. Bids will start at ten thousand five hundred. At the end of this round, Spittin' Image will go to the highest bidder. Best of luck to all of you."

"Well," said Kathryn, with a sigh. "That does it. It was a stupid dream. I shouldn't be so flippant. We've wasted the morning and now we have to go pick up an old dog that probably should have been put down. What are we going to do with the dog?"

"I've got two thousand saved up for college. We can use that."

"No, you don't. You're going to college, kiddo."

"Maybe we can charter the boat out for divers or something."

"Right. Like you said, I don't know the first thing about boats. This was just a stupid dream. Let's go."

"Wait, Mom. Maybe there's another way."

"How? Even if I maxed out my credit card and drained my savings, I'd still have only eleven thousand. The boat's going to go for fifteen, at least."

"Mom...,"

"Can't sell the car. Even if we did buy the boat, like you said, where are we going to keep it? Come on. Let's go pick up the dog."

Kathryn turned and headed for the car. Reluctant, Paul hesitated, wanting to get one more look at Spittin' Image. It called for attention and he was ready to jump in and make that happen.

"Paul!"

Turning, he spotted Melissa, from school. She smiled. "Are you bidding on the boat?"

"Not any more. It's too much."

"Us, too. We bid nine thousand. That's as high as we

can go. Too bad. I like the boat."

"Me too. Were you going to live on it?"

"No. Dad wanted it for diving."

"You dive?"

"He's going to teach me. We're you planning on living on it?"

Paul shrugged. "If I could."

"Wouldn't that be too small?"

"Not for me."

"Do you know how to sail?"

"No. But I can learn."

"Not according to Mr. Cobb."

"Why does that always come up? My mom's been harping on me about that all night."

"You do fall asleep in class."

"He's boring."

"Anyway, my dad knows how to sail. He's going to teach me."

"Is that who's coming over here?"

"Oh, yeah. Dad, this is Paul. He's in my Science class."

"Hi, Paul." He extended his hand. "I'm Sal. You were bidding on the boat?"

"We were."

"It's a pretty boat. I'll bet she's fun to sail."

"Is it hard to learn?"

"Some people pick it up right away."

"They were going to live on it."

"You and how many others? Boat's not that big."

"Just me and my mom. Oh, here she comes."

Kathryn joined them, putting her hand on Paul's shoulder. "What's up? I thought we were leaving."

"Mom, this is Melissa. She's in my Science class. And this is her dad, Sal. They were bidding on the boat, too."

"Wanted to use it for diving," said Sal, shaking Kathryn's hand. "You and Paul were going to live on it?"

"Just a dream."

"They bid nine thousand, Mom. I have an idea. It's crazy. How about if we pool our money and make one last bid? We live on it and pay slip fees. Sal and Melissa use it for diving and Sal can teach us how to sail. We own it fifty-fifty."

Kathryn laughed. "Right. They're going to risk nine grand after knowing us for thirty seconds? Nice try, Paul."

"Actually, it's not a bad idea," said Sal. "I like the boat. We'll both be on the title. You can live on it. We don't have to pay slip fees. We use it for diving and split the maintenance fees."

"What if," Kathryn asked, wanting to see all of the bad things that could come out of this, "you decide that you want the boat for yourselves? That leaves us out in the cold."

"That won't happen," said Sal. "We've got a nice little house with a pool and a great view. We're not going to move onto a boat."

"We each put in eight?" Kathryn suggested.

Sal held out his hand. "It's a deal. We'd better hurry or we won't even get a chance to bid."

"Ladies and gentlemen, bidder number two is now the proud owner of Spittin' Image. The purchase price is seventeen thousand, five hundred dollars. Please meet with us at the table to finalize the deal. We want to thank everyone for coming out today and supporting our efforts to...,"

"Well," said Kathryn, with a sigh. "There it is. Come on, Paul. Let's go pick up the dog." She extended her hand. "Nice meeting you Sal, Melissa."

"What kind of dog?" Melissa asked.

Paul laughed. "It's a smiley dog."

"Never heard of one."

"Mom, tell them."

"They don't want to hear it."

"Hear what?," Sal asked. "I always like an interesting story."

"Explain smiley dog," said Melissa.

"It was Mom's birthday. I forgot. So, my forced present to her was to read this book on a blue moon, which we did last night."

"In the story," Kathryn added, "there was a smiley dog that helped save a boy's life. At the end of the story the boy pleaded for anyone who read the story on a blue moon to try and help the dog."

"Which we've done," said Paul. "We picked up the dog this morning. That's when we found out that it was owned by the man that owned Spittin' Image."

"Wish that I'd known that earlier," said Sal. He motioned for them to follow him over to the table. "Let's go see if this deal is going to go through."

"I can't afford it," the man was saying. "Fifteen hundred bucks for sales tax? That puts me over nineteen thousand!"

The woman sitting behind the table, whose name tag said Nora, did not seem too concerned. "No problem. If you wish to pass, the boat will go to the next highest bidder."

"What number is that?" Paul asked.

Nora glanced down at her papers. "That would be lucky number seven. Is that you?"

"No. How much was that bid?"

"Sixteen thousand, five hundred. Sir, do you wish to pass on your bid?"

"I certainly do. The taxes are outrageous."

"What happens next?" Sal asked.

"I have a number here for bidder number two and I'm dialing. What number are you folks?"

"Twelve," Kathryn answered, almost in a whisper.

"Hello. This is Nora from the Coast Guard Station. Is this Mr. Pittman? It is? Mr. Pittman, the highest bidder has passed on his bid and you are next on the list. Are you still interested in purchasing Spittin' Image? You're what? Heading back to Arizona? I see. So, you defer to the next highest bidder? Yes, sir. Thank you, Mr. Pittman."

Nora looked up from her papers and smiled.

"Well, they say the third time's a charm. Are you folks still interested?"

Capn, ears perked and nose wet, pulled at his leash, looking several years younger. So many things to explore, so much to smell. Never seen a fire hydrant before.

Getting into the car was another matter. Last time he saw one it smeared his mother all across the road. Get into this thing? Nope.

Biscuits later, he was in the back seat with Paul, windows cracked just enough that he could stick his nose out while Kathryn drove back to the boat. Starting and stopping took a little bit of getting used to, not like on a boat at all.

When Kathryn pulled into the Coast Guard parking lot Capn knew the smell. Wagging his tail, pushing his nose even further out through the opening, he scratched at the door.

"Look at him," said Paul. "He knows where we are."

"Put that leash on him before you let him out."

"Well, duh."

Stepping onto Spittin' Image, they let him go. Capn ran below, checked all of the usual places, sniffing everything, and then came topside where he circled the perimeter of the deck, twice. No Ben. He looked up at Kathryn and Paul, expecting an answer.

"We should've cleaned the boat first," said Kathryn. "He's looking for his old master."

"I think he's just glad to be out of that cage," said Paul. "He's smiling."

"He always smiles."

"Yeah. But this is more. He makes me smile. Good dog! Come here for a pet."

Kathryn cast a motherly eye over the boat. "Well, if we're going to live on it, let's make it livable."

"When's Sal gonna be here?"

"He's going to call. I guess you two are going to learn all about the engine?"

"Yeah. This is cool. Hands on."

Kathryn felt like a little bit of magic had somehow slipped into her life. When she had told her boss that she was going to quit because the drive was now going to be too far, she got a promotion and a raise. The law finally caught up with her ex and suddenly he was paying child support again. The clunking noise in her car turned out to be a factory defect and was going to be fixed for free.

From apartment to boat, almost overnight. What things to throw away? What to keep? Lose all of the furniture. Cut possessions down to a fifth of what's left and that's about how much can be taken onto the boat, including groceries.

Paul moved into the forward cabin, laying claim to the chart room at the same time. Before long he was picking up the maps, figuring out how to use the compass, charting courses and learning how to use the radio.

Kathryn was busy learning where to put the dishes, how to cook on a gimbal stove and wondering why all of the flat spots were always taken whenever she wanted to set something down.

She had the feeling that she was somehow living in a dream, like all of her senses were plucked up from one world and dropped into another. Sleeping on the boat, her dreams were of crossing the sea, searching for some unknowable place and waking up in the morning remembering only that she had never found it.

Was it the gentle rocking of Spittin' Image as some boat or another passed by their slip in the wee hours? The clanging of the rigging hitting against the mast on a windy night? The gurgling sounds that came from everywhere? Or the tiny shrimp that snapped up against the hull? What was causing her dreams?

Back at the apartment, Kathryn had never dreamed. Living there seemed so long ago already. That entire existence had a dark feel to it, confined, dreary, and backward-looking.

But if that life had a dark side, so did this .There were too many coincidences, all in a tidy little row leading into the life that she and Paul were now living. And she was beginning to wonder just what she had gotten themselves into.

In her dreams, she became aware of him in pieces, a bit of an eye here, an ear there, brief glimpses of someone moving through a moonlit forest. Stepping out into the moon's light, carved black shadows across his face, beard disappearing entirely into the night, he carried a knife strapped to his hip, a coil of rope over his shoulder, a leather strap diagonally across his bare chest holding in place the leather bag close to his hips.

He was searching for something, his gaze steady, unblinking as he scanned the area. Kathryn, fearing that she might be found out, backed into the shadows. A twig snapped. He turned his head in her direction and in a heartbeat was coming her way.

Kathryn awoke with a gasp, heart pounding.

Did our eyes meet? Was he aware of me?

It was just a dream. That's all. Nothing more.

How come he seemed so real?

She turned over to her left side, pulled the sheet up to her chin and curled up into a loose fetal position.

Did he see me? Did he somehow notice that I was there?

Spittin' Image was pulled out of the water, blasted with a power sprayer to get the years of barnacles off, set on her keel over in a corner of the shipyard where stands were placed on either side of the boat to hold her in an upright position. To get onboard they rolled a big metal ladder over to one side of the boat. Access to Spittin' Image was now ten feet off of the ground.

"Feels like we have beach front property," said Paul, standing on top of the cabin, holding onto the mast and looking out over the rest of the shipyard. "Are we going to stay on her?"

"Where else we gonna go? This is home, kiddo."

"This is really cool, Mom. Thanks."

"It's for both of us."

"We're going to need a buffer. Buy one tomorrow?"

"It begins," said Kathryn, with a sigh. "Probably a couple bottles of polish and a few cans of wax."

"Extension cord, ladder, paint, brushes, masking tape, paint thinner...,"

"I feel broke already."

"Keep the receipts. They're paying half."

"What time are they coming?"

"Melissa said they'd be here by seven."

"Maybe they've got a ladder."

"I'll give her a call."

"Ask about brushes and rollers, too."

The next day, while helping to polish and buff out the hull, Kathryn was beginning to understand how Spittin' Image would react in the swells. She studied the contour of the fiberglass, saw how the bow looked like it could cut through the waves cleanly, a shape that would not cause too much of a splash yet was high enough to keep the waves off of the deck, and how the design provided good headroom in the forward cabin directly below, Paul's room.

The mast looked like it went up forever. Kathryn wondered what it would feel like to have wind hit all of that sail and worried how much it would tip the boat. Sal explained that the keel weighed over two thousand pounds and that it was not going to come out of the water.

"If you're flying too much sail on a windy day, that might do it. The fix is, don't fly too much sail on a windy day. You'll never have that problem."

"How fast will this boat go?" Paul asked.

"There's a formula for that, about one-dot-three-five times the square root of the waterline length."

"What?"

"I'll show you the math later. I'm guessing Spittin' Image will do about eight knots."

"That's it?"

"It'll feel like a lot more when we're doing it. If you think about it, if we traveled at eight knots for a day, how far would we have gone?"

"Don't ask Paul," said Melissa. "His mind is...,"

"One hundred and ninety-two," Paul interrupted.

Melissa laughed. "Didn't think you had it in you."

"The point I'm trying to make," said Sal, "is that you can travel about one hundred and fifty miles a day in this boat and you don't have to do much more than keep it on course. So, eight knots isn't too bad. You can go three hundred miles in a car but that's all you're doing for six hours, not to mention paying for gas. Who wants to tape the waterline and who's painting?"

The first coat was done within a couple of hours. After that, Paul put a wire brush on his drill and began buffing out the propeller while Melissa repainted Spittin' Image on the transom. Sal started on the second coat of bottom paint while Kathryn went for pizza.

At the end of the day, they all climbed up to the deck, congratulated themselves for a good day's work and talking about where they would go, deciding on short trips first, just out of the harbor and back. Once comfortable with that, sailing along the coastline while trailing a line out behind the boat and hoping to catch dinner. What's the cost if you're using the wind?

They spent the summer putting Spittin' Image through the drills, first testing the motor to ensure that it wouldn't overheat, that there were no water leaks and that the cabin ventilated well when the engine was running hard.

Next, the rigging. They learned how to work every type of connector used on the boat, making sure at the same time that the stays were in good condition, that the turn-buckles used to adjust the tension of the mast were in working order, which they were not. It took a day of oiling them and slowly turning them, one direction and then the other, until they loosened up and responded to a full turn.

Then came the sails. They laid them out on the dock and scrubbed them while Sal named the parts and explained the purpose of each differently sized sail. All of them signed up for the Coast Guard Sailing and Seamanship class and learned how to tie knots.

Paul was at the helm when they cleared the protection of Point Loma one windy day and got hit with gusts coming in from the north. The main sheet clacked loudly as the boom snapped stiffly to port, tugging at the pulley holding it in place while the wind whooshed between the two sails in a low, steady roar.

Spittin' Image rolled to port, water up to her rails. Kathryn, sitting on the low side, uttered something between a gasp and a scream as the water rushed by just a couple of feet away. Paul let out a whoop. Waves burst over the bow, rushed by the cockpit in a steady stream, while the spray came over the top of the cabin and covered them in a thin, salty mist.

Sal reached over to the main sheet a let out a couple of feet and then did the same with the jib. "Spittin' Image is showing us what she's made of. I think she's happy to be back in the sea."

"What a rush," said Paul, grinning from ear to ear. "Wow!"

"If you let out the sheet for the main, the pressure on the rudder decreases, the boat stands up and you have a much easier time steering."

"I can feel it," said Paul, with a smile that wouldn't go away.

Kathryn let out a relieved sigh. "I sure like it better when the boat's standing up. How fast are we going?"

Melissa glanced over at the knot meter. "Six and a half knots."

"Feels faster," said Paul.

They headed north to an area where, Sal informed them, a sunken ship was directly below. "When you're ready, if you want, we'll come out here one day and explore. Paul, you ready to give your Mom some time at the wheel?"

"She doesn't want to."

Kathryn got up and stood next to Paul. "You turn it around kiddo. I'll take it home."

Spittin' Image headed south with the wind at their backs and the swells coming in from the stern, Kathryn at the wheel. "Seems like we're going slower."

Melissa glanced over at the knot meter. "Eight knots, sometimes nine. But it doesn't feel like it."

"Wind's behind us," said Sal, sipping on his beer. "And we're surfing the swells. Both of you are good at holding your course."

"She yells at me if I don't do something right," said Paul.

"And if I'm wrong," said Kathryn, slightly turning the wheel to prolong her ride in that last swell. "He won't let me forget."

That night, after everyone had gone home and Paul had gone to bed, Kathryn made herself a cup of tea, wrapped a blanket around herself and found a comfortable spot out in the cockpit where she could look up at the stars.

So much had happened in such a short time that she was feeling a bit bewildered by it all. Everything seemed to be changing for the good. But life had already taught her that with everything good, something potentially bad is lurking close by.

The hatch was opened enough so that the night air, cool and damp with a slight smell of fish from the barge out in the harbor, drifted in with the moonlight, a thin shaft of light that moved back and forth across Kathryn's bedspread as the boat rocked gently in the glistening, glassy water.

Sounds of a late night party from somewhere down the dock drifted in. That would be Manny, still going on after the bars had closed.

Kathryn opened her eyes, surprised as always to find herself sleeping on the boat. She readjusted her pillow, bunching it up so that she could rest her head without it interfering with her breathing, tried that for a few minutes, then turned over to her other side and repeated the motion.

Minutes later, with an exasperated sigh, she pushed the pillow out of the way, laid on her back and looked up at the ceiling.

"Why am I so fricking worried?"

Manny crashed, died, or for some other reason turned off the music and the night suddenly became still. Off in the distance, a foghorn sounded out from the top of a buoy near the entrance to the harbor. One of the halyards thudded softly against the mast as a gentle breeze passed through. Spittin' Image tugged gently at the ropes holding her to the dock, the tide coming in.

There it is, the reason I'm here. That's more like it.

Blending with the shadows and filtering out the light, nooks and crannies becoming one and the same, water and night as one, the fog moved in like a wall of silence, thick at the bottom, billowy at the top, drifting across the glistening water, laying out like a fluffy blanket over the many fingers of docks and leaving only the tallest of masts exposed to the moon's light.

Capn, lying at the foot of Kathryn's bed, was either chasing or being chased in his dream, his legs twitching, him thinking he was uttering some kind of ferocious bark.

Kathryn smiled. The dog was a great pleasure. Everyone's humor stepped up a notch when they saw him, and he was happy to be a part of it all. The one time he growled at a cat when it hissed at him, people couldn't stop laughing, seeing a smiling dog growl.

Content that everything was OK, Kathryn finally drifted off into her dreams...,

Pea soup fog. She was sitting out in the cockpit, leaning back into the cushions that she'd piled up, blanket pulled over her lap, hot cup of tea by her side when it flew overhead. She couldn't see what it was, but was thinking it must've been a pelican, something with big wings to make that kind of sound, a quiet whoosh only ten or fifteen feet above.

It must've landed on the next dock, or the one after that, judging from the low level and angle of flight. Waiting for some kind of tell-tale sound to help confirm that thought, Kathryn sipped her tea.

It was too big for an egret.

And it was black..., wasn't it? Happened so fast, hard to see.

Must've been a Blue Heron or a Brown Pelican. Nothing else is big enough. But why would anything fly in this fog? If I can't see more than a few feet, how can they?

Some distance away, a metallic clink, like one of the metal gates between dock and land opened and closed. A minute later, the sound repeated at the gate of the dock next door. Kathryn sat quietly and watched, hoping for a break in the fog, some kind of clue as to who was out exploring at this time of night.

Several minutes passed without a sound. Kathryn decided that it must've been some drunk that went into the wrong gate, couldn't find his boat and, realizing that, went to the right dock, found his boat and crashed.

But when the gate to that dock opened and closed a second time, and a minute later when the gate to her dock opened and closed, Kathryn decided that it was time to go below, safer to look from behind a locked door.

174

Whoever it was, they were apparently looking for something. She got up, made her way through the companionway and down the four steps into the cabin, locked the door and pulled back the curtains just enough to see.

He was out there. She could feel the dock shift under his weight, a slight tug on the ropes holding Spittin' Image in place. He was walking alongside, silently, slowly, deliberately, and when he looked down at the dark space inside the cabin where the curtains had been pulled back, Kathryn screamed.

Capn was on his feet in a second, barking loudly, hair raised on the back of his neck. And then he looked around blankly, wondering what the fuss was all about.

Kathryn was sitting straight up, hands to her heart, eyes darting around the room. Just a dream she was thinking, just a dream.

She retrieved a flashlight from the head of her bed and walked through the boat slowly, checking things out. Paul was sleeping diagonally across his bed, covers kicked off, music still playing. She turned off the music, covered him and made her way back to the stern of the boat.

She paused in the galley. The curtain was open, slightly cracked, just like in her dream.

Peeking outside, pea soup fog.

She went to every window on the boat, pulling back the curtains and peering out into the darkness, seeing only the blurry shadow of her dock box, the boats in their slips on either side. Nothing.

Going up on deck and stepping over to the dock, she shined her light to where she had seen him. No one there, but shining her light down to the damp cement, it looked like someone had recently been standing there, little circular shaped pools of mist.

Just a mother worrying? Could it be as simple as that? Am I putting Paul's life in danger living on a boat? Can it sink at night while we're both asleep? What if one of the through-hull fittings suddenly gives way? Will we have time to get out? What if it happens when we're out at sea? What else can go wrong?

Paul was unaware of anything unusual. He put down four bowls of cereal, a glass of orange juice and said that he was going with Melissa to her martial arts class and watch.

After he had gone, Kathryn stepped back out onto the dock and went to where the man in her dream had been standing. There was nothing to suggest that anyone or anything had ever been there. That part of the dock looked like all of the rest.

My imagination? Or, what? Ever since we read that story. The problem with all of this is that there are too many unanswered questions and on a one-in-five billion chance, I have the dog and the boat he came in on.

I am fricking nuts. That's it. Back to Higgin's Bookstore. I'd better find book two or I'm going to yell at Higgins for selling me book one.

Higgins looked up from his newspaper when Kathryn asked about the book. He pushed his glasses down to the tip of his nose and looked over the top. "I remember that story. I searched everywhere for part two. I don't think it ever got written. And then it occurred to me that the story will never be finished."

"Why do you say that?"

"Say, for example, someone actually read that story on a blue moon and then saved that dog. Impossible, right? But if that happened, the stone, what did they call it, a firestone?"

"Yes."

"It would then have a link to this time and place."

"Say that happens..., someone reads the story and

saves the dog. What then?"

"I'd say the debt's repaid. Everybody moves on. But the one remaining question I would have is, who has the stone? Because if the rest of the story is true, doesn't it seem like the part about the stone is true as well?"

"I hadn't thought about it like that. If the story's true, so is the stone."

"Who has it? Do they know how to use it? Because, if they do..., wasn't there a trapper involved?"

"Bardolf."

"I guess that was him. He had the dog when it disappeared. Right?"

"Right."

"At the end of the story. Wasn't he going back to the island?"

"Right. Looking for the dog."

"You've got to wonder what he found."

"Didn't you say that once the debt is repaid it's over, a done deal? No more connection, right?"

"That's what I said. But who am I? I just read the book, that's all. You know as much as I do. More, I think."

"Say someone read the story on a blue moon, saved the dog, and that Bardolf has the stone. Could he come here?"

Higgins laughed. "I don't know if he can be here. But whoever has the stone probably has some kind connection to our time through the dog. But what are the odds of that?"

And there it is in a nutshell, Kathryn was thinking. What are the odds of all of this neatly lining up into some sort of new..., condition. Is that the word? A new reality slipping into the old one, a little here, a little there?

The following day, stopped at a red light while taking Paul to school, a man crossed in front of their car, peering inside as he passed by. He had wavy black hair and a close-cropped beard, heavy enough growth that Kathryn felt the chill of seeing Bardolf. Her hands tightened on the steering wheel.

This morning, putting gas into the tank, that guy at pump

six. He had the same kind of look.

Thinking about it, he was everywhere, walking his dog in the park yesterday, going into the bar while she was driving home with the groceries. Some did not even have beards or were bald. Something about them, the way that they looked at her, they were the eyes of Bardolf.

Never had this kind of feeling while living in the apartment, no feelings of impending danger, no moments of dread.

Boring, yes. Dark, yes. Living there sucked, yes. But I never felt impending doom. I am going nuts!

"Mom, go! The light's green!"

"Mom, you've got to hear this guy. What he says makes sense."

"Paul, martial arts are little more than glorified boxing. If you learn how to take care of yourself, that's good. But you don't need to be getting into any tournaments to prove how good you are."

"It's not like that. There are no tournaments."

"Oh. So your different colored belts are given after you pass some kind of test?"

"There are no tests."

"How do you get your next colored belt?"

"There are no colored belts. It's not about that. It's about balance, body language, learning how to move."

"Doesn't sound like martial arts. More like a school for wimps."

"Just come with me one time, next class."

Kathryn didn't really like the idea. This was going to be one more time slot out of any given day. How many times a week for practice? How much was it going to cost? How would Paul get to and from the studio? Nope. Didn't sound too good. "Paul...,"

"Just one time, Mom. Please?"

The instructor's name was Sam. He didn't look like a Sam, not according to Kathryn's preconceived notion of one, not with his olive colored skin, long curls of black hair and youthful, clean-shaven face.

He looked more like a Ricardo or Franco or Miguel or, and here Kathryn was careful to stop herself from saying anything to Paul, he looked like Kashif, in her mind anyway, minus the goatee.

"We don't know," he was saying, standing in the middle of the tatami mats with Paul at his side, "what direction life is going to take or what we will encounter along the way. It is important to be able bend with the turbulence."

And here he put his hand on Paul's shoulder and gently

rocked him side to side. Several times Paul took small steps to compensate.

"You are thinking that your balance is from your shoulders." Sam pushed Paul's slumped shoulders backward so that he was standing straight. "Shoulders back, relax, put your balance down here, in your abdomen." Sam repeated the rocking motion, Paul kept his balance, grinning ear to ear.

After demonstrating balance, Sam moved into the topic of motion, showing Paul how to fall forward and then backward, a controlled motion that, if one practiced it and it had become second nature, looked like it would work when needed. Paul was working up a sweat.

Sam asked Melissa to join him and, each standing with their right foot forward and right arm extended, touched hands and began to move in a slow circular motion, their hands forming a figure eight as they pivoted on their hips.

"The idea," said Sam, "is to feel your partner's energy, keep in touch with it, lightly, always keeping your balance. Don't try to control anything. If your partner pushes hard, simply guide it away. Test each other."

Sam put Paul and Melissa together to practice, watched for a few minutes, made a few corrections, and then looked over at Kathryn and invited her to join them.

"OK, Paul. You got me hooked. I think we need to know these things."

"Thought you'd like him."

"It's not just him. It's what he's saying. Everybody should learn this. We'd all be a lot happier."

"I'm pretty happy these days."

"Well, sit down, kiddo. I've got something to say."

"What did I do?"

"You didn't do anything. What if I told you that the story was true."

"What story?"

"The blue moon story, with the dog."

"I'd say you're crazy."

"I talked to Higgins."

"From the bookstore?"

"Right."

"He is crazy. Mom...,"

"Wait. Hear me out. The dog's dream was in eighteen-eighty-three, but he's living here with us."

"One in five billion, right?"

"Right. That's us."

"Oh..., boy."

"I think I've seen Bardolf."

"Now I know you're crazy. Mom...,"

"Call it what you want. Two times I've dreamed about the man. These are not your normal dreams. The man is creepy and he's looking for something."

"Mom...,"

"The second time he was looking in through those curtains, Paul. Scared the bee-geezies out of me."

"OK. Say it's him. What's he gonna do, kill us?"

"Looking for the dog, I suppose."

"Why would he want the dog?"

"I'm not sure. Why else is he in my dreams?"

"Oh-my-gosh. You really do believe this, don't you? I thought you were kidding."

"Paul, if you saw him you'd be worried, too. He looked in through *that* window. I think he's out there."

"How can he be out there? He lived in eighteen-eighty-three. That guy's long gone."

"OK. Who has the stone now? And what can they do with it?"

"*If* the story was true."

"Humor me."

Paul went over to the fridge and got himself a drink. He pulled out Kathryn's half empty bottle of chardonnay, looked over at her with raised eyebrows and a smile.

"Oh, sure. It's a little early."

He retrieved a glass, set it and the bottle in front of her and then wandered back to the cupboard.

"Where'd you put them?"

"What?"

"The bag of nuts."

"Bottom drawer on your right."

"Why way down there?"

"Because that's the only empty place left on this boat. Seems to get smaller everyday. We've gotta get rid of more stuff."

Paul seated himself across the table from Kathryn, opened the bag and poured some into a bowl. He popped open his soda, grabbed a handful of nuts and began chewing with a big grin. "He couldn't actually come here. We agree on that, right?"

"Bardolf? I don't know. He has most definitely been in my dreams. The first time, he acted like he was aware of my presence. He came *toward* me. The second time he was here at the boat."

"Right. But you were dreaming both times, right?"

"Right."

"How do you know it's him? Did he look the same both times?"

"The first time I saw his face piecemeal, like he was standing in the shadows of a moonlit forest. The second time was in pea-soup fog, kind of blurry. He was out on the dock."

"Have you ever seen him in real life?"

"No."

"OK. Say it's him. He's not *really* out there. More like a..., manifestation. What can he do?"

"Paul, he's scaring the hell out of me. That's what he's doing. I keep thinking I'm going to run into him. Who has that stone?"

Paul groaned. "Oh, we're back to that. Even in the story, looking through the stone, those people could not actually *go* to the island. They could only look. Remember?"

"Maybe that's what he's doing, looking."

"But only if he has the stone. We'll never know what happened to that."

"They were going back to Mogadishu. There must be a record of that somewhere, what ship they were on. Maybe it ran into trouble...,"

"If they ever existed."

"If Bardolf has the stone, he could track the dog. They're still linked until the debt has been repaid. Isn't that what Musheer said?"

"I don't remember that."

"I think you were reading in your sleep by that time. He was talking to Mahin."

"I'll take your word for it. Wait..., you said, until the debt's repaid. That's us."

"That's what I've been saying. So, in my thinking, Capn is ours free and clear. So, why am I having dreams of Bardolf looking for..., whatever he's looking for?"

"OK. Say you're right about everything. What are we going to do, buy guns? Kill him?"

"I think we need to get with Sam and get some extra training."

"You said it was for wimps."

"I'm a little wiser now."

Kathryn and Paul took off their shoes and followed Sam across the tatami mats, past the curtain leading into the hallway and into a small, windowless room at the back of the building.

Sam flipped on the switch and set the dimmer to low. A white paper and bamboo framed light hung over the table, a low table in the middle of the room with a pillow on each side.

Sam motioned for them to sit while he filled a teapot with water, placed it on a hotplate and then joined them. "May I ask what your expectations are for these lessons?"

Kathryn glanced over at Paul. "Coordination, certainly, self-defense, you know. What do you call it?"

"Hand-to-hand?"

"Yes. Does that include weapons?"

"It can. How often would you like lessons?"

"Three times a week, if that's possible."

"Three times. The workouts can be rather intense. Maybe twice a week would be better, at least to start. It will give you some time to recover."

"If that's what you recommend."

"You still have not told me why you feel the need to have this training. Are you in some kind of danger?"

"She thinks she's seeing a ghost," said Paul."

Sam smiled. "If that's the case, I cannot help you. I can only deal with what is real."

"There's more to it than that," said Kathryn, giving Paul a warning look.

"If he's going to teach us," Paul replied. "He needs to know what we're up against."

"I thought you didn't believe me."

"Mom, I always believe in you. Sometimes I think you're a little off, but you're always right."

Sam twisted around on his pillow, found three cups on the middle shelf of the cupboard behind him and set them on the table. "What are we talking about?"

"We read this book," said Paul. "And it said if you read the story on a blue moon that the story might come true."

"And..., you did?"

"Yes."

"Is the prediction coming true?"

"Yes," said Paul, glancing over at Kathryn. "Up to a point."

"We saved a smiling dog on a blue moon," said Kathryn. "I know that sounds crazy. In the story the dog was captured by this trapper, but it got away. The trapper may still be looking for it."

"I see. So, you think the trapper is going to harm you to get the dog?"

"It has crossed my mind."

"The story took place in 1883," said Paul.

Sam got up, retrieved the steaming pot of water and poured it into another pot, added a handful of tea leaves, grabbed a box of cookies and joined them back at the table. "These are kind of stale but they won't kill you. They're still pretty good. Where did this story take place?"

"Jakarta," said Paul, forgetting where Nerissa sailed from.

Sam set the pot down between them and opened the box of cookies. He spread them out on a napkin. "Sorry. I don't get too many visitors. Jakarta..., 1883. Krakatoa erupted, right?"

"Right."

"If the story took place in 1883 in Jakarta," Sam asked, looking over at Kathryn, "how can the trapper be here, a hundred and some odd years later?"

Paul nodded. "My question, exactly."

"Too many coincidences have already happened," said Kathryn. "And there was a stone, a firestone with some kind of magical properties."

"And you're thinking that the trapper is somehow transported to the other side of the world over a hundred years later and is still looking for the dog?"

"I know it sounds ridiculous."

Sam poured a little tea into each of their cups. "It's still a little weak. Kathryn, how do you propose that I teach you how to defend against such a thing? I cannot defend from a ghost any more than they can hurt me. We are a world apart."

"I did not say it was a ghost."

"Then, how else can he be here?"

"Did I not mention a stone with magical properties?"

"Wait," said Paul. "Oskar said that Bardolf did not have the stone."

"But he was going back to the island. Maybe he found some kind of clue."

"There wouldn't have been any clues on the island. The dog was already gone and the stone was going back to wherever it came from, with that family. We don't know if they ever left. The ship, what was her name?"

"Nerissa."

"Right. She was headed to, where was it?"

"Teluk Betung."

Sam poured a little more tea into his cup, tasted it, decided it was strong enough and served the others. "Teluk Betung. Some of my ancestors were wiped out by that eruption. A tidal wave got them."

Kathryn moved her cup closer to the edge of the table and turned it clockwise, absent mindedly watching the steam evaporate. "What if Nerissa went back to Teluk Betung, dropped off supplies and then came back to Jakarta? If they headed back to Mogadishu after that, Oskar and the family might have been on it."

Paul looked at Sam. "We're not really crazy. We just talk like this sometimes."

"If that happened," said Kathryn, "Bardolf might have had time to go explore the island, return to Jakarta and book passage back to Mogadishu on Nerissa. There's Bardolf's opportunity."

Paul devoured one cookie and was reaching for another. "Thanks for the cookies, Sam. As far as we know, Oskar went with Mahin and her family. They had the stone."

"Mahin?" Sam replied with a questioning look. "That's a

very unusual name."

"The daughter of...," Paul stopped. "I can't remember his name."

"Let me guess," said Sam. "Musheer?"

Kathryn almost spit out her tea. She swallowed quickly, coughing at the same time and spilling her drink onto the table. "I am so sorry."

Sam was not concerned. He got up, grabbed a couple of paper towels and set them over the spill.

"Kathryn, let me add to your list of coincidences."

"Oh, no."

"Musheer was my great-great grandfather. My great-great-great grandfather, Sameer, was murdered in his sleep and the stone was stolen. My name is also Sameer, Sam for short."

Paul threw up his hands. "Why did I not see this coming?"

"I am very interested in your story. My family has been waiting for generations to get back what is rightfully ours."

Kathryn was feeling a little dizzy. Instead of getting a little training to boost her self-confidence, she felt like she was stepping into quicksand. "The firestone?"

"Of course. We heard that an English speaking boy had accompanied my family back to Mogadishu. Your accounting of the trapper might very well be true. I'm going to check it out."

Kathryn mopped up the spill. Sam pointed to the cupboard door beneath the sink.

"Trash can's in there."

"If it's true," said Kathryn, coming back to the table, "if Bardolf was on the return voyage and..., say he murdered Sameer, so..., what? What are you going to do? What *can* you do?"

Paul enjoyed another cookie. "You're going to track down somebody who probably died a hundred years ago? This I gotta see."

Sam refilled Kathryn's cup, offered some to Paul, who shook his head, no, and then refilled his own.

"I don't think we have to do anything yet. If it is the trapper and he has some interest in the dog, he'll be back. In the meantime, we train."

"What kind of weapons?" Paul asked.

Sam smiled. "Don't worry. You won't be disappointed."

"It's for Mom, not me."

Kathryn laughed. "Right. You can't wait to get started."

"Kathryn. May I borrow that book?"

"Of course."

"First comes balance," said Sam. "We can never be ready if we don't have excellent balance. Everything we do involves balance, reaching for something, opening a door, every move we make has to start from somewhere. Any time that we are caught off-balance, our brain is busy trying to compensate, to readjust to the new, unexpected situation. That is lost time, precious time in a fast moving situation. So, we will start here, with balance."

"How come the pant legs are so short?" said Paul, looking down at his ankles. "Are they gonna shrink more after I wash them?"

"They're always like that," Sam answered, grinning. "You have to be able to move without anything getting in your way."

Kathryn finished tying her belt in place and stepped onto the mat, smiling. "You have beautiful legs, Paul. No need to be self-conscious."

Sam started them walking around the mat, testing their balance, making adjustments, and moving from there into rolls, forward, backward, testing their balance when they came out of a roll, and from there, basic hand techniques for getting control in hand to hand exchanges. Two hours later...,

"You each have a new relationship with the other, and on these grounds you must respect each other at that level. You are partners, now. I expect that you will test each other, practice together and help each other to get better. You both already do that. I am impressed."

"When will we be ready?" Paul asked.

"Ready? You must always be ready."

"You know what I mean, like for...,"

Kathryn opened her purse. "How should I pay you? Credit card? Check?"

Sam waved her offer away. "No charge. As far as I am concerned, we're in this together. My success depends on your success."

"Surely, something for your time."

Sam smiled. "My time is coming. The secret of the fire-stone has been passed down from generation to generation and every generation has raised one of their children for just this moment. It is me. I should be paying you."

Kathryn smiled. "Day after tomorrow? Same time?"

"Yes."

"Wait," said Paul. "What if that ghost comes back?"

Kathryn nudged him a bit, checking his balance, which was off. "Thought you didn't believe in ghosts,"

"My suggestion," said Sam, "would be to buy a can of mace. If he gets too close, hit him with it. If it doesn't bother him, then he probably can't hurt you either. Meanwhile, practice, practice, practice."

Kathryn and Paul met Sam at the studio, in the back room where Sam had spread out a pizza and salad. He motioned for them to sit. "What are you two drinking?"

"Soda," said Paul. "Unless it's diet. Then I'll just have water."

"Kathryn?"

"Water, thanks."

"I've read the book. Very interesting reading about my ancestors. I felt like I was there. Thank you for letting me read it."

"You're welcome. So, what do you think?"

Sam handed them their drinks and joined them at the table. "Please, dig in."

Paul was first to the pizza. "Music to my ears. Thanks, Sam."

"You didn't answer," said Kathryn, dishing salad onto her plate.

"Oskar's story is only one piece. First, some history. Musheer died while treating the local population from some kind of disease, died from it. Kashif went in pursuit of the murderer and thief. We don't know what happened to him. He was never heard from again. Kashif's wife had a son, my great grandfather. Mahin and Oskar, went into hiding.

Reading the story, my guess is that they returned to Oskar's home. That would be the safest place. All that we know of those two is that they were together when they disappeared.

Most of what I know of the stone has been passed down from generation to generation by word of mouth. Each generation believed the story a little less. And now you've come along."

Kathryn served herself a piece of pizza. "So, all of this is true?"

"There's more. Sanjay, do you remember him? There was some kind of altercation in Jakarta several months after Nerissa sailed back to Teluk Betung. A man was murdered and Sanjay was believed to be the killer."

Paul reached for another piece of pizza. "I thought he was going to hang when they got to port. You know, for mutiny."

"He argued that the crew thought they were sailing into their deaths and had a right to mutiny. They let him go."

Kathryn wiped her hands and reached for her water. "How is he involved?"

"I don't know that he is. But it proves that part of Oskar's journal is true. I found a record of Sanjay. He did exist. Nerissa was real. My family was on her when she sailed to Teluk Betung."

"OK," said Paul, between bites. "Why would anyone want to go to Teluk Betung?"

"Sameer's brother lived there. He was in failing health and there was some great urgency that the two meet before he died. Krakatoa put an early end to that."

"What was the reason?"

"All of that history died with the death of Musheer and destruction of the family. I think I want a beer. Anybody else?"

"I'll take one," said Paul.

"No, he won't."

"Kathryn?"

"No, thank you."

Sam popped off the cap. "A little history of the stone. This is what I have heard. A young girl, Kass, was very plain looking and very shy, so much so that she stayed inside all of the time. She dreamed of having lots of friends and wanted a lover, but knew that would never happen because she couldn't look any boy in the eye. She spent her days and nights in this fantasy world.

"One night, much to her surprise, they met in their dreams, each seeming as real as if they were in the same room. He was very much like her in that he couldn't talk to any girls. When they discovered that about each other they laughed and became very good friends. They agreed

192

to meet every night and talk about their days. They fell in love.

"One night, when he didn't show, Kass became very worried. He would always be there. He said forever and so did she. They had a pact. When he didn't show the next night or the next, she wondered if he had found someone else, someone prettier, more fun, someone more exciting. Maybe he found someone in real life and had no more use for her. Finally, in despair, she killed herself.

"When he arrived at their secret place the following night, anxious to tell her of his amazing adventure, all he found was this stone that had the words, "Love forever," scratched on the side.

"He waited for her to return, night after night he was there patiently waiting, each night ending with a bit more anxiety than before. After a month of waiting, he scratched the same words on the other side of the stone and then killed himself.

"The stone, I'm told, fell into the seam between the two worlds, the real one and the one of dreams."

Paul gulped his soda, burped. "Excuse me. So, the stone is from the world of dreams? What does the stone actually do?"

"All I know," said Sam, reaching for another piece of pizza, "is that the stone was capable of seeing dreams and we don't know who has it. They may not even know what it does."

"Could be," said Paul, "Nobody owns it anymore. It could be just laying on the ground, looking like every other rock."

Kathryn cut one of the pizza pieces in half and took half. "I doubt it. I think Bardolf has it. Have you tried to find the island?"

Sam shook his head. "Nerissa's log was destroyed when she succumbed to a storm in eighteen eighty-four, so we don't have the coordinates. But we do know when she left Mogadishu and how many days she had been at sea when she ran aground, so we can guess the area. But I've already looked. No islands. Nothing even close."

"Then..., what?"

"That makes me believe that Bardolf didn't find the island either. If you were Bardolf, where would you go next?"

Kathryn and Paul exchanged glances. Both answered at the same time. "Look for the stone."

"I'm thinking," said Sam, "that this island exists only on the night of a blue moon. It's an island of dreams. And it doesn't have to be near Teluk Betung."

Melissa was definitely pissed about something. She was hardly making eye contact, had been very quiet during the first half of the lesson, and when they were practicing pushing hands, she had been very aggressive, testing Paul's balance by pushing hard and sudden.

"What's the matter?" Paul asked, at last. "What are you angry about?"

"Nothing."

"Doesn't feel like nothing. Normally we have a lot of fun doing this. Today I feel like you want to beat me up."

Melissa waited until their hands were on a motion toward Paul and then shoved hard, trying to get him to lose his balance. "Nothing's wrong."

He guided her force away, turning his hips slightly. "Well, that's good. Cause if you were really mad, I'll bet you'd shove me right through that wall. Come on, Melissa. What's up?"

She dropped her hands and went to the side of the mat where she retrieved her water and then walked outside. Paul followed.

"I'm going to keep asking until you tell me."

She opened her water bottle, took a long sip and slowly screwed the lid back on. "You're holding out on me."

"What? How?"

"There's something going on with you, your mom and Sam and I'm not a part of it. I feel left out and it's not right. I introduced you to this."

"Ahh," said Paul, thumping his forehead with the heel of his hand. "I should've guessed. We're not leaving you out. I just didn't think you'd want to be part of it."

"I wouldn't know. You haven't let me in on the secret."

"I'm sorry. It has to do with Capn and that blue moon thing."

"What blue moon thing?"

"If we read the story on a blue moon and then save the dog, the story might come true. Remember? When we were first buying the boat?"

"I remember. Keep going."

"Mom thinks a ghost has been visiting, looking for the dog, I suppose."

"A ghost? How does Sam fit in?"

"She wants extra training from him."

"That's it?"

Paul sighed. "No. Turns out, Sam's ancestors owned the firestone that was mentioned in the story. He wants to get it back."

"I need to read this story. Can you loan me the book?"

"I guess. I'll talk to Mom."

"Didn't that take place a long time ago?"

"Right. Eighteen eighty-three."

"How's he going to find the stone after all this time?"

"Beats me. I'm just going along for the ride and getting extra training. That's pretty cool."

Without warning, Melissa slapped Paul, a good hard open handed smack on his cheek."

"Ow! What was that for?"

"For leaving me out. How could you?"

"I didn't know."

"Right. Something like this comes along once in a lifetime and you don't think to let me in on it?"

"I'm not sure about anything. I've never seen the ghost."

"And you think I wouldn't be *interested*?"

"I really didn't think about it much."

"And that's why you got slapped. When we're done with our lessons today you have to clue me in on everything."

"There's not much more to tell."

"I'll be the judge. How many times has she seen the ghost?"

"Twice, I guess."

"Have you set up any tests to see if it's real?"

"No. How do you do that?"

"See, Paul. That's your problem. You don't pay attention in class. A ghost is going to be a field of energy. Maybe we can't see it, but we have detectors that do."

"You know how to do that?"

"Yes. And Mr. Cobb will loan me the equipment."

"What kind of equipment?"

"Infrared temperature detectors, motion detectors that see in the dark. EMF meter...,"

"EMF?"

"We covered it in class last semester. You were sleeping."

"What does it mean?"

"Electromotive force. Look it up."

"I get it, a force that might be there but we can't see. Pretty cool, except we don't know when it's going to appear."

"Maybe we can coax it into view."

"How?"

"Paul, loan me the book and ask me when I'm done reading it."

Lights dimmed, their movements across the tatami mats were in slow motion. Kathryn, Sam and Melissa circled Paul, who was doing his best to keep all three in front of him.

Kathryn moved in first, slashing diagonally across Paul's chest with her wooden knife. Paul moved toward her, letting his hand rest lightly on Kathryn's arm so that he could guide the knife away.

He forced her fall into the path of the next attacker, Melissa, and then turned to face Sam who was coming at him with a bo. Paul sidestepped the lunge, moved into Sam's space, dropping the front end of the weapon down so that Sam was forced into a forward roll.

"Very good," said Sam. "Except next time make sure you get the weapon when I go by. I can still attack."

"Me, too," said Kathryn. She thrust the knife toward Paul's stomach.

Paul twisted sharply, guided the knife by and then held Kathryn's forearm lightly with one hand while using the other to twist her wrist upward, forcing Kathryn to her knees. He stepped to her side, twisted her arm behind her and forced her to lay out flat on her stomach. Still holding her arm behind her, he calmly took the knife.

"Nice," said Sam. "OK. Melissa. You're up."

And so went the next hour, each taking turns being the attacker and the one being attacked. The more they practiced, the faster their movements. Sam kept slowing them back down and sometimes stopped altogether to explain a certain move.

The last fifteen minutes of the two hour session was for discussion. Paul headed for his towel.

"I think I lost ten pounds. What's for dinner tonight, Mom?"

"Spinach salad."

"You're kidding, right? I need protein."

"I'll throw in some garbanzo beans and feta cheese."

"Mom…,"

"It's good for you, puts hair on your chest."

"I could use some of that."

"Not me," said Melissa. "We're having grilled fish."

"I'm going with her for dinner," said Paul. "Put my salad in the fridge and maybe I'll eat it tomorrow."

"How's your dad doing? We haven't seen much of him lately."

"He's in the middle of a big contract deal. He has to travel a lot and when he gets home, he just likes to stay."

"Well, he's welcome to come out to the boat sometime and have dinner."

"I'll tell him that. Thanks, Kathryn."

Sam got a quick drink, toweled himself off and sat up against the wall. "Anybody have anything they want to talk about?"

"I have a question," said Paul. "Melissa wants in, and I would like that. Can she be part of our team?"

Kathryn and Sam exchanged glances. "What team?"

"You know, the Blue Moon Strike Force Team."

"Didn't know there was one," said Sam. "Who's heading it up?"

"You are, for going after the firestone."

"Nobody's going after the firestone," said Kathryn.

"Not yet. But sooner or later you will. It's inevitable."

Melissa grabbed her water and joined Sam, sitting next to him on the mat. "Kathryn, Paul said that you saw a ghost?"

"I didn't actually see a ghost. It appeared in my dreams."

"Could you see its face?"

"No. The first time he was in shadows, the second on a foggy night."

"You said, he. You're sure of that?"

"Yes. Very much so."

"Do you think he will come back?"

"I don't know. I hope not."

"Have you thought about trying to detect its presence?"

199

"She knows how to do this stuff," said Paul.

Kathryn shook her head. "Never thought about it. You can do something like that?"

Sam held his hand up. "Wait. Kathryn saw him in a dream, not when she was conscious. How are you going to measure that?"

"Maybe we can coax him out."

Kathryn joined Sam and Melissa, sitting in front of them on the mat. She put the flats of her feet together, held them in place with her hands and leaned forward. "You want to go looking for the thing?"

"Why not?"

"How would you make that happen?"

"Set up detectors on the boat."

"What kind of detectors? Cameras? Because if it's a camera, I say no."

"Infrared, EMF and motion detectors."

"You're getting ahead of yourselves," said Sam. "This isn't your normal ghost hunting expedition. What if we become part of the dream?"

Paul grinned. "Wow. What would that be like?"

"Are you ready to confront him? What would you do, face-to-face with Bardolf?"

Paul nodded. "We need more weapons training."

"Exactly. I think Melissa's idea is something to consider, but we're not ready."

"Well," said Kathryn. "All of this scares the bee-geezies out of me."

Capn was acting strangely. All day long he had been restless, going up the companionway, standing in the cockpit and sniffing the air. Twice he went all the way up to the bow and sat next to the bow pulpit like he was waiting for something, looking up and down the dock several times before returning to his bed beneath the steps.

Watching him, Kathryn was getting a little concerned. Paul was spending the night at a friend's house, going to the movies, and his cell would be turned off until he got out at midnight.

The hair stood up on Capn's back and he uttered a low growl. Kathryn climbed the steps leading up to the cockpit and checked out the view. All of the boats were where they were supposed to be and there were no strangers lurking around, nothing to be growling about.

She went below, made herself a cup of tea and went topside for a bit of fresh air.

This is the best part of the day, when everyone goes home and the place is quiet.

Spittin' Image tugged at her dock lines, ropes tightening against the cleats as the tide moved through. Halyards thumped lazily against the mast, an onshore breeze. Kathryn sipped her tea.

Capn joined her, jumping up on the seat and putting his head on her lap. She scratched behind his ears, feeling secure with him around, even though she felt that he was as much a part of her troubles as he was her comfort.

Around nine, sticking up like toothpicks and creating long spaghetti-like shadows across the water, masts from the many sailboats captured the first light of the moon. When it was apparent that this was going to be a full moon, Capn got up, went to the top of the cabin, sat next to the mast and howled.

That's what it was. He knew it was going to be a full moon. How did he know? This isn't a blue moon, is it?

201

Another minute of that and she took him below. Late night clouds drifted in, thin and glowing, challenging the moon for control.

Back at the apartments, somebody would be arguing. Someone would be yelling out a window or banging on the floors or walls. There would be loud music, blaring television and car alarms.

Kathryn went through the boat, closed and locked the front hatch, closed and locked the companionway but left the hatch above her bed open, preferring the salty night air to the closed ventilation of her cabin.

Capn settled in at the foot of her bed. For unknown reasons, he chose to sleep in Kathryn's room at night, much to her comfort. Hearing him settle in, she drifted off into her dreams...,

She could not identify the sound. Something pulled against a latch, metal against wood. Whatever else, the action was not completed because the sound repeated. Scrape..., clunk.

She'd heard that sound before, many times. But the things that made those sounds were not coming to mind, such a disturbing feeling, to know something, but not be able to recall.

Creaking, something forcing something else apart. Fumbling, the sounds of a hand exploring the boundaries of the hatch, searching for a way to release the lock.

When the hinge of the hatch above her bed creaked like it always did when being opened, Kathryn knew exactly where the sound was coming from and was wide awake. She screamed when Bardolf peered inside...,

Capn put his front paws up on the bed and leaned forward to lick her face. She pushed him away. "Where were you in all of that? Aren't you supposed to protect me?"

The hatch was just as she had left it, open two inches and latched into place, enough for fresh air, not wide enough for someone to manipulate the mechanism from outside.

Capn sat next to her bed and waited. Finally, she reached over and gave him a pet, scratching behind his ears. Seeing that she was OK, he eventually wandered off for a drink from his water dish out in the main cabin.

Kathryn got up, ensured the boat was still secured and peeked out of all of the windows looking for anything unusual. Nothing.

Back in bed...,

OK. That does it. I can't do this anymore. Melissa's right. I have to face it. If all four of us were together when it happened, it wouldn't be so bad.

Maybe I need to see a psychiatrist first. Maybe I'm going crazy. Geez.

Sam handed Kathryn a plate, a stack of napkins, a bag of cookies, and then went about pouring tea into everyone's cups. "You had another dream?"

"Yes."

"And you think it was Bardolf?"

"Yes."

"What makes you so sure?"

"In my mind he was the same person as the first two times."

"What happened?"

"He opened the hatch over my bed and was looking in. Scared the bee-geezies out of me."

Paul took the unopened bag of cookies from Kathryn, opened them, poured some onto the plate and took two.

Melissa situated her pillow a bit farther away from the table and then sat back down. She grabbed a napkin, wiped up some spilled tea from the table and pulled the cup closer to her side. "Did you get a good look at his face?"

"No. It all happened so fast it was over before I really understood what was happening."

Paul looked over at Sam. "Guess it's time for weapons training, huh?"

"What weapons do we have that can be effective in a dream?"

"Maybe I just need to go see a shrink."

Melissa sat up. "Why don't we see if it's real? Until we can prove something one way or the other, we don't know what we're up against."

Kathryn nodded. "Got a point. I will bring wine to the event. And Sam, you're going to be there with all of your weapons, right?"

Paul grinned. "And I'll just be there."

Sam quietly blew the steam from his tea and took a cautious sip. "I think the three of you have no idea what you're up against." He looked over at Kathryn. "He wants

204

something and he's spending a lot energy to get it. If it's the dog, I would say give it up. You don't need the dog as much as you do your sanity."

"I believe I was the object of his attention this last time."

Paul laughed. "He wants *you*?"

Kathryn laughed. "Hard to believe, huh?"

"That was cruel," said Melissa, frowning at Paul.

"I didn't mean it like that. All along I was thinking he wanted the dog. So, is he just using the dog to find his way here?"

Melissa took a cookie from the plate and nibbled an edge. "Looks like."

"So, if we give the dog away...,"

"Then you haven't saved it," said Sam. "You can't guarantee its future."

Paul reached for another cookie. "If we didn't save the dog, none of this would have happened, right?"

"Right."

"You wouldn't be able to search for the firestone because you wouldn't have this lead, right?"

Sam nodded.

"But we've already saved the dog. The future is whatever it is, whether we have the dog, or not. Right?"

Sam nodded again. "Possibly. So, maybe I should take the dog and get you two out of the middle. That might stop her bad dreams."

"Where are you going to keep it?" Kathryn asked. "This dojo is also your home, right?"

"At the moment, yes."

"No. Neither one of you would be happy."

"I'd take him," said Melissa. "But I have three cats."

"Capn is at home on the boat. Giving him away is not an option."

"It's not that hard to set up detectors," said Melissa. "Why don't we do that? What's it going to hurt?"

Kathryn sipped her tea. "How big are they? Where would you put them?

"They're handheld. I could tape them to the walls."

"Bulkheads," Paul corrected. "No walls on a boat."

"Tape them to the bulkheads."

"What will they detect?"

"Energy fields. If there is any kind of disturbance, we'll record it."

"Where would you put it?"

"I'd get two. One for your cabin and one for the kitchen area."

"Galley," Paul corrected.

"Do they see images? This isn't like a camera, is it?"

"No. Nothing like that. What we'll see is some kind disturbance, like a sine wave."

"I don't think ghosts ride on sine waves," said Paul.

"I know that. I was trying to explain that whatever else we see, it won't be a picture."

"What'll happen? Will it set off an alarm, or what?"

"We can rig up an alarm. But do you want that? That'll scare off whatever the detector's detecting."

"I'll take it," said Kathryn.

"You're all talking like it's a ghost," said Sam. "It's not. It's a dream. Don't know how you're going to detect that."

Melissa did not tell them everything.

Why get into technical explanations? Everybody's eyes glaze over, they nod politely and wait for you to finish.

What she didn't tell them is that after installing the equipment on Spittin' Image she set up a link that she could log into from her computer back home, where she could run the signals through more sophisticated software.

Could be it's a composite signal. I'll sample at different intervals and see what else pops up. How many channels can I run at once?

Firestone. We don't know what we're getting into. That's what Sam said. Wonder if the stone's energy is a certain frequency?

If it's blue moon, magic, ghosts or some other phenomena, it's all energy. And if it's energy, I can measure it. I'm pretty sure of that. Question is, how to interpret the results?

So while Kathryn and Paul went about their business doing whatever they do after dinner, Melissa was taking readings, seeing what was normal, the fridge cycling on and off, lights on or off, the stereo playing.

Everything makes a difference. Got to set up a null program so this stuff won't interfere with what I'm trying to measure.

Calibrate, calibrate, calibrate. Make sure it's right. I may never get this chance again. One in five billion. Isn't that what Paul said?

And I get to be part of it.

The alarm came in at three twenty-six, "Might as well be walkin' on the sun", over and over. Melissa hit the remote that turned on the overhead light, got up and crossed the room to her computer.

The signal was coming from Kathryn's room, some kind of energy field that swept through the entire bandwidth of her measuring equipment, bottom to top and back again.

The interference repeated itself several times. Melissa ensured that she was recording everything and then checked the galley monitor. No disturbance was coming from there.

And then the signal was gone, all over within a couple of minutes. Melissa started running several programs, sampling bits and pieces of this signal and comparing it to that, multiplexing them together, taking them apart and searching for some kind of combination that might be coherent.

By six in the morning, just about the time she was nodding out in front of the monitor, a shape began to take place. It was just a crooked line, black and slightly curved, nothing unusual about that. But Melissa drifted off after seeing it and when she opened her eyes again, the shape was on the other side of the screen.

It repeated! I have to play that back. Hmm. What if I played it back slightly out of sync with the others so that it doesn't move.

What if I inverted this one and increased the output of that? What would happen?

By eight, Melissa was staring at the image on her screen, a black spot in the middle of her monitor, motionless while all of the lines of static spun erratically around it.

Hitting Pause, she selected the dot and began to magnify. Each new image had two changes, the dot grew longer, looking more like a crooked branch of a tree, and the static lines surrounding the dot changing from what looked like bursts of energy to thin dark lines sweeping across the screen.

Initial magnification showed red. Increased magnification changed the color to orange, and then to yellow, green and finally blue. At this magnification the dot looked more like a tunnel, glowing blue on the outside, dark in the middle.

Melissa pushed Play and watched, fascinated by the image as the tunnel twisted and pulsed in the middle of a brilliant, shimmering blue light.

Kathryn was sitting out in the cockpit under the shade of the tarp when Melissa waved from the dock. "Permission to come aboard?"

"Hop on," said Kathryn. "What brings you here so early in the morning?"

Melissa sat on the other side of the cockpit, keeping in the shade, pulled out her laptop and turned it on. "Did you have any dreams last night?"

"Not that I can remember, no. Why?"

"I set up a link for the detectors and monitored the signals from my house. At three twenty-six this morning I got an alarm. Look at this."

Kathryn stared at the shape as it twisted around, weaving itself back into the light where it faded into and out of view. "Play it again."

Melissa hit replay several times while Kathryn studied the image.

"Looks like it's alive."

"That's what I thought when I first saw it."

"This was in my room last night?"

"Well, in one form or another."

"But I don't remember anything."

"Maybe because nothing happened."

"I don't like it. This is not some place I'd go in my dreams. If I had been awake, could I have seen anything?"

"No. I don't think so. How about Capn? Was he acting unusual?"

"Yesterday. But..., turned out it was a full moon that he started howling at. Have you told Sam about this, yet?"

"No. I wanted you to see it first."

"If it is a tunnel, how does that help anything?"

"This might be what Sam's looking for. If it is a tunnel, maybe we can locate where in the room it is."

"You're kidding, right? I don't even like thinking about that."

"Where did Capn sleep last night?"

"In my room at the foot of my bed, as usual. Why?"

"Could you close the door to your room tonight and make him sleep somewhere else?"

"I get it. See if it happens out in the galley?"

"Right."

Melissa could hardly contain herself. A quick call to Sam got the OK for her to arrange a meeting with Kathryn and Paul at his dojo at noon. She even volunteered to bring lunch.

She handed Sam and Paul each a carne asada burrito, gave Kathryn her order of three rolled tacos with guacamole and set two fish tacos in front of herself. Reaching back into the bag...,

"I brought chips, extra salsa and hot carrots. Dig in."

Paul opened his burrito, poured salsa all over and wrapped it back up. "Thanks, Melissa. This looks really good."

Sam retrieved an assortment of sodas and bottles of water from the fridge and set them on the table. "What's this I hear about a tunnel?"

"Looks like a tunnel," said Kathryn, biting into her rolled taco. "Looks like it's alive, too."

"Cool," said Paul. "Fire it up. Let's see."

Sam bit off the top of his burrito and poured salsa inside. "How did you come about this image? Is this raw data?"

"No. I had to change a lot of things around, but everything I used came from raw data."

Melissa set up the laptop between Sam and Paul, played the video and set it to repeat.

"That is cool," said Paul, between bites. He grabbed a root beer, popped it open and gulped down about a third. "I wonder where it goes."

"Could be your worst nightmare," Sam cautioned. "If it goes anywhere at all."

Kathryn poured salsa over her second rolled taco and then down into the middle. "A path to the island?"

Sam laughed. "Right. How will we get in, jump through the screen?"

Melissa opened the bag of hot carrots, took one, grabbed a chip and ate the two together. "I don't know how we can use any of this. What I do know is that this video came from some kind of mysterious energy that was in Kathryn's room two nights ago.

"A fluke?" Sam asked. "What happened last night?'

"Funny thing," said Melissa, as she finally got around to squeezing lime juice across her fish taco. "To prove whether, or not, Capn was somehow part of this, Kathryn had him sleep in the galley last night. This energy field, whatever it is, goes where he goes. Let me show you what I recorded last night."

Sam was not in favor of the plan. The next full moon was going to be a blue moon, if the definition of the third full moon in a quarter that has four is used.

They wanted to congregate on Spittin' Image, have dinner, spend the night and see what the detectors detected first hand.

"You're tempting fate and you're not ready," Sam said. "Another year. That's what it's going to take, at least."

"I can't take another year of these dreams, Sam. Melissa's right. What's it going to hurt, just to look?"

"Just looking might just draw you into the dream. None of us know what the stone is capable of. All I'm saying is, you'd better be ready."

"Here's a thought," said Paul. "If it's been happening all along and nothing's happened...,"

"Speak for yourself, Paul."

"Except for Mom, the only difference is going to be that you two are there with us. People do spend nights at other people's houses."

Sam nodded in agreement. "On a blue moon, with all interested parties gathered in one place, on the boat that the dog came in on. You ever hear of Murphy's Law?"

"I'll do whatever Mom wants. I'm with you, Mom."

"Me, too," said Melissa.

"You need your dad's permission. I need to hear from him."

"Right."

"What are you going to tell him?" Paul asked.

"The truth. That the four of us are working on a puzzle."

Kathryn looked over at Sam. "What if we do this, but not on a blue moon?"

"You're tempting fate a little less."

"You really think this dangerous?"

"All I'm saying is that anything is possible. Look at the odds against what's happened already. It could be that everything turns out OK. More likely, nothing will happen and we'll all go home to get some rest. In any case, I'll be there if you guys are going to do it."

"Thanks, Sam. Then...," she looked over at Melissa and Paul, "let's do it."

Melissa stepped down into the galley carrying her sleeping bag and equipment. "Which bunk is mine?"

Paul pointed to the bunk on the starboard side. "Over there. You can use the counter top to set up your stuff."

"After dinner," said Kathryn. "I need the space for the lasagna."

Sam followed Melissa down the companionway. "You made it?"

"Nope. Bought it at Luigi's. He said if I bought the Chef Salad Special as well, he'd give me a bottle of Chianti for half price. His family has a winery back in Italy. So, I thought I'd give it a try. Glass of wine, Sam. Beer?"

"No, thanks. I'll just have water."

"Kids?"

Paul headed for the fridge. "Soda. I'll get it. Melissa?"

"Just water. Thanks."

After dinner, Melissa set up her laptop, got the program running and set the laptop so that it faced the rest of the room. They all went topside, sitting in the cockpit, talking quietly as the night began to unfold.

Capn joined them, making the rounds and getting his ears scratched before heading up to the cabin top where he sprawled out to wait for the first light of the moon.

"Late night and early morning low clouds," said Melissa, looking west. "We may not be able to see the moon at all if it doesn't hurry up."

"That comes in almost every night," said Paul.

"I don't think we have to see the moon to feel its effects," said Sam, getting up. "Think I will have a beer. Kathryn, more wine?"

"Sure. Why not?"

"I'll take a beer," said Paul. "Thanks, Sam."

"No, he won't. And you've had enough soda."

"Mom...,"

"Nope.

"You're drinking wine."

216

"It's red wine to prevent heart attacks. And If I'm ever going to have one, tonight's the night. Melissa, what did your dad say about you spending the night here?"

"He wanted to make sure that you were going to be here and then said, "Don't do anything I wouldn't do.""

"May I ask, where is your mom?"

"She was doing one of those things my dad said he'd never do, skydiving. Her chute got tangled. She didn't make it."

"Oh, Melissa!"

"It happened years ago. I'm kind of over it now."

"What was she like?"

"Very independent. She was always off doing something new. Dad's more of a stay-at-home kind of guy but he always joined us on our hikes. That was fun."

"Do you still hike?"

"Not as much. I'm really getting into computer technology. I do laps in the pool every day, though."

Sam joined them in the cockpit. "Your wine."

"Thanks, Sam. What about your family? Where are they. What do they do?"

"My dad was in Special Forces. Got killed by an IED. My mom married a jerk-off, excuse the expression, and we haven't talked much since. How about you?"

"Ex is a flake. My job keeps me busy. Running Paul all over the place keeps me busy...,"

"Makes you feel wanted," said Paul.

"A chauffeur. This boat keeps me busy. Walking the dog keeps me busy."

"Basically, her life's a zero," said Paul. "So, tonight's a real adventure."

As if that was the queue, Capn sat up, raised his head and howled, a low guttural sound that worked itself into and out of some note about an octave higher. Everybody laughed.

Sometime around eleven, when the cool air was covering everything with a light mist, they decided to go below and get some sleep.

Melissa had situated herself in the cockpit so that she could keep an eye on her screen. Nothing. Other than sitting out on Spittin' Image with friends and waiting for a full moon to rise, pretty cool all by itself with the seals swimming by, pelicans landing here and there, the docks creaking as the rollers traveled upward on their pylons, boats pulling at their tethers, nothing unusual had happened.

"It's going to be foggy again," said Kathryn, looking west. "It was like this last night. Rolled in around two."

Sam stood and stretched. "What were you doing up at two?"

"I wanted to see if the fog rolled in." She motioned for Sam to precede her down the steps and then for Melissa to do the same. Everybody said their good-nights and went to bed.

Sometime around two, the keel of Spittin' Image dragged across some kind of shoal, gravel or sand or, maybe rock. A scraping shudder resonated throughout the fiberglass hull, bringing everyone to the sitting position in their beds.

Kathryn was the first one up. She threw the door open and turned on the galley light.

"What the frick is that?"

Paul came out of his room. "Sounds like we're hitting bottom."

Kathryn pulled back a curtain and peered outside. "Pea soup fog. How can we hit bottom? We're tied to the dock!"

"If that's the case," said Sam. "We'd better be thinking tsunami."

Melissa cupped her hands against the window and stared outside. "I can't see the dock."

218

Another scraping sound echoed through the cabin.

"That sounded more like sand. Mom, we're moving!"

"Paul, hand me the flashlight from the drawer." Kathryn opened the companionway door and scrambled up the steps. She shined her light over to where the dock should be and, to her increasing distress, did not see anything. Her light bore out into the gray mist until it was absorbed. Shining her light down at the boat's cleats, she discovered that the dock lines were missing.

"I think somebody untied us."

Paul came up into the cockpit, went to the wheel and turned on the power to the instruments. "GPS is not working. It's giving me random coordinates. Radio's out, too. All I'm getting is static."

Sam joined them topside, looked around for a few seconds, cupped his hand behind his ear and leaned to the port side. "I keep hearing waves coming from over there. Anybody else hearing that?"

"We are moving," said Paul. "Knot meter says half a knot. We must've cleared the shoal. Depth gauge shows about fifty feet."

"Paul. Drop anchor. Do it now!"

Paul hurried to the bow, opened the hatch, pulled out the anchor and dropped it overboard. He waited for it to hit bottom and played out another thirty feet before tying off.

"Was this part of your dream?" Sam asked.

"I would like to say, no. But I can't."

Sam turned back to the companionway. "Melissa? You show anything on your screen?"

"Come on down. You won't believe this."

They gathered around the screen and watched as the tunnel grew longer, twisting and turning, contorting into different shapes, disappearing and then reappearing, the mouth of the tunnel always larger than before.

For a second or two it disappeared completely. When it reappeared, the mouth of the tunnel took up most of the screen. From somewhere deep inside, at the other end, a blue light blinked into and out of view.

Sam went to his backpack and began to open various pockets. "Kathryn, turn out the lights and get Paul down here. The three of you are going to get a crash course in weaponry. Hurry!"

The Other World

Sam lit a small glow light, placed it on the floor in the galley, retrieved four garments from his backpack and handed them out. "Put this on under your clothes. If someone tries to stab you, it might save your life. It won't stop a bullet."

Kathryn was feeling desolate. "I can't believe it. I've put everyone in danger. I am so sorry."

"Sorry? Mom, this is cool!"

"We'll see how cool it is," said Sam. "Melissa. Stay here and put that on. We don't have time to be modest."

"Mine's on," said Paul.

Sam turned him around and pushed a button on the lower end of the garment. "This will identify you as the proper wearer of the shield. It detects your pulse, breathing and blood pressure. If you remove it or die, it sends a signal telling us where you are.

He handed each of them a wrist strap that looked something like a watch. "I call it, Snitch. Put it on your left wrist, strap it firmly and don't take it off. The screen on the face is small, but it will let us know where everyone else is, should we get separated. The shields we're wearing transmit our locations back to Snitch."

"Wow," said Paul. "Did you invent that?"

"No. I have a friend who designs fun little gadgets." He handed each of them a belt with a holster. "Put these on. Each belt contains night vision goggles, on the left hand side, a can of mace here on the right, a flashlight, water, first aid kit and three air packs for these." Sam gave each of them a lightweight plastic pistol.

Paul looked disappointed. "Is this a toy?"

"Hardly. See the red LED on top? That means the safety is on. Here's the safety behind the trigger. Push the button and the led changes to green. It will shoot. With your hand holding the grip everybody push and hold the safety until the LED turns green and starts blinking. It will take about ten seconds."

"What does that do?"

"It programs the gun to recognize you. It won't shoot for anyone else."

"Can it be reprogrammed?"

"No."

"The barrel's not round," said Melissa. "What does it shoot?"

"Stars. There are ten per pack and they're accurate up to about a hundred feet. They cut and penetrate. The red pack is a power pack for a laser. It's only good for about thirty seconds but it will blind whoever's looking for about two hours. Never, never, never point it at your face or at any of us."

Kathryn strapped hers on. "When would we use that?"

"If you're under attack, point it at your adversary and push the button."

"Cool," said Paul, grinning. "What is the blue pack?"

"Darts. Get hit with one of these and you'll be asleep within a minute or so."

Melissa flipped the safety on and off and watched the led change colors. "How do we reload?"

"This latch right here," said Sam, pointing to the bottom of the grip. "Flip it. The old pack falls out. Slip in the new and push until it clicks. The LED stays off until the gun's properly loaded."

"Does it make a lot of noise?" Paul asked.

"Very quiet. That's why I chose these. You'll hardly hear more that a quiet "phhht." Lastly, they're air powered. You've got about twenty shots in each canister before you're out of air."

Sam flicked a latch at the rear of the gun and pulled out the tiny container of compressed air. "This comes out. Slip in the new and push until you hear it penetrate the membrane in the top of the cylinder. Latch it closed and you're good to go again."

Kathryn was falling more and more into the depths of dread. "Is all of this really necessary?"

Sam reached into his backpack and retrieved a collapsible crossbow and a belt containing several bolts. He strapped the belt diagonally across his chest and clipped the crossbow to it. "I hope not. What I'm hoping is that someone untied us from the dock and we're just drifting."

Paul holstered his weapon and snapped the strap into place. "That doesn't explain the GPS being out. Do we get a crossbow, too?"

"No."

Melissa found a button on the other side of Snitch. "What's this button here for?"

"Communications. Push it and a tiny red LED will light in the bottom corner indicating that you are connected to an encrypted loop. Just the four of us are on it. Talk quietly if you have to use it. If you yell into it, you could give away your partner's position."

Kathryn went back to the steps and peered out into the dim light. "Fog's not lifting. It's thicker than ever."

Sam turned off the glow light. "Let's go topside. Stay low. Don't make too much noise. Kathryn, that's a four man dinghy?"

"Yes. Where's Capn? I forgot all about him."

"I saw him go up the steps," said Melissa.

"I'll get him," said Sam. "I want to add a tracker to his collar."

They found Capn at the bow of the boat, nose wet, ears up and very interested in whatever was lurking out there in the fog.

Paul pulled the dinghy up to the side of Spittin' Image and held it in place with his foot. The inflatable was sturdy and fast, easy to row and he had done a lot of it. "Who else is going?"

Kathryn looked over. "Where are you going?"

"Over to see what's causing those waves."

"No, you're not. You don't just take off."

"What's to discuss? There are waves and rocks over there somewhere and it's too foggy to see. It can't be that far away. Maybe it'll tell us where we are."

"You're both right," said Sam. "Good to explore and fog is good cover. But we have to make group decisions."

"So, can I go?"

"I don't want you going out there by yourself. Sam?"

"I can go with him. But that leaves you two here alone."

Kathryn pointed her light down at the deck and clicked it on and off. "These weapons really do what you say they do?"

"Yes. Be careful. Like I said, you three need another year."

"Yeah, but this is hands on," said Paul with a smile.

"So is your life," Sam cautioned. "And you only have one of those. Kathryn?"

She studied the face of her watch. "K, P, S, M, that's us?"

"Right. For you, K is in the middle of the circle. The rest of us are in one place or another around you. Same goes for everyone else. You're in the middle. As Paul and I row away, you'll see the direction and distance, in yards. Kathryn?"

She nodded, doubtfully. "How long?"

"Thirty minutes."

"OK. Paul, be careful."

"Mom, I'm not a child."

"No. You're a teenager. That's worse."

Sam stepped into the dinghy and went to the forward seat. "You row, tiger. I'll be the look-out."

Paul untied from Spittin' Image, sat at the center seat and grabbed the oars. "Roger that."

"What if you don't come back?"

Sam laughed. "Then, I guess you'd better leave without us."

Sitting in the cockpit, Melissa and Kathryn watched them slowly disappear into the mist. They sat quietly for several more minutes, staring into the emptiness. Kathryn got up and walked the perimeter of the boat.

"All I see is fog. GPS is still out. Weird. Don't know about you, but I'm starting to think I got us into something far bigger than what I bargained for. I don't want anyone to get hurt. I just want that man, ghost, whatever, out of my

225

life. Everything else is good."

Melissa gave her a hug. "I love what we're doing. So does Paul. He's like a little puppy with a wet nose. You're the greatest."

"Thanks. How long have they been gone?"

"About fifteen minutes."

Kathryn glanced down at her monitor. "They went south for about a hundred yards and now it looks like they're heading west."

"They must've discovered what's causing the waves." Melissa held Snitch up close to her mouth and pushed the button. "Hey. What are you guys doing?"

"It's a peninsula," said Sam. "Waves are hitting from the other side and washing through. We're rowing parallel to see how far back it goes. Everything OK over there?"

"We're doing fine."

"We'll head back in a few."

Kathryn made a pot coffee, pulled a package of donuts out of the cupboard, orange juice and containers of yogurt out of the fridge and set them on the table. "Should I scramble some eggs?"

Sam shook his head. "I'm not even sure about the coffee. That scent will carry all the way to land."

"Oh. I didn't even think of that. Sorry."

"Fortunately," said Paul. "The wind's blowing the other way."

"We don't know what's over there, either," Melissa added.

Kathryn poured herself a cup of coffee and set it on the table.

"Since you already made it," said Sam. "Sure. I'll have a cup."

Paul got four plates out of the cupboard, placed them on the table and opened up the donut package. He looked at everyone questionably. "Donuts anyone? Going, going..., last chance before they're gone."

Kathryn handed Sam his coffee. "So..., what do you think? What's out there?"

"I think we need to follow this stretch as far back as it goes. Paul, can you quietly start the engine and idle us further in?"

"Piece of cake. I'll watch the depth gauge. When we get down to thirty or forty feet, drop anchor."

Paul got four glasses out of the cupboard, set them on the table. "Juice anybody?"

Melissa held up an empty glass. "I'll take some. So, are we in a cove?"

Sam sipped his coffee. "Don't know. Say we are. Do we go ashore? Or do we turn around and try to go the other way?"

"There aren't any islands around here," said Kathryn. "Except Coronado and Catalina. And I know we didn't drift that far overnight."

Paul devoured a donut and washed it down with a half glass of juice. "Say it is an island, cove, whatever. If we go explore it, who's going to stay with the boat?"

"First off," said Sam. "I don't think we're in California anymore. And if this is an island, I don't think it's in the Pacific."

Kathryn stared at her coffee cup. "You think we're at *the* island?"

"I don't see why we wouldn't be. Everything else has played out. Radio doesn't work. They didn't have radios back in eighteen eighty-three."

"Or satellites," said Paul. "That's why the GPS is out."

Sam took a chocolate donut from the package and placed it on one of the plates. "I think we have to go on the assumption that we are caught in the magic of the stone and the blue moon. You guys asked for it. Welcome to the other world."

Sam went over to his backpack and pulled out three pairs of boots. "Last night, nobody asked me why my backpack was so full. We were going to spend one night, right? It doesn't make sense. Question everything."

"I noticed it," said Paul. "Just didn't think much about it. Now..., if you were Bardolf. That'd be different."

"I hope so. Because it might come down to that." Sam handed everyone a pair of boots and two pairs of socks. "I took the liberty of looking at your shoe sizes when you came to visit. Melissa, you're always wearing sandals so I had to guess. If we go ashore, if there is a shore, sandals aren't going to make it."

Paul kicked off his tennis shoes and tried them on. "Cool. Thanks, Sam."

Melissa sat down to try hers on. "You're right. How naive of me. I come up with the technology that lets us see what we're getting into, but don't believe in it enough to bring boots. Duh."

"If we all have boots," said Kathryn. "Does that mean that we are all going onto land? That leaves the boat unprotected. Someone could board her and sail away. And then we'd be the ones stranded."

228

Paul grabbed another donut. "If it's eighteen eighty-three, they're not even gonna know what this thing is. Besides, we'll lock it up and take the keys. Boots fit."

"Mine are fine," said Melissa. "Thanks, Sam."

Kathryn headed for the cupboards. "Mine, too. Thanks, Sam. We'd better get a little more to eat. Granola? Lasagna? I've got some lunch meat and cheese. We can make sandwiches."

Spittin' Image quietly chugged alongside the peninsula. Kneeling at the bow, holding onto the bow pulpit, Sam gave Capn a good, long pet. He was certainly excited about something, ears forward, nose wet, wanting to bark but for Sam's insistence that he stay quiet.

Paul eased the engine into neutral and then into reverse. Spittin' Image drifted to a stop. Paul held Snitch up to his mouth. "OK, Sam. I'm at thirty feet. Drop anchor."

"Roger."

Sam quietly lowered the anchor into the water and let the rope play out until it hit bottom. He gave it a few more feet and tied off. Paul let the engine idle in reverse until he felt the anchor grab, then killed the engine.

They met back in the cockpit where everyone had various combinations of lasagna, granola and sandwiches.

"I think I saw cliffs," said Sam. "I suspect that we're in a cove."

Biting into a ham sandwich, Paul looked up. "I've seen a few stars. Maybe the fog is breaking."

"It's always worse right on the water," said Kathryn. "If we go on land, maybe we can climb above it."

"That's not going to help us discover if it's eighteen eighty-three," said Melissa. "I checked my laptop. No Internet, obviously."

"Looks like it's getting a little lighter," said Paul. "About two hours before sun-up."

"You don't know what pre-dawn looks like. You're never awake before ten unless I get you up."

"That's because I'm growing. I know what pre-dawn looks like."

Melissa laughed. "He saw a picture of it once."

Sam set his coffee cup down, wiped his hands on a napkin and looked at the others. "OK. We're fed. We're equipped and we're trained. I suggest that we all use the rest room one last time...,"

"It's called a head," Paul corrected.

"Let's all use the head one last time, put a leash on Capn and go see what's out there."

Kathryn began gathering things to take down to the sink. "Wouldn't it be better to wait until it gets light?"

"I'm for going now," said Paul.

"We could wait until the fog lifts and sail away," said Kathryn. "Why do we even need to go on the island?"

Paul picked up Melissa's plate and stacked it on top of his. "Yeah, but what year are we sailing into?"

"If we are caught in the Firestone's world," said Sam. "I think our path forward is on the island. I would like to see a little of it before they can see us, if there is someone out there."

"Let's do it," said Kathryn, heading down the stairs. "Paul, hand me the dirty dishes. I'll just stack them in the sink."

They pulled the raft ashore, carried it across the sand and tied the rope around the trunk of an old, weathered pine. Capn led them toward what sounded like a waterfall.

He turned inland before they could actually see it and then sniffed his way upward. Shadowy hunched figures, wind-worn pines loomed into view, ghostly and gray in the thick, wet mist.

Capn, tugging at his leash, led them up to a small grove of similar pines enveloping a flat area that they thought would overlook the cove, if they could see that far. Glimpses of the night sky passed overhead, a moonbeam here, Venus over there, thinning wisps of fog drifting by.

Capn led them back into the trees, quite sure about where he wanted to go. He sniffed his way forward, pulling Paul along.

"Keep it slow," Sam whispered. "You control him, not the other way around."

"He'd take off running, if I let him."

"I'm with Sam," said Kathryn. "Go slow and keep an eye out for traps."

"Traps? Like, what?"

"Trip wires," said Sam. "Look for anything suspicious in front of Capn. Don't think they had infrared back in eighteen eighty-three.

"Bear traps," said Kathryn. "You don't want one of those thing clamping down on you. You'll probably lose a leg."

"Geeez."

"Pit," said Melissa. "You don't want to fall into a ten foot pit, either."

"Somebody else want to lead?"

Kathryn patted Paul on the head. "You're doing just fine. I'm looking over your shoulder."

When they reached the stream, Capn turned left and followed the bank upward. Another hundred feet of elevation and they were looking down on the fog, puffs of silver light and gray shadows drifting by with an occasional treetop poking through.

To the northeast, the mountain dominated much of the sky, a looming black silhouette outlined with the silvery-blue light of the moon.

Kathryn stopped. "This must be the place Oskar was talking about. He was on the mountain side, over there, looking this way when the dog disappeared."

Sam moved closer to the bank and looked down. "Pretty good drop. Probably hard to cross right after a storm."

Capn splashed into the water and started across, making his way to the first few rocks before turning and running back. Paul, caught off-guard by the dog's sudden action was tugged into the water.

"Nice balance," said Melissa.

"I wanted to do that..., see if the boots are waterproof. They are. Thanks, Sam."

Capn continued upward, sniffing his way along the riverbank, around patches of scrub pine, and when the trail ran along the stream, through thick brush and tangled vines, urging Paul to keep up.

Ahead, the trail split, the one on the right followed the riverbank, but because of the turn in the shoreline was impossible to see where it led. The other trail led across an open, flat, rocky area and, further up, into a patch of scraggly trees. Capn headed left. Sam reached past Kathryn and tapped Paul on the shoulder. "Stop."

"Just following the dog," said Paul.

"Wait here." Sam followed the trail to the right, down through the brush and around the curve. It continued on, but some of the path was through wet, treacherous rock. He returned to the group and pointed left. "Capn seems to know the way."

At a snail's pace, they quietly worked their way around clumps of tall brush, through the trees and the tangled remains of higher water times.

"Looks like this stream has overflowed a few times," Melissa whispered.

"Heavy rain," said Sam.

Paul did not notice the tiny string stretched across the trail. Three of Capn's four feet cleared it, but his last foot snagged the wire. Something sounding like a big snake streaked through the grass, coiled itself around Paul's ankle and pulled his left leg out from under him.

"Holy crap! Help!"

A bearded man, tall and thin with deep set dark eyes stepped out from the brush, from the direction that they had been heading, and pointed his rifle at them.

"Back away from the boy or I'll shoot him."

Kathryn backed into Melissa, put her arm around her and guided her over to Sam, who had been bringing up the rear.

"Not behind him! Git over there." He pointed his rifle in the direction of the stream, to a flat, wide slightly curved rock. "Stand there until I say you can move. Toby, where are you?"

Another man approached from their rear, heavy set, stocky, his long black hair pulled back behind his shoulders and held in place with a leather strap. "Drop yur weapons, nice and slow. You with the crossbow..., go first. Any funny moves and I'll just start shootin'."

Sam removed his crossbow and bolts and set them down by his feet.

Toby motioned with his gun. "Not *by* yur feet! Move it away..., with yur feet. Next the belt."

The first man, keeping his gun trained on Paul, walked across the clearing. "Hands up. Keep both of 'em on the rope that's got your foot. Let go and I'll shoot. Move!"

He unsnapped Paul's holster and pulled out the gun. "This thing ain't real."

"Right," said Paul. "It's just for looks."

"Don't lie to me, boy! What's it for? It sure ain't no gun."

"Don't know why I was carrying it. It doesn't work."

"We'll see about that." "My name's Brock. I'm the man that's gonna shoot you in the foot. Yur still sayin' it don't work?"

"Right."

Brock pointed the gun just to the left of Paul's foot and pulled the trigger. Nothing. Inspecting the gun a little closer, he found the safety button and pushed it. The LED switched from red to green. "Ain't that fancy? What kinda fire you got in there that it can change colors?"

"Don't know. Like I said, it don't work."

"You think green means somethin' different than red?"

Paul hoped not. Green meant that it would shoot. But didn't Sam say that the gun would only shoot for the owner? "I don't know. It did that for me, too. But it never shot."

Brock pointed the gun at Paul's foot again and pulled the trigger. Paul flinched. Nothing happened.

"You got gypped, boy. This thing's worthless. What's yur name?"

"Paul."

"Paul? I want you to take that belt off and let it fall to the ground. No funny stuff cause this gun here works."

When the belt fell to the ground, Brock kicked it away. "Now put yur hands behind yur back. That's right. Nice and slow."

With Paul's hands tied behind his back, Brock cut his foot loose. "Sit down and don't move. You try and run away, I'll shoot them. And then I'll come lookin' for you."

When all four had their hands tied, Brock gathered up their weapons and started heading upstream. Toby motioned with his gun for them to follow.

"Where are you taking us?" Kathryn asked.

"You wouldn't know even if I told ya," said Toby. "What I'm wonderin' is, how did ya get here? And how many more are there?"

Nobody answered. Toby smiled. "You'll all be talkin' before long."

The trees thinned quickly as they approached the shore of the lake. A thin mist covered the water, golden with the reflected light from the upper ridge of the island.

They trekked west along the shoreline, working their way through another grove of trees, hiking in silence at a good clip. Paul spotted what he thought was a chimpanzee way back in the shadows, motionless, watching them, but said nothing.

Coming out of the trees, the trail cut back to the water and followed the shoreline across a higher terrain, about twenty feet above the lake.

They reached a fork in the trail, one continuing west up toward the ridge, the other following the shoreline. Brock motioned for them to stop.

"What do you think, Toby? Long or short?"

"Long," Toby replied. "They can't climb good with their hands tied and we'll be havin' to pick 'em up."

"That's what I was thinking." Brock took the footpath on the left, heading up.

The trail eventually veered north, up and down through the rolling terrain until they hit flat ground a couple of hundred feet above the lake. Another hundred yards and they marched up to a make-shift log cabin.

Kathryn, Melissa and Sam were told to sit next to the trunk of a large tree and were then tied to it. Once secured, Toby offered water. Brock motioned for Paul to head toward the cabin.

"Where are you taking him?" Kathryn demanded.

Brock put his hand on Paul's shoulder, stopped him, and then turned and studied Kathryn. "I expect you'll be more polite when you address me next time. You want to try again?"

"He's my son. I'm afraid for him."

"He's gonna answer a few questions. As long as he does, he'll be fine."

"Take me instead."

Brock smiled. "Your turn is coming."

"Take me," said Sam. "I'm the one you want to talk to."

"Oh, yeah," said Brock. "Every one of you is going to get a chance, especially you. But I'm the one who says who goes first." He turned and nudged Paul toward the door. "And he's the lucky one."

Rhett was sitting over at a makeshift table by a hole in the wall when Paul and Bock entered the room. A canvas cover for the opening had been pulled out of the way, allowing the only other light into the room. He stood and moved from the window to the other end of the bench, closest to Paul.

"What's yur name?"

"Paul."

"Paul, you gonna answer me truthfully?"

"Yes, sir."

"Cause every one of you is gonna tell me a story and if they don't match up, we're gonna find out who's lying. Got it?"

"Yes, sir"

"Where are you from?"

Paul had a sinking feeling, a knot forming down in his gut. If this was eighteen eighty-three, they wouldn't know. "California."

"Never heard of it. By Africa?"

"No. The other side of the world. America."

"Heard of that. How did you get here?"

"By sailboat."

"Ship? How big?"

"Forty-two feet."

"Feet? What's feet?"

"Fifteen meters," said Paul, figuring that was pretty much right. Three feet per meter. Three times fifteen is forty-five. Close enough.

"You sailed around the world in a fifteen meter ship? How big's your crew?"

"Just us four."

"Where is your ship?"

"I can't tell you, exactly. We sailed into fog and dropped

anchor when we heard the bottom hitting. We think we're in a cove."

"Caught them just above the crossing," said Brock.

"How'd you keep from hitting the rocks?"

"Just lucky, I guess."

"Where were you headed?"

"We weren't heading anywhere."

"Destination, Paul. Where were you going?"

"We weren't going anywhere. We just arrived."

Rhett stood, put his face very close to Paul's and said, almost in a whisper. "You don't sail around the world in a fifteen meter boat with a crew of four and not have a destination. What do you take me for? I'll give you one more chance to answer that question. Destination?"

"We never left the dock. There was no destination."

The backhand came without warning. Paul stumbled backward into Brock's arms. His face stung and he could taste blood. He had bit his tongue.

Brock stood him back up. "Don't make sense to me either. Guess we'll have to go look at that ship. Must be some kind of toy."

"Take him outside," said Rhett. "Who's next?"

"His mother."

"I've told the truth," said Paul. "We don't know where we are. Can you tell us that?"

"Your clothes are funny," said Rhett. "Everybody dress like that where you're from?"

"Pretty much. Can you tell me what year it is?"

"What year do you think it is?"

"Eighteen eighty-three?"

"You got that part right. Take him out. Tie him up. Bring in his mother."

"What's yur name?"

"Kathryn."

"I'm going to tell you the same thing I told Paul. I expect the truth. You lie to me, I'm going to find out. Understand, Kathryn?"

"Yes."

"Where you from?"

"America."

"Where is yur ship anchored?"

"We think we're in a cove. We don't know for sure. It was foggy when we arrived."

"What is yur destination?"

"We didn't have one."

"You sail all the way from America, clear around the world and you don't have a destination?"

"We never untied from the dock."

Sitting on the end of the bench, Rhett rubbed his hands together. He looked down at his boots, let his gaze follow the floor all the way over to Kathryn's boots and slowly shook his head. "That just don't make sense." He stood slowly and got in her face. "How did you get here?"

"We don't know. Last night we had dinner on the boat, went to bed and woke up when our keel scraped across some rocks. We dropped anchor and came ashore to see if we could figure out where we were. And then we ran into you."

"And you expect me to believe that?"

"Yes, because it's the truth."

"Brock?"

"Yes, sir?"

"Bring the girl in. Kathryn, go sit in the corner and don't say a word until I say you can. You make any noise, I'm going to hurt the girl. Understand?"

"Yes."

"Brock, help her over there."

"I don't need any help. Thank you."

"That's the last time you speak. Got it?"

Kathryn nodded, went to the corner and, using the walls for support, lowered herself to the floor. She sat on the underside of her left foot, leg tucked under while keeping her right foot flat on the floor, knee bent upward.

From this position, Sam had taught them, you can roll in any direction, stand straight in an instant and have the ability to move quickly when needed.

The only problem with this position, Kathryn had experienced many times, was that if you stayed like this for too long, your foot goes to sleep.

Melissa came through the door, spotted Kathryn in the corner and went to her. "You OK?"

Kathryn nodded and smiled.

"Over here," said Rhett. "I'm the one you need to be talkin' to."

"You hurt her and I'll...,"

"Shut up. Bring yur self over here and face me or I *will* hurt her."

Melissa hesitated. If only her hands were free, she could get to that laser, blind the bums and steal the gun that Brock kept at his side. If only...,

Rhett's face was getting red. "NOW!"

It wasn't just the volume of the command, it was the tone, his demeanor, red face and fingers working that told Melissa that she had overstepped her bounds.

"Pick your battles," Sam had always said. "Show your enemy that you respect them and you've gained an advantage."

Melissa crossed the floor quickly, stopped in front of him and smiled. "I am sorry. I did not mean to offend you."

"What's yur name?"

"Melissa."

"Where you from?"

"The United States."

"Is that near Africa?"

"No. North America."

"You're from America?"

"Yes."

"What is your destination?"

"Destination? We didn't have one. We were tied to the dock when we went to bed. We woke up when our keel scraped over some rocks. That's when we dropped anchor and came ashore."

"Brock?"

"Yes, sir?"

"Bring those stumps over here and go get Kathryn."

"Right."

"Melissa? Sit down."

When they were seated, Rhett leaned back against the table, crossed his legs and studied the two them. "Start from the beginning. I want to know everything leading up to you sitting on these chairs. Kathryn, you go first. Melissa, you fill in the details. I've got the whole day."

"It was my birthday," said Kathryn. "My son, Paul, didn't remember, so I made him read this book with me."

"What book?"

"It was called, The Other World. It said, "Beware if you read this story on a blue moon." We read it on a blue moon."

"Beware of what?"

"If the story is read on the night of a blue moon, the events might transcend time."

"Is that so? What events?"

"It has to do with a dog."

"A dog?"

"A diary written by a boy named Oskar who lived in eighteen eight-three...,"

"Lived? What year do you think it is?"

"I'm guessing eighteen eighty-three."

"Go on."

"He was on a ship called Nerissa when it got caught in a storm. The ship ran aground on an uncharted island. The boy and a man named Bardolf came to the island to get some of his animals back. Bardolf captured the dog. But when he was taking it back to the ship, it disappeared."

241

"What do you mean, disappeared?"

"Oskar wrote that the dog disappeared into thin air. It had saved his life and he wanted to repay the favor."

"If the dog disappeared, what debt was there to repay?"

"He knew that it was not possible for him to do that, so he asked one of us, whoever read the story on a blue moon, to try and help the dog if it was in trouble."

"How would you know the dog?"

"He said it was smiling."

"Except..., you don't have a dog."

"They did," said Brock. "It got away when the boy got caught up in the trap."

Rhett studied Kathryn. "You think this is the dog from the story?"

"Yes."

"Are you bringing it to Bardolf?"

"No."

"Then, why are you here?"

"I bought the boat that this dog lived on. His master was killed and the dog was going to be put to sleep. Paul, the dog and I moved onto the boat. Then I started having dreams. Some man kept coming into my dreams, lurking around. He was looking for something. It scared me. We finally guessed that the man was Bardolf."

Rhett laughed. "And you think you're just going to walk in here and tell him that?"

"I was hoping to."

"Lucky you came up this side of the stream. Had you come up the other side, you'd be talkin' to him. But it wouldn't be pretty. Who's your other friend?"

"Sam."

"What's in it for him?"

"I don't understand."

"Why is he here?"

"In case we run into trouble."

"No other reasons?"

'No."

"He your lover?"

242

'No."

Rhett studied Melissa. "Is he your lover?"

"No."

"So you're telling me that the four of you had dinner last night, went to bed, slept alone, were tied to a dock and you all woke up on the other side of the world overnight when you sailed into this cove?"

Both Melissa and Kathryn nodded. "Yes."

"What kind of magic is that?"

Melissa cleared her throat. "It has something to do with a blue moon."

"Nothing but blue moon's since Krakatoa. Nothing special about it. You sure that's all it is?"

Melissa nodded. "Must be. I can't think of anything else."

Rhett sat up and faced Melissa, about a foot away and, looking into her eyes, asked, "You ever hear anything about a firestone?"

She didn't answer. But she did flinch. Rhett smiled. "I thought so. Now we're getting somewhere. Brock, take these two outside, tie them to the tree and bring Sam in."

"Sam, I'm going to ask a few questions and I want you to answer me honestly. Will you do that?"

Sam studied Rhett. This was a man that was very sure of himself. He looked like he could be very thorough, short tempered and mean. Even though Paul hadn't said anything, he had been hit. Sam noticed the red welt on his cheek. "Yes."

"Good. Where are you from?"

"America."

"How many in your crew?"

"Four."

"What is your destination?"

Sam hesitated. Surely he had asked the others the same question. Paul probably said he didn't have one because he really didn't. Melissa would have had a better idea of where or when they were going but probably said that they didn't have one. Kathryn, somewhere in the back of her mind probably always knew what the destination was but wouldn't tell this man. "We did not have a destination."

"How long did you sail to get here?"

"We never raised the sails."

"When did you leave your home port?"

"We never untied from the dock."

"Sam, do you really expect me to believe that?"

"No. I don't. I don't expect anyone to believe that. But it's the truth."

"How do you explain your presence on this island?"

Sam let out a long sigh. "Kathryn read a story on a blue moon and got caught up in some kind of..., I don't know what to call it, an unusual string of events."

"The magic of a blue moon?"

"Something like that, yes."

"And how is it that you got involved?"

"I was afraid that she might get in over her head and need some help."

"So, you volunteered?"

"Yes."

"What made you think that you could be of assistance?"

"I didn't know that I could. Apparently, I've failed."

"This story..., have you read it?"

"Yes."

"Is it a story of fiction?"

"It should be. But..., here we are."

"Reading the story makes you part of it. What's the purpose?"

"I don't know. That was one of the reasons that I came along."

"This, Bardolf, that Kathryn spoke of. What do you make of him?"

"If the story is true, he left Oskar on the island to die. He tried to kill Oskar. If he is that kind of man, I have no use for him."

"That is a very bold statement. You could be put to death for that."

"You asked that I speak truthfully."

"In this story, what happened to Bardolf?"

"He was going to charter a ship and search for the island. There was no more information after that."

"Why was it so important that he came back?"

"To look for the dog, I suppose."

"All of that, just for a dog?"

"Some men are driven."

"Yes, some are. Tell me, are you one of those people?"

"If I have a goal, I strive my hardest to attain it."

"Other than your desire to help Kathryn and feed your curiosity, do you have any other reasons for coming to this island?"

Sam was hoping that this question would never be asked. He knew that he could take out Rhett with one or two kicks. But with Brock behind him, holding the gun, and with his hands still tied behind his back, he didn't have much of a chance.

Even if he was successful, Toby was still outside with

the other three, tied up, and he had a gun. Now was not the time. "I've always had a spirit of adventure."

"Sam, I'm going to ask that question again. Do you have any other reasons for coming to this island?"

"My ancestors were killed, murdered in their sleep. If there is an opportunity for me to find the murderer, I will do that."

"And you think it's Bardolf?"

"I don't know."

"If Bardolf is guilty, then what?"

"I want to see him brought to justice."

"You think there are courts on this island?"

"No."

"So..., how will you bring him to justice?"

"First, I have to find out if he's guilty."

"How will you know that?"

"I don't know."

Rhett leaned back against the table. "What would be Bardolf's motive?"

"My guess, money. My family had some wealth, or so I've been told."

"Where did this murder take place?"

"Mogadishu. At their home."

"Toby was on Nerissa's crew when it sailed from Mogadishu to Teluk Betung. Bardolf was on that voyage with his animals. And he said that there was an odd group of passengers that had their own cabin. Were they part of your family?"

"That might be true."

"But then Krakatoa wiped out Teluk Betung. We have a connect between Bardolf and your family. But why would he follow them all the way back to Mogadishu to murder them?"

"As I've said, money."

"Nothing more? Be honest."

"In the story, Oskar mentioned something about a magical stone, only a rumor. I am curious about that."

"A magical stone. Toby also mentioned the stone, Firestone, is what they were calling it. It was rumored that your family had it. What do you know about that?"

"Nothing, everything is only a rumor until I learn the facts."

"You remind me of someone I know. Does the name 'Kashif' mean anything to you?"

"Many generations ago, my grandfather had that name. You know of him?"

"Many generations ago. Hmm. He's on the other side of the island, prisoner of Bardolf."

"We never knew what happened to him."

"Brock, untie this man. And then untie the others and give them back their weapons. It's my turn to bring you up to date. How odd that you sail into the past to learn your future."

Kathryn rubbed the red welts on her wrists. Toby had coiled the rope tightly and tied the knots in such a way that there was no slack at all. Her fingers tingled with the fresh blood entering the area. There would be bruises later, for sure.

They were seated on split log benches around a makeshift table comprised of several smaller saplings tied together to fashion a somewhat flat surface.

"All of us here have a story," said Rhett, nodding toward the front door. "Toby likes being alone. He's got family in Indonesia and wants to go home. What's stopping that from happening is that Nerissa is sitting out there in the harbor, guarded by Bardolf's men."

Brock retrieved a basket of what Paul thought was beef jerky when he placed it on the table. He took a stick of it and broke off a piece and began to chew. Frowning, "What is this stuff?"

"Squirrel," said Brock. "Or rat. You get used to it. Rabbit's good when we can catch 'em."

"Bardolf's men?" Sam asked. "How many? Where are they?"

"The lake divides us. They're on the east and us the west. North side is passable, but there aren't many places to hide when you cross. It's barren and flat with low grass. South side divider is the stream. You came up on our side."

"What's the conflict?"

"We want to leave. Bardolf has Kashif prisoner and isn't about to leave until Kashif gives up his secrets."

"What secrets?"

"We suspect that it has something to do with the firestone. They live over in the mountain. There's a cave with good protection. We've seen bright lights at night but we can't get close enough to see what's causing it."

"The Firestone?"

"Don't know."

248

"Why don't you just board the ship from this side and sail away?"

"It's guarded day and night and they've anchored her on their side of the cove. Besides, I won't leave Kashif behind."

"How many of you are there?"

"Five. Toby, Brock, me. We have look-outs, Mickey on the south, Turk on the north."

"How many of them?"

"Twelve, as far as we can remember. There was a mutiny. The Captain and his crew were killed, and Bardolf took over the ship. A man named Sanjay controls the crew."

"How long have you been here?"

"No way of knowing. If we had a normal moon I could tell you how many months. But..., on this island every night is a full moon."

"So...," said Kathryn, "you must've been part of the mutiny in order to get as far as here. How did you become isolated?"

"Kashif was his prisoner. Some heard my objections to his treatment and reported to Bardolf."

"Why don't they just attack? You're outnumbered."

"Why? When they get what they want from Kashif, they'll just leave. And then we'll be stranded. No sense risking their lives to kill us. My question to you is, where are you anchored in relation to Nerissa? They will seize your ship as soon as the see it. That, or blow it up."

"If Nerissa was more than ten meters away from our ship, we wouldn't know. We anchored about a hundred meters north of what we thought was a jetty."

"The cove is about three hundred meters wide. They have Nerissa pulled in close to the shore on the north side. So, there's about a hundred and fifty meters between you."

"It all depends on the fog," said Kathryn.

Rhett looked over at Brock. "How quickly can you get down to the cove?"

"About an hour, little more."

249

"What are you going to do?"

"Sail your ship out of the cove. Take it around the jetty on the south end of the island and anchor over here on the west side. You'll be out in the swells, but chances are they'll never see your ship because we control this part. That's if you can get out of the cove without being seen. How many cannons do you have?"

"Cannons?"

"That's what I thought. A fifteen meter ship can't be much. I'd say that's your first step, save your boat. Then, if you want to come back and help us, we'd welcome it."

Paul untied the dinghy while Sam and Brock collected the oars. Running across the sand, they pulled it into the water and climbed inside.

Brock ran his hand over the smooth, slick surface. "What's this thing made of?"

"Vinyl," said Paul taking the oars. "UV resistant, tough, durable."

"Never heard of vinyl,' said Brock. "This thing just floats on top of the water?"

"Yep," said Paul. He dipped the oars deep and put his back into rowing. The dinghy surged ahead. "No draft. That's why it rows so good."

Sunlight was breaking through the fog here and there exposing patches of glistening water. Brock kept his eye on the north side of the cove, looking for Nerissa. "Soon as they see us, they're gonna shoot. How far out, are you?"

"About a hundred meters," Paul replied. "A little more, maybe."

"How many guns do you have?"

Sam shook his head. "No guns. But we do have weapons."

"What kind of weapons?"

"We'll explain later. First, let's get to the boat."

"Fog's lifting. No wind. How are you going to sail out of here with no wind?"

Paul smiled. "We don't need wind to make the boat move."

"How's that?"

"We've got a motor."

"Don't know motor, either. You are some strange folks."

"Uh, oh," said Sam. "There's Nerissa."

The ship stood tall in the cove, all three masts glowing brightly in the morning sun, most of her hull still hidden in the lingering fog. She was just as Paul imagined and he slowed for a moment to check out her lines. It was impossible to think that anything bad could come from that ship.

Brock noticed Paul's slowing and, sitting in the rear of the dinghy, looked over at Paul nervously. Beyond Paul, the shadowy silhouette of Spittin' Image came into view, tiny compared to Nerissa.

"That's it? Hardly big enough for four people. It can go around the world?"

"It's a really good boat," Sam replied. "It has all the latest technology and...,"

A projectile of some ilk whizzed by Paul's head. A split second later they heard the shot. Instinctively, Paul ducked, letting go of the oars and leaning forward, putting his head between his legs. "Holy crap! They're shooting!"

Sam moved from the front of the dinghy over to sit by Paul. "Keep rowing! I'll take one side. Move!"

Brock poured some powder into his rifle, jammed in a small piece of leather and dropped the ball in after. "This won't hit anything but at least it will let them know we've got some firepower." He pulled back the hammer and squeezed the trigger. A loud explosion filled the air along with the smell of gunpowder.

"They've got a couple of Springfields over there. We're going to take another couple of bullets before we get to your toy boat. I sure hope you've got some tricks up your sleeve because there's a guy named Ollie onboard who's real good with that cannon."

Another shot. The bullet hit the side of the dinghy with a loud thud. It popped with a horrific whoosh and deflated.

"The dinghy's got six chambers," said Paul, between breaths. "We won't sink."

"A rowboat made of air," said Brock, shaking his head. "I think I like the old kind better."

They reached Spittin' Image without taking another shot. Paul raced over to the ignition switch, inserted the key and turned it. The engine sputtered to life as Sam ran to the bow and began pulling up the anchor.

252

Putting the engine to full throttle, Paul spun the boat around and headed out of the cove. Brock, keeping his eye on Nerissa, groaned. "They're positioning the cannon!"

A puff of white smoke emerged from the ship. The cannon ball hit just short of Spittin' Image, soaking the three of them. Then came the sound.

BOOM!

"Sam," Paul yelled. "I have an idea. Get the flare gun from the drawer. It's on the left hand side after you go down the companionway. Fire a shot over their ship."

Another shot. The cannon ball hit a few yards behind the stern.

BOOM!

"A flare gun?" Brock asked. "What's it going to do?"

"It will send a fireball up into the air and linger over their ship for about fifteen minutes. It might distract them."

Sam did better than that. Rather than shoot high, the way a flare should be fired, he calculated the arc and put one right on the ship's deck. Suddenly, Nerissa's guards had other problems.

Kathryn followed Rhett up to the top of the ridge and turned to check out the view. Melissa brought up the rear and joined her, extracting a bottle of water from her belt at the same time.

Sun now directly overhead, the western slopes of the mountain reflected across the lake, smooth and glassy in the still air.

Rhett pointed to a flat area extending off of the south side of the mountain. "There's a cave over there. That's where we've seen the light coming from. We think that's where they're holding Kashif."

"Do you have any idea how you're going to get him out?"

"It's going to have to be a shoot-out. The problems are that we're outnumbered, they have better firepower..., and they have that bird."

"Bird?"

"A red one. It keeps an eye out for trespassers and lets everyone know when it sees one. Nearly impossible to get by her."

"Maybe at night?"

"Like I said, every night on this island is a full moon. It's almost as bright, only blue."

"Do you have many cloudy nights?"

"When we do, it's black as night. The lake sits inside the crater. No light comes in. It's just as hard to attack as it is to defend if you can't see. I think...,"

BOOM! The sound echoed across the lake and back again. Boom..., boom.

Kathryn pointed toward the cove. "It came from over there!"

Rhett took a deep breath. "Cannon. Sounds like your friends have stirred up some action."

"What!" Kathryn started down the trail. "We've got to go help!"

"By the time we get there, it'll be all over. You're going

to have to trust that they..,"

"That's my son down there!"

"By the time you get to them...,"

BOOM! Boom..., boom.

Checking Snitch, Melissa noticed that the 'S' and 'P' were missing, no communications. "Snitch is out. I'm going to higher ground to see if we can make contact."

Rhett stared at the contraption strapped to her wrist. "What's that thing do?"

"At the moment, nothing."

Reluctantly, Kathryn followed Rhett and Melissa. He was right. Sam and Paul and Brock can take care of themselves. Still..., a cannon?

Melissa kept Snitch close to her mouth. "Sam? Paul? Hello. Anybody hear me?"

Another five minutes standing on high ground, and Kathryn was going crazy. She put Snitch up to her mouth and yelled. "Paul! Answer the freaking phone! This is your mother!"

A crackling sound, laughter. "Hi, Mom. Read you loud and clear. Sam just about jumped out of the boat." More laughter.

"Are you OK? What were those Booms?"

"Cannon. They shot cannon balls at us! Wow!"

"I take it they missed?"

"Right. We're heading out of the harbor. I've got Spittin' Image at full throttle. We're at the tip of the peninsula. I'm about ready to head south and go around. Where are you?"

"We're up on the western ridge. I guess we'll be heading down to where you're going to anchor. We'll meet you there."

"There they are!" Melissa yelled. "I see them!"

"We see you," said Kathryn. "Be careful!"

"Aw, Mom."

"Hey!"

"What?"

"Have you seen Capn?"

"No. I was going to ask you the same thing."

"Nothing. He's still on his leash, right?"

"Afraid so. Hope he doesn't get caught on something."

"Me, too."

When they were done talking, Rhett motioned for Kathryn to show him Snitch. She held up her wrist. He examined the piece carefully, puzzling over the material, black plastic with a black glass front that had red letters 'K' and 'M' together in one corner and 'S' and 'P' in the other.

"That's quite the contraption." Rhett turned back toward the trail. "And I see your boat's moving without wind. How does it do that?"

Kathryn stepped in behind Rhett and followed him back down the trail. "We're full of surprises."

Back at the cabin, Kathryn put a pot of steaming macaroni and cheese on the table. "Three packages. That's all I had."

While everyone was serving themselves, she returned to her little propane stove, retrieved the pot of steaming hot dogs and cut them up into pieces. "Didn't think I'd be serving an army. You can thank Paul for the hot dogs."

Rhett popped a piece into his mouth. "It's dog meat?"

"No," said Paul. They just call it that."

"Never tasted anything like it. Chicken?"

Sam shook his head. "No. Not sure what it is these days. It used to be pork. Then they went to beef."

Brock tried a piece. "So, this is how meat tastes in the future?"

"Hot dogs, anyway," said Paul.

They ate mostly in silence for the next several minutes. Before long, all of the food was gone and everybody was using their fingers to get the last of the cheese sauce off of their plates. After that, coffee and chocolate chip cookies.

"I'm moving to the future," said Brock. "We've been living like animals." He wiped his hands on his pants. "Right after we get Kashif."

Rhett had been watching them, quietly studying them. These people were in great shape, agile and they had weapons that he had no idea what they did.

Who is in charge? Who to address? The role of women in the future seemed to have changed. They carried more power. "Kathryn, have you decided whether or not you'd like to help?"

She looked over at Sam. "Of course, we're going to help. Sam?"

"I have no choice. Kashif is family. I will not leave until I know that he is safe. Paul?"

"Are you kidding? I wouldn't miss this for anything."

"Me either," said Melissa.

"They're shooting real lead." Rhett reminded them. "Any of you ever been shot?"

Silence and shaking of heads from all four.

"I didn't think so. I got a bullet through my leg once. Didn't hit the bone but it's been killing me ever since. I tell you this because I know what you're up against. Every one of them has got a rifle that can out-shoot us three to one. That's a lot of lead."

"It will have to be a surprise attack," said Sam.

"No surprising them anymore, said Brock. "That cannon woke up the whole island. They'll be ready."

"Question is," said Paul. "What are they doing right now? Will they come looking for our boat?"

"Not with Nerissa. There's no wind. If they did put sail to her, that would take most of their crew and that would be our time to attack."

"They could be attacking as we speak," said Kathryn.

"Toby will let us know," said Rhett. "He's up at the look out. If he sees anything, he'll fire a shot. Way I see it, our best advantage would be to attack from north and south at the same time. Problem is, we can't get across the northern end without being seen."

"We could use the dinghy to go around, stay close to shore."

"Brock shook his head. "You already got one hole in that thing. Should've seen that, Rhett. The side just went poof."

"They shot my dinghy?"

"Oh, yeah. Sorry, Mom. I forgot to tell you. There's a patch kit onboard. And we've got that little compressor."

"They shot it? Where were you?"

"Rowing. Brock was in the stern and Sam up at the bow.

"I have an idea," said Melissa. "Anybody care to hear it?"

"We're open to anything," said Rhett. "Until now, we're trapped."

"Make Spittin' Image black, same with the dinghy, and split into two groups, one that motors around the north side of the island tonight, staying close to shore, not *that* close, but close enough, anchor her out of sight and take the dinghy in. That group comes up to the cave from the east side."

"Before we go any further with that," said Rhett. "We don't know if that side's scalable. None of us has ever tried it."

"Even if it isn't, continue down the coast until you reach the cove. They would never expect you to come in from that side. If we can get by Nerissa, we'll just take that path up to the cave. The other group goes in from the south at the crossing."

"It's guarded."

"We've got the flare gun," said Sam. "Shoot it out over their area and while they're looking at that, slip across. What is that, thirty meters?"

"Thirty meters with lead," said Brock. "Jumping from rock to rock, you're a pretty big target."

Paul sat up and looked at everyone with a big grin. "Lasers! Sam, how far are they good for?"

"They should do a hundred meters."

"Once we get to the crossing, shoot the flare. They'll see where it came from and while they're looking for us, hit them with the lasers."

Both Rhett and Brock look confused. "What's a laser?"

Melissa jumped into this one. "It's a concentrated beam of polarized light. It's produced by electromagnetic radiation and...,"

"It's light that hurts your eyes," said Paul. "Never look at it."

"Doesn't sound too good," said Brock. "You send a flare up, give them plenty of light to see, give away your position and then shoot them with light that hurts their eyes while they're shooting lead?"

"They won't be able to see," said Kathryn. "Can't aim if you can't see."

"You're going to *blind* them?"

"It only lasts for a couple of hours. How many guards at the crossing?"

"Usually, two," said Brock. "But they work shifts so if we catch them at a shift change, there's gonna be more."

"When does that happen?"

Mickey'll know better than the rest of us. There's a night shift and a day shift. I'd guess sometime after breakfast and sometime after dinner."

"Do you change shifts with Mickey?"

"No. He likes it down there. He's got himself a fishing spot where he can watch the crossing. He doesn't want to come up here."

"Did he see us come up the bank this morning?"

"Probably. He wouldn't pick a fight, though. Not when it's four to one. But I'd guess that he followed you up the bank until he saw that me and Toby had you tied up. He'd be backing us up."

"OK," said Paul. "Say it all goes well. We cross the river, the other team comes up the other side and then..., what?"

"We head for the cave. That's where the light's coming from."

Paul looked at everybody with a big grin. "And we all know how to get to the cave, right?"

"I'm pretty sure all trails going up lead to the cave," said Rhett. "Unless you've come over the top. Seems like a lotta work for..., what kind of advantage?"

"They won't expect to get hit from two sides. If one of our groups catches fire, the other one will have an easier time getting through."

"That just don't make sense. Wouldn't it be better to have all of us attack at one place?"

"Stealth," said Sam. "I hope that we don't have to confront them. I'd rather go around their guards quietly. That way no one gets hurt."

"What about that flare you were talkin' about? That's not stealth."

"That's from our 'bag of tricks' department," said Paul. "To catch them by surprise if stealth doesn't work."

"In case we have to come into the cove, how many are on Nerissa?"

"We think there are two, sometimes four if they're being relieved."

Sam started counting on his fingers. "Two at the crossing, maybe four, two on Nerissa, maybe four. That's four or eight. You said there were twelve?"

"As best we can remember."

"Does that include Bardolf and Sanjay?"

"Yes."

"Hold on," said Brock. "A lot of these people don't want to be doing what they're doing. They'd change sides if they thought it would get them home."

"Why don't they mutiny?"

"Sanjay..., him and his brother-in-law, Raja. Each of them have relatives by their side and they're all good fighters, ruthless."

"So, they're the ones guarding the cave?"

"That's our guess," said Rhett. "And we're thinkin' that they'll kill Bardolf once he figures out the secret of the stone."

Spittin Image rolled lazily in the swells. Paul. Kathryn and Rhett said their good-byes, climbed into the dinghy and rowed out through the waves to the boat.

It didn't look like much of a boat anymore. They had harvested pine tree branches, placed them across the top of the deck and held them in place with fishing line tied onto the stanchions. From those limbs they tied kelp, seaweed and anything else that was dark and not too stinky. With her black mast, Spittin' Image looked like a tiny island that just emerged from the sea.

Kathryn started the engine while Paul went forward to weigh anchor. Rhett, sitting in the cockpit and looking nervous about the whole affair, studied the area beneath his feet. "What's making that sound?"

"That's our motor."

"What's it do?"

"It's what makes the boat go without wind."

"Is it dangerous?"

Kathryn smiled. "On a boat, everything's dangerous."

"Can it blow up?"

"I hope not."

"How far will it go?"

"Until we run out of gas. And don't ask me what that is because I don't know."

Paul coiled the rope on top of the newly acquired vegetation and laid the anchor on top of that. Kathryn eased Spittin' Image further out and then headed north.

They were in no hurry. Looking at the island from the western ridge earlier that morning, she guessed that it was about five miles long and about four wide, though it was impossible to see how far east the mountain extended. So she figured it would take an hour, maybe two, before they could even consider crossing the north side And she didn't want to do that until dark.

Paul joined them in the cockpit. "I just tried talking to them. No communications. I think the island's getting in the way."

"I hope it works later. Otherwise, how are we going to coordinate?"

"We start at midnight, right?"

"That's the plan."

"They should be at the lake by now," said Rhett. It's another hour down to the crossing." He studied the wristbands that Kathryn and Paul were wearing. "How do those work?"

"Transceivers. They send signals through the air."

"All these new things. Are those guns real? Brock said they didn't work."

Kathryn and Paul exchanged glances. None of these weapons had been tested. That's what Sam was warning her about. She wasn't even sure if she remembered how to use the gun and wondered if Paul was thinking the same thing.

Was it going to be one bullet from Rhett's gun that saves them against the two or three defenders? What if the lasers didn't work? What if these guns didn't shoot?

A whole bunch of doubts entered into Kathryn's mind. What if the cliffs weren't scalable? What if they were spotted coming around the east side and began taking fire?

"Sam designed these guns," said Paul. "So, you know they work."

"What do they do?"

Paul pulled out his gun and flipped the safety off. The LED changed from red to green. "What they don't do, is make noise. We're hoping that you never have to shoot your gun."

"The barrel's not round. What do they shoot?"

"Different things, depending on what we run into."

"Like?"

"If we can get close enough to a guard, this will shoot a tranquilizer dart. He'll be asleep in a minute. No sound."

"Does it shoot lead?"

"No. Nothing like that. You'll see."

"And so will I," Kathryn was thinking.

Rhett tapped the cockpit with his fingernail. "This boat,

what's it made of?"

"Fiberglass."

"*Glass*? Will it shatter if we take a hit?"

"Not with bullets," said Kathryn. "It won't stop a cannonball. They don't have a cannon on land, do they?"

"Not that I know of. Just stay out of Nerissa's line of fire."

"I don't plan on going that far down the coast."

"If we can sneak into their side of the cove, that would be cool," said Paul.

"Not in this boat."

"Of course, not. The dinghy."

Rhett stood, held onto the corner of the companionway to steady himself from the slow rolling motion of the swells and studied Spittin' Image's rigging. "Just one mast. Two sails? Is that the most you can fly?"

"Right. But we have different sizes."

"How fast will she go?"

"We've had her up to eight knots."

"She can't outrun Nerissa."

"No, but she can turn on a dime."

"I don't know what a dime is."

"A very small coin."

Rhett pointed to the array of gauges next to the wheel. "What do all of those things tell you?"

Kathryn pointed them out, one by one. "Knot meter, depth finder...,"

"It says how deep?"

"Yes, twenty meters right now. This one here is for wind speed. This one is our compass. These switches are for running lights, which we won't use tonight. We have a tri-light up on top of the mast, radar deflector, radio...,"

"All of this in the future?"

"Things you can't even imagine," said Paul.

"What year are you from?"

Paul laughed. "What year do you think?"

"Paul, I have to apologize. Your story was so completely unbelievable, I had to hit you."

"That's OK. I probably would've done the same thing."

"You're not a bad kid. I can see that. You four are on a mission and I can see that you've trained for it." He sat back down. "I just hope all of these things work for us tonight."

"Everybody's taking a chance," said Kathryn.

Paul was grinning. "What year?"

"I don't know. Nineteen hundred?"

"You think all of these things are going to happen in the next seventeen years?"

"You're right. Nineteen hundred and fifty."

"Getting closer."

"Two thousand?"

"Keep going."

"What else are you doing after the year two thousand?"

"We've put a man up on the moon...,"

"*What*?"

"News travels from one side of Earth to the other in seconds...,"

"How?"

"They have satellites that orbit Earth and...,"

"Never mind. I don't want to know these things."

It was dark by the time they reached the north end of the island. Watching the depth gauge and hugging the coast, being careful to stay out of the breakers, Kathryn turned Spittin' Image toward the east, motoring at five knots into enemy territory. She motioned for Paul to take the wheel and then sat down next to Rhett.

"Please tell me, How did you and Kashif become friends?"

"He was following Bardolf. I think he knew that Bardolf had the stone and was waiting for the opportunity to get his revenge. He signed on as crew for the voyage, but during the mutiny fought on the losing side. They were going to throw him overboard but somebody recognized him and he became Bardolf's prisoner. I was the one delegated to make sure he stayed captured..., and to keep him alive. He told me how his family was murdered. We've become friends."

"And now you're the hunted?"

"Not hunted, just unwanted. They will still shoot to kill."

The night vision goggles did not look like goggles at all, more like sleeping eye masks. What they really were was a collection of flexible light sensors on the outside connected to an array of flexible LED's on the inside that repeated what the sensors detected.

What Melissa actually saw was that her entire field of vision was presented in a light yellowish, green glow, sharp resolution in the middle, blurry around the edges.

She had taken them off and tried hiking without them. But with the moon not yet clearing the eastern ridge of the island, it was too dark to safely keep up with Sam and Brock. There were too many ankle twisters, thorny branches and snakes.

Sam had given Brock a flashlight so that he could lead the way. At first he was afraid to touch it, thinking that it was hot. After he got used to the light, he didn't want to put it down. His first impulse was to shine it at everything, just to see what kinds of things were lurking out there in the black night.

"Keep it pointed down," Sam warned. "Otherwise they'll be able to see the light from the other side of the lake."

"How does it work?"

"It's got batteries."

"What's a battery?"

"An electrical charge."

"What's that?"

"It's kind of like lightning," said Melissa, who was hiking behind Sam.

"This has lightning inside?"

Melissa was beginning to see the futility of any explanation concerning any of their equipment. All of it had been developed after eighteen eighty-three. What would Brock think of the Internet, satellite communications, space exploration? "Not lightning, exactly. It has power without the thunder."

A call from the trees, something that sounded like,

"Whoo - la - lee - loo."

"That's Mickey," Brock whispered. "He's wantin' to know who's coming through." He stopped, cupped his hands and made the sound, "Who - whoee. Who - whoee."

"Whoo, whoo."

Brock smiled. "He says, "Hello."

"Is he going to join us?"

"No. He'll follow, keep an eye on our backs. If we need him, he'll be there."

The terrain flattened out at the crossing, allowing the water to gush shallow but turbulent across the entire one hundred and fifty foot wide stretch from bank to bank. Fifty feet further downstream, the banks narrowed again and formed a sudden, rocky descent heading for the cove. Keeping hidden in the brush, they studied the different possibilities.

"Fastest way across is on top," said Brock, reluctantly switching off the light. "But you're begging for lead if you go that way." He pointed downstream another thirty feet, "Over there, you're less of a target, but you'll have to be light on your feet. Any lower than that is a nasty fall if you make a mistake."

Looking across the stream, Melissa thought she saw movement in the brush, something larger than a dog anyway, heading toward a cluster of trees located a ways back from the crossing, on higher ground. "Sam," she pointed. "Over there. There's something heading for the trees."

"That's their look-out," said Brock. "I don't have yur fancy glasses. How many are there?"

"I only saw one. And I'm not even sure it was a human."

"It'll be a human, all right. After that cannon this morning, you can bet they'll be waiting."

Sam held Snitch up near his mouth. "Kathryn, Paul? Either of you read me? Hello."

"I couldn't get them, either," said Melissa. "Their positions aren't displaying on the face."

"There's two of them," said Sam. "I just saw the other

268

one come around from behind the tree."

"What's it look like, looking through those things? Doesn't look like you should be able to see anything."

"Everything's kind of yellow-green," said Melissa. "Not high resolution, but I can see basic figures."

"Can you tell it's me and not them before you shoot?"

"Oh, yeah."

"Good."

"It's after eleven," said Melissa. "They should be looking for a place to anchor by now, you think?"

Sam glanced down at Snitch. Eleven twenty-three, still no contact. "I hope everything's going OK."

Rhett pointed to the glow of blue light emanating from the top of the mountain. "Here comes the moon. We start at midnight, right?"

"Right."

For three hours they'd been traveling down the east side, the kelp and seaweed camouflage glowing blue with the newly acquired moonlight.

"It's working against us," said Paul. "I'd rather come down this side in the dark, but the moon's lighting our way. And when we go up into the island, it's going to be light when we'd want it to be dark."

The knot meter was showing five knots, but they were going against the current. Adjusting for that, Kathryn was figuring that, by land, they were only making two knots, about six miles. She figured that the south end on the island must be right around the next bend.

Paul pointed Spittin' Image into the swells and eased back on the throttle. "Well, are we close enough?"

"See if you can bring it in a little closer."

"I don't want to get too close to the breakers."

"How deep is it?"

"Sixty feet."

"OK. I'll drop anchor. Put it in reverse to make sure it sets good."

"Right."

"I'll give it some extra slack. We'll drift in a bit closer anyway."

"Not too much."

They were about two hundred feet off shore. The plan was to row the dinghy just outside the surf until they either spotted the cove or spotted a good place to access the island. For the last five miles, most all of what they'd seen was steep, rocky cliffs.

Rhett, now feeling a little more comfortable on Spittin' Image, reached past the stanchion and pulled in the rope that was keeping the dinghy in tow.

With the deflated section, the dinghy didn't look safe. Being in tow at five knots for several hours had filled the thing up with water, and with his boots on, Rhett knew that he couldn't stay afloat, much less keep his gunpowder dry.

"Got a problem here."

Paul groaned when he saw it. "I forgot! I was going to fix that."

"How are you going to do that?"

"We have a patch kit." Paul pulled up one of the hinged seats in the cockpit and retrieved one end of a one inch rubber hose. "Here. Put this in the dinghy. Hold it in the water."

"What's it going to do?"

"Suck all of the water out."

"How does it do that?"

"No time to explain now."

When he saw that Rhett had the hose in place, Paul turned on the pump. It started sucking water out of the dinghy and sending it out the back of the Spittin' Image.

Rhett shook his head in disbelief. "Amazing."

"Mom, can you get the patch kit out of the navigator room? It's in the bottom right hand side drawer."

While she was searching for that, Rhett and Paul finished draining out the dinghy and pulled it onboard. Paul found a towel and started drying off the hole where the bullet went in, rubbing it vigorously. "Looks like it didn't come out the other side. That's good."

They rubbed the scraper over the surface surrounding the hole, roughing it up, applied the glue and pressed the patch on top of that. A few minutes more of keeping pressure on the patch, Paul got Rhett to take over while he went for the compressor. "Good thing we've got these breakers making all of that noise. The compressor is noisy."

"What's a compressor?"

"Something that pumps air."

"So, you got one for air and one for water, huh?"

Paul smiled. "Yeah, we're brilliant." He returned with the unit, unwound the hose, plugged the plug into an outlet down by their feet, hooked up the hose to the dinghy and flipped the switch.

Rhett jumped away when it started. "Holy...! Sounds

like a giant rattlesnake!"

A steady whooosh sound accompanied the rattle of the compressor. Rhett kept his distance but was amazed to see the deflated chamber fill, looking like it was coming to life. About the time he was getting worried that it was going to explode, Paul turned the compressor off.

They lowered the raft back into the water while Kathryn locked up. She set the alarm on the boat as well, thinking that maybe the noise might scare anyone off if they tried to get inside.

They climbed into the dinghy, Paul took the oars, and headed south down the coast, being careful to stay out of the breakers.

Kathryn pointed to a small inlet. "How about there? Looks pretty safe."

Paul nodded. "Yeah. But look at the climb after that."

"I'm with Paul," said Rhett. "Let's go as far south as we can. If we can get to the cove, that would be good."

Before long, Nerissa's stern came into view. As soon as they saw it, Paul turned the dinghy around and went the other way.

Kathryn pointed to the first cove north of the main cove, out of view. "There! Take us in. I think our time has come."

Rhett pointed to Snitch. "What time is it?"

"Twelve fifteen."

Sam glanced down at Snitch, still no contact. That would definitely have to be improved on the next revision, work on how to make signals go through rock. All of these things tested fine on flat ground and even around buildings and hilly terrain.

Rock is a whole different animal. Fix that, and figure out how to make Snitch's display information visible while wearing night vision goggles, a flaw in the design. You think you have it all covered...,

Melissa nudged Sam with her elbow. "I've been thinking. Why don't I go up to higher ground or maybe climb a tree and see if I can make contact?"

"Too dangerous. We don't know what's out there."

"I'll be quiet. Even twenty feet higher might make a difference."

"I don't like it. We should stick together."

"There's nothing happening. And we're going to wait for how much longer?"

"We have to give them enough time."

"It keeps getting brighter. We should've crossed when it was dark."

"That wasn't going to give them enough time."

"Maybe they're in trouble."

"Maybe they're doing fine and are quietly working their way up to the cave as planned. We have to wait a little longer."

"Haven't heard anything over there," said Brock. "Either they haven't been spotted or haven't made it to land."

"Or, the boat broke down and they're still at the other end of the island. Come on, Sam. Let me go. I'll just be a minute."

"This whole thing was a bad idea from the start."

Melissa turned away. "I'll be right back."

"Where are you going?"

"To find a bush that I can pee behind."

"You're not going to climb a tree or something?"

"No. You told me not to."

She headed for an area where she could keep an eye on things, back into the brush on slightly higher ground. Snitch quietly beeped that it had re-established contact with the others.

"Kathryn," she whispered. "Do you read me?"

She heard her voice but it was breaking up and unintelligible. With hardly another thought, Melissa found a thick tree trunk where she could get up onto the first branch.

"Kathryn. Can you hear me?"

"Hi Melissa."

"Where are you?"

"We're on the north side of the cove where Nerissa's anchored, looking for a way up. Where are you?"

"We're at the crossing. We haven't crossed yet."

"Snitch is telling me that you're about a thousand yards away. That's about half a mile, right?"

"Little more, I think. OK. I'll tell Sam."

"We've got to get by Nerissa first. Don't know what that's going to take."

"I'll tell Sam where you are. I think we're about ready to cross."

"Keep it quiet."

"We're all hoping for that. Be careful."

"You, too."

From the other side of the crossing, Klicker was eyeing the rocks, studying the trees, wondering when and if something was going to happen.

He had heard the cannon in the morning, same as everyone else on the island, and had hurried up to the rock where, from high above the cave, they had a view of the cove. Everyone saw the tiny boat leaving, moving along quite well without any wind.

When it cleared the jetty on the south side and disappeared behind the island, everyone pretty much assumed that, whoever it was, they were with the other side. The shift change after dinner put him back at the crossing.

Klicker had been given the Springfield but had been

told not to waste any ammunition. He knew how to work the gun and had pointed it at several different targets but had never actually pulled the trigger.

It was a glint of the moon's bright light off of the black glass on the face of Snitch that caught his eye, a momentary flash of blue light. Before he could stop himself, he put the gun up to his shoulder, aimed and pulled the trigger.

Melissa heard gunfire but it didn't register in her brain. Her left arm twitched involuntarily. Something warm was dripping off of her elbow. She climbed back down to the ground and hurried over to Brock and Sam.

"They've landed. They're on the north side of the cove and working their way up."

Sam stared at her arm. "What the hell, Melissa! What happened?"

"I had intermittent contact with Kathryn. We...,"

"Sit down!" Sam pulled bandages from his pack and quickly wrapped them around her wound. "This will have to do for now. Brock?"

"Yeah?"

"Your gun's loaded? You're ready to go?"

"I'm itching to go."

Sam retrieved the flare gun, aimed it high and fired. The hot, glowing reddish, orange ball streaked up into the sky and hung out at about one hundred yards. A bullet ripped through their hiding place.

"Brock, set the flashlight on that rock, point it toward them and duck."

"What are you going to do?"

"It's time for the laser. Melissa, you still bleeding?"

"Yeah..., a little. I'm OK."

Brock set the flashlight in place and turned it on. When another bullet came through, Sam aimed Snitch toward the location of the last flash and pushed the button. A brilliant yellowish, green beam of light flashed around and through the bushes on the other side.

Except for the sounds of the river passing between them, gurgling through the rocks, all else went quiet.

"I'll go first," said Sam. "If I can make it to that log, that'll give me a better angle at their hideout. Brock, you next?"

"Sure."

"You come to the log and I'll work my way up to their position."

"Melissa, you remember how to use your gun?"

"Right. Turn the safety off. It's loaded with stars."

Brock looked down at the plastic gun still in her holster. "That shoots stars?"

"Not like what you think," said Sam, turning to go. "You two got me covered?"

Leading, Rhett stayed up against the rocks, quietly working his way toward the mouth of the cove, Kathryn second, Paul bringing up the rear, scurrying one by one across the numerous inlets, getting onto higher ground before the next wave washed in.

Joining up, the three of them paused behind the last of the hiding places before they crossed the beach to get to the trail leading up onto the island.

They all had taken the time to rub ash over their faces and arms and were wearing dark clothes. Yet, crawling across the sandy beach, the camouflage wasn't going to make much difference with the moon's bright light.

Nerissa was anchored only fifty yards away and there were a million places where someone could stand in the shadows of her rigging, look out and not be seen.

"Another hour," said Rhett, looking up. "And this side of the island will be in the moon's shadow."

Kathryn shook her head. "We don't have that long. Paul? Are you getting any signals from Snitch?"

"No."

"Me either."

"Weren't they going to shoot a flare?"

Rhett looked at the elevation doubtfully. "Probably can't see it from down here."

Paul spotted someone moving up in the shadows of Nerissa's deck. "Look! What's he doing?"

One of the guards walked over to the bow, grabbed hold of a line and pulled himself up onto the rail, looking interested in something further up on the island. Pointing, he spoke to someone else out of view.

"Easy target," said Rhett. "I can hit him."

"But..," Kathryn nudged Paul out of the way and peered around the rock. "Who was he talking to? And how many?"

"You won't get a better chance."

"Paul?"

"Yeah, Mom.?"

"Put in your blue pack. You think you can hit him?"

"I have no idea. But I've got ten shots, right?"

"Just do one. We don't want to kill him."

"This, blue pack. What is that?"

"Shoots darts," said Paul. "If I hit him, he'll be asleep within a minute."

"If he falls backward, he'll drown. I might as well just shoot him and be done with it."

"Too much noise," said Kathryn. "And he might fall forward onto the deck where he won't die. At least we're not intentionally killing him."

"Unlike them," Rhett muttered. "Go ahead. Do what you've got to do. I'll be here with lead when things get serious."

Paul switched packs and turned the safety to OFF. Something he hadn't noticed before, the silver LED that he thought meant that the gun was turned on, was now blue, indicating what kind of pack he had loaded. He showed this to Kathryn, leaned out past his cover, aimed and pulled the trigger.

Hardly a sound, certainly not loud enough to be heard above the water washing up onto shore.

"Did I get him?"

"Don't know. I thought I saw him twitch."

Rhett was doubtful. "Are you sure *anything* happened?"

"I felt it kick," said Paul. "Something came out but I couldn't see what it was. Wait. He's getting down..., scratching at something in his ribs, wobbling..., I think I got him!"

"That might be one," said Rhett. "But where's the other?"

"Mom. You know what we need? An infrared heat sensor. We'd know right where he is."

"Put it on the list," said Kathryn. "Meanwhile...,"

"There's no way you can cover me," said Rhett. "Not if it takes a minute after you shoot for your victim to go down. He could shoot me two or three times."

Kathryn pulled out her gun and switched the safety off. "I've got stars loaded. That's just like lead."

"Stars? You're gonna shoot stars?"

"Not like what you think."

"Mom. How about the laser?"

"That might work."

"What's a laser?"

"We're going to temporarily blind him."

"How's it do that?"

"Paul, get your laser ready. I'll get his attention with a flashlight."

"What's a flashlight?"

Kathryn messed around with the contraption that was keeping her flashlight attached to her belt. It seemed to have a mind of its own. Sam was right, another year before they're ready, at least six more months.

Turned out, it was a simple latch that held the light in place by a magnet until the user pulled it away. "This is a flashlight." She pointed it down at the ground and turned it on. Rhett jumped away. "It won't hurt you." She held her hand in front of the beam and waved it around.

"Then what's it good for?"

"If it was pitch black out you'd be happy to have it."

"How does it work?"

"We don't have time for that. But I'm going to shine the light toward Nerissa and get somebody's attention. When they're looking, Paul's going to shine a laser his way."

"What's a laser?"

"It's like lightning in a bottle," said Paul. "Except no noise."

"It's light?"

"Right."

"They're both light. One'll hurt you and the other won't?"

"Right."

Rhett shook his head. "You live in a crazy world."

"I'm ready when you are, Mom."

The second guard onboard Nerissa went over to examine the first who had fallen. They were both out of view.

Kathryn shined the light toward the ship but the beam was so wide that it hardly made a difference in the moon's bright light.

"See if it has a focus," said Paul.

"A focus?"

"Turn the rim around the light. See if you can focus it."

Kathryn was surprised that it did. She turned the rim until the beam of light about the size of a pregnant basketball reflected through the rigging.

Seeing it, the guard stood, watched the light for a second or two, turned to see where it was coming from and took aim. Paul pushed the button.

A steady brilliant yellowish, green beam of light shot out and lit up the area where the guard stood. Blinded, he pulled the trigger.

The flashlight was blown off of the top of the rock. Kathryn, who had been holding it in place, felt her hand go numb. She ducked down, holding her wrist and trying to work her fingers.

"Damn!"

"Mom, are you OK?"

"No. I'm not. All of my fingers are tingling!"

"You're lucky," said Rhett. "You coulda lost your whole hand. Why you want to give them a target and then stand behind it?"

"Because I'm stupid! This is not where I want to be or what I want to be doing. All I wanted was sleep without nightmares."

"How's your hand, Mom?"

"I'm not bleeding. It just tingles. I'm OK, and a little wiser."

"I think I got him. I don't see anything."

"Maybe he's reloading," said Rhett.

"He shouldn't be able to see."

"You want to be the first to run across the beach?"

Kathryn stood, rubbing her hand. "Let's try it again. Paul, give me your flashlight."

Paul fumbled with the latch for a minute. "This could

be less complicated."

"Put it on the list," said Rhett with a slight smile.

Paul finally figured it out, turned the light on and handed it to Kathryn. "Don't stand behind it."

"Well..., duh."

Kathryn focused the beam and shined it through Nerissa's rigging. No response. Paul retrieved his flashlight, attached it to his belt, changed the gun's pack from blue to silver and moved over by Rhett.

"Cover me?"

Rhett raised his rifle and pointed it toward the ship. "Got you covered."

"Paul, be careful."

"Well..., duh." He turned and gave her a hug and a smile. "I'm heading for the trees at the bottom of the trail. As soon as I get to one big enough to hide behind, I'll wave. Who's next?"

"It makes no difference to me. Kathryn?"

"I'll go next. Think of it, Rhett. You'll have two of us shooting stars on your behalf."

"Just don't shoot me." He turned his attention back to Nerissa, found a comfortable place to steady his arm, and looked down the barrel of his gun. "Good luck, Paul."

Paul figured he could run the distance in about ten seconds if he were on hard ground. But it appeared that, about halfway across, the sand was thick and dry. Add three or four more seconds. The terrain was also going up. Add another couple of seconds.

He would be running away from Nerissa so the further he got the better his chances of them missing. What did Brock say? Accurate up to one hundred and fifty meters? These guns would be accurate all of the way to the trees. Better to run zigzag. Add another couple of seconds.

He took a deep breath, ensured that the safety on his gun was off and, crouching low, ran at full speed toward the trees.

The first few yards were easy. Sam jumped from rock to rock, hardly getting his boots wet even though he was running at a pretty good clip.

But the next few yards required quick decisions about staying out in the open too long by taking the easier route, stepping into the current to be less of a target, hoping that the smooth rocks below were not too slippery, or taking a chance with the long jumps from rock to rock.

Sam knew that he could make the long jumps, but also figured that Melissa and Brock were watching and guessed that they would try to follow the same path as he. He didn't know if either of them could make the jumps, so he took the easier, longer route.

The bullet hit him in the side of his ribs just below his right arm. The lead caught in his vest and spun him around clockwise. Down on the rocks, water gushing all around, Sam stumbled toward the bank, heading for the log.

Diving in behind it, he heard another shot, this time from the other side of the bank, Brock's gun. He opened his vest and checked the wound, superficial. The lead had been slightly deflected by the webbing of the material. It got caught by the webbing on the other side as it was leaving.

Snitch came alive.

"Sam! You OK?"

"Just a scratch. Did you see where the shot came from?"

"Both of us did. Brock shot at it and I gave it two stars. No idea what happened."

"Don't try to cross. I've got a good angle on their location. I'm going to work my way up. Don't use the laser. You might get me."

"Right."

The grass growing in the area surrounding the log was high enough that, staying on his belly, Sam could inch toward the bottom of the knoll beneath their position.

Peering out from the grass, he saw someone moving in the shadows of the trees, but not looking in his direction. Gun drawn, Sam made a run for the bottom of the embankment and then to a cluster of rocks, bringing him to within fifty feet of their position.

Once at the rocks, Sam could see that the man was moving, but he seemed disoriented. He held onto a tree trunk, let himself down to the ground and then sat there rubbing his eyes. Another man was laid out flat on his back, not moving at all.

Sam advanced slowly, quietly. When he was sure that there were only two at the site, he moved in.

"You by the tree, lay face down on the ground."

"I can't see."

"Lay face down on the ground or I'll shoot."

"You might as well. If I can't see, I'm as good as dead. Go ahead, shoot."

Sam entered the clearing and checked the other man, dead. He had a bullet through his chest and a star in the side of his head. Sam retrieved handcuffs from his pack and snapped them onto the wrists of the sitting man, hands behind his back.

"What's your name?"

"Piss off."

Sam walked out into the open, shined his flashlight in Brock's and Melissa's position and waved. A moment later, Melissa worked her way across the stream.

With her gone, Brock did one last take of the area before following. Looking down, he spotted the flare gun, opened the chamber and removed the spent cartridge, smelling the gunpowder before he threw it to the ground. And then he noticed a fresh cartridge attached to the handle. After carefully tucking the gun into his pants to conceal it, he hurried across the stream and joined them up in the hideout.

Melissa stared at the blood coming from Sam's wound. "That doesn't look good."

"It's not bad."

"Better than him," said Brock, pointing to the dead man. "That's Keenan." He leaned down and inspected the star embedded in his skull. "So, that's a star, huh?"

"Careful. They're razor sharp." Sam turned his attention back to the handcuffed man. "What's your name?"

"I already told ya, piss off."

"His name is Klicker," said Brock. "Makes these clicking sounds when he's tryin' to concentrate on something."

Sam kneeled next to Klicker. "Concentrate on this. How many are up at the cave?"

"Like I said, piss off."

"Klicker, we're going to play a little game. I'm going to ask a question and you're going to answer...,"

"I'm not telling you nothin'."

"I'll ask three times, just so you can change your mind. If I don't get an answer by the third try, I'm going to cut something off. I think I'll start with your left ear."

"I'm not saying nothin'."

"How many more up at the cave?"

"Piss off."

"Strike one. Do you remember the question? Or, do I need to ask it again?"

"Piss off."

"Strike two. How many up at the cave?"

"I don't know who you are. I'm blind. And even if I told you, they would shoot me if they thought I did. So..., piss off."

Sam pulled out his knife, grabbed Klicker's ear and pulled it away from his skull. "I guess you won't be needing this earring anymore."

Brock put his hand on Sam's shoulder. "Wait. Klicker, this is Brock."

"I know who you are."

"You're gonna get your sight back. Isn't that right, Sam?"

"In about another hour or two."

"What caused it?"

"A laser."

"A what? All I saw was a bright light."

"That's all that's necessary," said Sam.

"Klicker," said Brock. "Listen to me. You're gonna get your sight back so don't try and be a hero. I don't know about you, but I'm sick of this island and I'd love to sail out of here. Don't you want that, too?"

"Everybody does."

"Wouldn't you like to have both ears when you go?"

"I see what you're trying to do. Piss off."

"What's the one thing between you and going home?"

"Two, Sanjay and Bardolf."

"We're going up there to kill them. Whose side do you want to be on?"

"The one that's leaving. But you won't kill them. He's got that magical stone. He can see everything. He's probably watching us right now."

"He can do that?"

"I've seen him appear, just like a ghost. Right out of thin air. Don't know that he can hurt me, but I do know he's watching. I'm already a dead man for telling you that."

"Klicker, listen to me. This is our chance, our only chance to get out of here. These folks are on a mission. They're green and they're very odd..., but they're good. We all want the same thing, to be rid of Bardolf. Who was that girl in Mogadishu that you left behind? Don't you want to see her again?"

A long moment of silence passed between them, the calming sound of the stream nearby, Klicker squirming in his handcuffs.

"Take these off, will you? I can't hurt nobody."

"First, answer me one question. I thought we were on the same side. Why were you part of the mutiny?"

"I didn't want to be. Sanjay said he'd cut me up if I didn't help." A long sigh. "If somebody can guide me, I'll show you the way. But you have to give me protection and you have to promise to kill me if you think you're gonna lose. Cause I don't want to be alive if they win."

It was the glint of light reflecting off of the star that caught Melissa's eye, a razor edged, polished piece of steel glowing in the moon's light, wedged into the pool of blood from what used to be a living man's face.

There was no way of denying that she had done it, no way of convincing herself that it had come from some other gun.

What did it feel like, getting hit with a piece of razor sharp steel traveling as fast as a bullet? Would it hurt? Or, would it just cut it's way through, severing everything down to the bone, painless until the nerves had a chance to catch up?

What kind of life did he have? Where was his family? Were they expecting him? Did he have any children? A wife? What will they think when he never comes home?

The moon was directly overhead now, blue shafts of light cutting sharply through the branches of the trees, splitting the undergrowth into an abstract pattern of black and blue, a place where, just minutes ago was the dead man's protection.

He had looked out over that stream. And he had heard those sounds of water gushing through the rocks, giving the false impression that everything was OK.

It was not. Melissa began to cry. "What was his name?"

"Keenan," Brock replied, quietly.

"Did he have family?"

"A girlfriend," said Klicker. "He signed up to get enough money so they could get married. He didn't want to be part of the mutiny either."

"I killed him."

"No, you didn't. I shot first. It went straight through his heart. He was already dying before you pulled the trigger."

"I did not help his cause."

"His cause," said Sam, "was to keep us from crossing

286

the stream. He paid for that and, if anything, you put him out of his misery a little sooner."

Melissa removed the silver pack from her gun and replaced it with the blue. "I'm not shooting stars anymore."

Hands free, Klicker went back to rubbing his eyes. He stopped long enough to shake his head and stared blankly at the ground. "I'm hearing a young girl saying she won't shoot stars? I don't understand."

Brock extended his hand and helped Klicker to his feet. "You don't have to. I don't either. But at least now I'm on this side of the stream. And that's one step closer to boarding Nerissa and heading for home."

Only twenty feet to go and this man steps out of the trees and points the gun.

Sam had spent excessive amounts of time teaching them about that, the line of attack, the moment of intent, the peak of the action.

Don't look at their hands or feet, they're too fast. You'll be in a react rather than an act mode. Shoulders move more slowly and give the same information. Go with the flow.

They had spent hours, eyes closed, standing before a partner, tapping their leg when they thought the strike was coming.

Wait for their mind to create intent. You will feel it.

At first, all three of them thought Sam had gone over the line, professing to know when the attacker would cut with a knife, strike a blow, pull the trigger.

But what they found was that, after hours and hours of training, standing a foot away from someone, that there was a disturbance in their own minds, much like a pebble falling into a calm pond, creating a ripple, the moment of attack.

When Paul saw the barrel swing into his line of sight, and when he saw the gun being leveled, he dove into a forward roll moving to his right as the shot rang out.

The next forward roll took him left, within striking distance. He used his forward momentum, hitting with his shoulder against the man's knees while holding his heels with his hands. The man went down like a sawed off tree trunk.

Still on his back, the man brought the rifle butt straight down onto Paul, who turned his head sideways. The wood missed his face but tore over his left ear.

Struggling over the gun, Paul got to his feet and tried to pull it away. The man stumbled upward and, still maintaining his grip on the gun, charged into Paul.

He wasn't expecting it, Paul suddenly going down in

the same direction, rolling backwards, kicking his foot up between the man's legs and flipping him over the top. He hit flat on his back with a hefty thud.

Kathryn arrived, gun drawn, grabbed the man's hair and put the gun up to his temple. "Don't make me pull this trigger. Paul, you OK?"

"I'm fine."

"Your ear is bleeding."

"Is it? It burns a little bit."

"Scared the bee-geezies out of me. You sure you're not shot?"

Paul checked himself, looking for blood, moving this way or that, brushing himself off. "Nope. Perfect, as usual."

"Not your ear."

Rhett joined them and tied the man's hands behind his back. "His name is Raja. He is Sanjay's brother-in law."

"And you are a dead man, traitor Rhett. Wait until you see what we have in store for you."

Capn didn't know how he did it. Somehow the leash got caught on something over there, and circling around and around and around, no matter which way he tried to go, the tangle only got worse.

There was nothing to do but wait. Surely somebody will come along and lend a hand, somebody that understands the complexities of a twenty foot leash. Problem is, it's night. Everybody's asleep.

The frog was nowhere to be found. Surely it wouldn't have left this perfect spot, not with the long protective trunk of the tree laying out into the water, plenty of places to hide, lots of mud, a stretch of shade no matter what time of the day and, judging from the multitude of bugs, plenty to eat.

"Hello, frog. Are you here?"

It was this nagging feeling, constant, unrelenting, the steady pulling pressure around his neck that was most bothersome. And it was apparent that the leash had a mind of its own. Capn laid down in the mud next to the trunk, picked up a section of the leather and began to chew.

Far had heard the humans long before he saw them and followed their sounds until they came up out of the fog. He noticed that the dog was tethered and was wondering about that. When the dog escaped, he followed.

This dog attracts attention. Easier and safer to not get involved. Best to stay away. Still, he helped us when we needed it...,

"Do you remember me?"

Capn dropped the leash, stood and shook off the mud. "Of course. Mother and baby."

"Do you want help?"

"Don't know how this happened. Do you know how it works?"

Precisely the thing that Far liked most, having to figure things out, just like that lock back in Nerissa's belly.

He studied the tangled mess, pushing here, pulling there and attempting to figure out how it would come loose.

"You have to go back the other way."

"I would, but I'm stuck."

"Wait." Far studied all of the complicated things the dog had done to where get he was and then looked at Capn's collar, where all of the trouble seemed to originate. Easier to look there first. "I'll try to remove this thing.

"My collar? Are you sure?"

"Yes. It's what's keeping you stuck to that."

"I've been told that a collar is a good thing."

"Who said that?"

"I was told that to get out of a cage, you have to have a collar."

"Well, it's not helping you now."

"And I'm not in a cage. Can you do it?"

Holding the leash, Far pulled Capn toward the trunk, trying to get enough slack to undo the first tangle, a nub of a broken branch wedged down into the mud. "If we get this loose, I can look at the collar. Tell me, why did you come back?"

They stopped at a fork in the trail, Sam looking in the direction heading north while Brock inspected the one heading east, up. Melissa offered water to Klicker, who gratefully accepted.

"I think my eyesight is getting better. I'm starting to be able to focus."

"Probably another hour," said Sam. "We're at a fork in the trail. Which way?"

"Is there a stand of pines blocking our view of the lake?"

"Yes."

"The trail splits?"

"Yes."

"Take the one going up. It's a short hike. You'll come to a very large rock, almost vertical. Don't approach it directly. Sometimes they post a guard on top. They'll have one there tonight."

"Is there a way around?"

"If we stay on the left side of the trail, we'll be on the lower side. That's the way I would go. There's better cover than if we take the higher side. The disadvantage is, if we're discovered, they're on higher ground."

"What kind of cover?"

Klicker smiled. "You're asking a blind man? Rocks, trees, the usual. I don't know. I've always taken the trail. You've got that, what was it? A laser?"

"Right."

"Use that. It worked on me. I couldn't even shoot my foot right now if I had a gun."

"We'll use it if we have to. I'm hoping we can just sneak by. Any idea on how many might be there?"

"Probably just one...,"

Smitty was laid out on top of the big rock. He had seen the flare, thought he heard gunshots coming from down by the crossing, but if they were heading this way they'd have to be blind to take this long.

He was tired of sitting on top of the rock, it was round and hard to sit on. Not a little round, no, bigger than that. This was big enough that he could find several places to sit, all of them uncomfortable and out in the open.

The rest of the rock wasn't that round. Parts of it were quite comfortable if you have to stay on the rock for four or five hours. But from those places you couldn't see what you were supposed to be looking for.

So it was a steady trip up and down most of the time, being uncomfortable but aware of who was on the trail or being comfortable twenty feet lower but afraid to linger.

Laying out near the top wasn't too bad, but since that whole area was uniformly round, it was hard to lay out differently to give yourself a break. But that's what he was doing now, laying out on top of the rock uncomfortably.

He didn't know exactly what he was supposed to do if somebody unauthorized came up the road. Nobody had ever done that. He figured that he'd shoot first and ask questions later. Safer that way.

But he started thinking, if I shoot the wrong person..., well, I could get killed for that. Better to know who you're going to shoot.

He decided to practice. He raised his head above the rock and looked down on the trail. "Halt! Who goes there?"

Down in the brush, Sam stopped, turned and motioned for the others to be quiet. "Did you hear something?"

"I thought I did," Melissa whispered. "But it was weak. I don't know. I was concentrating on where I was stepping."

Smitty was thinking that just telling someone to halt and not giving them a good reason was just not smart. Better to sound more authoritative, something louder like, "Stop! Or I'll shoot!"

Yeah, that's better.

"I heard *that*," Melissa whispered. "Do you think he saw us?"

"I don't see how," Sam admitted. "We're totally under cover and we've been quiet."

"Must've," said Brock. "But I don't see how either."

"That's Smitty," said Klicker. "Don't hurt him. He's a good guy."

"He's got a gun," said Sam.

Just for grins, Smitty decided to try the ultimate, since there was nothing else to do. "Last warning! Hands up or I'll shoot! Come on out!"

"Let me talk to him," said Klicker. "He knows me. He won't shoot."

Everybody looked at Sam. "I don't like it. We should just take him out."

"Not with a star," said Melissa. "I won't ever forgive you. How about a tranquilizer?"

"You haven't been on that rock," said Klicker. "You put him to sleep and he'll break his neck. Might as well just shoot him and be done with it. Like I said, let me talk to him."

Sam didn't like it, but nodded. "Go for it."

Klicker cupped his hands. "Smitty, it's me, Klicker. Don't shoot."

Smitty wasn't even looking over there. "What?"

"It's me, Klicker. Don't shoot."

"Klicker? What are you doing down there?"

"I'm, uh, taking a leak."

"I didn't see you come up the trail."

"Yeah, uh, I didn't know when I'd need to piss."

"You're gettin' old, Klicker. Come on up when you're done. I need help stayin' awake."

"I'd like to, Smitty. But I gotta go see the boss man."

"What was that fireball? You know anything about it?"

"I saw it. Came from the other side of the stream. Not sure what caused it."

"Did I hear gunshots a while ago?"

"That was me. I tripped while I had the safety off."

"Thought I heard two shots."

"Might've been an echo."

"When you're finished there, Klicker. Come up here for a minute. We gotta talk."

"Uh, right." Klicker turned back to the others and whispered, "What am I gonna do? I still can't see."

"Tell him you'll come back after you've talked to the boss," said Sam.

"Right. He's going to expect me to take the trail after I take my leak. How will I explain that?"

"I'll go with him," said Brock. "We'll tell him I was gonna give myself up and you fell while arresting me. You banged your head and can't see very well so I'm helping you back to your camp."

Klicker was making those sounds again, putting his tongue against the front of his teeth and sucking air in through the back. Click, click. "Won't work. We've got orders to shoot you on sight. He'll know something's up."

"We could leave you here to talk with Smitty," said Sam. "We'll go on ahead and...,"

"No. You don't. You can't leave me unprotected. It will be a horrible death."

Melissa was beginning to lose patience. "Let's just tell him the truth. Does he want to go home?"

Everybody stopped and stared at Melissa.

"What?"

"No, we can't do that. He'd never believe us."

"He has to believe us. We're here."

"He'll shoot you."

"He only has one shot."

"Right. Who's going to take it?"

"I knew this was a bad idea," said Sam. "Now, let's think of it like this...,"

Smitty laughed. "Klicker, you OK? You didn't poop yourself to death, did ya?"

"Smitty, you wouldn't believe it even if I told you."

"Did you get some of Sulley's stew? I thought it burned pretty bad going in, but the worst part was still to come. Whew! Coulda burned down the whole island if someone had lit a fire."

"Smitty, I'm gonna tell you something, and you're not going to believe me. But I want you to try."

Smitty laughed. "I don't believe anything anybody says anymore."

"Try this. I've been blinded by a beam of light. I can't see. Keenan's dead. I've been abducted by Brock and visitors from the future. How does that grab ya?"

"What've you been drinkin', Klicker? I want some of that."

"I'm not lying, Smitty. Answer me this, do you want to go home?"

Funny how that works. Everybody is a good friend as long as you're on the same side. Suspicion is a twisting, slippery sort of thing.

Smitty quietly nudged his rifle close enough that he could get his finger on the trigger and pointed his gun down toward Klicker's voice. "What?"

Paul was sick of Raja. Ever since they'd made him their prisoner, he'd made a lot of noise, misled them several times about the way up, and now he was making lewd comments about his mother's body.

Paul stopped abruptly, turned around and slapped Raja. "Watch your mouth, scum bag."

"For you," said Raja, grimacing under the sting. "We'll cut off one piece at a time and watch you bleed to death. For you mother, we have other plans. We will...,"

"Mom, why don't you walk back there with Rhett?"

"It's OK. I don't listen to him anyway."

"But..., I do."

Kathryn nudged Paul ahead. "We have more important things to do. Keep going."

Paul turned and headed up the trail. It had taken them a while to find this one. Raja was deceitful with his eyes, shifty and smiling, having fun with their confusion, laughing at their ignorance. Moving up the trail, Paul quietly removed the star pack and inserted the blue.

"Yes," said Raja. "Your mother and me, we will dance under the moon and...,"

Paul clicked off the safety, turned around and shot him. "Now, you'll be quiet."

Raja doubled over and fell to the ground with a string of curses. His hands were tied behind his back and there was a short rope tied between his ankles so he couldn't run. He writhed on the ground like a snake, convulsing and screaming.

He was shot in the leg, but it wasn't a bullet. It shouldn't hurt that much. The man on Nerissa, didn't he react like it was a sting? Of course, this was fifty yards closer.

"Paul! I can't believe you did that!"

"Mom, he was slowing us down."

"We could have used him for bargaining."

Raja was slurring his words now. His eyes were starting to glaze over.

"He was dangerous to us. Now we can move."

"What are we going to do with him?"

"Nothing. He's got to sleep it off."

"And leave him tied up? What if the animals get him?"

"Oh, well. Mom, he tried to shoot me. Whose side are you on?"

"That's a dumb question."

"I agree with Paul," said Rhett. "And I think we should gag him, just to make sure he stays quiet."

"He could die here."

"Kathryn, I've seen this man stab another just for looking at him the wrong way. It won't bother me if the animals eat him alive."

"Me, either. Mom, we have to come back this way. We can decide what to do with him then."

Kathryn didn't like it, but there wasn't much she could do. Raja was now dead weight. "OK. Let's move him off of the trail. How about over there in the bushes? And then we'll mark the spot. How can we do that?"

Rhett grabbed hold of a small sapling and snapped the trunk so that it laid across the trail.

"There. Paul. Grab his feet. I'll get his shoulders."

With Raja out of the way, their progress was much faster. Glancing down at Snitch, Kathryn could see that they were catching up to Sam and Melissa. "We're only a quarter mile behind them. I'll feel a whole lot better when we're all together again."

Paul quickened his pace. "What did we gain by splitting up?"

"What?"

"We split up into two groups, Mom. How did that help us?"

Hiking behind Kathryn, Rhett cleared his throat. "We've got control of the path from Nerissa up to the cave. Nerissa's probably ours for the taking, and Raja can't help them now. That's a good start."

A mist began to form across the trail between Smitty and the others, glowing thinly with a touch of blue.

"What the heck is that?" Melissa whispered, peering up between the branches.

Carefully inching his way forward, taking baby steps so he wouldn't trip over anything, Klicker moved out into the opening to get a better view. "I can see a blue glow. Is there a shape forming inside?"

The mist began to gather, swirling back upon itself, creating a window of light inside of which a form began to take shape.

"Something's happening," said Sam."

Klicker was rubbing his eyes again. "What does it look like?"

"Something's glowing," said Melissa. "What is it?"

Click. Click. "That, my friends, is Bardolf."

"It's just an image," said Sam. "He cannot physically harm us."

"An energy field," said Melissa. "He must be projecting through the fire stone!"

Bardolf casually turned and looked down at Klicker, shaking his head slowly side to side, made a gesture, left thumb up, forefinger pointing down at Klicker, and then turned back to Smitty with a nod of his head to shoot.

"I..., I'm wondering whose side he's on," Smitty stammered.

Bardolf made the motion again, this time a bit more forcefully.

"He's my friend."

"Don't mind him," said Klicker. "He's just a ghost. He can't hurt you."

Bardolf pointed up at Smitty with a look of disgust and made a gesture that his throat would be cut.

"Dang it, Klicker. I don't want to shoot you!"

"Then, don't!"

"He's gonna kill me if I don't."

"He's just a ghost, Smitty. Besides I still owe you twenty...,"

"You owe me forty," said Smitty. "You keep tryin' to cheat me out of that."

"Don't you remember when I doubled down and won?"

"No."

"That's because you were drunk. I kept trying to get you to stop."

"You kept given' me the bottle."

"I don't believe this," Sam whispered. "Let's break for a commercial."

"Smitty. We're going up to the cave, me and Brock and two others. Go with us."

Sam rolled his eyes, shook his head and whispered angrily. "Don't say that! Don't tell him anything!"

"What happened to Keenan?"

"I shot him," said Brock. "I didn't mean to kill him. He shot first. Not that it makes it any better."

"What are you going to do at the cave?"

Bardolf had been following the conversation with amusement, smiling at the exchange of information. With that last question, he put his hands on his hips, cocked his head in a sarcastic manner and looked down at Klicker questionably, eyebrows raised.

Click, click..., click. "Well, first I have to get there."

Bardolf opened his arms in a welcoming gesture, inviting them up to the trail. Klicker looked back at the others. "Uh, guys?"

"I'd rather eat poisonous snakes," said Brock. "It's a trap."

Melissa shook her head. "I'm with Brock on this one. Sam?"

Sam was shaking his head. "No. We're not going up on the trail. So much for stealth. Brock? How about you take Klicker up on the trail? Easier for him to walk. We'll cover from down here."

Click..., click. "Excuse me. He's pointing that gun and they're looking for an answer."

Sam turned sharply. "You're the one who walked out

into the open! You're the one who wanted to talk to the nice man!"

"Laser?" Brock suggested.

Melissa didn't like that idea. "He'll fall off of the rock."

Sam was about ready to take off on his own. None of this would have happened if it was just him. Let them argue it out. "You can't have compassion for someone who's holding a gun on you."

"OK. I agree. Brock goes up there with Klicker and they take the trail with Bardolf. We follow and keep an eye out from down here."

Brock sucked in his next breath through clenched teeth. "We're going to be dead men walking. I'm keeping my gun."

Click, click. "I heard that."

Hairs on the back of his neck suddenly tingling at the thought of it, Sam turned. How simple. Effective. Bardolf's a ruse! He motioned for Brock and Melissa to get down and be ready. Something was back there, back in the trees where the shadows prevail.

Snitch came to life. "Anybody home?"

"Kathryn," Melissa whispered. "Snitch is saying you're about a quarter mile away. How are you doing?"

"Working our way up. How about you?"

"We've got a blind prisoner who claims to be on our side, Bardolf's ghost glowing up there on the ridge and a gun aimed at us. If you happen onto a trail that leads up to a large rock, about thirty feet high, go around, stay quiet. Unlike us."

"We're on our way."

Paul stopped, looked over his shoulder and whispered. "We're joining another trail."

Kathryn, looking left and right, stopped to check Snitch. "Go right."

"Looks like it's pretty well traveled. Should we stay on it? Or, off to the side?"

Rhett caught up to them. "We're going up, right? Looks like that's the way."

Paul exchanged the blue pack for the silver, pushing until he heard it click into place. The LED displayed the change, now glowing white.

"Don't know if anybody's noticed yet," said Rhett. "But we've got some clouds coming in."

"Good cover for us," said Kathryn.

Rhett nudged Paul and Kathryn ahead. "Make tracks while we can. If those clouds keep coming in, we won't be able to see."

"We've got night vision goggles," said Kathryn, nudging Paul forward. "Let's go."

"What are those?"

"We put them over our eyes. We can see in the dark."

"There is such a thing? How does it work?"

"Ask Sam, if we ever catch up to them. Come on, Paul. Move it."

"On or off the trail. That was the question."

Kathryn glanced over at Rhett. "On?"

"On. Hurry, before it gets dark."

"For you," said Paul turning right and heading up. "We have a flashlight."

"Is that the same thing she had before it got shot up?"

"Right."

"Good point," said Kathryn. "If you're holding a light, don't hold it in front of you."

Mountain looming up on their right, with it's ridges and gullies, stands of trees and pockets of coastal shrub glowing in the moonlight, and a forest on their left growing up from the downward sloping terrain, they crunched their way upward, catching only intermittent views of the lake.

Paul glanced down at Snitch. "They're only a few hundred yards ahead of us."

"I've been watching," said Kathryn. "They've come to a stop."

"Think I just heard a gunshot," said Rhett.

Snitch came to life. "Hey, guys. Melissa here. We see you're coming up behind us. We've got someone shooting at us from our rear, somewhere between you and us. A little help?"

"We're on it," said Paul. "Any idea where they are?"

"The shot came straight through, parallel to the trail, I think."

"How can you know that?"

"Simple, dummy. Where the sound came from and where the bullet went. They're probably only fifty feet off of the trail, same as us."

"OK. We're on our way."

"Hey!"

"What?"

"Don't use your laser. You might get us."

"Right. Hey!"

"What?"

"You're on the downhill side, right?"

"Right. Watch where you shoot those stars, too. I hate those things."

Stepping off of the path, they hiked around and through the undergrowth that hogged the area between the trail, rocks and trees. Their progress was slow but quiet.

Pop!

Something zipped through the leaves above their heads, knocking branches loose and ending with a thud into a tree trunk somewhere behind them.

Paul ducked left and hit the ground, Kathryn right behind. Rhett quietly went down to one knee, aimed his rifle and waited. Everyone remained motionless, listening.

"Either they know that we're here," Kathryn whispered.

"Or Sam and Melissa have attackers front and rear." Talking into Snitch, "Bullet just came through. What's happening?"

Melissa: "I'm hiding in a pile of rocks watching our rear, hoping to see you. Brock's guarding our front and Sam has headed back into the trees, says there's something out there."

"Are you being attacked from the front, up toward the cave?"

"Yes. That's where that last shot came from."

"I'll see if Rhett can get to the other side of the trail and come in behind the ones in front of you."

"Right. Sam? You hear all of that?"

"Got it."

Kathryn turned back to Rhett. "Rhett, could you go on the other side of the trail and...,"

"I heard it." He glanced up at the sky. "Clouds are almost on top of us. I won't be able to see. You say you had a light?"

Paul unclipped it from his belt. "Right. Good luck."

Snitch had been a distraction. There was someone just off to the left, over behind those trees, but listening to Kathryn's and Melissa's conversation, whoever was over there had moved. Sam turned Snitch off.

Did they go left or right? Further back?

Staying low, Sam waited, gun in hand, loaded with stars.

Rustling, something moving in the brush to his left. Sam knew he could hit it but didn't want to shoot until he knew who or what it was. He followed the sounds with his gun.

Behind, a twig snapped. Instinctively, Sam rolled to one side as the blade came down. It slashed through the shrubs and then was back in the air, waving menacingly as the attacker charged.

Phht! Phht! Two stars, one in the stomach, one into the shoulder holding the sword. Screaming, the attacker fell to the ground. Sam ran back into the brush, changed the weapons pack to blue, turned and shot him again.

Where's the other one? There were two.

BAM!

The gun was blown out of his hand, Sam's thumb bent over backward with the force, certainly out of the socket. Springfield's, right? They only have one shot.

Holding his hand up against his chest, Sam rushed the shooter's location. He found an older man trying to load another bullet when he came around the tree. Two kicks, one to the groin, one to the head and he was out. Sam took all of his ammo, scattered it out into the trees, broke down the rifle and scattered the parts in different directions. The sword attacker muttered a few more curses and then fell quiet.

Sam's gun was destroyed. The end of the barrel was blown off and what remained was bent, too dangerous even to try and use. He removed the power pack, left the gun where he found it and sat down to figure out how to

305

get his thumb back into its' socket.

Have to use the crossbow now. Can't do it without my thumb.

OK. Take a deep breath. Don't think about it, pull fast and hard, no flinching. This won't hurt.

Rhett was as fascinated with the flashlight as Brock. He also stepped back when Paul first turned it on and thought it would burn if he put his hand in front of the beam. Seeing that it was harmless, he wanted to shine it everywhere.

"That'll get you killed," said Paul. "Point it down at the ground so no one else can see it. And keep it turned off if you don't need it. That'll save the batteries."

"Batteries? Like a battering ram? I know about those."

"Kind of. It pushes the light out into the dark."

When they came upon the big rock, they backed up out of view, Rhett crossed the trail and then all three continued forward. Snitch was showing that Melissa was only a hundred yards ahead.

Nobody was at the big rock. Clouds, drifting in, began snuffing out the moon's light, a little here, a little there, a steady blue glow quietly fading back into the shadows.

Smitty was noticing the clouds as well. Pretty soon it was going to be too dark. Bardolf's instructions were to follow the intruders and shoot to kill. But if they don't show themselves again, it's gonna be too dark.

Am I expected to go after them? Easy for Bardolf to say go do this or go do that. He's not looking at the wrong end of a barrel.

But if I don't like it, what am I gonna do? Nothing, that's right. Easier to do than to have it done to you.

Brock and Klicker, friends on the ship, enemies here. What he said, true? People from the future? Why come here? Don't want to be on the wrong side when this is over.

On the other side of the trail Rhett stopped dead in his tracks. Something had moved in front of him. It wasn't so bright that he could see what, but it was big enough that its motion caught his eye.

He clicked on the flashlight, discovered that he was about to step on a large, coiled up snake, jumped away

307

and fell backward over the rock that he had just stepped around.

Falling, he was careful to not lose or bang the light. But while trying to break his fall, he swung his arms backward in a motion that flashed the beam of light down toward Smitty, hiding in the brush.

That was like nothing Smitty had ever seen, something bright as day coming out of a little tiny opening.

To shoot, or not? Nobody knows where I am. There's nobody around to say that I saw something and didn't shoot. What the heck was that?

Getting up, Rhett kept the light on the snake until it crawled back into the brush. While watching, he discovered that the rim of the light turned. Twisting it this way or that, he realized that the light either grew wider and dimmer, or smaller and brighter.

Would it do that far away as well? He aimed the beam at a more distant rock and discovered that, readjusting the rim, he could bring the beam into focus again.

See how wide it gets? If I turn the rim just a little, it gets smaller, brighter. How does it do that?

Hiding within the leaves and feeling increasingly uncomfortable with this strange light, Smitty pulled the trigger. Whatever it was, he shot it. There was a bright flash of light, more like an explosion actually, and then it was gone.

Paul stopped, turned back to his mother and whispered. "I think Rhett just took a hit. I saw a flash up there."

"Crap! What are we gonna do?"

"I think I know where the shot came from. I'll see if I can get a little closer. Cover me."

"I hope Rhett's OK."

"We gotta get this guy first."

Staying low, running in a crouched position, Paul made his way through the trees, stopping here and there and waiting for Kathryn to join him. Snitch was saying that Melissa was only about fifty yards away.

"There he is!" Paul whispered. He pointed to a slightly built, balding man hiding down in the brush.

"If you can distract him," Paul whispered. "I can circle around and come in from behind."

"And what? Take another prisoner?" Kathryn removed the silver star pack, put in the blue and shot him. Phht! "This way no one gets hurt. All we have to do is wait a minute."

Smitty felt the sting in his shoulder, leaned his gun against a tree trunk and attempted to reach whatever it was that got him. It felt like that bumble bee that stung him on top of his head when he was climbing over a wood-pile last summer, like the sting from the wasps that got him when he dove into a pond back home, not as painful as the nail that he stepped on when he was four. There were lots of times when...,

Rhett was right about the clouds. There is no light on the island once the clouds roll in. Approaching the trail on her belly, Kathryn looked both ways, everything glowing green through her night vision lens. Nobody. She scurried across the flat area and moved up into the rocks.

She was trying to figure out how many were out of the picture. Two on the ship and Raja, that's three. The one they just shot, four. Melissa said they had a blind prisoner and that they shot one, that's six. Didn't Rhett say there were twelve?

"Mom. I got this guy all tied up, turned around and you weren't there. Where are you?"

"I'm on the other side of the trail, looking for Rhett."

"I'm coming across."

"No. Go find Melissa."

"It's not safe for you to...,"

"She needs help. Get over there."

"Mom...,"

"I can take care of myself."

"Hey! Melissa here. We can take care of ourselves, me and Brock."

"We got the shooter at your rear. Shot him with a blue."

"Sam here. Break down his weapon and scatter his ammo."

"Doing that right now," said Paul.

"Sam. I'm trying to keep count. Paul, Rhett and I got four. How many with you guys?"

"Two," said Melissa. "That's six. Sam?"

"Add two more. That's eight. It's going to be nine in a minute."

"Are you killing them?" Melissa asked.

"Only if necessary. I'm going to take out the one in front of you and move up to the cave."

"Are you going to kill him?"

"No, Melissa. Sleep works well if I can get away with it.

It's my first choice. Follow me up?"

"How will we know when?"

"I'll call on Snitch."

"I've found Rhett," said Kathryn. He's down, but conscious. Paul, get over by the trail and I'll try and bring him across."

"Right."

The flashlight had been hit, blown into pieces, one of which appeared to have ricocheted off of the rock and back into the side of Rhett's head, leaving a big gash behind his right ear.

Kathryn sat him up, which helped stop the bleeding, and dug through her first aid kit until she found a bandage large enough to cover it.

"How are you doing, Rhett?"

"What?"

"How are you doing?"

"Feels like my head is split open. How does it look?"

He was speaking loudly, too loudly. Kathryn motioned for him to lower his voice and put her finger to her lips. "Shh."

She cleaned the wound as best she could, applied some antibacterial salve to the area and wrapped gauze around his head to hold it all in place.

Rhett was slow to get up and his balance was not good. She put his arm around her shoulder and held it there while she worked their way down to the trail. Having no moonlight to guide the way, he was hesitant with every step.

"Paul. Where are you?"

"About fifty yards up the trail from the big rock. I don't see you."

"Further back, approaching the trail about twenty yards shy of where I think you are."

"Coming to meet you."

Rhett pulled his arm away from Kathryn. "I can walk. I'm OK. It's too dark. Just can't see."

Kathryn grabbed his hand and led him across the trail. Snitch indicated Paul was located ten yards to her

311

right. Follow the little red 'P' on Snitch's shiny black face. "Paul?"

"Over here."

Paul checked Rhett's wound. "I'm not a doctor, but I think Mom did a pretty good job. How are you feeling?"

"Probably better than it looks. I'm walking. Thanks, Kathryn. Did you get my gun?"

"I didn't even think about it. I'll go get it."

"Mom, let it go."

"No. He's got to have a gun. I'll just be a...,"

"Sam here. I hear your conversation. Add number nine to your list, Kathryn. I'll leave this guy's gun and ammo here for Rhett. If you touch and hold the 'S' on Snitch's face, it will put this position into memory and from then on it will show where I am in relation to it. After you get the gun, push and hold again and this point will be erased."

"Melissa here. What happened to number nine?"

Sam wanted to say, "Sleeping soundly, tied up." But without his gun, the best he could say was, "He met with an accident. Sorry, Melissa. It was quick." Actually, it was a bolt from his crossbow straight through the man's heart. "I'm going to scout ahead a little bit. I'll meet you back at this spot."

Staying on the west side of the clearing, downhill from the surrounding terrain, Sam was watching. There was a man positioned in the trees above the cave, one on the other side of the clearing hunkered down in the rocks, and one lingering around the mouth of the cave. All were armed.

Could take them out right now if I had my gun. Three tranquilizers, no noise.

Let that be a lesson. Next time, if there ever is one, I'll design the guns so that each of us can use the other person's weapon..., and bring a spare.

None of them appeared to be Bardolf, if the image he projected earlier was accurate. That image showed a man with a close-cropped beard, shoulder length hair, stocky build, about six feet tall, big for a man in eighteen eighty-three, black eyes and a crooked, taunting smile.

How long ago was it that they were sitting in the cockpit laughing and joking? Was that only last night? No one had addressed this yet, but even if they were successful at saving Kashif, getting possession of the stone, having Nerissa sail back to her home port, what then?

If a blue moon and the stone combined in some strange way to bring them here, what was their new destiny going to be?

Were they now the new inhabitants of the island, stuck until some new combination of things took them away? How to get back to the future?

Sam turned and headed back down. Clouds were beginning to stir.

Before long everyone will be able to see. Better to attack now while it's still dark.

"Sam here. The coast should be clear. If you head up, I'll meet you somewhere in the middle."

"We're on our way."

"Snitch is showing about two hundred yards between us."

"Anything we need to look out for?"

"No, it's clear. I still wouldn't walk on the trail. There are three guards around the mouth of the cave. As you approach, one is on the east side, up in the rocks. Someone needs to come in above him...,"

"Melissa here. I'll do it."

"I'll go with her," said Paul.

"Not if you're going to shoot stars."

"Sam? How do I answer that?"

"Let Melissa lead and let her make the shot, blue pack. If your lives are in danger, Paul, shoot stars. That work for you, Melissa?"

"Perfect. Thank you."

"Kathryn here. Where are the other two?"

"One is above the cave. I'll get that one. The other is in and out of the entrance. I'll close in from above."

"Sounds like a laser moment," said Paul.

"Not before we take out the other two."

"OK, everybody. Radio silence unless it's an emergency. Report in when you've got your man."

Melissa wanted to get a little closer, just to be sure she wouldn't miss. He was hiding in the rocks overlooking the entrance to the cave, fifty feet below their position.

Coming out of nowhere, Ekko swooped over their heads, squawking like a murder of crows. Both of them were looking up when the guard turned, spotted them and got off a quick shot. The bullet zipped through the empty space between them, hit some distant rock and ricocheted off. Melissa hit the ground and crawled for the next available rock.

Paul shot off two stars, both misses, then joined Melissa behind the rock. "Holy crap! He almost got us!"

Melissa pulled him to the ground. "Get down, you fool!"

"So much for surprise. Flippin' bird!"

Ekko circled above them making as much noise as she could. Paul took aim. Melissa pushed his arm off target.

"No! You're not going to shoot it."

"What? Are you crazy? It's giving our position away!"

"She's already done that. No reason to shoot her now."

"I can't believe it. You're killing us!"

"Kathryn here. You two OK?"

"We're OK. The bird spotted us and..., Paul. Where are you going?"

"Away from you. You're going to get me killed."

"What?"

"I'm going to get on the other side of that guy. Cover me."

"Stay here."

"If I stay, he's got one target. We're better off splitting up. He'll have two of us to worry about."

"The bird's just going to follow you."

"It'll have to go back and forth between us. That guy will know where we are, but he'll have to turn his back on one of us."

"Paul, stay where you are."

"Mom, she won't even let me shoot the bird. I gotta get away."

"Sam here. Will all three of you please be quiet? Paul, stay there. We'll get him in a minute."

"Did you hear that?" Melissa whispered.

Paul turned his head slightly, listening. "Hear what? Take off your goggles. We can see better without them now."

"Thought I heard a crunching sound."

"Crunching? Like..., what?"

"Like boots on the ground, dummy."

"I didn't hear it."

"Shh. Just listen."

"Take off your goggles."

"You're right. Tranquilizers won't work, will they?"

"It's a good idea until they know where you are."

"He could shoot a couple of times before he's asleep."

"Yep."

"You have my permission to use stars."

"Thank you. I was going to anyway. How about the bird?"

"No. It's only doing what it's been trained to..., there! I heard it again! Did you hear...,"

"Shh. Stay close to the rock. First thing I see move is going to get it."

Grub approached Paul's and Melissa's hiding place on his hands and knees. He would have gone up the hill with his hands above his head, but if someone down at the cave saw him doing that he would be shot. Crawling was the only option.

"Hey!" He whispered. "Don't shoot. I'm unarmed."

"Stand up where I can see you," Paul replied, trying to make his voice deep and authoritative.

Melissa started to laugh.

"I can't stand up. If they see me giving up, they'll shoot me."

"Show yourself."

"You won't shoot?"

"My finger's on the trigger. Show yourself."

"I can't put my hands up. I'm crawling."

"Then keep your hands on the ground. Show yourself."

Grub crawled into view. If standing, Paul figured that he'd be a small man, about five-five, slim build, wearing dirty, ragged clothes and missing a front tooth. "I'm giving myself up. Take me prisoner."

"I don't want a prisoner."

"Well, you got one now."

"Where's your gun?"

Grub pointed back to his old spot. "Down there."

"You have any other weapons?

"Just my bad breath."

"Get back down there, get your gun and let's battle it out."

"I don't want to battle it out. I want to go home and you're the best thing that's come along since we got here."

"How long you been here?" Melissa asked.

Grub looked over at Melissa, seeing her for the first time. "A girl? I'm being rescued by a girl?"

"We're not rescuing you."

"You're going to get shot by a girl in just a second. Yeah. I'm a girl. What about it?"

"I just thought that..., that."

"Thought what? That a girl can't *do* anything?"

"Let it go," said Paul. "We don't want a prisoner."

"OK," said Grub, with a sigh. "I guess I'll just tag along."

"Sam here. Charley's on vacation."

Grub looked around. "Who said that?"

"You don't need to know," Paul replied.

"The voice came out of nowhere."

"Yes. It did. Now, you have to go away."

"I'm your prisoner."

"No. You're not."

"Would you shoot Bardolf if you got a chance?" Melissa asked.

"It won't do any good. Bullets go right through him. Doesn't bother him a bit."

"You've tried it?"

"No. Robbins did. He's dead. Throat got cut night after he tried it. Sanjay doesn't care who he kills..., or why."

"Why don't all of you mutiny and kill Sanjay?"

"Lady, we don't know who's on what side. Talk to the wrong person and you'll be dead before morning."

"Sam here. I think we can all start closing in on the cave."

"This is a better way to go," said Grub, crawling alongside Paul and Melissa. "If you go that way, you're gonna be out in the open when you get to the cave."

"What am I, nuts?" Paul asked. "I can't trust you."

"You're going to take us right into the line of fire. You're putting my life in danger."

"You are not my prisoner. Go away."

"Which way would you go?" Melissa asked.

Grub pointed to another path, going up and north, looking like it had never been traveled. "This way gives you better cover and it comes out just to the right of the cave. You'll have cover when you get there, too."

"Paul? Sounds good to me."

"We can't trust him. He's not one of us."

"But I am tagging along," said Grub. "So I'm kinda worried about me. If we go that way, I might get shot."

"Then don't tag along. Get out of here."

"If you haven't noticed," said Grub. "The bird is gone. He thinks it's OK 'cause you're with me. If we split up, he's comin' back."

"Crap!" Paul talked into Snitch, "Sam? We got us a prisoner here. What do you want us to do with him?"

"Tie him up and break down his weapon."

Grub stared at Paul's and Melissa's wrists, where the voice had come from. "I don't have a weapon. And I'm not his prisoner. I'm just tagging along."

"Who is this?"

"I don't know," said Paul. "He just crawled out of the bushes and said he was my prisoner."

"Is he? Or, isn't he?"

Grub nodded approvingly and looked over at Paul with a big grin. "Name's Grub. Who are you? And how come you're talkin' out of this guy's wrist?"

"Grub," said Sam. "Listen to me. You are endangering our mission and if you interfere, we will have to kill you. Understand?"

319

"I'm just tryin' to help. They're gonna walk into a trap and I'm tryin' to warn them."

"What kind of trap?"

"If they go the way they're gonna go, they're going to walk right into the open with no cover. One of them, for sure, is gonna get shot. I'm sayin' come in from the side."

"Paul? What do you think of that?"

"I don't know. That's why I called you."

"Paul. Let Grub lead the way. If you run into trouble, he's the first one you shoot. And shoot to kill. Grub? You hear that?"

"Yeah, Boss. I heard that loud and clear."

"Kathryn here. Do you want us to go straight up the trail?"

"No. Approach the cave, stay off the trail. Detain anyone coming or going if at all possible."

"Look like you got a whole army in that wrist of yours," said Grub. "I hear voices, but no one's around."

Paul nudged Grub forward. "And that's the way we're going to keep it. OK, Sam. We're following Grub. Meet you at the cave."

Sulley came out of the cave holding a rifle and looking confused. He had been told to shoot anything that moves. He had never actually shot the gun before but he had been shown how to aim, pull the trigger and reload. He had been given ten bullets, nine of which were in his pocket.

Sulley was not too happy about his new situation. Kill or be killed was something he had always believed in. But this set of orders implied that if he didn't kill or be killed by his enemy, he would be killed by those three men back in the cave with guns pointed at him.

Bullets from the front? Or bullets from the rear? Which is better? Which hurts less and makes it easier to die? That's the real question here.

He wandered out through the entrance, couldn't see anyone coming up the trail, noticed that the moon was already sinking into the west and, glancing up at Grub's position, saw no one over there either. Somebody got off a shot. He looked longingly to his right, into the shadows of the trees leading down to the lake.

If I'm gonna go, that would be a good place, drinking and fishing. Better to die doin' that than what I'm doin' now.

Thought I'd killed them with the mushrooms in the stew but they wanted more. Finding non-poisonous mushrooms. What are the odds of that?

The voice, a man's voice, came from above the mouth of the cave. "Drop your weapon or I'll shoot."

Sulley lowered his rifle and started to turn. "Don't shoot. I'm...,"

"Stop! Do *not* turn around or I *will* shoot."

"Is it gonna hurt?" Sulley asked.

"What?"

"Is it gonna hurt? If I drop my gun, them guys in the cave are gonna shoot me. If I don't drop it, yer gonna shoot me. Either way I'm gonna get shot so I'm wonderin' which is gonna hurt less and which one might let me live.

Can't ya just shoot me in the leg?"

"Shut up. Stand still. Don't move. Paul, Melissa? Where are you?"

"Climbing down toward the cave," said Paul. "The other way would've been faster."

"I'm covering the guy who might've shot you."

"Kathryn here. Snitch is saying you're only a hundred feet in front of us, but we can't see you."

"Do not come up on the trail. You'll be in their line of fire."

"Including me," said Sulley. "Who are ya talkin' to?"

"Paul here. We're at the bottom. We see the guy you're talking to. Grub says his name is Sulley."

"Approaching from below," said Kathryn. "We see the cave. We can see Sulley. What now?"

"Who has laser capacity?"

Melissa clicked on. "I do."

"Me, too," said Kathryn.

"Sulley, how far back does the cave go?"

"I can't tell ya that."

"How many are in there?"

"I can't tell ya that either."

"Can they hear our conversation?"

"I can't say nothin'. How'd ya know my name? I don't know ya."

"Doesn't matter," said Sam, speaking a bit more softly. "When I say run, I want you to go left, over to those rocks as fast as you can."

"I can't run, got bad knees."

"Then maybe you can get low and hobble."

"If I get low, I fall down."

"Then stay there, close your eyes and...,"

"I got it," said Sulley. "Kiss my rear end good bye. That's what yer sayin', ain't it?"

"All I'm saying is...,"

"I'm just the cook! Why am I the one that's gotta get shot when all of ya have the problem?"

"I'm trying to help you, Sulley."

"Well, it ain't workin'." Looking over his shoulder, Sulley yelled back into the cave. "Mister Bardolf, what do ya want from these people? And you up there, what is it ya want? Ya gotta talk and get me outta the middle!"

For a moment it was so quiet that even the moonbeams seemed to make sounds, humming softly onto Sulley's hunched shoulders and wincing face. He held his gun pointed down, finger off of the trigger.

A soft breeze worked its way up through the trees, fresh, clean and, if not for the situation, peaceful. Everyone waited.

"Bardolf," Sam yelled. "We've come for Kashif and we've come for the stone. Hand them over and we'll let you live."

"Not good," said Sulley.

"We give you Kashif for the dog. We keep the stone and we let you live."

Sulley looked left, to where he had been told to run and spotted Grub, who waved and ducked back behind the rocks. There were voices out there in the trees, sounds like a woman's, but too muffled to hear any words.

"Kathryn here. Where is Capn? Anybody seen him?"

"Paul here. No. Why would he want the dog?"

"It's obviously connected to the stone," said Melissa. "Maybe they've gotten all they can get out of Kashif and Capn is the key."

"But why?"

"Doesn't matter," said Sam. "None of us have him. They're counter offer is non-negotiable. How to proceed?"

"I think we...," said Kathryn. "Wait. Rhett and Brock are leaving. Where are you two going?"

"Kathryn. You got us this far and it's much appreciated. Now, it's our turn."

"What are you going to do?"

"We're going to light up the inside of that cave."

"How?"

Brock pulled out Sam's flare gun from inside his shirt, opened the chamber and inserted the new cartridge. "I got one shot. I just need to get close enough to put it in

323

there."

"Hey Brock," said Grub. "I hear you talking out of this guy's wrist. You OK?"

"Grub? Whose side you on?"

"Yours, you old fart! You going into the cave?"

"Hope to."

"Wait. I'll get my gun and join you."

"Don't shoot the flare into the cave," said Sam. "It burns very hot. The fumes are toxic and...,"

"They're leaving," said Kathryn.

"Grub. This is Sam. How far back does that cave go?"

"About thirty meters," said Grub, turning to go. "And about ten wide, once you get inside."

"The range on that flare is about a hundred yards," said Sam. "It might ricochet around and come right back out. Wait before we go in."

"Same thing for lead," said Paul.

"Or stars," said Melissa.

"The air will be toxic. You three, stay outside and stop anybody trying to leave. I'll go in and get Kashif."

"I want to go in," said Paul.

"If Brock and Rhett want to take care of business, that's fine with me. We'll be their backups."

"Melissa here. Grub's back with his rifle. Looks like they're going to rush the cave."

Grub held his rifle up and waved from the other side of the trail. Brock confirmed that his own gun was loaded and ready, cradled it in his left arm and made his way over to the left side of the mouth of the cave.

The entrance was only about twenty feet across. Brock figured that he had about one second to peer inside and get his shot off. How far back were they? If it was only a few feet, they could take aim quickly.

Sulley spotted Brock as soon as he stepped up onto the trail but looked away, down the path toward Nerissa, up at the sky and over to the rocks where he had spotted Grub.

Whatever was going to happen was going to take place in the next few seconds and his heart was pounding. As soon as the first shot was fired he was going to drop to the ground and crawl away if he still could.

Above the mouth of the cave, Sam quietly waited, watching everyone get into place. He would've preferred his gun. Next time, bring a spare. It wouldn't have been that hard to make one more.

He held the crossbow at the ready. It was a lightweight model, only eighteen inches tip to tip on the bow, but the tension on the loaded bolt was tremendous. This would shoot quite accurately up to about fifty feet, still pretty good even at a hundred. Also, in his belt were two throwing knives, accurate up to about thirty feet.

Coming in behind Sulley, Brock, crouching low and holding the flare gun in his right hand, looked into the cave and shot the flare.

A sizzling white flame streaked into the dark confines of the cave. The flare sizzled past Kashif's head, hit the back wall, deflected over toward Sanjay and shot up into the rocks where it finally came to rest, glowing brightly, spewing smoke and casting a brilliant orange glow into the main chamber of the cave.

Sulley hit the ground and started crawling. A bullet

ricocheted off of the rock where Brock's head had been. Grub rushed into the cave, hoping to get to the one rock that he knew could provide cover, but got shot before he got there, bullet ripping through his clothing on the left side of his stomach. Hanging onto his gun, he fell in behind the rock.

"Two bullets, ten seconds," Sam was thinking as he made his way down. "They're both probably reloading right now. How hard is that in a smoke filled cave? Can anyone see anything?"

He jumped down to the ground and with a diving leap and forward roll, joined Grub behind the rock, who was busy placing a rag over his bloody wound.

"How are you doing, partner?"

"Better than getting hit between the eyes, I think."

"How many are back there?"

"Three, plus Kashif."

Rhett came into the cave hugging the left side, seeing the interior through the sights of his gun. He spotted Sanjay's cousin back in the smoke and shot him.

Brock stormed the cave straight in, saw Bardolf and took a shot. The bullet clipped his shoulder but was not enough to keep Bardolf from firing back. Brock went down.

Sam ran to one of several large rocks near the center of the cave, to the one holding Kashif and started cutting the ropes away from his wrists. He tried to give him a knife but Kashif fell to the ground as soon as his hands were free.

Coming out of the smoke and coughing, Sanjay stumbled forward, holding one hand in front of his nose, the other carrying his gun. He had tried putting the flame out, but even the bucket of water had failed.

Sam spotted him first and threw the knife. It went in just below Sanjay's breast plate, quiet, but effective. Looking at it and watching his blood gush away, Sanjay was stunned.

How could that happen? His whole life he'd always been in control, killing his drunken father in his sleep after he'd been abused, killing the policeman who said he was out of control, cutting up those who had bad things to say about him. There was always someone who needed to be put back in their place. How could it now be him?

Gagging from the smoke, eyes watering and wanting to know who had done such a foul deed, he looked at Sam, who was waiting with his crossbow. Sanjay tried raising his gun, but collapsed down into the dirt.

Bardolf reloaded first. As he pointed the gun at Sam, he was hit by a shot from Grub. Seconds later, both Brock and Rhett got off another shot. Staggering backward, Bardolf fell to the ground, wiggled around a little bit and died.

Kashif couldn't get up. The cave was spinning uncontrollably, flashing with orange light and spewing some kind of harsh, sulfur smoke. Suddenly there were people everywhere, swarming inside the cave, picking him up and helping him out into the cool morning air.

"Kashif. This is Rhett. Can you hear me?"

Someone's hand, a woman's hand began to wipe his face with a cool, damp towel. Someone was trying to drip water into his mouth.

Water? Not too fast, can't swallow. "Who...?"

"Rhett. Remember me?"

"Rhett?"

"You're safe now. Bardolf's dead."

"I..., I can't believe. Sure?"

"I checked him myself."

"Sanjay?"

"Dead."

"Who..., people?"

"Get some rest, Kashif. We'll watch over you. You're safe now."

Kashif glanced over at Kathryn, the woman who was adding a bit of water to the towel. She wrung it out, looked down at him and smiled.

A smile? So long since he'd seen one that he didn't know how to respond. It used to be so easy. Tears came to his eyes.

Oskar, too, had cried when pulled out of the water and into the boat, and now he understood why. How long ago was that? Oskar and Mahin together, hugging and laughing and crying all at once.

Their eyes met when Kashif looked up at Melissa as she attempted to give him a bit more water. Kashif swallowed, coughed a bit and then accepted more.

She's older than Mahin. Both have those burning eyes, Mahin's, brown. This girl's, blue? Who are these people? Where...?

"Kashif. Get some rest. We found Sulley over in the bushes, and he's going to make you some stew. We'll wake you up when it's ready."

Hearing that, Kashif coughed, started laughing and then went into a fit of coughing and laughing. The one thing about dying, he kept telling himself when tied to the rock, was that he'd no longer have to eat Sulley's cooking, especially the stew.

Rhett started laughing. "I guess that's not good news."

Kathryn, thinking about Flabby Max telling Oskar as he handed him some of Sulley's stew, "This probably won't help either but it's better than the poop deck," also started laughing.

Pretty soon everyone was laughing and, relieved that he was among friends, Kashif fell into a deep sleep.

They had built three houses, one for each family, and a forth, smaller building used for a studio, meeting place, whatever, all built into a 'U' shaped configuration so that the back side of each house formed part the ten foot high wall that surrounded their property. They built covered walkways between the houses, each with their own path out through the gardens and to the pond in the middle, a common gathering place.

Oskar was commissioned to continue his English lessons with the family and was given a corner of the studio for his living quarters.

When the family was notified that Musheer had contracted the disease that the village was fighting, and that he was in isolation, Kashif set out to see how he could help.

Upon his arrival, Kashif learned that Musheer had already died and was buried. With nothing left to do, he returned home to discover that it had been burned to the ground.

Sifting through the ashes, he found the bodies of his parents, both with head wounds. Musheer's pregnant wife was visiting her sister at the time and was spared the fate of his own wife. Oskar and Mahin were missing. Searching through the family's secret hiding places, Kashif discovered that both their money and the stone were gone.

The police said that their residence was not in their jurisdiction and offered little help. Neighbors said that two days before they had seen three men traveling in the area, two with few identifying features, the third, a large, bearded man with a red macaw.

Kashif disguised himself and followed them back to Mogadishu where they booked passage on Nerissa. Kashif signed on as crew.

The mutiny took place on the third day out. Many on the crew were relatives of Sanjay, Bardolf's right hand man, and were well-prepared for action. Fourteen walked the plank.

Kashif would have been next, but just before he was pushed onto the plank, he and Bardolf stood eye to eye. Bardolf reached up, smiled, and slowly removed Kashif's disguise. "Lock him in a hold. Make sure he doesn't escape. This one's special. Rhett, you're in charge."

Countless days passed. There were rats and endless gurgling sounds, the steady rolling of Nerissa as she sailed across the sea, but with no light, nothing with which to measure time. The only contact was Rhett who, when he could, listened to Kashif's plight.

Let him loose? No. Certain death for both. No place to hide on a ship. Kill Bardolf? Sure. Kill most of the crew and get by Sanjay and his friends first. Impossible.

The torture began when they got to the cave. Bardolf needed information about the stone and became more and more insistent about getting it. Unable to bear it any longer and unable to do anything about it, Rhett and a few others left in the middle of the night.

Rhett is here. Who are these people? Where did they come from? How did they come to know Rhett? How did they get past Bardolf's guard?

All of these questions moments before Kashif opened his eyes.

"Kashif. This is Rhett. Can you hear me?"

He nodded slightly without opening his eyes. Rhett was talking in a whisper.

"Just wanted to put your mind at ease. I have the stone."

He nodded again.

"You have a relative in the crowd."

Looking up, Kashif studied Sam, who was sitting opposite Rhett. Certainly there was a resemblance, Sameer's deep set eyes, a stubborn chin, his mother's nose and the hands of working man. "How?"

"My name is Sam, short for Sameer, my birth name. Your brother's wife had a son named Musheer, after his father. He is my great, great grandfather."

330

Kashif looked over at Rhett. "What year..., today?"

"Eighteen eighty-four."

Kashif turned his attention back to Sam. "How?"

Sam smiled "This is going to be hard to swallow, but easier than what she's about to give you."

Kathryn moved closer holding a cup of Sulley's stew. Kashif frowned when she put a bit up to his lips, but soon wanted more.

Sam waited until Kashif had had enough. "Would you like to see some pictures of your descendents?"

Klicker stepped out into the open. "Ain't that something? The shootin' stops and my eyesight comes back."

Rhett glanced over at Brock. "Coincidence?"

Brock finished tying off the bandage around his rib cage. He had been lucky. The bullet missed the bone. "Sounds fishy to me."

"I ain't lyin'. That light went past my eyes and straight into my brain. Powerful stuff."

Rhett smiled. "Messed you up, huh?"

"Fried his brain," said Brock, wincing with his own laughter.

"Try it. You'll see."

"Don't think so, " said Rhett. "But you can make up for doin' nothing by carrying supplies down to the ship."

Sam came out of the cave wiping the blade of his knife. He put it back in its sheath as he approached them. "Everybody ready?"

Kashif insisted on walking on his own, but within minutes of attempting to navigate some of the steeper drops or the patches of loose rock, he succumbed to the makeshift stretcher they had prepared and let himself be carried down toward the ship.

When Smitty heard people up on the trail, he stopped squirming, trying to get untied. He didn't recognize some of these voices, but when he finally heard Klicker's voice, he started squealing like two cats squaring off for a fight.

"Who tied me up? I'm gonna skin 'em alive! Who was it?"

"Me," said Kathryn. "It was either that or shoot you. I thought I was being nice."

Turning, Smitty stared at Kathryn, seeing her for the first time. "Well," he stammered. "Those were some mighty good knots. I appreciate you not shooting me."

"Bardolf's dead.," said Klicker. "All of 'em up there."

"Sanjay?"

"Bled to death, back in the cave."

Rhett and Paul set Kashif down and waited for everyone to move on. Brock found a rock good enough for sitting and sat down with a sigh.

Melissa went over to check his bandages and, seeing that they were holding, moved on to Grub, who held up his hand. "It just stopped bleeding. I don't want to mess with it. Thanks."

Standing next to Klicker, Smitty watched the odd looking group. "You weren't lying last night, were you?"

"Nope."

"I almost shot you."

"I appreciate that you didn't. You ready to go home?"

"You still owe me forty."

"It's twenty. I keep telling you."

They continued down the trail, but when they arrived at the broken sapling, Raja was gone.

Rhett pointed to a trail of broken branches, crushed plants and wiggle marks in the dirt. "Looks like he's heading back down to the ship."

"Probably heard the gunfire," said Brock.

"He was guarding the trail over by Nerissa," said Klicker. "How'd he get way up here?"

"We took him prisoner," Rhett explained. "He had a big mouth. Paul shot him with a tranquilizer. You shoulda seen that kid dodge a bullet. Hit Raja at the knees and took him down."

"Dumb question," said Smitty. "What did you do with his gun?"

Rhett shook his head. "We didn't even think about it. We took *him* and went looking for the trail up. Should've shot him right then."

Click. Click. "He's out there. He's got a gun and he's mad."

Rhett shook his head. "We don't even know if he's untied. Don't get hysterical."

"Did you pass by the ship?"

"Right."

"How did you get by the guards? There were two."

"We blinded one and tranquilized the other."

"Blinded? Like you did to me?"

"I guess."

"Tranquilized, like what you did to me?" Smitty asked.

"Right."

Click…, click. "So, there's three of them in between us and the ship."

Sam joined them. "Rhett, how about you and Smitty go find Raja? We'll stay on the trail with Kashif."

"I don't have a gun," said Smitty.

"Paul, give Smitty Sanjay's gun, will you?" And then he handed Bardolf's gun and ammo to Klicker. "OK. Everybody's armed. Stay sharp. Let's go."

Easier to roll downhill, than up. More brush, more cover, more places to hide until I can get to that knife in my boot and cut these ropes away.

Slimy pig kid. Who does he think he is that he can slap me? If I have only one bullet left, I will save it for him. I will make him beg.

Hog tied, ankles and wrists bound together, Raja rolled like a pumpkin, slithered like a snake and wiggled like a caterpillar down to a place that felt secure, safe from bullets and far enough away that he could make a little noise while he attempted to retrieve his knife.

He had heard the gunshots and was pretty sure that he knew what had happened. They had stormed the cave. Eight shots, all within a minute or two and nothing after that. Whatever happened, it was over quickly.

Better now to go to the ship and defend it. We'll see who comes out of the trees and wants to come onboard. Sanjay and Bardolf? Welcome aboard. If not? Shoot..., and aim for that boy.

The knife was not actually in the boot. The sheath was strapped to his ankle at the lower end of his calf on the inside section of his right leg. Rolling up against one of the largest rocks, chest and face against the stone, Raja slowly pulled his pant leg up and began to fumble with the leather tie holding the knife in place.

Minutes later, he began to saw the rope connecting his ankles to his wrists. This was tough stuff, not ordinary rope, like nothing he'd ever felt before.

He cut the connection between his ankles and wrists and then brought his hands up beneath his feet to where he could see what he was cutting. A few minutes later and he was free.

Staying off of the trail, Raja headed down to the ship, stopped at his hiding spot near the trail head where he found his gun and ammunition untouched.

Gotta get to the ship and aim one of the cannons at the

trail, see who comes along. Nobody's gonna stop a cannon ball.

They crossed the beach from the far side. Must've landed somewhere around the point. Where is their boat? Why didn't the guards shoot them?

Raja loaded his rifle, picked up his belongings, hurried out to the longboat and pushed it into the water. And then he went back for the second one, dragged it into the water and tied it to the first.

Can't get to the ship unless you can walk on water. And I don't think any of them can do that. And if they can, we'll see if they can dodge bullets at the same time.

Slimy little pig of a kid. Humiliate me? Bring it on. I'll be waiting.

The last thing Ollie remembered was hitting the floor. Some drunken idiot had spun him around and laid a roundhouse punch square on his jaw.

Remembering that, Ollie moved his chin side to side, wanting to know if it was broken. Oddly, there was no pain.

So you can imagine his surprise when he opened his eyes, looked up and spotted the masts of a ship instead of the ceiling of the Mad Hunter Bar in Mogadishu.

Confused, Ollie sat up, looked around and slowly became aware of Nerissa's wooden deck, railing, rigging, rat ropes, things that he'd come to hate after being kidnapped from the bar and put to work on the ship.

Sleeping? I've been sleeping? What was I doing? What's my job? Don't want to get caught slackin'. I saw what happened to Jake.

Jake. Where is Jake? We're supposed to be guarding the ship!

Jake was passed out face down in Bardolf's cabin when Ollie found him. A mostly empty bottle of rum lay on its side in the middle of the room, held in place by Jake's lifeless hand.

"Jake! Wake up! Jake!"

Moaning with the effort, Jake rolled over. "I can't see, Ollie. I can't see."

"That's cause your eyes are closed, dimwit."

"No. That light got me. What was that?"

"What light? I didn't see a light."

"Burned my eyeballs. That's bad, Ollie. They're gonna shoot me if I can't see."

"Jake, open your eyes."

"It's no good. It's..., it's...," Jake blinked several times. "Hey. I can see again! It's back!"

"We better get this cleaned up or they're going to shoot both of us. Come on. Sober up!"

Jake tried standing but even before he got halfway up,

he fell back down. And then he felt a terrible upsurge in his stomach. Crawling like a pig being chased by a pack of wolves all the way out of the cabin door and over to the rail, Jake stuck his head over the side just in time and let it loose.

Ollie picked up the bottle and followed. That's when he spotted Raja rowing toward the ship.

"Jake! Here comes Raja."

"Crap!"

"He's bringing both boats. Somethin' happened. Remember last night? There was some kind of light comin' from the island?"

"I heard a lot of shootin'. Sounded like it was comin' from up by the cave. Don't know for sure. I was blinded! What was that?"

"So you went lookin' for a bottle?"

"If I can't see to shoot. I'm just an extra mouth to feed. I'd rather die drunk than sober."

Raja tied off to the rope ladder, grabbed his gun and hurried up the side. They met him at the railing. "Jake, go below and aim a cannon at the trail head. Let me know when you're ready."

"At the trail head?"

"Right. Go! Ollie, get up in the crow's nest and let me know when they're coming."

"When who's coming?"

"Anybody. If you don't recognize them, shoot."

"What's happening?"

"We got some intruders trying to take over."

Jake was feeling sick again. He swallowed twice to keep it down. "I heard shooting."

"So?"

"What happened?"

"Didn't I say to get that cannon ready? Why are you still standing here? Go!"

Jake hurried away, not wanting to speak because he was feeling like throwing up again. He hoped he could go in a straight line and that he wouldn't fall down. He was seeing two doors, kind of overlapping, so he closed his left eye and aimed for the one that was still there.

Raja didn't notice. He hurried off to the locked cabinet where the extra weapons were kept, three pistols, two rifles and three swords. He grabbed all of it and returned to the railing closest to the trail head, about a hundred yards away. The cannon that Jake would be firing was directly below. Raja leaned over the side. "Jake, you ready?"

"Workin' on it."

And that's what Jake was doing. Can't keep the cannons loaded all the time. Gunpowder gets damp, especially in this cove where everything gets dripping wet from the fog most every morning. The powder keg was mid-ship and, both it and Jake being wobbly, took a while to go get and roll back.

Dropped the cannon ball on his big toe, twenty pounds of joy, and while he was chasing after the ball, fell and got a hand full of slivers for the effort. The fuse hole was smaller than he remembered, or moving, or maybe there was more than one. Jake was working on all of it.

Directly above, Raja made sure he had good cover and that all weapons were loaded and strategically placed down by his feet. Holding one of the rifles, resting the barrel on the railing, he quietly watched and waited.

Up in the crow's nest, Ollie could see above the first few stands of trees that peppered the shoreline all the way back to the trail that led up toward the cave.

If he used his spyglass he could even see the expressions on the faces of anyone coming down the trail or, if they turned and looked back toward the cove, those heading up.

But the spyglass had its drawbacks. Any motion on the deck of Nerissa, such as the commotion in the water caused by the occasional large set of breakers that washed over the rocks on the south side, caused a couple of feet of motion up in the crow's nest.

Looking through his spyglass, Ollie was getting seasick. He never liked boats and, since he couldn't swim, the whole idea of being on any liquid that was deeper than he was tall, made him queasy. Yet, here was something compelling to see.

The trail up to the cave, after disappearing into the trees near the beach, reappeared above the trees about three hundred yards away and again, further up the mountain at about a thousand yards.

On the higher slope, Ollie spotted a whole group of people coming down the trail. The optics were not that good in this scope and, combined with the motion of the crow's nest and minimal pre-dawn light, he could not identify who they were. He counted seven, but even then he wasn't sure.

Looking down, he watched Raja prepare for the defense of Nerissa. If there were seven in this approaching group, and if they were the enemy and they all had guns, who were they most likely to shoot first?

Raja had not answered Jake's question about the gun battle so, Ollie was thinking, either it didn't go well or he didn't know. More likely he didn't know because he also didn't know who might appear at the trail head.

Worst case, it doesn't go well, strangers show up, all

of them having guns and stupid Raja takes a pot shot. Raja ducks behind the railing and then seven bullets are searching for a target.

When the group reappeared at the lower section of the trail, Ollie spotted a woman leading the way and behind her, a young man carrying the front end of a stretcher upon which someone was tied. The other end of the stretcher was being carried by Klicker. Following him was a beautiful young girl, blonde hair, carrying some kind of back pack. He also spotted Brock, Grub and another man.

Ollie decided not to warn Raja. That would just get him more trigger happy and more likely to mess things up. Let's talk it out first and see what both sides want. This might be the opportunity that everyone was waiting for, a chance to go home.

And if this new group did not include Bardolf, Sanjay and friends, Ollie figured that he was going to be on the wrong side of the conflict.

Now skeptical about the entire situation, he looked down at Raja, who happened to look up at the same time. "Anything?"

"Not yet," Ollie replied, thinking that nobody better shoot that girl. That would be a tragedy.

Jake didn't mean to spill the gunpowder.

Sometimes that happens. I get in a hurry and then I have to heave. Life is like that.

Didn't really want to drink the whole bottle either. But I was blind and the rum just happened to find its way into my hand. What are you gonna do?

Sit and wait and know that I'm gonna get shot soon as they see that I'm blind. I won't even see it comin'.

It wasn't like he spilled the whole keg. Just what he was going to pour into the cannon. It scattered out pretty well since he tripped over the breech rope at the same time and, breaking his fall, let go of the container. It bounced away emptying its contents.

Hmmm. Is that dangerous? There's nothing to light it down there. I'll clean it up later. Don't need Raja gettin' all worked up cause I'm not ready.

What does he expect? There's supposed to be three of us down here. The cannon weighs a ton. I have to move it all by myself?

Powder successfully poured down into the barrel, Jake looked around for something to use for the wad. It was not morning yet and the area was very dark. He found some old rope but it was too long. The search for a knife began.

Can't see what I'm doin'. I need a lantern and..., guess I'll get that one from the crew's quarters. Half the crew's dead anyway, lot's of old stuff laying around.

Lighting the lantern was another problem. It had been left burning when they reached the island and was empty. Stumbling around, Jake searched for some oil. He had never been in charge of keeping the lantern lit so he had no idea where it was kept, not to mention the problem of lighting it.

He abandoned that idea and instead found an old knife, cut up somebody's oilskin for a canvas wad and, bouncing off of the bunks, stumbled back to the cannon.

Every cannon did not have its own rammer. Jake retrieved one from two positions down, tripped over it, returned and rammed the wad down on top of the gunpowder. Turning, he discovered that the cannon ball had rolled away somewhere.

Once the cannon ball was in the cannon and after Jake had packed another wad of canvas down the barrel to keep it from falling out, he went in search of primer powder for the touch hole at the breech of the cannon. Nearby, he also found the flintlock used to supply spark.

Won't be long now. When this thing goes off, I'm gonna wake up the whole island.

Wonder what happened last night. Hmm.

Looking out through the opening, wanting to aim the cannon, Jake discovered fog rolling in, just like it had done since forever, cutting visibility down to about fifty feet. Can't aim nothing if you can't see.

Sitting up in the crow's nest, Ollie quietly waited. This was a good thing. Certainly no one on shore was going to be able to spot him.

He wondered how things were going for Jake. Even under normal circumstances he was not good with the cannon, twice let the ball drop into the sea before the cannon went off, once forgot to run out the carriage before he fired it, almost blew a hole in the side of the ship.

Raja got it wrong. If he'd a been thinking, he'd have sent me down there and Jake up here.

Not that Jake could've made it. And I've got no need to fire a cannon, especially if that girl's in the line of fire. Who are those people?

Ollie watched Raja with interest, now barely more than a foggy silhouette down on the deck, wondering at the same time if he just shot the guy, would all of this be over?

If Klicker, Brock and Grub are traveling together, are we going home? Is Raja the only one stopping us? That's worth a bullet.

"Cut himself loose," said Rhett. "We found the rope behind some rocks not far from where we tied him up. Tracked him down to the ship. He took both boats."

They had gathered back in the trees in Raja's old hideout. Coming up out of the fog, Sam joined them. "Even if I stand next to the water, I still can't see the ship."

"Fog's thick now," said Grub. "But sometimes it clears out fast. Whatever we're planning, let's do it."

"How about this?" Paul asked. "Some of us go back to the dinghy and row over to the ship. In this fog, it should be safe."

"I'll be part of that," said Sam. "How far to the dinghy?"

"About a fifty yards of sand, and then we have to climb over the rocks to get to the next inlet. The dinghy's tied up in there. About ten minutes if we move fast."

"I'm goin'," said Rhett. "Should've shot Raja the first time."

"I'll tag along," said Grub. "If Nerissa's heading home, I want to make sure I'm on it."

Melissa, who had been very quiet, cleared her throat. "Who are the guards? Are they like you, Grub? Will they join us?"

"Jake and Ollie," said Klicker. "They're not Raja's friends. At least not until today, now that he needs them."

Paul checked his gun, made sure the light was glowing white. "Let's do it."

Inside Nerissa, Jake was feeling queasy again. It's not easy staying below deck with a hangover. Actually, just becoming a hangover. The drunker than a skunk part was still there. He leaned up against the bulkhead and closed his eyes.

Fog can take forever to clear. No sense standin' and waitin'. Nothing's going to happen until the fog clears. Can't shoot nothin' if you can't see.

Through the fog, Raja heard muffled voices over by the

shoreline, but couldn't see anything to shoot. Ollie heard them as well, sounded like several people out there, but he wasn't about to shoot blindly. Don't want to make enemies of the very ones that might be your ride home.

Sam and Paul found the dinghy. They manned the oars with Rhett in the bow and Grub at the stern. With two of them rowing, they rounded the point quickly, headed into the cove, found Nerissa's hull and began to ascend the rope ladder. Grub covered Rhett as he made his way up. On deck, Rhett covered Grub's ascent. Sam started up next but stopped Paul from joining them.

"Go back to Spittin' Image," he whispered. "Get her ready to go."

"Where's your gun, Sam?"

"It got shot."

"You don't even have a gun. Let me go."

"No. Your mother would never forgive me if...,"

"Sam, that's not fair."

"You're right. But I don't know how to run the boat. You do. Can you please get it ready for us? We're going to need it. I'll call on Snitch when it's safe to bring her in."

"Sam...,"

"Don't argue. Paul, I really need you to do this. I'll explain later. Go!"

Standing up in the crow's nest, Ollie watched with great interest. Yep. He could pick off one of them, but then he'd be a sitting target while he tried to reload. Nothing to gain there. Almost better to shoot Raja and be done with it.

Looking down at the man, hunkering near Nerissa's bow with all of his weapons, Ollie concluded that this was the best way to end it all, shoot him.

He watched Paul row away in that quick little boat, odd shaped, but light and fast, until he disappeared into the fog. When he looked back down at Raja, readying his rifle, he saw that Raja had already done the same but that it was aimed up at him.

The bullet shattered an entire plank of the crow's nest, which crashed into Ollie's hunched figure. He felt the wood slam into his body, felt a lot of pain in his arms, thought he was bleeding.

Shoot back? Of course, shoot back!

But he's got lots of loaded guns.

I'm a sittin' duck.

Another shot rang out, and then another. Ollie cringed inside the tiny wooden loft and waited for the bottom to fall out. Nothing happened, silence. He dared a look.

Raja was gone. Somebody was down mid-ship by the ladder. In a panic, Ollie did a quick scan of the ship, hoping Raja didn't have him in his sights again. No Raja. He ducked back down.

Climb down? Hardly.

That's like sayin', shoot me! Shoot me!

Nasty fall.

Stay here? Hardly.

What kind of crap is that? All I want to do is go home! I'm bleeding all over the place!

Climb down? Hardly.

Raja ran from his hiding spot behind the bulwark, across the bow and over to the other side of the ship.

Should've been watchin' the ladder. Got one of 'em. Saw two more come on board. Ollie should've said somethin', should've shot them. I know whose side he's on. Think I got him. My shoulder's bleeding.

Keeping close to the cabins, Raja ran to the crew's quarters, down the steps and then cut left, heading toward the forward hold.

Can't find me in the dark. Gotta have a lantern and I'll shoot anybody who's carrying one.

Grub went forward, hugging the cabin, rifle ready. Sam went aft, crossbow leading the way, hoping to catch Raja coming around the corner.

Shot in the leg, Rhett decided that sitting was just fine. He scooted back into the shadows as far as he could, reloaded and waited.

Sam spotted blood on the deck in front of the door, just a drop or two, enough to know which way he had gone. Standing on the side, he swung the door open, and stepped back into cover.

Four steps going down..., into what?

A second glance showed that, on either side of the stairs there was cover behind the stairwell.

Question is, which side of the stairs to go?

Sam shifted to the other side of the door, peered into the darkness and discovered the crew's quarters.

Very dark, hiding places everywhere. This is going to be slow.

He put on his night vision goggles, took a deep breath and descended quickly, jumping off of the middle step over to the cover of the first available bunk.

Waiting, listening, he spotted another drop of blood in the aisle way between the bunks heading toward the bow. Most every bunk had something in it, many of them looking like someone hiding. Sam moved through the area cautiously, checking out every suspicious object that could either be a human or hide one.

OK. He's not in here.

Peering into the next area, the forward hold, Sam spotted someone's foot sticking out from behind a stack of crates on the port side of the ship, about thirty feet away.

Straight out from the foot in the middle of the room, was some sort of stairway going down, surrounded on three sides by railing. Sam quietly lifted his goggles, scanned the room and then put them back on.

Too dark. He doesn't know his foot is showing. If I had my gun, it'd be a tranquilizer. Whoever that is, this bolt only going to make them madder. I hit his foot. He has a gun. How fast can I reload?

The crossbow was designed to hold a clip of three bolts. After firing one, the cocking mechanism that drew back the string also cleared the way for the next bolt to spring into position, an operation that took about as long as it would to operate the pump mechanism of a shotgun, about two seconds.

"Raja. My name is Sam. Let's talk."

Sam waited, hearing his own breath, muffled voices from somewhere outside, distant waves washing ashore.

"Raja, it's over. Sanjay and Bardolf are dead. Give yourself up. Let's avoid the bloodshed. Everybody wants to go home."

"I will be killed before Nerissa's sails are raised."

"We'll make sure you have a fair trial."

"So that I can be hanged?"

"At least you'll have a fair trial. You have my word."

"Who are you to make such a guarantee? I don't know you."

"I am a relative of Kashif. He is with us now. Nerissa's going home."

Raja still had two loaded pistols. There wasn't enough time to reload the rifles. His arm throbbed and the bleeding hadn't stopped, sticky and wet, dripping off of his elbow, finger sticky on the trigger.

He had no reason to disbelieve Sam. There had been a shoot-out. His claim about having Kashif, if true, also meant that Bardolf's scheme of power and fortune was over, and now his time was up. A fair trail and then hanging was worse than dying now. More time to think about it.

"Sam? Is that your name?"

"Yes."

"I challenge you to a duel. You win, you take me back. I win, I go free on the island."

"I don't want to duel."

"You are a coward?"

"I'm smarter than that."

"So..., I'm stupid?"

"You choose your own path."

Grub cautiously descended the steps and, being the one in charge to keep the lantern burning out at sea, knew exactly where the supplies were kept. He filled the lantern, got it lit as fast as anybody could, grabbed his rifle and headed through the crew's quarters toward Sam.

Peering around the edge of the crate, Raja spotted Sam's silhouette in front of the light, raised his pistol and shot.

Wearing the goggles, Sam saw it all clear as day. When he saw the pistol, he slipped back behind cover as the bullet whizzed by, catching Grub by surprise. He fell and dropped the lantern.

Sam fired his first bolt, hitting Raja in the hip as he was running down the stairs. Following, they played cat and mouse running from cannon to cannon through the dimly lit room.

Jake didn't wake with the first gunshots up on deck, but the one at the forward end of the room seconds ago caused his eyes to blink open. His head felt like it was split in half, about five miles apart, and his eyes were still seeing double. He didn't bother to get up, but one thing he surely knew, there were other people in the room.

Jake had put his gun down seconds after being blinded and had never found it again. All he had now was the flintlock and a one ton cannon, both not good for self defense in a closed room.

Backing quietly away from an adjacent cannon, Raja was unaware of Jake's presence. When he looked down and spotted the keg of gunpowder, only one thing crossed his mind. If I'm not going home, neither is anyone else.

When he raised his pistol and aimed, Jake let out a short scream and, in a convulsive reaction, squeezed the flintlock that accidentally lit the spilled gunpowder.

A tremendous 'Whoosh!' filled the chamber and sent up a fireball that torched the wood above. Raja, standing in the middle of it, screamed. Sam fired a second bolt that hit him in the chest. Raja collapsed down onto the blackened floor.

Snitch came alive. "Sam! Paul! Kathryn here. What's going on? You guys OK?"

"Paul here. I'm on Spittin' Image, engine running, waiting on Sam. Sam?"

"I'm OK."

"We're seeing what looks like flames coming out of Nerissa. Not sure. It's still too foggy."

"A blast of gunpowder," said Sam. "It burnt itself out." He aimed the crossbow at Jake, who raised his hands.

"I'm unarmed."

"Whose side are you on?"

"Whichever one's goin' home."

Sam motioned for him to stand and then to lead the way back toward the stairs.

"We're still seeing what looks like flames, Sam."

"We'll check it out."

They smelled the smoke when they reached the top of the steps. Jake hesitated. Sam nudged him forward. "Go! Now!"

Holding their hands over their noses, stumbling through the smoke filled room, they found Grub in between the rows of bunks, hunched into a ball.

"Got me in the stomach. That hurts *real* bad."

"I'll get his shoulders," said Sam. "You get his legs."

They carried him to the exit. Jake, sobering up quickly now, struggled to get him up the stairs and laid out on the deck.

Going back inside, Jake found the lantern too hot to pick up. He tried smothering it with a blanket, but it too started to burn. He raced up the stairs and threw the whole thing overboard.

The fire below was spreading quickly, burning blankets and clothes, flames lapping up against the wood.

"Paul, bring Spittin' Image alongside Nerissa. We need fire extinguishers."

"Got it. On my way."

Paul brought Spittin' Image alongside Nerissa, put her in reverse and waited for her to come to a stop. Sam, hanging onto Nerissa's rope ladder, grabbed hold of Spittin' Image's bow pulpit and kept her from drifting away.

Paul ran below deck and retrieved the first of three fire extinguishers, the one in the forward cabin. He opened the hatch, climbed up on deck and handed it to Sam, who handed it up to Ollie, who had no idea what to do with it other than set it on the deck. Next came the extinguisher from the engine compartment and then the one from the lazerette. Paul started to tie up. Sam waved him away.

"Go get whoever's able to help. We need to get a bucket brigade going."

Gunning the engine, Paul pulled away. The shore line was about a hundred yards away but it would be the depth finder that told him how close he could get. Currently, it was reading fifty feet.

"Mom, coming toward you. Need help putting out a fire."

"I'll see who's able. Swing the stern around. We'll get in the dinghy and you can tow us out."

As soon as Smitty, Kathryn and Klicker were in the dinghy, Paul gunned it. How good it felt to be back on Spittin' Image! The GPS was still out, as was the radio. But feeling technology come back into his life was a good thing, a very good thing. It was nice to hear the engine chugging away, seeing the depth finder's readings change from eight feet to fifteen, twenty-five to fifty. Nerissa emerged out of the fog.

Tied up to the ship, Kathryn climbed up onto Spittin' Image and grabbed the two buckets she kept onboard. She dipped them into the water and handed them to Paul, who handed them up to Smitty. Klicker carried the buckets over to Jake and Ollie who poured them onto the fire. Sam was throwing burning bedding and clothes overboard. Still, they were losing control.

Paul jumped back on board Spittin' Image, retrieved the sump pump out of the hold, threw it into the water and, holding it by the electrical cord, handed the hose end to Kathryn who handed it up to Klicker, who had no idea what to do with it until Paul flipped the switch.

Gushing water coming out of the end, he handed it up to Ollie. There wasn't enough hose to reach the cabin but the buckets were now being filled on deck. Soon, with the faster operation, the cabin was reduced to a smoke filled, smoldering room.

Hearing all of the commotion outside, Raja, breathing heavily, pulled the bolt out from his chest, and seeing the blood rushing out, knew he was done. He crawled over to the opening in front of cannon, looked down and saw Paul.

Giddy with what he was going to do, he smiled, more like an evil kind of laugh in between the gurgling sounds of blood, salty and warm, causing him to cough, as he crawled back to get his pistol.

One bullet. Perfect.

He was fading in and out now and he had to rest several times before he got back to the opening. With enormous effort and concentration, he cocked the pistol, aimed at Paul's chest, only thirty feet away, and said, "Remember me?"

When Paul looked up, Raja pulled the trigger.

"I'll get my laptop. Maybe we can identify what he hit."

"Missed the ribs and heart. What's below the heart?"

"Stomach, isn't it?"

"I think the liver's in there somewhere."

"Spleen. I think the spleen is right there, too. What happens if he hit that?"

"Why is this so slow powering up?"

"It didn't come out the back. There's no hole."

"Lucky he was wearing the vest."

"It still went in. Vest is not designed to stop a bullet."

"At least it didn't go all the way through."

"Right. But now we've got to get it out."

"Can you tell where it went?"

"I'm following the angle."

"Looks like the vest deflected it down. That's why it missed the heart."

"Paul. You still with us? Paul?"

"His face is white. Paul?"

"Here's the illustration. The lungs are on either side of the heart."

"No. It didn't go in the lung. It went in here. It's his stomach."

"How will we get it out?"

"He's going to squirm if we start looking. We'll have to tie him down."

"How about a tranquilizer?"

"I don't know. He's lost a lot of blood. Paul? Can you hear me?"

"No reaction. How are we going to grab the bullet, once we find it?"

"Don't know. Do you have any tongs onboard?"

"Tongs. Like for cooking?"

"Right."

"The bullet hole's not that big. You'd have to cut."

"OK. Long nose pliers?"

"Maybe. Paul keeps the tools over by the engine."

"We have to sterilize them somehow."

"If we have them. I'll go check."

"How about chopsticks?"

"Probably not enough grip."

"How do we stop the bleeding?"

"First we've got to find the bullet."

"Here's a long nose. Will this work?

"Maybe. We need to sterilize them."

"Give them to me. I'll scrub them with soap."

"That's not going to sterilize them."

"I've got a bottle of alcohol in the cupboard."

"He's squirming as soon as I touch him."

"Tranquilizer?"

"I don't know. Actually, the chopstick idea is good, plastic if you've got them. I can poke around until I feel it hit something hard."

"Just one?"

"It's just as easy to bring two. Sterilize them."

"Here's the alcohol."

"We need a wide bowl."

"My pasta bowl. I'll get it."

"Here are the chopsticks."

"Soon as she comes back, throw them in there and pour alcohol over them."

"Paul, this is Melissa. Can you hear me?"

"I think I saw him nod."

"I think that was more of a grimace. I'm poking around.

"Here's the bowl."

"Throw everything in there. Soak them."

"I talked to Rhett. They're going to leave with the morning tide. They want to know if we're going to follow."

"No way. We'll be stuck in eighteen eighty-four."

"I think we are already. How do we get out of here?"

"I'm still trying to figure out how we got in."

"I'm so sorry for all of this. When I think back, that old apartment wasn't so bad after all. None of this would've happened."

"Paul wanted this too. You can't feel guilty."

"Of course I can. He's my son! I never should've taken the chance."

"You didn't know."

"Here's the chopstick."

"Hold his arms. I'll see what I can find."

"He keeps bleeding."

"We'll stitch him up after we get the bullet out."

"He's squirming."

"Hold his arms. I think I felt it."

"He's really strong!"

"Sit on his arms. Hold him down."

"Paul, hang in there."

"I feel it. Hand me the long nose."

"Paul. Relax. We know it hurts. We're trying to get the bullet out."

"How are we going to stitch him up?"

"I've got a little emergency sewing kit."

"As soon as I'm done here, go get it."

"He's not going to like this."

"I've got the bullet."

Sam quietly knocked on the door, opened it part way and stuck his head inside. Kashif was lying in a bed that was positioned near an opened port hole on the starboard side of the cabin.

"You wanted to see me?"

Kashif motioned to a chair next to the bed. "You go..., Mogadishu?"

"No. We stay."

He looked puzzled. "Why? Here..., nothing. You go Mogadishu. Together, we go."

Sam shook his head. "No. We stay."

Kashif leaned over toward the table, with much effort, toward a cup of water. Sam retrieved it for him.

"What will you do when you get to Mogadishu?"

Kashif held the cup with both hands, tried hard to swallow. "Find Mahin. I must find Mahin."

"Do you know where she is?"

He shook his head. "No. But I have stone. I will find."

"And Oskar?"

"How you know Oskar and Mahin?"

"Oskar wrote it down and sent the manuscript to London."

He frowned. "Yes..., I remember. You read?"

"All four of us did."

"You from London?"

"No. America."

"This place. Is good?"

"Yes," said Sam, thinking of his studio and of the classes that he had yet to teach. How long had it been? Were they missed? It was impossible to know. This place, this island...,

Kashif cleared his throat. "The dog. You have?"

Sam shook his head. "No. We haven't been able to find him."

"He..., go away?"

"He's on the island somewhere."

"Oskar say, disappear. Same?"

"Until we find him, yes."

"You must find dog. Dreams, come here. Dog come here, this place. No dog..., you stay, I think."

"Why?"

"Mahin ask stone for help, for Oskar. Must pay back. You say..., equal?"

"But we didn't take anything from the stone."

"Dog, stone and blue moon, together, this place. No dog. You cannot leave."

Kathryn poured coffee into Sam's cup and offered more to Melissa, who declined. She returned the decanter to the coffee maker and joined them back in the nook. "Nerissa's gone. It's just us now. What's next?"

Sam stirred a second spoonful of sugar into his coffee. "Well, the blue moon got us here. I think it needs to take us away."

"Crap. All of this is my fault."

"We all wanted this," said Melissa. "Except...," she glanced in Paul's direction. "Except for that."

"The wound looks OK."

"There's too much swelling."

"I agree with Melissa. Looks like he's getting an infection. We need antibiotics."

"If we had the Internet, we could take pictures and get advice."

"Not for another hundred years."

Melissa watched Sam test his coffee, blowing off the steam and taking a cautious sip. "That coffee maker runs on AC. Right?"

Kathryn nodded. "Right."

"How are we getting AC on a boat that runs on batteries?"

"I'd ask Paul," said Kathryn. "He was quick to learn all about that stuff."

"I think it's called an inverter," said Sam. "It runs on either propane or batteries and makes AC. Spittin' Image must have one."

"How much of that do we have before we run out?"

"Engine charges the batteries," said Sam. "That's good until we run out of fuel. How much do we have?"

"We're down to less than half a tank. We used a lot coming around the island."

"Do you have solar panels?"

"Yes."

"Good. So we have batteries until they die out. How long

are they good for?"

"I think I saw five years marked on the battery. But it could be that a couple have already gone by."

"How about propane?"

"No idea. If I'd of known we were leaving the century, I'd have filled up the spare."

"Well," said Sam. "Sooner or later, we're going to run out of supplies and convenient ways to cook. How are your survival skills?"

"I can't start a fire from scratch, if that's what you mean."

Sam nodded knowingly. "All of the above. How cold does it get here? What's the weather like? What kinds of food are available?"

"Fish," said Melissa. "Lots of fish."

"What can we grow?"

"Grow? I live on a boat. It's not like I was thinking about having a garden."

"We should go back and locate those guns, put them back together and look for the bullets."

"And what? Move into the cave? Is that what we're going to do, live like them?"

"We could sail away," said Sam. "But I don't know if that gets us out of eighteen eighty-four."

"Way I see it," said Melissa. "We're going to be here until the next ship comes along."

This was a different kind of puzzle. Nothing like Baby's toy that unlocked the cages. Not like that thing the dog was attached to. No. This one is different. This one has no parts.

The dog had circled the lake twice, sniffing along the shoreline, looking under logs and into the tall grass, searching for something. Both times he came back to the same log on the west side and hung around the area.

Far did not consider this behavior dangerous, not like that of the bird spying for the humans. But he did consider it odd behavior and, as with all puzzles, was curious.

When Capn finally settled in on a patch of ground just out of the water, Far came down to the shoreline, jumped up on top of the log, found a spot above the dog and sat down.

"Did you hear them fighting?"

"Yes."

"The big ship is gone."

"I didn't know that."

"Your humans are on their boat."

"Good. That's how we got here."

"Are you going with them?"

"Are they leaving?"

"I don't know. Aren't you worried that they'll leave without you?"

"Yes."

"I don't understand. What's keeping you here?"

"I'm looking for a friend."

"Who?"

"Someone who probably died for warning me about the human. I don't want to leave until I know what happened to him."

"Why do you think he died?"

"That bird caught him."

"The human's bird?"

"Right."

"Why don't you go ask her?"

"I don't know where she is."

"Up at the cave."

"I don't know where that is."

"I'll take you. She's harmless now. Her master is dead."

"Why would she tell me anything?"

"I don't know. Let's ask."

Ekko was perched on top of one of the larger boulders at the entrance to the cave. She watched with interest as Far and Capn made their way toward her.

And even though there was eye contact, she said nothing as they cautiously entered the cave. Minutes later, Far and Capn came back out into the clearing and turned to face her.

"What are you going to do now?" Far asked.

She quietly studied them, nodding her head side to side. "There is nothing left to do."

"Why didn't you leave with the ship?"

"I would become dinner."

"This island's not so bad," said Far. "You'll get used to it."

"I want to go places." Glancing at Capn, she cocked her head again. "And you. You came on a boat this time. How did you leave last time?"

"I remember being here, but I was somewhere else, too."

Ekko and Far exchanged glances.

"Where were you?" Far asked, thinking the puzzle was getting better and better.

"In a cage. I dreamed about this place when I was trapped in that cage."

Far scratched his head. "How did you get out of the cage?"

"The humans that I'm with saved me."

Ekko was thinking the dog loony, but for the fact that he had actually disappeared. She was witness.

"I have a question," said Capn. "What happened to the

frog?"

"Frog? What frog?"

"That night. Down by the water. He warned me that it was a trap."

Ekko made a sound very much like a witch's cackle. "Oh, that frog! I'd forgotten."

"What happened to him?"

"He wanted to fly. So I dropped him into the highest tree."

"And...?"

"I don't know. We left that morning. I forgot all about him."

"Which tree?" Far asked.

Sam pulled the dinghy up onto shore and dragged it to higher ground. Melissa placed the oars beneath the seats, grabbed their gear, handed Sam his backpack and headed for the trail.

"Where do you think we should look first?"

Still strapping on his pack, Sam stepped in behind her. "I'd guess by the lake. Everybody's got to have water. He's bound to leave footprints."

"Which side of the crossing?"

"I put a tracker on his collar. We should be able to walk right to him, once we get within range."

"What if we don't find him?"

"Kashif said the dog, island and stone are linked. If we want to go home, we have to have the dog."

"Let's go."

Heading up, Melissa set a fast pace. "I'm worried about Paul. That's why I wanted to come along. I couldn't stand being confined on the boat any longer. It's depressing."

"He's not getting better. Kathryn says he is."

"I agree with you. He needs antibiotics. Operate? See if we can find out what's wrong?"

"We don't have the right equipment. None of us are doctors and we don't have any medicine. We'd only make him worse."

Capn's tracks were all around the crossing. Studying them, they determined that the dog was either traveling with one of the chimpanzees, or that they had crossed separately traveling in the same direction.

The problem was, the tracker said that he was west of their position, in the opposite direction from where they thought he was now going.

Sam studied Snitch. "It says he's about a quarter mile over there. We should check that out first."

"Has he moved?"

"Either he's sleeping, trapped, dead or missing a collar. Let's go."

They discovered the collar still attached to the leash and still wound around the log. Melissa freed it up and examined it.

"It's been unbuckled. How would a dog do that?"

"Chimpanzee?" Sam turned. "Let's get back to the crossing. We've got some catching up to do."

They took the easy way across the stream, staying out in the open. Stopping at the old lookout where Klicker had been blinded, they spotted the grave that the men had dug for Keenan on their way down to the ship. Melissa felt a terrible wave of sadness flow through her and pushed back her tears. "I'm sorry, Keenan. Safe journey, my friend."

Sam said nothing. Maybe it wasn't such a good idea to bring her along. If this bothered her, she wasn't going to like the other bodies coming up. He was going to gather their weapons but now, seeing her, "Looks like both of them are heading up toward the cave."

"What an odd thing."

"What? Them traveling together? Or, us being stuck on the island?"

"All of it."

The cave was just as they had left it. Melissa spotted Capn's tracks. Both the dog and the chimp had been there.

She found a good sitting rock and reached for her water. "It's futile. We could walk this island another ten years and not see the dog. In fact, the odds of that are pretty good."

"We have to keep looking. What else are we going to do?"

"Dumb dog. Doesn't it have any loyalty to Paul and Kathryn? All of us have given it snacks and fed it and taken it for walks. If he doesn't come back, what's going to happen to Paul? What's going to happen to any of us?"

Sam sat down in the dirt beside her. "I don't want to ask either of those questions."

"Paul, can you hear me?"

He was looking pale, and his voice, the last time she had heard it, was weak. Kathryn didn't want to admit it, but she also felt that Paul's health was failing. He seemed to be doing an awful lot of resting and not too much recovering.

"Paul?"

A slight, weak smile. "Hey, Mom. Are we home yet?"

She put the back of her hand up against his forehead, fever. "Working on it. How are you feeling?"

"Never felt better."

"I think you're a liar."

Paul turned his head slightly side to side, checking out the cabin. "We're on the boat."

"Right."

"Are we under sail?"

"Not at the moment."

A long sigh. "We're still in the cove, aren't we?"

Kathryn nodded.

"Nerissa's gone?"

"Yes." He had asked this question the last time he was awake. "They were anxious to be on their way. Not sure if they know how to sail her though. They had a hard time turning Nerissa around to get her out of the cove."

Paul started to laugh, wound up coughing. "Hard to sail something that big."

"You should've seen them celebrate when they got her turned around. Fired off a cannon."

"Did you tell them good-bye for me?"

Hearing this, Kathryn had to turn away before Paul saw her sudden tears. "I did. They all thought you were pretty cool."

Every one of them, on crutches, bandaged, still bleeding, whatever, gave her a hug and said Paul was about the finest example of a young man that they had ever seen.

Kathryn reached for Paul's water glass. "I'll freshen this up."

"I'm not thirsty."

"You need to keep taking in fluids."

"Relax, Mom."

"I can't. I'm worried about you."

"Don't."

"I'm so sorry for all this, Paul. I shouldn't have been so flippant."

"I think it's pretty cool that you were."

"We weren't ready. Sam was right."

Paul managed a smile. "I thought we were pretty good."

"I've endangered everyone's lives."

"Mom. Stop worrying. We all took the bait."

"But I'm responsible for you. You're not even of age yet."

"But...," Paul grimaced with a sudden shooting pain in his gut. "I've had more adventures than most people do in a lifetime."

"You're just getting started, kiddo."

"Where's Sam and Melissa?"

"Out looking for Capn."

"Strange, him just running away like that."

"I think it was a mistake saving him. Everything would be OK if we'd left him there."

"We'd be living in the apartment and be bored out of our skulls."

"Paul, you're hurt. I'll take boredom every time."

Paul did not say that his insides felt like they were on fire. Or that the pain was starting to become unbearable. Or that he thought his condition was getting worse. There was nothing anybody could do about it anyway. "I think you're the coolest Mom in the world. No one else would let their kids do this."

"Melissa's dad."

"She told him we were going to see a movie and was going to spend the night on the boat."

"Great. I'm going to jail for child endangerment."

"Enhancement, Mom. Go relax. I'm fine."

Kathryn smiled a motherly smile and kissed him on the cheek. "Get well, kiddo."

"Working on it."

"I'm leaving the door open so I can check on you."

"Right."

Paul watched her from his berth as she passed in and out of his view while she made herself a cup of tea.

He did not tell her that whatever it was that was inside him was spreading. He could feel it growing, little tentacles here, a nerve tingling over there. Then the pain, a little bit here, a little more over there. Yes. It was growing and there was nothing anybody could do.

People always said he didn't listen, but some things he picked up. Antibiotics weren't invented until nineteen twenty-nine by Alexander Fleming, forty-five more years to go.

Tracks leading down through the trees were hard to follow across the carpet of moist leaves and thick undergrowth. Getting the general idea that he was heading for the lake, Melissa and Sam gave up on following and instead just looked for the easiest way down.

They found his footprints all along the shoreline, coming and going every which way and in both directions. After several frustrating minutes trying to figure out which way he went, Melissa threw her hands up.

"No way. I'm not a tracker! The dog's here, yet he's not. He's got a collar. Oops, no he doesn't. The magic stone was here, but now it's gone. They're all gone. Everyone but us. What's up, Sam? What are we going to do?"

Sam patted her on the back. "I'd say that's a pretty good question." He pointed to the upper ridge on the western side of the island, to the clouds rolling in. "They weren't there when we left the cave. Maybe we ought to start heading back."

"Crap. We're never going to find him."

"Let's think of some kind of trap. What can we use?"

"I know one thing. My gun's set on tranquilizer. If I see him, I'm going to shoot him. I'll carry him on my shoulders all the way to the cove and swim him out to the boat, if I have to."

Sam laughed. "Me, too."

They followed the shoreline south and then hiked along the bank of the stream until they reached the crossing. Both Sam and Melissa agreed that his most recent tracks appeared to go back across, and that the chimpanzee was with him.

"Shoot me now," said Melissa. "Put me out of my misery. What's next?"

"Dog or storm. You choose."

"Storm?" Looking up, Melissa was surprised to see how far the clouds had advanced. But these were high clouds, thin, wind blown. "Doesn't look like rain."

368

"That's just a sign of what's coming." Sam pointed to the high western side of the island I bet if we climbed up there, we'd...,"

"We'd be tired. I'll take your word for it, whatever it is you were going to say."

"If we keep going, we'll be tracking him in the dark."

"If it's the dog that we need, then it's the dog we should go get."

"I see Snitch is showing out of range. We'll have to get to higher ground to check in with Kathryn."

"Let's go."

They followed the dog's tracks to the other side of the crossing and then lost them about half the distance heading back up to the lake.

Frustrated, Melissa stopped, found a rock to sit on and uncapped her water. "He's gone into the trees. We'll never be able to track him."

Sam joined her on the rock. "Getting dark. What say we head back, regroup on the boat and head out early tomorrow morning?"

Melissa nodded. "I'm sure Kathryn wants some company. Here's something, if it rains, all tracks will be fresh, right?"

Sam stood and held out a hand for Melissa. "I hope it works like that."

Kathryn was sitting in the cockpit when Sam and Melissa tied up to the boat. She looked up and smiled when they climbed aboard, but it was the hunched figure with crossed arms that gave her mood away. They joined her in the cockpit.

"No dog, huh?"

"Not yet," said Sam, shaking his head. "But his tracks are all over the place and we know the area."

"We're going back out tomorrow morning, early."

Anchored in the island's shadow, darkness was already setting in even though sunlight, squeezing in between the western ridge and the clouds, was lighting up the sky.

"Looks like rain," said Sam, looking up. "We might want to set out a second anchor, just in case."

"Wait," said Kathryn, sitting up. "You started with rain and ended up with a second anchor. What's up?"

"I think we've got some weather coming. And I was just remembering the book."

"What book?"

"The one we all read. There was a storm. Nerissa was caught in it and ran aground here." Sam held out his hands for emphasis. "This cove."

"What are you saying?"

"We should be prepared for whatever might come. Set out a second anchor. Is this the best part of the cove to be in if bigger waves wash through? Is everything tied down?"

Kathryn checked out the clouds and nodded in agreement. "Coming in from the west?"

"Right."

"So, we're sheltered from the wind right where we are." She turned and studied the shoreline. "I don't want to be any closer to shore. I think we're good right where we are." And then she went back to her crossed arms, hunched position. "Paul's not getting better."

Sam and Melissa exchanged glances. Melissa moved

beside Kathryn and gave her a hug. "What makes you say that?"

"He's not...," Kathryn started crying. "He's not waking up as often. And his voice is weak."

"He's just getting lots of rest."

"His breathing is labored. I can't deny it and neither can either of you. So, let's not sugarcoat it. I can't stand that."

Sam stood. "I agree." He pulled Kathryn up and gave her a hug.

Kathryn let herself be held for a minute, garnering a little comfort from Sam's presence but not nearly enough to overcome the utterly helpless feelings she had. "I made steamed rice, you guys. And I caught some fish. It's baking. Should be ready any minute."

Melissa stood and hugged the two them. And then she kissed Kathryn on the cheek. "You're freaking amazing."

"I'll start tying everything down," said Sam, breaking away. "And drop another anchor while you two get things ready?"

"Sounds good," said Melissa, heading for the companionway. "I'm famished." She grabbed Kathryn's hand and pulled her along. "Guess I should start calling you Mom. You're always there for us."

"Call me a fool."

Sam went to the lazerette at the stern of Spittin' Image and retrieved the anchor. After tying off the loose end to a cleat, he coiled the anchor side and heaved it as far away from the boat as possible and, after waiting for it to hit bottom, started pulling it in until it caught. And then he played out another thirty feet before tying that off, just in case a large swell came over the rocks.

Ekko circled the tree a few times, comparing the branches with other surrounding trees. It was the configuration of the upper limbs, a hammock shape formed by three individual sprigs nestled under a canopy of leaves, that confirmed her decision.

Capn arrived at the trunk of the tree and it was to there, to a low hanging branch just above the dog that she flew. "This is the tree."

"And...?"

"He's not in it."

"Are you sure?"

"I'd guess he fell," said Far, looking up. "I can't imagine a frog climbing down."

"The branches are much closer up at the top," said Ekko. "He could practice."

Far glanced over at Capn. "I say, let it go. Go back to your humans and go home."

"I want to know what happened to him. If I can help him get home, I will."

"There's nothing you can do. If he's not in the tree...,"

"Could he see the lake from up there?"

"Of course," said Ekko.

"Then he would know which way to go."

"If he could get down."

"Which way is the lake?"

Ekko flew to the next tree. "As I would fly, this way."

With nose to ground, zigzagging his way toward Ekko, Capn decided that the trail was cold, nothing. He looked up at Ekko. "Next?"

Following, Far scratched his head. "You're going to check every tree from here to the lake?"

"Not every tree. Just the straightest path. If I don't find him, I'll give up."

"It's going to rain," said Ekko. "You won't be able to follow."

"Don't frogs love rain?"

Normally, by now, Far would throw up his arms in frustration and walk away. But this was so compelling that he just had to hang around and see how it ended.

Ekko forged the direction from trees to rocks to shrubs and all that led back toward the lake. Far kept one eye on the dog, one on Ekko, who was also searching from the air, and before long he even found himself scanning the forest floor for signs of the frog.

The first few drops came through the canopy of leaves sounding like spot or spit or hiss, a little here, more over there until the rain came down like a liquid veil through the trees, blowing this way and that.

*R*ain!

Croaker hopped out from beneath one of the last few obstacles between him and the lake, a low hanging bush crowding a large rock.

Wet rock. Wet leaves, wet ground..., wet, wet, wet. I can smell the lake! Mud..., coming up! Finally! Never thought I'd make it.

It hadn't been easy. Looking down from the treetops, high up was a new concept. Learning how to hop from twig to twig, tiptoe across leaves, jump branch to branch and climb down the trunk was all brand new.

Ground. How good it felt to be standing on something that would not allow him to fall, even if he tried.

Water, wet, mud, moss, decaying logs, bugs..., yes! All of it coming up!

Ekko landed in front of the frog, talons crunching across the gravel. "We've been looking for you."

"Get away."

"I'm here to help."

Croaker hopped left. "I have my doubts."

She moved to block him. "The dog is looking for you."

"What dog?"

"That night. You told him to run."

"The night you put me up in the tree?"

"Yes."

"I deny everything. Step aside."

"He wants to help you get home."

"Then he should tell you to get out of my way."

"I can take you."

"Do I look crazy?"

"I know where the log is, on the other side of the lake. Do you know how far away that is? It will take forever for you to get there."

"If I can climb trees, I can get home."

Capn and Far came out of the trees and, seeing that Ekko had found the frog, hurried down to join them. Far, chin in hand, came to a squatting position on one side of the frog. Capn sat on the other.

Croaker quietly studied the three of them. "What's wrong with all of you? It's raining!"

"I agree with him," said Far.

Ekko shook off her feathers and stepped from foot to foot. "Me, too. You've found your frog. I need to get out of the rain." She looked down at Croaker. "Sorry I put you up in the tree. I was going to help you fly, but we left that morning."

"And I'm sorry I got you involved," said Capn. "You warned me."

Croaker looked over at Far. "What about you? What are you sorry for?"

"I'm just sorry I'm wet."

"Then, why don't you leave?"

"I have to see how this ends."

"You know what I'm sorry for?" Croaker asked. "I'm sorry that there are three of you that don't want to be in the rain blocking my way to the one thing I haven't seen since the last time I saw you. Now that we're all sorry, I'm leaving."

Croaker hopped between the bird and the dog and when he was only a few hops from the water, turned back to face them. "I did enjoy flying. But this is home."

"That's it?" Far asked as he watched the frog disappear into the water.

"I had to make sure he was OK."

"I'll take him flying again some day," said Ekko, shaking her feathers again. "I'm drenched. I have to go. That was fun."

Capn and Far watched Ekko hurry into the trees and then they worked their way up the bank and back onto the trail. Capn shook the water off of his fur from time to time. Far, shielding his eyes, was anxious to get out of the rain. He hurried to get beneath a tree and then turned to wait for the dog.

"Are you going back to the humans?"

"Yes."

"There's no more to this?"

Capn shook his head. "No. Thanks for your help."

Perhaps it was the rain that cut everything short. Perhaps there was nothing more to say. Everyone had played a part and none of it would have been complete without all of the players.

Understanding that, Far smiled a quick smile. "It was fun." He turned and disappeared into the forest, heading back to Amber and Baby hidden in their makeshift home.

By the time that Capn made his way down to the cove, rain was being whipped around by the wind, sometimes coming in from behind and sometimes straight at his face.

Searching for Spittin' Image, he discovered that they had moved it to the other side of the cove. To get to it, he would have to go all the way back up to the crossing and come back down, or swim across.

Being very tired and very hungry, Capn chose the easiest way. He got as close to the boat as possible and started barking.

Melissa cocked her head to one side, attention turned in the direction of the narrow window above the sink. "I think I just heard thunder."

Sam went to the companionway, slid the cover slightly aside, stepped up to the second step and looked out. "Storm's moving in. Hear that roar coming through the trees? Wind's really blowing."

White caps were beginning to appear across the cove. Bits of sand hit the windows, sounding like a quiet static against the whistling and banging sound of the halyards hitting the mast.

"We've got two things happening," said Kathryn, pulling the curtain away from a window. "We've got the wind driving us toward the southern peninsula and the swells coming over the south side driving us toward the other side of the cove.

Melissa returned to her laptop, busy with a game of Solitaire. "Let's hope it all evens out."

Sam returned to his coffee at the table. Kathryn remained standing at the window, working her hands nervously. "I hope we're anchored in the right spot. Don't want to get washed up on the rocks."

"Too late to change anything," said Melissa. "Can you imagine pulling up the anchors now?"

Kathryn went to a window on the starboard side of the boat and looked out. "Can't see much. Maybe we ought to take turns going topside with a flashlight and see if we're getting closer to shore."

"I was looking at that earlier," said Sam, getting up. "It's hard to tell. We've got thirty feet of play on the anchors so we can swing sixty feet." He went to the small closet where they kept the foul weather gear, retrieved a jacket and put it on as he headed for the companionway. "Got a good strong light?"

Kathryn went to another compartment near the engine area and found the light that plugged into one of three outlets topside. "This is like a headlight on high beam. Watch out. It gets hot."

Standing out in the rain, Sam plugged the light into the outlet located in the cockpit and shined the beam out into the storm.

The southern peninsula was two hundred yards away. Waves, washing over the rocks, were much larger than usual and easily found their way to Spittin' Image before they rolled on by. Looking, Sam wasn't sure, but thought that the water level was higher in the cove. There was less beach than he remembered.

So that's what it is. We have a rising sea filling up the cove. The wind can't stop that. I wonder if thirty extra feet on the anchor is enough. Maybe I should let out another thirty.

But if I let out more, we could wind up way too close to shore. If a big swell makes it through though, our anchors are going to float right along with us. Hmm.

Getting closer to shore? Impossible to tell. I'll just keep checking. If we break free, I don't think that little motor's going to do us much good.

Going forward, Sam used the lifeline for support and hung on to the anchor hold cover. It was when he was playing out more anchor rope that he thought he heard the barking of a dog. Turning, he squinted toward the sound.

If there was anything over there, it was going to be hard to get to, about two hundred yards of angry, choppy water.

He double checked his work and went aft to retrieve the light. Shining it back in that direction, he thought he spotted Capn running along the shoreline.

Going below, Sam was going to say, "I think Capn's out there." But a brilliant flash of light and instantaneous thunder muffled his words.

"I have a question," said Melissa. "If this boat has an aluminum mast and aluminum is a conductor, can we get electrocuted sitting here inside the boat?"

"I don't think so," said Sam. "We're inside a fiberglass

shell."

"So, easiest path, right?"

"I think so. The boat's wet and water's a conductor, so if lightning hits the mast it probably just travels down until it finds the sea."

"So, we shouldn't be standing around the mast during a storm."

"I'd say so. I think I heard...,"

Kathryn came out of Paul's cabin, shaking and white, her eyes red and swollen, arms crossed, fists clenched. "We're losing him. He's hardly breathing. I don't know what to do!"

There was nothing to do. All of them knew what would fix the problem but no one had thought to bring along antibiotics. They stood where they were in silence for a moment, until Melissa went over to give Kathryn a hug.

Sam grabbed Capn's leash and his backpack and headed for the companionway. "I think I heard Capn over on the south shore. I'm going to go check it out."

Melissa looked at him like he was nuts. "In this weather? We just had a discussion about lightning. You'll be a sitting duck out there."

"Kashif said we had to have the dog if we want to leave. Anybody here voting to stay?"

Paul could see it in their faces. Don't need a doctor to tell you how you're doing. Just read the faces of your friends. Of course, they're encouraging, optimistic, hopeful, all of the good things. But look in their eyes and the fluff goes away.

I'm dying. I know I'm dying and there's nothing anyone can do about it.

"Mom, you are so cool for letting me do this."

"Paul. Don't talk like that. You're sick, very sick. And I'm the one that got you into this."

"Thank you for the opportunity."

"Paul. There's nothing I can do. You understand?"

"Right. But if I've had the greatest adventure ever, why should I regret it? I don't."

"I just don't want the price to be too high."

Kathryn picked up the glass and offered a drink. Paul smiled and nodded, no. "Are we under sail?"

Kathryn smiled, more like a grimace. "No. We're still stuck here in the cove."

Paul closed his eyes and listened to the wind, heard the rain pelting down onto the deck above, felt the waves splashing against the hull.

"Mom. Something's wrong."

"What's that?"

"The boat. If we're at anchor, the bow should be pointing into the wind."

"Layman's terms."

It was getting harder and harder to speak. With swollen tongue, it was becoming difficult to swallow. "Are there two anchors out there?"

"Right. Sam dropped the stern anchor in case the other one didn't hold."

"You need to pull it up."

"Why? I thought it was a good idea. Aren't two anchors better than one?"

"Wind and water are hitting us broadside. We're a target. How close to shore, are we?"

"About where Nerissa was, a little closer to the beach."

"Storm's getting worse?"

"Seems like it."

Pain was everywhere and Paul felt like he was slowly slipping into some other place. The world of Sam, Melissa and Mom seemed more foreign, a place that he liked to visit when he could. He took a deep breath and collected his thoughts.

"Mom. Spittin' Image needs to anchor in the middle of the cove. Let out lots of line. One anchor."

"I don't know if we should try to move the boat in this weather."

"Storm surge. Get Sam to help."

"He's out looking for Capn."

"Melissa?"

"I'll go talk to her. I'll be right back."

Paul watched Kathryn leave and sighed heavily when she disappeared out into the galley. He didn't want her to be around when it happened, not anyone. When you take your last breath, you want to be alone. Who needs an audience to witness the inevitable?

So when he heard their muffled voices filtering through the sounds of rain, the halyards banging against the mast, felt Spittin' Image, the boat he'd come to love, tugging against her anchors, he smiled as he recollected their accomplishments..., and let himself go.

Capn did not want to get into the dinghy. It was too wet and wild and the thing was blowing all over the place, not to mention that there was already about six inches of water in it.

Sam was ready for the occasion and offered a treat. That brought the dog up to the boat, but it wasn't enough to coax him in or even to stand still long enough for Sam to get a grip on him. Reluctantly, Sam pulled the dinghy out of the water and up onto shore.

Once he had the collar back on Capn, he picked the dog up, put him in the dinghy and gave him a very short leash because he kept trying to jump out. Sam pulled the dinghy back into the water and began rowing back out to Spittin' Image.

Lightning flashed across the sky, fiery fingers of white light streaking together, snaking back into the trees with a hair-raising, crackling and thunderous boom.

Looking over at the southern peninsula, Sam was appreciative of the swells washing over the rocks. It was helping to drive them back toward Spittin' Image, better progress against the wind.

The dinghy that worked so well in calm weather was not quite as stable with the bigger waves. Designed with the idea of folding up when not in use, the various pieces of floorboard, held together by flexible rubber, rolled one way or another as the swells passed by.

The dinghy also had no keel. Sam, Capn and the dinghy were all an easy target for the wind blowing them back toward the peninsula. Capn, feeling trapped in this life threatening situation, started howling his full moon howl.

Snitch came alive. "Sam! Sam! Can you hear me?"

Sam let go of the oars and put Snitch up to his ear. "What's up? You sound...,"

"I shot Kathryn with a tranquilizer!"

"*What?*"

"I had to shoot her. She was going berserk!"

"Melissa!"

"I think Paul's dead! He's not breathing! Kathryn had a knife. She was going to cut her wrists!"

"I've got the dog. I'm on my way. I'll be there in a minute."

"Hurry, Sam! I'm going *crazy!*"

To safely approach Spittin' Image, Sam was forced to row past the boat and let the wind push them into the hull, slightly less dangerous than the other side, swells doing the same thing.

Capn was squirming and whining and anything but cooperative. Sam braced his legs against the dinghy's wooden seats for support, used one hand to hold onto the stanchion so they wouldn't drift away, cradled Capn under his other arm and held the dog up for Melissa to grab.

She was standing in the cockpit, sobbing like a baby, soaking wet. She opened the lifeline, unsnapping it from the stanchion and, leaning out, reached for the dog.

It was a struggle. It seemed that when Spittin' Image was up, the dinghy was down. Seconds later, the opposite was happening. Sometimes the two drifted out of reach.

When she finally had a good grip on Capn and was pulling him in, just as Sam was letting go, a blinding white flash lit up the sky.

When the storm surge came through, the anchors snagged into the rocks on the north side of the cove and ripped the cleats right out of the deck as Spittin' Image was washed out to sea.

Kathryn figured that there were a couple of holes topside and, peering out through the narrow window that overlooked the bow, confirmed one for sure.

That explains the sump pump running non-stop. Water in the bilge. We're slowly sinking, probably good until the batteries give out.

She didn't know if they still had a mast. Something was thumping against the hull as the boat rolled around in the angry sea.

If it is the mast, please don't poke a hole in our side.

Nothing to do but wait. Hope the dinghy's attached to the boat if we have to bail.

We? Sam's gone. Melissa's gone. Paul is..., Paul.

Don't want to think about Paul.

We? No such thing anymore.

Maybe I should just jump overboard and be done with it.

I don't want to go it alone...,

*T*hey were sitting around a short square table in the middle of a small, dimly lit room. Sam recognized the soft feel of the tatami mats making up the floor, much like what was in his studio back home.

Mahin elegantly poured tea into Sam's cup, keeping her eyes on the process until finished. She met Sam's inquisitive look with a smile and then, turning to face Kashif, poured tea into his empty cup.

The room was lit by three candles on a table in one corner of the room and, in the far corner, another table with four lit candles. There was only one door, behind Kashif. There were no decorations on any of the walls.

Mahin filled the two empty cups in front of her place at the table and slid one across to Oskar. When everyone had their tea, Kashif raised his cup and waited for the others to do the same.

"To Sam."

Sam nodded as they clinked glasses. "To Kashif."

Oskar set his tea down, cleared his throat and offered his hand. "My name is Oskar. I am a friend of Kashif."

"I have heard of you," said Sam,. "I read the account of your voyage aboard Nerissa. You were very brave."

Oskar, slightly embarrassed with the compliment, looked down at his hands, flushing. "I was only trying to stay alive."

"Good man," said Kashif, patting Oskar on the shoulder. "Very brave."

Sam turned his gaze to the girl. "And you are Mahin. You are even more beautiful than Oskar described."

When Oskar translated, Mahin's face became very red. Sam reached across the table and took her hand. "You are my great, great aunt. I am your brother's great, great grandson. If anyone can call you beautiful, it should be me."

Kashif, quietly sipping his tea, studied Sam as the three of them talked. There is much to be said when there are so many generations in between.

They named off relatives and spouses and places where they planned to live or, as corrected by Sam who knew the history of the family, where they wound up, and connecting the lines linking the future with those of the past.

When it seemed that enough had been said about such things, Kashif reached into a small black box and retrieved a soft leather bundle from within.

Carefully setting it on the table, he untied the string at the top, unfolded the protection, and left the stone exposed. "This..., for you."

Sam studied the firestone with great interest. Its surface was smooth, like a translucent, milky glass stone, but with hard edges like quartz.

"May I hold it?"

Kashif nodded. "It is yours."

The stone was warm to the touch and, closing his eyes, Sam could feel the inner energy surging outward. A tingling sensation, feeling much like a hand or arm or foot that has been asleep and is now coming awake, beginning in his fingertips, flowing up his arms and encompassing his being.

Sam found himself back in the dinghy, standing in water, handing Capn up to a very distressed Melissa in the middle of the storm when lightning hit the mast.

The easiest path. Isn't that what she said? Poor Melissa. Never knew what happened. Gone before she had a chance to test all of her ingenious skills.

And Paul. Dead? What is it about fate that takes away someone extremely valuable and leaves the scum behind? What will Kathryn do when she wakes up and discovers the grisly scene?

Sam felt the anguish of a thousand dreams gone wrong. The despair of millions of lives that never had a chance to bloom, all of the loves lost, children gone and dreams shattered...,

Sobbing involuntarily, Sam carefully set the stone back on the table, wiped his eyes with his sleeve and said, "This does not belong to me."

Kashif seemed a bit confused. "For you, yes?"

Sam shook his head. "I cannot. I do not have such great power as you. You keep it."

Both Mahin and Kashif started talking to Oskar at the same time. He seemed to be taking it all in, a little here, a little more over there.

Finally, with a determined look, he turned his attention to Sam. "They say that the stone would no longer be theirs, if not for you. Kashif says he owes his life to you and that the stone should be payment for such a brave act."

"It is not my time to own the stone. If anyone should own it, I would elect Mahin. It was her brave act that saved you. She has more power than I."

As Oskar translated, Kashif, eyes looking down at his hands, took it all in with a nod. When Oskar finished, he looked up and met Sam's eyes. He spoke quickly to Oskar, who translated.

"He says that he also believes that Mahin has great power and that she is worthy of the stone. But he cannot guarantee that this will pass on to you."

"I do not ask for it."

"He says, what is it that you want?"

"To be safe at home with my friends."

Sam, sitting in the dinghy, was in the middle of some-where, visibility through the fog about twenty feet, seas calm, flat and glassy.

Checking Snitch for position or contacts, he discovered that he wasn't wearing one. His watch showed the time to be, if he were in the real world, about four in the morning.

That's what it felt like. Sam could not see the moon through the fog, but its distant, silver-blue glow gave away its location deep in the western horizon.

That would make sense. We were up until sometime around eleven, moon still rising.

Capn, up at the bow, nose wet, anxious to move along, turned back and, with his big smile, barked for Sam's attention. When he had it, he pointed with his nose to where Sam was supposed to go, forward and slightly to the left.

Sam laughed. Why not? He seems to know the way. He set off in a slow, easy rowing motion, one that allowed the dinghy to glide effortlessly over the glassy water. Fog opened to let them in and then quietly closed the door behind.

Capn would have jumped off of the dinghy as soon as it hit the rocks, if allowed, but Sam had wisely wrapped the leash around one of the dinghy's seats.

The rocks were thick chunks of granite piled up against the bank, a rocky buffer from sea to land.

Sam secured the dinghy while Capn marked this new territory. When they reached a sidewalk, Capn immediately went left, sniffing his way through the fog, tugging at his leash.

Sidewalk lights were spaced about a hundred feet apart, one invisible from the other as they made their way forward.

If not for the watery surge coming up into and draining back through the rocks, and the distant blare of a fog horn, Sam felt like he was walking through the clouds.

But then a familiar light came into view, that of KBL Donuts, a tiny shop located in the marina where Spittin' Image was docked.

The place was not open, but in the back of the shop Jimmy was busy cranking out donuts, turning the handle as the dough shaped O's fell from the aluminum hopper and plopped into the hot grease of the fryer, thirty per tray, five rows of six, to the sounds of rock and roll blasting into the room.

Jimmy did not own the place. KBL Donuts was owned by Kim Ber Lee, his mother, known as Kim to the locals, or Lee, or Kimberly, or KB, or the donut queen, anything. She didn't care as long as you bought donuts. She would smile her gold-tooth customer smile and answer to almost anything you called her as she put your money into the cash register.

The place also made excellent donuts. Jimmy, anal in many ways, took pride in getting the formula, water temperature versus flour temperature, just right so that the dough would react perfectly with the hot grease, as measured by the star shaped hole in the middle of the donut. No star? Wrong temp, unprofessional.

Good donuts, view of the waterfront, coffee, always freshly brewed because it sold so fast, made KBL Donuts a hot spot. Customers bring in customers, the idea that if everyone else likes it, it must be good. In this case it was. KBL Donuts was open, and pretty much packed from five in the morning until they closed, at noon.

Sam looked at his watch. It was four-thirty. "Too early, Capn. We've got to wait half an hour."

That didn't make sense to Capn. You walk all the way to the door, you go through. That's the next thing humans do.

Capn liked donuts, plain donuts in particular. He didn't care for the frosting, but a well made plain donut was something that he could eat right now. And this place had them. He looked up at Sam with a big smile. Sam laughed, but took a seat at a table near the front door.

Jimmy appreciated that. Open at five means exactly that. Customers always arrive a little early and expect you to drop what you're doing so that you can serve them, even though you're not open yet.

If the sign said four-thirty, customers would start arriving at four-fifteen. No. Five means five and there's a reason for that. Everything takes a certain amount of time and it all works if there are no interruptions.

Capn understood none of this. Getting a good pet from Sam was nice, but plain donuts were just on the other side of that door. What is *wrong* with this picture? Wanting to get a better assessment of the situation, he moved toward the door, tugged at his leash, and when nothing happened, sat right there and leaned toward the door.

It's impossible to train this dog, Sam was thinking. He's too old. How old? Old when he's resting, young in an adventure. Uncanny.

He gave Capn a few more feet of leash, hoping he would take the hint and lie down. But Capn moved closer to the door and assumed the same sitting, leaning position. There was no one else around and, tired of fighting it, Sam allowed Capn enough leash to get to the front door.

Pulling the donuts out of the fryer and setting them on the stainless steel drain pan, out of the corner of his eye, Jimmy spotted Capn sitting next to the glass, first in line, smiling.

Moving the tray of donuts over to the icing area, he saw that Capn had changed his position and was now facing the other way. When, looking out of the corner of his eye, Capn noticed that Jimmy was looking, he turned his head to face him and smiled. Too hard to resist.

"You guys heading out today?" Jimmy asked, handing Sam the box of donuts.

"I hope not," Sam replied as he handed Jimmy a twenty. "I think we partied a little too hard last night."

Jimmy started to give him change but Sam waved it off. "You opened early. Thanks."

"You didn't ask me to open early. He did."

"Yeah, but he doesn't have any money. Otherwise he'd

give all of it to you."

Donuts in hand, Capn decided that Sam was now his best friend and the last obstacle between him and his donut. He diligently led Sam back to the dinghy, hopped in and assumed his position at the bow.

Yes, it was still foggy. Yes, it was early, much too early for breakfast. And, yes, this human probably wouldn't be able to follow his nose back to the boat until the fog lifted. He barked for Sam's attention and, when he had it, pointed the way.

E yes blinking open, taking in the small, dimly lit area, gazing into the mirror hanging on the wall next to her bed, Kathryn spotted her tiny closet across the room.

So..., quiet. Storm is gone?

It's..., too calm.

Keeping the covers pulled up to her shoulders, she sat up.

Sam was looking for the dog. Paul was..., was...,

Getting out of bed, she was surprised to see that she was wearing pajamas.

When did that happen?

She opened her door and peered into the galley. Melissa was asleep in her bunk. Sam's bunk was out of view. Paul's door was closed.

"Melissa? Paul? Sam? Anybody awake?"

Melissa rolled over to face her. "Kathryn! What?"

"Go check on Paul, will you please?"

Melissa sat up with a start, suddenly wide awake, hair as wild as her eyes as she studied the room. She too had that puzzled look. Sam's bunk was empty. "Where's Sam?"

Kathryn glanced down at her wrist, wondering if Snitch would know, but was surprised to see that she was not wearing it. Nor was Melissa wearing hers. "I don't know. I just woke up. I'm worried about Paul."

"Sam had Capn in the dinghy. He was bringing him back to the boat."

Kathryn looked confused. "I don't remember that. Where was I?"

"It was right after," Melissa stopped.

"Right after what?"

"You know."

"No. I don't know. After what?"

"I..., I shot you."

"Me? You shot me?"

"With a tranquilizer. I'm so sorry."

"Why?"

"You..., you were going to kill yourself. You had a knife."

Kathryn looked utterly baffled. "What?"

"Paul. His breathing was, was...,"

Kathryn stared at Paul's closed door. "Before I open that, what happened with Sam and Capn? Apparently I missed it."

"Sam had Capn in the dinghy. I opened the lifeline and was reaching for the dog. It was very windy and everything was shifting around. I finally got my arms around him. Sam was letting go. That's all I remember until now."

"Lightning?"

"I would be dead, I would think."

"So..., where's Sam?"

"Where are we?"

They went to opposite sides, Melissa to the window above her bunk, Kathryn to the window above the galley sink. Looking out, both of them were speechless.

Kathryn broke the silence. "I don't know what to say."

"Me either. I..., I'm at a total loss for words..., or under-standing."

Kathryn went to the companionway, opened it up and stood at the top of the steps, assessing. "We're at the dock, very foggy. No Sam. No Capn."

Heart pounding, she slowly came back down into the galley and stared at Paul's closed door. "Do me a favor, will you?"

Melissa shook her head. "I can't do it."

Kathryn started for the door. This was a small galley, maximum fourteen feet from bottom of the steps to door. Yet it took her a full minute to get there. Neither of them spoke. Kathryn, feeling like she was going to be sick, swallowed twice to convince herself that she was in control.

As she was reaching for the handle, the door swung open with a bang and Paul came out, hair looking like it was styled by a tornado, bleary eyed, wearing red boxer shorts and a rather dingy looking T-shirt. "I'm freaking *famished!*"

They both screamed, Melissa wide-eyed, hands to her mouth, Kathryn jumping backward.

Paul looked at both of them, mystified. "What?"

"We thought you were dead!"

"Me? No, but I am starving. What's for..., what is it? Morning? It feels like morning."

"You don't remember?"

"Remember what?"

"We were on the island." Kathryn looked over at Melissa with a desperate look. "We *were* on an island, weren't we?"

"I killed a man," said Melissa, sitting down on her bunk. "His name was Keenan."

Paul scratched his head. "I thought all of that was a dream, my dream. You guys were in it, yeah, but..., where's Sam?"

"Do you remember being shot?" Melissa asked.

"Shot? Now that you mention it, yeah. What a scum bag."

"Do you remember his name?"

"No. What time is it?"

Kathryn glanced at her watch. "About five. Why?"

"I was trying to figure out if it was breakfast, lunch or dinner. Why is it so gloomy outside?"

"Fog."

"You were dead! I can't believe this discussion. I died a thousand times in that storm. Melissa shot me!"

"You shot Mom?"

"I had to. She was...,"

"And then you died! And now we're discussing what to eat?"

"I died? I don't remember that."

"You can't remember your own death," said Melissa. "What's the last thing you remember?"

Paul looked over at Kathryn, opening his arms for a hug. "Talking with you, Mom. You've always been there."

Kathryn burst into tears. While they were hugging, Melissa went over to Sam's berth.

"His backpack is still here. His water glass is still full.

It's all coming back to me. I remember him putting it up there last night so Capn wouldn't drink out of it. Paul, where do you think we are, right now?"

"Um, correct me if I'm wrong, on Spittin' Image?"

"You know what I mean."

"I'm hoping we're at the dock. Where's Sam?"

"That's what I'm trying to figure out. The dinghy's gone, he's gone and Capn is gone."

"When did we get Capn? I don't remember any of that."

"You were shot, remember? Your Mom was taking care of you. Sam and I were out looking for Capn."

"You found him?"

"Right."

"Then, where is he?"

"That's what I'm trying to figure out! Catch up, will you?"

"I've been dead. I think I have an excuse."

"Wait," said Kathryn, holding up her hand. "I'm going to put on a pot of coffee, make some breakfast...,"

"Yes!"

"You two, go topside and find out what you can. I'll call when breakfast is ready. Paul, put some pants on."

"I'm not going outside looking like this," said Melissa. "Dibs on the bathroom."

"It's called a head."

"What island?" Paul replied. "It doesn't exist."

Kathryn looked up from her coffee. "Yes, it does. We were all there."

Paul, in between bites of cereal. "Prove it."

"We all have the same memories. That proves something."

Melissa looked up from her laptop. She was attempting to get caught up on all of the worldly events since she'd been out of touch. "We each have our own memories, but we don't know if they're the same."

"But it's of the same place and people. Nerissa did exist!"

"None of this explains Sam."

Kathryn glanced over at Sam's backpack, empty bunk and the untouched glass of water. "He died to save us."

"We don't know that he died."

"What if he never shows up again? Will they try to pin a murder on us?"

"No body. No motive."

"He was the only one not on the boat," said Melissa. "The dinghy was not attached. Sam was in it and Capn was in between. Those are the three things that are missing. It has something to do with being on the boat, or not."

"It was a blue moon," said Kathryn. "Oskar warned us. Beware."

"Don't forget the firestone. Maybe that had something to do with it."

"It could be," said Paul, "that he wanted to stay and help Kashif. He was pretty vulnerable."

Kathryn shook her head. "No. Nerissa had already sailed. After that, Sam and Melissa went to the island looking for Capn. Whatever else happened, he didn't go with them."

"It always comes back to when Sam was handing Capn to me. Whatever happened, it happened then."

"That doesn't explain my riding out the storm in this boat."

"That was your imagination, Mom. It never happened."

"Something happened. Sam is gone."

"Way I see it," said Paul. "We sailed to the ends of Earth to stop an injustice, had to kill a few to get the job done, were wildly successful, and now we're safely back home. They'll write stories about us. I think it'll be an adventure comic series, the fantastic four and the firestone, adventures on a blue moon."

Kathryn headed for the coffee pot with her empty cup. "Except there aren't four. Sam is missing, probably dead."

"Mom, we can't do anything until the fog lifts. We can't even see land yet. Are you going to make breakfast?"

"You're eating it."

"No. I'm eating cereal in preparation for breakfast. I saw eggs in there. I'll cook up an omelet."

"How can you think of eating when Sam's gone?"

"I can't think of anything until my stomach gives back control."

Melissa motioned for them to be quiet, waited a few seconds and finally got up. She headed for the companionway and scaled the steps.

Kathryn watched. "What?"

"I think I heard Capn."

They emerged from the fog about fifty feet away, dark silhouettes, hard to distinguish, but it soon became apparent that Capn was at the bow giving them his big, "I'm ready for donuts," smile.

Sam pulled up to the transom of Spittin' Image and tied off. Paul spotted the box.

"Donuts! Sam, you're my hero!"

With a slight smile, Sam handed Capn to Paul, who was actually reaching for the donuts, climbed onboard, gave everybody hugs and motioned for them to go below.

Capn rushed down the steps ahead of everyone and, beaming, sat next to his bowl.

Kathryn turned. "I'll make a fresh pot."

397

"I'll get some plates," said Melissa. "And napkins. Paul's a pig."

Paul motioned for Sam to go next. "I'll keep an eye on the donuts."

Sam handed the box to Paul and nudged him ahead. "Anybody have anything they want to talk about?"

* * * *